BEYOND THE SILENCE

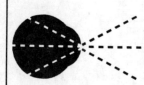

BEYOND THE SILENCE

TRACIE PETERSON
KIMBERLEY WOODHOUSE

THORNDIKE PRESS
A part of Gale, Cengage Learning

GALE
CENGAGE Learning®

Farmington Hills, Mich • San Francisco • New York • Waterville, Maine
Meriden, Conn • Mason, Ohio • Chicago

GALE
CENGAGE Learning

LIBRARY OF CONGRESS CATALOGING-IN-PUBLICATION DATA

Names: Peterson, Tracie, author. | Woodhouse, Kimberley, 1973- author.
Title: Beyond the silence / Tracie Peterson and Kimberley Woodhouse.
Description: Large print edition. | Waterville, Maine : Thorndike Press, 2016. |
  © 2016 | Series: Thorndike Press large print Christian fiction
Identifiers: LCCN 2015042660| ISBN 9781410485588 (hardback) | ISBN 1410485587
  (hardcover)
Subjects: LCSH: Large type books. | BISAC: FICTION / Christian / General. | GSAFD:
  Christian fiction.
Classification: LCC PS3566.E7717 B49 2016 | DDC 813/.54—dc23
LC record available at http://lccn.loc.gov/2015042660

Published in 2016 by arrangement with Bethany House Publishers, a division of Baker Publishing Group

Printed in the United States of America
1 2 3 4 5 6 7 20 19 18 17 16

This book is dedicated to and
in loving memory of:
JAMES WILLIAM (WOODY)
WOODHOUSE

One of the very best men
I've ever known.
My beloved father-in-law. For
twenty-three plus years,
you called me daughter, told me
you loved me, and gave me a
hard time whenever you had
the chance.
It was priceless.
Even though you left a gaping hole
(who will I debate and
discuss music with?),
I'm rejoicing that you are with
our Lord and Savior.
Thank you for all the
quiet encouragement

and support you bestowed on me
over the years —
telling me you were proud of me
and that I "did well."
Miss you, Dad. Can't wait to
see you again.

PROLOGUE

1890

Far-off screams filled the air and rattled six-year-old Jimmy Colton's bones.

Mama?

Jimmy paused to listen again and looked back toward the house. Another scream echoed across the yard. Something was wrong! He dropped his bucket of dirt and took off toward the house as fast as his legs could carry him, following the long path through the olive trees and gardens. Why did he go so far from the house? Mama had told him to stay close, but he'd wanted to chase the butterflies.

He tripped and fell on a tree root. Dirt filled his mouth and his knees hurt.

Another scream split the air and made his heart beat faster. He had to get to Mama. Something bad was happening. Real bad.

He pushed to his feet and ran. Harder and harder.

There. The house was in sight once he cleared the trees. He raced to the back porch, jumped up the stairs, and yanked open the screen door.

A stitch in his side made him stop and bend over for air. "Mama?"

Silence.

"Mama? Where are you?"

A mean voice from upstairs said something he didn't understand. *Slap! Smack!* The sounds scared him and urged him forward.

The backstairs door was locked, so Jimmy raced from the kitchen to the parlor and then to the front of the house and looked at the big staircase. His mother lay at the top, whimpering.

"Now, where is it?" The mean voice belonged to a pair of dirty boots that kicked his mama. "You took it, didn't you?"

Jimmy bolted forward and saw the man. Ugly. Dirty. Big. "Don't you hurt my mama!"

The man's head snapped up and squinted down. "Shut up, you little runt. You're next!" His ugly hands grabbed Mama's shoulders and then her neck. He forced her to her feet. "I won't hurt the boy if you'll just tell me where you hid it." The ugly man spat on the floor. Then he shook her again and again, raised his fist, and reared back —

"No!" Jimmy couldn't move. What was happening? He looked down at his feet as a whirring sound started in his head.

Laughter trickled down to him. But it wasn't nice laughter. "What? Aren't you gonna come get me?" He dropped Mama to the floor again. "Aw, are you afraid? Cat got your tongue?" The bad man yanked Mama's limp form up again and lowered his voice. "I'm gonna count to three and then I'm gonna kill your kid if you don't tell me." He looked down at Jimmy and snarled. "One . . ."

Jimmy's hands balled into fists at his sides but he couldn't seem to breathe or even move. His chest tightened. The whirring got louder. Where was Papa? Mama wasn't moving. Was she asleep?

"Two . . ."

Slap! The sound shook Jimmy to his knees. But this time it was Mama's hand doing the hitting. She hit the man's face again and then she clawed at him. Blood trickled down from the corner of his eye. She'd scratched him good.

"Run, Jimmy!" Her words were raspy.

"Why, you little . . ." The man's words grew louder until a roar filled Jimmy's ears and blotted out everything else.

9

Spots danced in front of his eyes as he gasped for air and watched the terrible man throw his mother down the stairs. Jimmy felt himself falling with her. He hit his head hard on the foyer floor and opened his eyes. But he couldn't see.

Mama! Clamping his eyes shut, his head hurt worse than he could ever remember. He tried to open his eyes again. To see her. Was she okay? His breaths were fast but he still couldn't get any air. Heavy thumps sounded on the stairs. The man was coming.

No! Jimmy lifted his eyelids a little and saw Mama. She was on the floor not too far from him. Her face was swollen and red and blood ran from her mouth.

Her hand reached out to his. "I . . . love you . . . Jimmy."

He cried. "I love you too, Mama."

The footsteps came closer. "Now, ain't this special?"

Mama closed her eyes and squeezed his hand. She wheezed, "Run!"

CHAPTER ONE

INDIANAPOLIS, INDIANA, 1891

"I forbid you to go!" Spittle flew from Adam Fletcher's mouth, his face a mottled red.

"My decision is made, Grandfather. I'm sorry." Two could play at this game. Lillian Porter wasn't a mouse to be trampled any longer by her stampeding-elephant-like-temper-tantrum-throwing grandparent. If she could just convince her heart to slow its tempo and stop breaking in two, she might survive this.

His eyes narrowed as the red of his face deepened. "How dare you speak back to me like that, child? You were not raised by your grandmother — God rest her soul — to ever speak to an elder in such a way." He stomped across the room and stopped mere inches from her.

She lowered her face. "I don't mean to be disrespectful, Grandfather. I only want to do something meaningful with my life."

"Meaningful? Bah. A woman's place is in the house, not gallivanting off to a place she's never been. And by herself!" His bony finger pointed at her nose. "I'll cut you off without a cent, I will!" Turning in a huff, he began to pace the room like a caged animal.

"Please, Grandfather, don't upset yourself so much."

He turned and looked at her oddly. "You're the one upsetting me."

Deep sorrow coursed through her. "I don't want to upset you, but can't you see that this is a good thing?"

"No, not at all. You won't be safe out there."

Lillian sighed. He wasn't going to hear reason no matter what she said, but she had to try. "Grandfather, for years you've cut me off from the world. After Grandmother died you wouldn't let me associate with my friends or even go shopping. You've jailed me up in this castle, not even allowing me to go to finishing school. The only time I ever get out of the house is to attend church with you."

"I've kept you safe," he countered and began pacing again.

"Safe? I suppose most prisons are, but they certainly aren't happy places."

In earlier years, while her beloved grandmother still lived, Grandfather had been doting and kind. As soon as she heard him come in the door each evening, she'd race down the grand staircase and hug him with all her might. He often had a peppermint stick or ribbon in his coat pocket for her. They'd laugh and talk and she'd follow him to his study and search maps in the atlas as he smoked his pipe. But after Grandmother passed, the smiling, doting, loving man turned into a beast. Lillian envisioned him transforming into a lion the way he roared his commands. On other days, she imagined him like a monstrous, huge elephant with red eyes and tusks sharp as sword blades as he stomped around the house grumbling his displeasure about everyone and everything.

Lillian took a deep breath and rubbed the locket at her throat. It contained the only picture she had of her mother and father — young and happy. Ready to follow their dreams to California. She wanted to follow their dreams, make some of her own, and actually *do* something with her life. Being locked up in a mansion surrounded by grief and no hope for the future would be her undoing.

Grandmother had always encouraged her to be herself — that it was okay to be strong and stand up for what she believed in. She'd often spoken of the tenacity it took to put up with a strong-willed, stubborn man. But she also modeled the behavior of a submissive, loving, and humble wife. How she ever balanced it all baffled Lillian to this day — especially after seeing the other side of her grandfather. If only she had her grandmother's wisdom at this moment. Standing up to this man she loved so dearly had taken years of bottled-up bravery. "Grandfather —"

"Do *not* call me 'Grandfather' with that tone that always got you whatever you wanted whenever your grandmother was alive. I will disown you and never speak to you again." He waved at her as if in dismissal.

Lillian stiffened her shoulders. All these years . . . she'd put up with his bullying and anger because she loved him. She knew he was grieved over his loss, but she always hoped and prayed that one day, maybe, he'd allow her *real* grandfather to take up residence again.

"If that's what you wish." She thought of all the angry things she might say to wound him as much as he was wounding her. But she didn't want to hurt him or anyone else.

Her grandfather looked up at her, the

scowl still lining his forehead, tears dampening his eyes. His grief radiated in waves off of him for all to feel. The man's misery was of his own doing. Rather than sharing in their grief together, he shut Lillian — and everyone else — out. In denying himself love and relationships, he'd found security in his anger and sorrow. As he turned his back toward her again, his shoulders slumped.

Lillian wanted only to comfort him — reassure him that she would always love him. "I do not wish to hurt you, Grandfather. And I don't care one whit about your money. I care about *you.* You are my blood, my kin, and I love you."

"Your words and actions here today would suggest otherwise." He turned slowly. "I've done the best I could by you."

"But you can't cage a person up just because you fear something bad might happen to them. Grandmother was afraid you might fret like this. She told me so. But her dying words were encouragement to live a life of purpose and value. To seek my dreams — my mother's dream. And . . . I intend to follow through."

The old man turned in a rage with his teeth bared. "How dare you! You know your mother's dream ended in death. Death!" he

15

screamed. "My only child." He choked the words, then clenched his jaw. "And I will not allow for you to follow in her footsteps, no matter what you *think* your grandmother said to you."

"I've already accepted —"

"I don't care what you've accepted! I *said* I forbid it and that's final!"

"Ahem." Stanton, their trusted butler, interrupted. "Your carriage is here, miss."

Lillian turned to the door of the library and found the bags she'd packed in the butler's hands. Two trunks sat behind him. "I guess that's it, then. Ask the driver to load my bags, please." She glanced one more time at her grandfather. Maybe, just maybe, she could get through to him.

"What do you mean —" her grandfather whirled around. "Stanton, what is this?"

"Miss Lillian's things, sir." The butler stood rigid.

"I'm on the next train, Grandfather." If only he would try to stop her. Tell her that he loved her. Please. Not that she wouldn't still go, but at least she would see some sign that the man she'd loved with all her heart resided within that hard shell somewhere. But he didn't respond. She sucked in a breath and held her grief in check. "I had hoped we could part on good terms. I won't be gone forever. I will write to you every week, and maybe one day you will even want to come for a visit."

For a long moment he stared at her. His expression a mix of anger and disbelief. No one ever defied him for fear of losing their position or his financial support, yet she had just done so without regard for his money.

The mahogany walls and shelves lined with books seemed to close in on Lillian. This had once been her favorite room. The floor-to-ceiling windows on the east side that drenched her in sunlight. The maps and ship models. And the books. She loved the books. She'd often followed the housekeeper around as the shelves were dusted and polished, breathing in the scent of leather, wood, and lemon oil. She held her breath. How could a room that held so much love and so many beautiful memories now strangle her with regret?

Grandfather took several steps toward her and then stopped, his hands balled into fists at his sides. "Then so be it." His face hardened even more. "Get out."

"Grandfather." She let out her breath in shock. Must he always be so thickheaded and stubborn? "Please. We don't want to say good-bye like this. As I said, I will write to you. And, when I can, I will be back to visit."

"No." Adam Fletcher's booming voice suddenly lowered. "I don't want to hear from you. And I never want to see you again." His eyes flashed like fire as he brushed past her and stormed from the room just as Stanton returned.

The tears came then. Big fat rolling tears. She suppressed a sob as Stanton looked at her with compassion.

"He's a hard man, miss." The butler stayed in his position at the door, but his features had softened significantly since his employer had left. "I'm sure he doesn't mean it."

Lillian took a deep breath and swiped her face with her gloved hands. "Oh, he meant it. Be assured of that, Stanton. I don't know who he is anymore. But it's no matter. I've made up my mind, and I know that God has given me a peace about this decision. I'm certain if I continue to seek Him above all else, that I will stay on the correct path."

The man nodded. He'd been a part of her life for as long as she could remember. "Yes, miss. The good Lord will guide and keep you." He turned toward the foyer. "I believe the driver is ready to get you to the station."

"I'm sorry to leave you all like this,

Stanton. You . . . well, all of the staff have been there for me since I was a baby. It's been so difficult the past few years, and he refuses to listen to anyone. Please don't think I'm abandoning you." She sighed. No use chattering any longer or attempting to explain.

The butler's expression said it all. He understood. Probably better than most.

"I'd like to keep in touch with you and the other staff, if that's all right?" Her steps slowed on the marble floor as she gazed at her home for what could be the last time. As she looked up at the upper landing, she envisioned her grandmother waving her hankie and smiling. The good memories this great big house contained. If only she could box them up and keep them with her always, blotting out all the sad ones of late.

"Yes, miss. We would like that very much." The rigid set of his stance never faltered as he paused at the door. "You are like a cherished daughter to us all. I'm certain you will make an outstanding nanny to the little mute boy. He'll need some joy in his life, and you will most undoubtedly bring it. Never forget that we will all be praying for you. Don't hesitate to send us word if you need anything."

Lillian took the smaller of the two bags

from Stanton, then headed through the open door to the carriage. She managed to swallow around the lump in her throat. These people were so dear to her. Why, they and this house were all she'd ever known. Pressing a hand to her locket, she heard what she thought were footsteps and turned on her heel. But the empty foyer mocked her. Her love for the old man must've conjured up the sounds in her mind. Hoping that he'd change his mind.

She turned around to face the carriage, but then glanced over her shoulder once more.

Not a sign of him.

Taking a few more steps toward the carriage, she allowed her gaze to glance up to her grandfather's bedroom window. A slight rustling of the curtains told Lillian he was watching. The ache in her chest built. She wanted so much to ease his pain and worry . . . and to have his approval.

"Good-bye, Grandfather. I love you." Her whispered words seemed to bounce back from the brick walls of the house. The curtain above went still. The tall clock down the hall chimed the hour. As it echoed through the foyer and out the door, the finality of the moment struck her. A hollow loneliness engulfed her. Lillian's time here had come to an end.

With a deep breath and lift of her chin, Lillian turned and headed down the steps to the hired carriage. Could she really leave like this? With her grandfather — her only living relative — so angry? And all because of her? Tears threatened to spill once again, but she held them at bay.

Stanton helped her into the carriage while the driver who'd already packed the two trunks came and took the bag Stanton held. Lillian could see the sadness in the butler's eyes. She wished she could say something to comfort him — all of them. The staff were like family to her, and she would miss them.

Stanton closed the small carriage door. He leaned toward the open window. As if reading her mind, he spoke with a smile. "You will be greatly missed, Miss Lillian. Fletcher Manor won't be the same without you."

She nodded and bit her lip to stave off the tears yet again as she gazed up at the red-brick exterior of her home. Would she ever see this beautiful place again? Would her grandmother be proud of her for following her dreams, or would she scold her for abandoning her grandfather?

As the driver maneuvered the carriage

away from the immaculate house and grounds, Lillian closed her eyes. She could almost see her grandmother again reaching out to her in those last moments. *"Your mother . . . she wasn't wrong in leaving. . . . The Lord just had a different plan than we expected, and He gave us you. Follow your dreams, dear girl. . . ."*

Tears choked her as they exited the gates outside her home of twenty-one years.

Lord, please make my paths straight. Forgive me for leaving Grandfather in such a way. I want to follow You.

She checked her small overnight bag and then patted her reticule containing her money and train ticket. The blessed peace that filled her heart soothed the aching places inside. There was a seven-year-old boy who awaited her on the other end of her journey. A little boy who needed healing. A little boy whose tragic story had pricked her heart from the very beginning. Lillian nodded. God's plan for her was in California. She knew it deep inside. But she couldn't rid her mind of one rather sickening thought.

Her grandfather had made it perfectly clear . . . she could never return.

Woody Colton found himself in Clark's general store in the small town of Angels Camp against his better judgment. Most times when he was in need of supplies, he trekked twice the distance to Copperopolis or put in his order with the Stickle brothers' mercantile, but he didn't have the time this month to spare, and Stickle Bros. was closed. So he'd had no choice. And now he was paying for it. Most people with a lick of common sense would have thought all the rumors and gossip would've died down by now. But no. They had only gotten worse.

Herman Clark, the owner of the general store, scowled across the room at Woody. Twelve customers had come and gone since he entered, and yet he still waited to be helped.

"That's him. He's the one I was tellin' you about," one lady whispered to another as they swished by, their chins high in the air.

"Do you think he'd hurt anyone else?" The lady's response cut him to the quick as they left the store.

The bell jangled over the door, and Woody glanced around the room. He'd been waiting thirty minutes. Guess his business wasn't as good as everyone else's.

After three more customers left with their goods, Woody could take no more and rang the bell on the counter. The Lord had given him enough patience to make it this far, but good grief, he wasn't a saint.

The shopkeeper just glared. "What do you want, Colton?"

"Herman, now I've held my tongue while you served everyone else who walked into your store, but I've had just about enough. You've known me for six years, and I've done a lot of business with you. What is it going to take to get my supplies?"

"Just because the judge let you go doesn't mean that anyone in this town has to trust you." This man he'd once called friend sneered at him, his face full of disgust.

So that was it. Everyone believed the accusations, even though he'd been found innocent. Not only had his heart been ripped out, but now they'd decided to trample it into the dust. As if his loss wasn't enough. "I'm not here to cause any trouble, Herman. I just need some supplies. And I'm paying cash."

Herman's eyes narrowed. "I don't know why I am even talking to you —"

"Herman!" Carla Clark's shrill voice from the back of the store shut the man up. With her hands on her ample hips, she shook her head at her husband. "I can't believe you are treating Woody that way. Why, we sat next to him and his wife in church for years. We prayed together and ate together and served together."

"*Humph.* Sittin' next to someone in church don't mean nothin', woman! Just because someone sits in church don't make them God-fearing."

"Well, then, you wouldn't mind sleepin' down here in the storeroom, would ya?" Carla reached for Woody's list. " 'Cause I shore don't want anyone but my *God-fearing* husband upstairs with me. And the man next to me right now ain't actin' like *he's* God-fearing. Especially when his opinion seems to be based on a bunch of malicious whispers rather than fact. As I recall, maliciousness and whisperings are sins that are listed right there with murder as to being disfavored in the eyes of God. It's all right there in Romans chapter one."

Herman sputtered as his face turned red. "We will discuss this later."

"Sure, we will." Carla handed Herman the list. "Right after you fill this customer's list and remind yourself what John chapter thirteen says in the Good Book." She turned toward the door as two more ladies walked in but threw over her shoulder, "Verses thirty-four and thirty-five, I believe."

"Stop throwing your Bible Scriptures at me, woman."

As soon as Carla mentioned the reference, the verses floated through Woody's mind. *A new commandment I give unto you, that ye love one another; as I have loved you, that ye also love one another. By this shall all men know that ye are my disciples, if ye have love one to another.*

Herman must've known the verses by heart, as well, because he began filling Woody's order without another word. A lot of slamming and thudding accompanied his work, but no words. Woody'd heard enough words today anyway. No wonder his orders for olive oil had all but diminished from Angels Camp. Granted, there was great demand for it in neighboring areas, but his own town ostracized him.

He hauled out all the bags and boxes to his wagon and noticed a small crowd of people out of the corner of his eye. As they inched closer with every trip he made to the wagon, he figured it would be prudent to head out of town as soon as possible. Maybe staying away from Angels Camp would be the best idea from now on. No matter what. He couldn't put Jimmy through this.

As he left the store for the last time, Carla

caught him at the door and patted his shoulder. "How's little Jimmy? We miss seeing him."

"He's fine." Liar. His son was thin as a rail and wouldn't speak.

"Well, good." She stuck a small brown sack in his shirt pocket. "It's candy for the boy. You're welcome here anytime, Woody."

He shook his head. "I wish that were true, Carla. But thank you for your help today."

"You know I'm a stubborn old biddy and can hold my own. I won't stand for people treatin' you wrong. It ain't right." She said this loud enough for the bystanders to hear.

Woody noted that a few of the gatherers left the group, while the others seemed fixed to the place where they stood. Carla blinked a few times, and Woody spotted the tears in her eyes.

"It stabs me in the heart when I see and hear these good folks believin' the lies. The good Lord done taught me a powerful lesson about gossipin', but by then I'd done too much damage with my tongue. I may never see my daughter again because of it, but I aim to shuck gossip and malicious whisperings clean out of Angels Camp." She crossed her arms and eyed the remaining crowd across the street. "They'll come around. Just have faith. Which reminds me, when can we expect to see you and Jimmy back in church?"

Woody pasted on a smile. "I don't think the church folks are ready to have us back."

"Stuff and nonsense. I'm gonna speak to the reverend about this right away."

Mrs. McCarthy approached the door and sidestepped Woody. "Good morning, Mrs. Clark." She rushed inside the store like her dress was on fire.

"Good morning." Carla turned to go inside but looked back at Woody. "We'll get it all straightened out. These are good folks."

Good folks. Who gossiped and allowed their fear to guide them.

He nodded as the door closed and turned to his wagon. Across the street, the crowd that had gathered moved toward him. When they were within ten feet, three men walked to the front of the group. The ringleaders, no doubt. Arms crossed, eyes narrowed, it was clear they weren't a welcoming committee.

"We don't want you in our town, Colton." The biggest of the group spat on the ground.

"Well, I'm leaving, so you get your wish." Woody climbed up into his wagon and took the reins.

The men made a half circle around his

horses. "What we're sayin' is that we don't want you back here. Ever. Not after what you did."

Woody took a deep breath and lowered his head. He knew these people. Each and every one of them in the group. A new ache crushed his chest. He looked back up at the men and shook his head. "I'm sorry you feel that way, but let's get one thing straight, right now" — he released the brake, then lifted the reins to signal the horses — "I did *not* kill my wife."

CHAPTER TWO

The train's whistle woke Lillian from a fitful sleep. Every inch of exposed skin felt gritty and covered in dirt as she attempted to work the kinks from her limbs. Ouch! And her neck didn't appreciate the hours it'd spent on her makeshift pillow, either.

The conductor strode through the car as if on a Sunday walk. Lillian had tried to master walking with the lurching and swaying of the train, but with little success. He reached her seat and tipped his cap toward her as she adjusted her hat. "We're still in Nebraska, miss," he blurted out before Lillian had a chance to ask the question on her mind.

"Thank you." She hoped her smile would help to smooth over his agitated demeanor that she'd apparently caused. It hadn't been her intent to nag the poor man every time he passed through. Honestly. She'd just have to put more effort into keeping her curiosity at bay.

Nebraska proved to be a wider state than she remembered learning from her schooling days, as the train had traveled for many hours already. At this rate, she'd be able to finish reading her book, eat dinner, and still be in the same state by bedtime.

Oh, why couldn't they be to California already? Impatience frayed the last of her nerves. Nerves that reminded her of all the what-ifs. It was bad enough that she'd deserted her grandfather and defied him in such a way, but now she had to endure the endless hours of the rocking train day in and day out with nothing to occupy her but her guilty thoughts.

Lillian stood, all the while holding tight to the back of the seat lest she fall flat on her face. She stretched, attempting to get rid of the remorse, as well as her stiffness. Grandfather's words returned again and again to haunt her. "*. . . your mother's dream ended in death. Death . . .*" The reminder of following her mother's dream — her own dream now — filled her with a sense of dread. Was she doomed to repeat her mother's mistakes? Grandfather Fletcher was a wealthy man. He'd made a fortune in all his business ventures over the years and couldn't bear it when his only child left to pursue her dreams of the West.

The story told throughout the household of Fletcher Manor was that when Lillian was only a few months old, her father died and her mother Mary fell apart. The grief too much to bear, she resorted to memories of happier years and all the dreams she'd shared with her husband. Dreams of owning land in fertile California. Dreams of fruit orchards and olive groves on their own prosperous farm. And dreams of vacations on the famed Pacific Ocean. So Mary had left in the middle of the night with a small purse full of money from her mother. Her only good-bye had been in the form of a note on the fireplace mantel that said she would send for Lillian once she was settled. But disaster had struck before Mary could ever see the beloved ocean.

Thoughts of her mother brought Lillian full circle and back to her present situation. Two months ago, an advertisement for a nanny position on an olive farm in California ignited a spark of memories and the desire to follow her parents' dreams. All the stories about beautiful, headstrong — always the dreamer — Mary came rushing back. Granted, she had no real memories of the woman who'd given birth to her, but oh, the tales her grandmother had told her as a child. The elderly woman grieved the loss of her only child and often mentioned that she wondered if she had been at fault by giving precious Mary the money. Would she still be alive? With them? But Grandmother always ended her stories with a smile and poured her heart and soul into Lillian and loved her unconditionally.

When Grandmother passed and Grandfather turned into a mean and angry old man who held no resemblance to the man who'd raised and loved her, Lillian's mind wandered to thoughts of the man and woman who gave her life and their westward dreams.

All she really longed for was a life that mattered. To make a difference. Grandmother understood that. Even though they'd sheltered and guarded young Lillian for so long, Grandmother shared her heart on her deathbed and knew that Lillian needed to spread her wings and fly.

Grandfather *had* understood it while his wife still lived. Adam Fletcher — wealthy widower, angry and bitter tyrant drowning in his grief — did not.

The train car passed over a rough span that nearly sent Lillian to the floor. She felt her face redden as several men glanced her way as if to lend aid should the need arise.

Taking her seat again, Lillian ducked her head, thankful for the brim of her hat. The last thing she'd wanted to do was draw attention to the fact that she was traveling alone. Proper young women didn't do such things, but then this entire trip hadn't exactly been what a proper young woman might do.

Doubt crept in. Had she made a mistake?

To ease her worries, Lillian opened her carpetbag and pulled out the correspondence from Mr. Woodward Colton she'd stacked and tied with a ribbon. Stanton had secreted the letters to her as well as posted her responses. With plenty of time to dispose of, she decided to study the letters and see what she could do to better prepare herself for her upcoming position.

The stationery was high quality and his penmanship that of an educated gentleman. It had impressed Lillian from the start. As she opened the crisp letters and placed them in order of date, she allowed a little thrill to jolt through her and diminish the doubt. How exciting to be on her own and away from the domineering, overbearing, and suffocating presence of her grandfather. With a gasp, she glanced heavenward, almost expecting a bolt of lightning to strike for her disrespectful, ungrateful attitude.

She allowed her breath to release and closed her eyes. *Lord, forgive me for my horrible thoughts. I promise to work on my love toward Grandfather.*

The train jerked over another rough stretch of rail, causing Lillian to glance out the window. The vast expanse of prairie rolled by in what seemed an incredible speed. Train travel was such an amazing thing and one she had always wanted to experience. However, the comfort wasn't as great as she'd hoped. Of course, Mr. Colton had purchased her standard tickets, and why wouldn't he? She was traveling to be a nanny, not as the wealthy granddaughter of Adam Fletcher. But if she had the opportunity — and funds — next time, she'd prefer traveling in style, using one of the grand and glorious Pullman cars. She'd heard tell they provided a traveler with cushioned chairs and beds to sleep in. How wonderful that would be. Her aching backside attested to the fact.

The train began to slow for what seemed like the hundredth time. No doubt they were approaching yet another tiny town whose very existence relied upon the railroad. They'd just taken on water at the last stop, so perhaps this would be nothing more than a slowing to grab the mail off the high hooks next to the tracks. The conductor had informed Lillian that this was one of the best ways for them to keep the mail moving. Once the mail was snagged, they immediately took it to the mail car, where a clerk would sort through it. That way they could leave letters off at the various towns as they headed west. It was all quite fascinating.

Just as she'd suspected, the train only slowed, and the tiny town passed by with nothing more than a blur. Once they'd regained their speed, Lillian refocused on the letters in her hands. Reading through them, she wondered about the family she would be serving.

Thirty-year-old Woodward Colton was a widower with a seven-year-old son named Jimmy. There was no mention of how his wife had died or how long she'd been gone, but it had been devastating to their little boy. It seemed the child hadn't spoken since his mother's death. Mr. Colton wanted her to be a nanny, teacher, and companion to the young boy, since they lived quite a ways from town and the elder Colton was busy long hours each day tending his olive groves. He'd requested that she come as soon as possible — *immediately* was his exact wordage. Concern for the lad oozed through the pages. The man must care a great deal for his son.

Her heart broke just a little more as she thought of little Jimmy. Losing his beloved mother at such a young age and no longer able to speak. Was it his grief that kept him from using his tongue? Or did he feel all alone? Abandoned? She certainly had felt that way, even though she'd never known her parents. Her grandparents had been wonderful to lavish her with attention and love, but there was still that hole in her heart where her mother and father should have been. If Jimmy felt the same way, then Lillian knew she could use this to help them grow close.

Lillian vowed then and there that she would do whatever was necessary to help the young boy heal. Children were her soft spot. She loved to work with them at church whenever she had a chance. Reverend Owens, back in Indianapolis, had often asked her to schedule special children's events since their church had grown so large. A wave of grief washed over her. She hadn't even said good-bye to the children in person. Hopefully Reverend Owens would read her letter to them, but would they, too, feel abandoned? Another wave hit her — this time filled with guilt. Grandfather's face — the face that she had kissed countless times as a child — appeared before her. Sad eyes. Tears pooling at the corners where he used to say his wrinkles multiplied every time she made him laugh or smile.

She'd abandoned him in his grief. Yes, he'd been miserable to live with the past few years. Yes, she had reached her majority in years and wanted to escape. But the dull ache that pounded in her chest now reminded her of how much she loved the old man. Would the chasm between them ever be bridged?

Lillian wiped at her eyes and shook her head. She couldn't afford to wallow. It was prudent to keep looking ahead.

"Miss?"

She looked up to find a young man looking down at her.

"Are you quite all right? I saw that you were crying." He didn't wait for an answer but took the wooden seat opposite her.

Lillian stiffened, once again very aware that she traveled alone. "I'm fine. Thank you." She looked back at the letters in her hands, hoping it would dissuade him from further conversation.

"I couldn't help but notice that you're traveling alone."

Lillian squared her shoulders and lifted her gaze to meet his smiling face. He couldn't have been more than eighteen or nineteen, if that. "I do not see that it is any of your concern."

"Well, I just thought maybe we could travel together." He leaned forward with a smirk. "After all, you must be the kind of gal that enjoys a good time. Otherwise, you wouldn't be here all by yourself. I heard tell that women who travel alone are always looking for fun. Believe me, we could have a lot of fun together." He winked.

She drew in a deep breath and prayed for wisdom. "I do not know from whom you might have received such errant direction, but I assure you that ladies can and do travel alone when necessity dictates, and they are neither looking for fun nor . . . a good time. Furthermore, I cannot imagine that your mother raised you to act in such a manner. How it must grieve her." The man looked confused, but Lillian continued. "I will pray for you to find your way back to being a respectable sort of man who would make her proud."

The stranger looked at her as if she'd slapped him. "If you didn't want to have a good time, you coulda just said so. Didn't have to bring my ma into it." He got to his feet and shook his head. "Women sure make no sense."

Lillian forced back a smile. She waited until the dejected young man headed back to the far end of the car before she let herself relax. This was the first time she'd encountered such behavior, and it had shaken her more than she cared to realize. Again she wondered if perhaps this entire trip had been a mistake. Had she only agreed in order to assert her will upon her grandfather? Was this young man's behavior the kind of thing she could expect all the long way to California?

She remembered the preacher speaking of how people often acted foolishly and took themselves out of safety for the sake of indulging sinful behavior. Was she guilty of that?

Lord, I'm really not trying to act in defiance. I brought this matter to You and felt confident that this was Your direction for me. If I was wrong, please forgive me and help me to make the best of it. Again that same peace she'd known when first bringing the idea to God in prayer engulfed Lillian and gave her a sense of comfort.

She focused back on the letters and read through the rest, perusing the terms and wages. It seemed more than fair. At least in her opinion. But what would she know? She'd never worked outside of her grandfather's mansion a day in her life. And in the last five years, she'd rarely left the manor except to go to church. Mr. Colton seemed pleased that she came from affluence and didn't mind that she had no experience. He assured her she would be comfortable in quarters on the main level of the house along with his housekeeper, Mrs. Goodman. And that the utmost of propriety was to be shown at all times.

A more perfect situation couldn't be found. Lillian refolded the missives and tucked them in their envelopes. As she stacked the letters and retied the ribbon, she couldn't help but smile.

A new life awaited her.

Darwin Longstreet hated waiting. First, he'd waited for Pa to die. Then he'd waited to strike it rich. Next, he'd waited in jail. Now he waited to find his gold. All he'd done was wait, wait, wait. And he was sick of it.

Sick of that and being hunted, and because he was hunted, he had to hide with relatives he hated who ordered him about. His father's no-good brother, John, had no business bossing him around. And his varmint cousins, Saul and David, weren't any better. Thinking they could do it just because he and Harry lived with them. Well, they had another think coming, that was for sure. Darwin would show them. He'd seen and done a lot in his twenty-seven years. Things that would make Uncle John's hair curl. They thought he was just an ignorant thief who'd been accused of murder . . . well, if they knew how many lives he'd taken, maybe they'd respect him more. Or turn him in for the reward money.

He frowned. No-good relatives. He couldn't allow them to ruin his plans. He hadn't spent all his time evading the law for nothing. That old miner he'd killed didn't deserve the gold he'd found. He would've died soon anyway. He was old and worn out. Darwin just sped up the process. At least he'd been able to hide the gold on his family's former property before the law caught up to him. Then they'd locked him up. In that lonely little town.

Escape had been easy. Darwin wasn't sure there was a jail built that he couldn't find a way out of.

So now his only problems were not getting caught and finding the gold that somehow had gotten moved. That Colton woman sure didn't know. But Darwin would bet every last sack of gold that her husband *did* know. He had to. Otherwise, why would he stay? His wife was dead, and the town thought he'd done the dirty deed. There was no reason for Colton to hang around unless he knew there was a payout waiting.

Darwin smiled as he remembered the fear he'd struck in her and her boy. It made him feel powerful — able to lick the world. They were living on *his* family's property. Property that should have come to him. But his mother had died and then the bank foreclosed when Darwin had no money for the mortgage. He'd asked for just a little more time, but they refused. Now that Colton man had his property. Not only that, but he'd torn down the house where Darwin's family once lived and built an enormous two-story home in its place.

Anger surged through him, and Darwin made himself a promise that if he got the chance, he'd kill Colton and maybe even that uppity banker who kicked him off the land. But not before he found his gold.

Darwin thought back to when he'd run across that old miner buying drinks for everybody and flashing around his gold. The man was sitting on a small fortune, and Darwin figured he might as well have it rather than let the old man go on with it.

When the drunken old man headed home to his gold mine, Darwin simply followed him and helped himself to the man's fortune. After he'd bashed his head in, Darwin hightailed it back to the property just ahead of the sheriff, having no idea how the man had caught wind of the old-timer's murder so fast. There'd barely been time to bury the multiple bags of gold in various places around the property. He'd taken them on a merry chase halfway across the state before the sheriff and posse caught up to him. It might have been easy for the sheriff to find out about the murder, but the chase was anything but easy. They would never have caught him, in fact, had his horse not gone lame.

And now he was playing the same game, only this time it was men seeking him in order to claim the reward. If Darwin could just keep the bounty hunters off his own trail, he'd be able to get his money and hightail it out of town. Possibly even the country. Mexico was warm and welcoming to wealthy men like him. He could build himself a stone house with a wall around it and have whatever he wanted. With plenty of señoritas to keep him company.

But the waiting was killing him. He knew when he broke out that he couldn't just go to the farm and collect his gold. The law would have known where Darwin had once lived. They'd expect him to go there. Well, he wasn't that stupid. He'd waited this long to retrieve his treasure. He could wait a little longer. Once the excitement of his breaking out settled down, folks would start looking for him elsewhere, and then he could go to the farm.

He spat his chewing tobacco onto the floor in the tiny cabin and sat back in the chair. Let someone else clean it up. He didn't care. He propped his boots up on the table in front of him. As soon as he got his hands on his gold —

"Brother! Brother, where are you?" Stomping accompanied Harry's childish voice.

"Harry, quit yer stompin'." At six feet, four inches, his twenty-year-old brother was huge like a brown bear, but his brain was stuck somewhere back in his childhood years. Ma had a name for it, but Darwin didn't ever care to listen. All he knew was that he'd been burdened with the boy since she died.

His simpleminded brother put a finger to his lips. "Sh . . . okay," he half whispered, half yelled. "But you told me not to sneak up on ya ever again." Harry's head shook

45

back and forth.

"But that don't mean you gotta stomp everywhere ya go." When he promised Ma he'd take care of Harry, he'd done it out of guilt. Ma loved the dumb man-child and had protected him from their beast of a father all those years. Darwin didn't understand why. The kid wasn't any kind of a help to anyone; he just got in the way. "Where you been?"

Harry shrugged. "I like explorin' and lookin' at things." He crouched down and pointed to the slop of tobacco. "I'll clean this up. You might fall down." He shuffled across the room and picked up a rag out of the corner. Three mice scattered. "Can we leave here soon?"

"No. Why ya in such a hurry, anyway?"

His younger brother sucked in his bottom lip. "I don't like it here. When Ma died, she said I'd get to live with you." He looked toward the door, his eyes wide as he lowered his voice. "Not with Uncle John."

Darwin narrowed his eyes and leaned forward. "They been mean to ya while I'm gone?"

Harry cocked his head to the side, looked at the floor, and frowned.

"Tell me, Harry. What have those lowlifes done to ya?"

Another vigorous shaking of his head. They probably threatened simpleminded Harry.

"I'll get ya out of here as soon as I find my stuff, kid."

"What stuff you lookin' for?" Harry came closer and knelt on the floor in front of him. "Can I help? I like lookin' for stuff."

Darwin sighed. "It's stuff I hid a long time ago before the sheriff took me away." Why did he ever open his big mouth in front of the kid? Now there'd be nothing but questions.

"On Pa's property?"

Darwin sat up straight. "How'd you know it was on Pa's property?"

" 'Cause I followed you. Long, long, long time ago. You had a bunch of sacks." Harry giggled and covered his mouth like a little girl. "Just like I did last year. But I thought you said you was payin' 'spects to Ma."

Darwin pulled Harry closer. "Did anyone else see you?"

Harry's eyes went wide and he leaned back. " 'Course not. It was like hide-n-seek."

Releasing his hold, Darwin stared up at the big dumb boy and narrowed his eyes. "Well, yeah. That's the stuff I'm lookin' for.

It's not where I left it, and so I've got to find it."

Harry stood up and smiled. "I can help you!" He clapped his hands together.

"No, Harry. You can't help me." Just what he needed. His imbecile brother following him around. He'd get caught for sure.

"Yes, I can." Arms folded across his chest, Harry stuck out his chin. " 'Cause I know where it is."

"I done told ya" — Darwin raised his voice as he stood — "it's not where I left it."

"That's 'cause I moved it." The grin on his brother's face was like he'd won the prize at a carnival. He shoved his hands in his pockets and laughed. "See? I can help you!"

Moving forward, Darwin put his hands on Harry's shoulders. "This isn't a game, Harry. You *moved* it?"

He nodded and his silly grin grew.

"Why'd you move it?"

" 'Cause men came to look for it."

"And you know where it is?"

He nodded again and then skipped around the room, singing, "I'm gonna help Brother, I'm gonna help Brother —"

"Gonna help him do what?" Uncle John's gruff voice interrupted. His even larger frame filled the doorway, and the two filthy shadows behind him had to be Saul and David.

Harry stilled and backed toward the corner.

Darwin stepped in front of his brother. "Nothin'. You know he can't help do nothin'."

Uncle John moved into the room and got in Darwin's face. The stench of rotten teeth and alcohol consumed him. "That simple-minded fool better not bring any attention out here. You got it?" He shoved Darwin aside and pushed Harry down into the corner.

Another reason to get out of here as soon as possible. Darwin's temper flared and he clenched his fists. No one treated him that way and got away with it. They deserved to pay.

And pay they would. Kin or not. They deserved it.

Harry looked up at him, his eyes wide. Darwin forced himself to take a deep breath. He'd never killed anyone in front of his brother. So with the news Harry had just given him, he calculated his next move. A slow burn started in his gut. Revenge was always sweet.

Yes, they would pay.

CHAPTER THREE

The wagon bounced down the road toward Woody's farm. He allowed the horses to plod along as his thoughts were elsewhere. How could God have permitted all this to happen? Hadn't he followed Him? Studied the Word? And what did he get in return? Unbearable loss. Grief. A damaged son who wouldn't speak, and now everyone he knew thought he'd killed his own beloved wife.

God, why do I have to bear up under all this misery? Haven't I lost enough?

As soon as he let the words float heavenward, he regretted them. God, the Father of all creation, had allowed His own Son to be sacrificed for Woody — and the rest of the world. The ultimate price had been paid because He loved them that much. Woody knew that suffering and trials were part of this time on earth, but he hadn't expected it to hit him so hard. And to feel so weak and unprepared for it. There were days that he didn't think he could go on without Rebecca. Especially knowing how she'd been murdered and that he hadn't been there. No chance for good-bye.

And then, there was little Jimmy. He hadn't spoken since they'd found him curled up in the locked closet. Bruised and shaking. Not only was his sweet wife gone, but so was his son. Had the boy witnessed what happened to his mother? Or had he been locked up during that time and heard it all? Both scenarios were torturous to Woody. He couldn't undo the past. He couldn't undo the pain. And he certainly couldn't undo the damage the rumors had done.

As the weight of all the burdens pressed down on him, Woody pulled the horses to a stop. Wouldn't it be easier for everyone if he just ended it all? His housekeeper would see to Jimmy. She was a good woman who loved the boy as if he were her own grandchild. It would be so much easier to just lie down and die. For several long, painful moments the ominous thoughts refused to lift. Finally, Woody straightened and shook his head.

No. A deep sigh pushed out of the depths of his chest. He couldn't take his own life and leave Jimmy an orphan. But sometimes, keeping the darkness from closing in was more than he could bear.

With a flick of the reins, he started the horses again toward home. The dark thoughts — thoughts of ending his own life — had come with more frequency of late. *God, You know I believe in You with my whole heart. I know You love me. But I'm just not strong enough. I'm tired and I'm worn out. And little Jimmy isn't getting any better. . . .* His prayer trailed off. The words were gone. He hated feeling weak. Feeling vulnerable. And yet, that's exactly what he was.

The dark thoughts pressed in again. Miserable. Wretched. Worthless. They all described him. And he was useless to fight it any longer. Regret and anger were so much stronger.

As the horses rounded the corner toward home, he saw the gate with the archway and the olive trees beyond. Rebecca stood by his side to make this place not only a thriving farm, but also beautiful. What was the use of it now? To try to sell his goods to people who didn't know him, while his own neighbors and friends thought him to be a murderer? What good was that?

Once he was through the gate, he slowed the horses again. Jimmy sat in the dirt ahead under an olive tree. Cradling something in his arms. The wind tugged for a moment on the light brown hair of Woody's boy. And his heart ached. How could he possibly think of himself at a time like this? His son was suffering through the grief of losing his mama the year before. He'd suffered enough. He needed his father.

Woody closed his eyes for a moment and offered a prayer of thanks as new strength took residence and chased the black cloud away. He didn't understand God's plan, but he knew that the good Lord had given Jimmy to him. Right then and there, Woody decided that no matter what, he would do everything in his power to help his son heal. He just wasn't sure his power was all that useful.

Woody pulled the wagon to a complete stop and hopped down. "Whatcha got there, Jimmy?"

His son turned, a tear dripping down his cheek. He held the bundle in his arms up to his pa.

As Woody stepped closer, he saw a tiny rabbit with a torn ear. The little guy seemed to be alive, if the little nose twitching up and down was any indication. "We should get him home. I bet Mrs. Goodman can help us find a box for him to place by the stove. We'll get him all fixed up."

Jimmy nodded. But as he tried to stand,

he couldn't get up with the animal in his arms.

Woody lifted his son and the rabbit in one fell swoop and headed to the wagon. The boy weighed next to nothing. Dirt covered him and his small bundle. Woody settled Jimmy in on the seat beside him, then headed the wagon back toward the house. He looked down at Jimmy and squeezed his hand. They might all be damaged and grieving, but they wouldn't give up.

Mrs. Goodman knocked on the doorjamb into the library, which he used as his office. "Sorry to interrupt, Woody, but the mail was tucked into one of the supply boxes." She laid it down on his desk. "Thought you might like to see it."

"Thank you, Mrs. Goodman." Woody looked up at his housekeeper and felt the need to say more. "And not just for the mail. You've been wonderful to us all these years and have had to go through so much with us. Thank you. I don't say it enough, but I'm grateful."

If he wasn't mistaken, he'd shocked her, because his stoic and no-nonsense housekeeper had tears in her eyes. "I've hated watching you boys suffer. That's for sure.

And lately, you've had this dark cloud following you around. I've been quite worried." She sniffed. "It's much appreciated to hear your words of kindness."

"I'm sorry they're so overdue."

"Stuff and nonsense. We both know that's not true." She straightened her shoulders. "Now before I head back to the kitchen, do you need anything? I promised Jimmy that we would check on the bunny before he went to bed."

"No, I'm fine." Using a letter opener, he opened the envelope from Indiana, praying that it was what he hoped.

"You just let me know, if you do." Her feet shuffled away.

"Wait, Mrs. Goodman?" A sliver of hope started in his chest after reading the first few lines.

"Yes?"

"Would you mind coming back after checking on the rabbit? I have some news."

"Not at all. I'll be back in a little bit."

Woody nodded and went back to the letter. It seemed Miss Lillian Porter accepted his offer of the nanny position and was on her way. After weeks of waiting and no word, he'd given up hope. He glanced at the postmark. Apparently, it'd been his own fault. Had he not avoided town for so long, he could have gotten his mail sooner. He checked the calendar on the wall. Good grief! And she would arrive in just two days' time.

Woody jumped up from his desk and thought of all the things they'd need to accomplish in two days. Excitement surged through him. Maybe Jimmy would finally speak again. Oh, it might take time, but Woody just knew that Miss Porter was the answer.

As he paced the room, Mrs. Goodman entered. "All right, Woody, so what's this news?"

"The lady I was telling you about in Indianapolis?"

"Yes?"

"She's coming. She's on her way right now."

"Why, that's wonderful news! Jimmy needs someone so badly." Mrs. Goodman pulled a pencil from behind her ear and her tattered notepad from out of her apron pocket. "And goodness knows, I'm too old to keep up with the lad. Oh, this will be just what we need. I'll have to get the room ready for her and I think new curtains would be nice . . . and —"

"She'll be here the day after tomorrow," Woody threw out.

"Oh my." Mrs. Goodman dropped her pencil, then picked it up again. "Yes. Well, then . . ." She scribbled furiously on the notepad.

"Don't go to any unnecessary trouble. I know how you like to do things, but I'm sure Miss Porter will be happy with the room as it is. You've done a wonderful job keeping up the house."

Mrs. Goodman left the room, nodding and talking to herself. If he were to guess, the older woman would have the room totally redone and have enough baked goods for an army of soldiers by the time Miss Porter arrived.

Now if he could just get to her before the town rumors did, he'd be doing well.

"Run!" Mama's voice sounded weak. But one look at her eyes told him she meant it. And Jimmy didn't want to disobey. A sob caught in his throat. Why couldn't he breathe? But, Mama! Her eyes closed and her hand went limp. She just lay there. He couldn't leave her.

The bad man yanked Jimmy up by his arm. "I don't suppose you know where my treasure is, you snot-nosed kid. . . ." His large hands wrapped around Jimmy's shoulders and squeezed.

His breaths came faster and faster. He

shook his head.

The man shook him. Hard. "You sure? You better not be lyin' to me." He shook him again and again until his teeth rattled.

The shaking helped him breathe, though. He had to help Mama. This man scared him. More than spiders and snakes. More than anything. "I don't know. . . . Mama doesn't know, either. She always tells the truth. Why'd you hurt her?"

The man made a face by scrunching up his nose and frowning too big. His voice changed as he made fun of Jimmy. "She always tells the truth." His big hands shook him again and the mean voice came back. "And I hurt her because she couldn't help me and got in my way. That's why." He looked around the foyer. "And now you're in my way, and I gotta dispose of you too, you little snoop." With that, he smacked Jimmy on top of the head with one hand and dragged him by the arm with the other.

The bad man stopped in front of the closet Mrs. Goodman used for cleaning supplies and mousetraps. He yanked open the door and muttered, "Too small to hide your mother's body in, but it would do for you, runt."

"No, mister, please! Don't put me in the closet." Jimmy started to cry. He glanced over at Mama. She hadn't moved.

"Shut up!" He yanked harder on Jimmy's arm. "Might as well just shoot you right here." It took him less than a second to pull out the revolver from his belt.

The whirring started in Jimmy's head again. This time, the spots came faster.

"Brother . . . Brother . . ." Another voice from outside sang the words.

The bad man said a word that Papa had told Jimmy never to say. Both of the big man's hands came around his throat and squeezed until he couldn't breathe. He whispered, "You better not say a word about me to anyone, you hear me? I'll kill your pa and your little housekeeper, and I'll kill everyone in town if you say one word." And with that, he slapped Jimmy hard in the face.

Pain shot through his whole head. Tears burned the corners of his eyes.

"Did you hear me?" The man's breath smelled rotten. "Not one word. Or I'll kill them all. It will be all your fault. Just like it's your fault that your mama's dead."

Mama was dead? No. He shook his head and tears slid down his cheeks.

"All your fault. If you hadn't come in here when you did." He pushed Jimmy into the closet.

More calls came from outside. Someone was looking for their brother.

The man's head jerked to the door and then back to Jimmy. "Not *one* word. Ever." Then he slammed the door shut and Jimmy's world went dark.

Jimmy sat up in bed with a gasp. The bad dreams wouldn't stop. Always the same, remembering the day that Mama died. The bad man's face was burned into his memory, but he couldn't say anything. Not even if he wanted to.

He sneaked down the stairs to check on the baby bunny he'd found in the olive grove. It was so tiny. Just like Jimmy. And without its mama. Just like him.

The big old hawk had been attacking the baby bunny's mama when Jimmy tried his best to scare off the big bird. But it took off with the mama and left the baby injured and all alone.

As Jimmy brushed his fingers over the soft little head, Jimmy wanted to cry. His new little friend had watched his mama get hurt, too.

The nightmare lingered in his mind. The memories were so bad. He wanted to tell Papa everything, but he couldn't.

If he talked, everyone would die.

CHAPTER FOUR

Warm June air hit Lillian in the face as she exited the stagecoach. The train ride had been arduous, but the stagecoach had been almost inhumane. Six people had been stuffed inside a space where four would have been more than plenty. She'd even had to give the care of her overnight bag to the driver as there wasn't room to hold it on her lap.

Lillian marveled that they'd managed to get all of the luggage stowed on the stage, since overhead another four men had taken up residence due to a lack of space inside. All of the travelers had been men with the exception of one other woman, wife to one of the men. Thankfully, Lillian had been able to sit against the wall of the coach with this woman on her left. The men used decent manners, much to her relief, but never had she known such an uncomfortable ride. She sighed and did her best to put it all behind her. Their arrival in Angels Camp signaled that the worst was behind her.

It was the first day of a new month and the first day of the rest of her life. She dusted the skirt of her deep green traveling suit with her gloved hands and clouds of dirt surrounded her. What a wonderful way to meet her new employer. Exhausted and filthy. She glanced down at her once-white gloves that were now a dingy brown and rechecked her reticule. The drawstring bag was just as dirty. Could she be more of a mess?

"Excuse me, miss." The stage driver climbed back up the stage to unload the bags and trunks.

Lillian turned. Two other passengers still waited inside the stage, hats in hand. At least they were gentlemen, but oh, goodness, she hadn't realized she'd stood in everyone's way as she'd worried over her appearance. What a horrible impression she must have made. She felt the flush rise up her neck. "My apologies." She moved away, hoping the red in her cheeks would subside before she had to meet Mr. Colton.

Glancing around, Lillian couldn't spot anyone waiting for her. The others who'd shared the stage with her had already left.

As people bustled along the street, she realized that she waited alone.

"Need anything else, miss?" The driver stood in front of her, holding out the smallest of her bags.

"Oh, um . . . no. Thank you." Lillian took the bag and tightened her grip. "Wait, sir?"

He turned back around. "Yes?"

"Are we early?"

"No, miss. Quite late in fact. I best be going."

Lillian watched the stage pull away and then glanced at her pile of trunks and bag sitting in the dirt in front of the general store. Maybe she should make inquiries around town. It wouldn't hurt to get to know her surroundings in the little town of Angels Camp. She looked beyond the main road with all its buildings. Rolling hills encircled the town, and everything was lush and green. She hadn't been able to see much from the stage, but now she could survey it all.

"Welcome to Angels, miss. Can I help you?" A burly man in a sharp white shirt and black vest with a white apron tied around his waist awaited her answer.

"It appears my ride isn't here yet. Is it all right to leave my things in front of the store for now?"

"Of course, of course. Why don't you come on in and have a cup of coffee?"

"That sounds lovely, thank you." Lillian took up the smallest of her bags and headed up the steps. At least she'd have a chance to freshen up. Maybe she should pick up a few items while she was here. She hadn't inquired of Mr. Colton about how often they made it back to town from the farm.

The man held the door for her as she entered. "Name's Clark. Herman Clark. And this here is my store. We've got a room in the back for ladies to fix themselves after the long journey. There's a basin in there, too." His chest puffed out just a little. "My wife and I wanted the very best here for our travelers."

"Why, thank you, Mr. Clark. My name is Miss Porter." She walked up to the gleaming wood counter. "It's a lovely establishment."

The bell jangled over the door. Mr. Clark pointed toward the rear of the store. "Just head on back if you'd like. There's pink curtains. You can't miss it. When you return I'll have that coffee for you."

"Could you make it water?"

He slapped his forehead. "I plumb wasn't thinkin'. Of course, you'd want something cool to drink. You just go on ahead, and I'll have it ready for you when you get back."

Lillian headed toward the back. She heard the chattering of women as she looked for the special ladies' room. If the storekeeper thought she needed cleaning up, then she must be quite a sight. What she wouldn't give for a long, hot bath right now. The voices behind her motivated her to move a bit quicker. She had no intention of meeting anyone else in the sad condition she found herself. She took off her hat and assessed the situation. First she'd wash her face and repin her hair; then, if there was time, she'd try to brush some of the dust from her skirt.

The pleasant little room wasn't hard to find. Nothing like the elaborate rooms back east, but it was very suitable and clean. Removing her gloves, she took a deep breath. She could do this. This was her dream, and she was here! In California. All on her own. The cool water from the basin felt glorious on her skin, and she scrubbed her hands and face, forgetting for the moment about all the dust residing in her traveling clothes. But when she looked in the glass hanging on the wall, she realized the once deep and beautiful green of her suit had turned an ugly greenish gray from all the filth.

Lillian dug at once into her bag and found the brush. It would take a while, but she was determined to look clean and presentable to her new employer.

A good bit later, after seeing to herself and cleaning up the mess she'd made, Lillian decided she could face the world. She felt at least partially put back together and walked out to the store, hoping she'd find Mr. Colton waiting for her.

"I thought maybe you got lost in there." Mr. Clark chuckled. He extended a glass of water.

"Oh my. I do apologize for the delay." Lillian glanced at the clock. Had a half hour passed already? She looked around the store. "Has anyone come for me?" She placed her bag on the floor and took the offered glass. "Thank you." She immediately drank it down in a most unladylike fashion.

"Nobody's come askin' for you. Not a soul." The bell jangled again, and he moved to help his customers.

Placing a hand on her waist, Lillian worked to ease the discomfort growing in her stomach. What if Mr. Colton had decided not to hire her after all? What if something happened to little Jimmy and her services were no longer needed? What if —

"Miss?"

She looked up. "Hm?" There, she did it again. Her imagination had taken off without her. She put the glass on the counter and gave him a smile.

"You all right? You look awfully pale." Mr. Clark headed toward her with three young women following him like sheep.

Lillian breathed deep. "Goodness, I do apologize. I'm fine. Just a little tired from all the travel." She'd come this far. Certainly she could find accommodations for the night if Mr. Colton didn't arrive. In the morning, she would be sure to hear something.

"Where did you come from?" The youngest of the three ladies poked her head through the others' shoulders.

"Ginny, let's not pester the poor woman. It's none of our business." The taller girl with dark hair lifted her nose a smidge.

"It's quite all right, I don't mind. Today I came in from Copperopolis. But originally, I came from Indiana." She watched the smallest of the trio's eyes go wide.

"Indiana!" The young girl gasped and bounced on her toes. "That's got to be thousands of miles from here."

"I'm not sure how far it is in miles, but it did take many days to arrive in California." Lillian worked to stifle a giggle.

"Girls, girls, I think we should leave Miss Porter alone. I'm sure she's got lots on her mind." Mr. Clark tried to shoo the girls away, but it didn't work.

"I've always wanted to go to Chicago or New York." The dark-haired girl leaned in and sighed.

"Well, I'm from Indianapolis." Lillian smiled.

*Ooh*s and *aah*s emanated from the trio.

She picked up her bag and began to peruse the store. It fascinated her, since she'd never had to buy anything for herself. Grandmother had seen to everything when she was alive, and once she passed on to glory, Grandfather had all the staff attend to any needs, including arranging for dressmakers to visit Lillian at the house. He made it very clear that he thought it inappropriate for Lillian to go shopping and didn't like her to leave the mansion except on Sundays. She shook her head. What rubbish. She'd have to learn how to do so many things now. How awful to feel so unprepared for the world.

As she rounded the corner of an aisle, the school items caught her eye. Hmm, maybe a slate and some chalk would be a good idea to help the boy with his lessons. Footsteps followed her down the long row of amenities and she realized she had a following. The bell jangled again. My, but the store was busy.

"So why are you out here?" the smallest girl chimed in again after greeting the newcomers.

"I'm going to be a nanny."

"A nanny?"

"A nanny?"

All the other girls and Mr. Clark responded at once.

Lillian nodded.

"Who would need a nanny out here?" The youngest one turned up her nose. "You don't look like a nanny, either. You look like one of the wealthy tourists."

"Ginny, that's not polite," the dark-haired, older girl scolded. She turned to Lillian. "I apologize for my sister's behavior, Miss Porter."

Lillian smiled at the girls. "It's quite all right. I've been known to be curious myself."

Just then the bell over the door jangled yet again.

"Girls!" A tall and severe-looking woman entered. "Girls, it's time to go. Did you get your ribbons?"

Amidst gasps and murmurs, the girls scurried to gather their things.

The woman walked up to Lillian. "Good evening. I don't believe we've met."

Lillian thrust out her hand. "Good evening. I'm Lillian Porter. I've just arrived from Indianapolis."

"Nice to make your acquaintance, Miss Porter. I'm Mrs. Sabotini, the mother of these girls. And what brings you to these beautiful parts?" One pristine eyebrow on the woman's face rose.

The middle girl, who hadn't spoken yet, jumped into the conversation. "She's going to be a nanny."

"My, my." The mother clucked. "A nanny. You don't look like a . . . umm . . . nanny. In fact, you hardly look old enough to be away from home."

Lillian smiled. "This is actually my first position." The woman had been sizing her up ever since she entered the building. Eyeing her clothes and her bag. No wonder the girls were inquisitive. They received that trait honestly from their mother. Lillian tried not to giggle.

"Ah, and what fine family of ours will have the privilege of your services?" Curious indeed.

"Mr. Woodward Colton." As soon as the words left her lips, she could have heard a pin drop. Everyone in the store turned and stared. In silence.

Then the frowns came amidst a few gasps. Whispers followed.

After a few awkward moments, Mrs. Sabotini found her tongue. The severity of the woman increased with her wrinkled brow. "Miss Porter, is it?"

Lillian nodded.

"Begging your pardon, but you look as though you've come from a good family, and I would hate for them to lose you." The older lady grabbed Lillian's elbow and pulled her toward the counter. "It's best you buy a return ticket this instant."

"Lose me?" Lillian was tired, but not so tired to abandon common sense. "What on earth are you speaking of?" She brushed the front of her skirt again and tried to recompose her thoughts around the niggle of fear building in the back of her mind.

Another lady joined them at the counter and tapped it with her index finger. "You'd best be listening to sound advice, miss, and get yourself out of town before he finds out you're here."

"Before *who* finds out?" Had they all gone mad? "I most certainly will not be leaving. Good gracious, I just arrived, and I've made a commitment to work for Mr. Colton."

The once-congenial storekeeper leaned

over the counter, his face red and his scowl meaner than any she'd ever seen. "You will *not* honor that commitment, Miss Porter. You need to go home." He smacked the counter with his hand.

Everyone started talking at once, and Lillian couldn't understand one word of it. These people were out of their minds. The fight with her grandfather came crashing down around her. People had been telling her what to do far too long. Besides that, she had no home to return to. Ever. Which meant she had no place to go other than the job she'd committed to. And to make matters worse, after all those days on the train and then the stage, she was dirty, tired, and felt like she'd been run over by a team of horses.

"Would somebody *please* tell me what's going on?" She hadn't meant to yell, but the last of her nerves had frayed into oblivion.

A new hush covered the room.

Mrs. Sabotini moved forward with her hands on her hips, her eyes narrow slits. "What's going *on,* Miss Porter, is that these good people here are trying to save you."

"I don't understand. What is it you feel you must save me from?"

The woman's fiery gaze intensified.

"Woodward Colton. You don't know him, but we do, and it is our duty to intercede. We can't in good conscience allow you to be misled. You simply cannot work for that murderer!"

CHAPTER FIVE

Darwin brought his horse to a stop in the middle of the road as he recognized the two incoming riders. He leaned over the horn and rested his elbow. "Well, well, well . . . if it ain't Uncle John and Cousin David."

"Shut up, Darwin." Uncle John sat a little straighter in the saddle, but it couldn't hide the large paunch the man carried. "You're drunk."

"Yeah, maybe I am. But that's where you two are headed, ain't it?" Darwin spat on the ground and wiped his mouth with his sleeve. "So don't tell me to shut up."

"Get out of the way, Darwin." Uncle John pulled his pistol. "I'm in no mood to mess with you. But I won't mind shootin' ya."

David laughed behind Uncle John. "Yeah." He sneered. "I wouldn't mind shootin' ya, either."

If Darwin got himself shot while he was drunk, he might not feel it, but he wouldn't be able to go find his gold. That thought was enough to keep him from beating them both senseless for talking to him that way. His no-good family wasn't worth it. "Be my guest." Darwin moved his horse to the side and waved them on with his arm. At least he'd had a chance to get something to drink. He'd needed it after the last week.

Uncle John stared at him as he rode by. "Go sleep it off, Darwin. Then the stalls need to be mucked."

"Yeah, muck the stalls." David spat tobacco and it hit Darwin's boot. "That's the perfect job for you."

Just once, Darwin wanted to slide his hands around his sniveling cousin's throat and squeeze. He sneered at them but held his temper in check. Right now, he needed to focus on finding his gold. Dealing with his idiot family could come later.

When their horses' hoofbeats could no longer be heard, Darwin continued on. The last few days had been the worst. After Harry's confession of moving the sacks, Darwin was ready to go get them. One big problem stood in his way, though — Harry couldn't remember where he hid all of the sacks.

The day after Harry revealed he'd moved Darwin's bags, Uncle John had sent Darwin out on a stupid errand, and when he'd returned, he found his brother in the barn holding his head. When he questioned Harry, the boy just moaned, and then Saul appeared out of nowhere and said that Harry had fallen from a tree and hit his head. Right. Likely story.

Then Harry couldn't remember things.

Darwin was ready to pound Saul into the ground. No doubt he'd done something to Harry. He didn't just fall from a tree. Of that, Darwin was certain.

Once again he was forced to wait. But all he wanted to do was find his gold and then rub his family's noses in it. They'd pay. That's for sure.

As he reached the shack they all lived in, Darwin heard cries for help. It sounded like Harry.

He jumped from his horse and ran toward the barn. The door squeaked as he opened it, but that didn't keep Saul from hitting Harry again.

A roar rumbled out of Darwin's throat as he lunged for his despicable cousin and tackled him to the ground. "You no-good, mean cuss." He wrapped his hands around Saul's throat. "You been hurtin' my brother, haven't you?"

Saul laughed through the constriction.

"He's dumber than the pigs out there." Then he spat in Darwin's face.

That was the final straw, and within minutes Saul lay dead on the ground.

Harry, curled up in the corner, cried and continued saying only one thing. "Uncle John will be so mad."

Mad wasn't the word for it. Darwin had just killed his uncle's pride and joy. Uncle John would never let him live after that. It made Darwin think. What would he do now?

Then an idea struck.

It would solve all his problems, too. Well, at least most of them.

He dragged Harry back to the shack and packed their meager possessions. He scribbled a note to Uncle John:

Pa,
    A man came today lookin for Darwin. Said the law was bearin down on him and if we got cot, they'd hang us for hidin a killer. I'm gonna get rid of Darwin and Harry. Told em we had to go fetch those pigs you bot. Will be gone for a week or so. We ain't gettin cot by the law for them varmits.

Saul

Darwin read the note again and hoped his

uncle would buy it. It even looked a little like Saul's handwriting. Of course, when any of them wrote, it looked like chicken scratch, so how would Uncle John know?

He stripped off his own clothes and put on a shirt and pair of pants that were Saul's. Running back to the barn, he wanted to laugh. This plan would work. Darwin ripped the clothes off of his cousin and then dressed the body in his own clothes. What else could he do to help them believe the body was him? He ran back to the cabin and found a letter addressed to him in jail about the death of his mother. That would do it.

Darwin went back to the barn again and placed the letter into his old pants that were now on Saul. He saddled his own horse for Harry, and Saul's horse for himself. Taking the blood-soaked clothes that he'd ripped off of Saul, he shoved them in a saddlebag and then tied a rope around his cousin's ankles and looped it around the saddle horn. Going back to the cabin, he grabbed their few belongings and told Harry to go hide in the hayloft until he returned.

Harry whimpered but followed him to the barn.

"I'll be back in a little bit for you. Stay hidden."

"All right, Brother." Harry still held his head and lay down in the hay. "It hurts, hurts, hurts, hurts, hurts, hurts, Brother . . ."

At least the kid could still talk. Maybe if he just got enough rest, he'd remember where he'd hidden the sacks.

Darwin went back and checked the house one more time. It had to be believable. And if Uncle John and David came back as drunk as Darwin hoped, they wouldn't check anything else until morning.

After one last look, he headed back to Saul's horse and climbed up into the saddle. He kicked the horse into a trot and dragged his cousin's body out to the road heading north toward Sacramento. It might take a while for someone to find him, but that would only be better for his plan to work. He'd leave the body in a gulley somewhere and then go back and get Harry. They could live in one of the abandoned mines until they found his gold. And then . . .

Well, then he could do whatever he wanted to do. And make Uncle John and David pay.

And the farmer and his kid.

And anyone else who got in his way.

"What in tarnation is all this ruckus about?" A plump woman descended the stairs in the store and walked up to Lillian.

"I'm not at all certain." Lillian placed a hand on her head. Hearing the news that her would-be employer was a murderer had rendered her speechless for several moments. Then the room had spun as everyone seemed to talk at once again. What had she gotten herself into?

The woman held out her hand. "Come here, dear. My name's Carla Clark. My husband and I run this place." She deposited Lillian in a chair by the checkerboard barrel. Then she looked at the rest of the room. "Now, would someone mind telling me what is going on? It sounded like a stampede of voices."

Mr. Clark whispered in his wife's ear.

"What?"

His face turned deep red again.

It was her turn to narrow her gaze. "Are you telling me that all of you are standing in my store gossiping about Mr. Colton?"

"It ain't gossip, Carla, and you know it," a male voice from the back erupted.

"Oh, Stewart, hush your mouth." Carla returned to Lillian's side and placed a hand on her shoulder.

The warmth seeped in and soothed all the ragged places where words just didn't make sense.

"The man killed his wife!" a woman piped up from another corner.

Lillian's heart began to race. The man had been accused of killing his own wife? Oh no. What *had* she gotten herself into?

"Oh, he did not," Carla huffed. "You all know very well that there was a witness to Mr. Colton's whereabouts and that the judge said there wasn't a lick of evidence for a case against him." Mrs. Clark's hand pressed harder on Lillian's shoulder. "Now, how long are you going to be treating that poor man with such ill behavior? And gossiping behind his back?"

"He paid off the judge!" another voice echoed in the store. They were drawing quite a crowd.

Carla turned toward Lillian and rolled her eyes. "He did *not* kill his wife, nor did he pay off the judge."

"He beat her and pushed her down the stairs. We all heard the story." Affirming comments raced through the mob.

"Exactly." Mrs. Clark's voice lowered and she held a hand up to the crowd. "Heard. *Heard* the story. Were any of you actually there? Did you see it happen?"

The murmurs stopped.

"Don't you see what's happening here?"

Lillian breathed deep and watched the

crowd. This was not at all what she had planned when she arrived in Angels Camp. In a matter of minutes, her dreams of the West and of beautiful California crumpled at her feet. She no longer had a home to return to. And the man she was supposed to work for had been accused of murder.

CHAPTER SIX

Woody crawled out from under the wagon and tossed his tools in the back. He sighed and dusted off his hands. Of all the times the reach could break, it had to happen today. The one day he wanted to get to town early. Not only was he now three hours behind schedule, but he was covered in dirt, thanks to rolling around under the wagon. He'd known the reach needed to be replaced — had even bought the new part and put it in the wagon bed with his tools — but he hadn't had the time. So, of course, it happened today, and it took much longer to fix than he thought it would. His new nanny was sure to have heard all manner of rumors about him — if she hadn't already left town — and would hate him as soon as they met. Mrs. Goodman would be a nervous wreck by the time he returned home with or without Miss Porter, and little Jimmy would probably be asleep.

Life just kept getting better and better.

The job finished, he stood and wiped his forehead with his kerchief. Even with all the doubts swimming around him, he had to go see for himself if Miss Porter had come.

He brushed as much dirt as he could off his clothes and plopped his hat back into place. Might as well get it over with. He couldn't do anything about the circumstances. Either God had a really good sense of humor, or Woody had become a modern-day Job.

Or it could be both.

He clucked the horses back into motion and headed toward Angels Camp.

Memories washed over him on the drive through the fine treelined country. Rebecca had loved this area. Loved their little town of Angels. Loved their church and their neighbors. She found the history of the area fascinating, telling him all about how a man named Henry Angel set up a trading post for the gold miners and made his fortune without having to use a pick and shovel. She thought that quite ingenious and used it to encourage him in the planting of their olives.

"There's obviously more than one way to strike it rich," she'd told him.

Woody looked toward the sky. "I still don't

understand why, Lord. Maybe I'm not meant to. And maybe there's some great lesson you'd like me to learn. . . ." His words trailed off as the ache in his chest intensified again. "But, frankly, I think I've learned enough."

These things I have spoken unto you, that in me ye might have peace. In the world ye shall have tribulation: but be of good cheer; I have overcome the world. The words he'd read that morning from John, chapter sixteen, overwhelmed him. Irritated him a little, too. Of course Jesus had overcome the world. He was the Son of God. There was nothing He couldn't overcome. But Woody was just a man. A very tired and discouraged man.

He drove on in silence, doing his best to put disheartening thoughts aside. In the distance he could see the town, and there would be enough negativity there that he certainly didn't need to add his own. Time to face the task at hand head on. "Lord, help me. I need to forgive and love these people no matter what they say or do to me. I need to strengthen my walk with You. I know I fail miserably every day, but I keep making the same mistakes, and so often I don't even know for sure what those mistakes are. I need Your wisdom and forgiveness." If he wanted to move on with his life, he had to start there. With God's love and forgiveness. One step at a time.

"And please let Miss Porter still be there. If you could keep all those rumors from reaching her ears, I sure would appreciate it."

No matter what, he had to do things differently. Jimmy needed him — needed help. And the only way to help his son heal was to truly go through the healing process himself. It would probably be like ripping the scab off a large wound, but he needed to get the festering wound cleaned out so it could heal properly. Otherwise, the grief and guilt would eat him alive. And he was tired of it and all the pain. It was time to let go.

A couple trunks and a large traveling bag sat in front of the general store as he pulled the wagon to a halt. Woody could only hope that meant good news for him.

Two men left the store and watched him approach. They shook their heads and scowled in his direction and then walked the other way.

At least he wouldn't have to talk to them. He could be thankful for that.

All right, Lord. I know You've got control of this situation. Woody climbed down from the wagon and walked to the door. The bell jangled overhead as he opened it, and Carla sent him a smile from behind the counter.

"Good evening, Woody. We've been waitin' on you."

Her husband *harrumphed* in the corner as he dusted shelves.

Woody removed his hat. "So I'm hoping that means Miss Porter arrived?"

"She did indeed." Carla patted his arm. "But it wasn't pretty there for a while, I must say. I'm sorry."

He could only imagine and nodded. Tendrils of fear raced through his limbs, trying to take root. *I have overcome . . .* Peace engulfed him again, and he stood straighter. "Is she all right?"

"She's fine. That one's made of strong stuff." She walked around the counter. "But I'm sad to say that she did get an earful from the townsfolk."

"I had a feeling she would." He shook his head. "I had intended to get here early but had a wagon repair on the way into town."

"No matter. She's here and has had a little time to rest." Carla motioned for him to sit by the checkerboard. The pungent aroma of the pickle barrel made his mouth water. "Let me go get her."

Herman continued to dust and kept his back to Woody, probably in an attempt to

87

keep his mouth shut. Which was for the best. Woody struggled with his own feelings but knew he had to forgive the man for his treatment the week prior.

Time to forgive him for his doubts about Woody, as well. God knew he had enough doubts for them both.

The butcher's daughter entered the store and greeted Mr. Clark. But as she turned, Woody recognized the horror on her face when she spotted him. She spun on her heel and walked right out the door.

Herman turned then and marched toward him. "You've cost me enough customers today, Colton." The shopkeeper looked over his shoulder to where his wife had disappeared, then stepped closer and poked Woody in the chest with his finger. "Now, get out!"

"Get out!" Was that Grandfather? What was he doing here in California?

A soft touch on her shoulder woke Lillian from a deep sleep. "What? Where am I?"

"In the general store in Angels, Lillian." Carla Clark helped her to sit up. "It's been quite a day, hasn't it? And it's not over. Mr. Colton has come to fetch ya. So we best get you freshened up." The robust woman bustled around the tiny cot and brought her a washcloth and basin of water.

As Lillian washed her face, the events of the afternoon after her arrival came rushing back. After Mrs. Clark — who insisted she be called Carla — shooed away the "gossiping herd," she had taken Lillian to a room in the back and sat her down. The woman had been kind and honest with her about the horrible death of Rebecca Colton. She never painted Mr. Colton as a saint, but did share her own memories of the man they'd known several years. It wasn't until the mysterious and awful death of Rebecca that people had anything against Woodward Colton. And even though Judge Morgan had declared him innocent of any wrongdoing, once the rumors started, there didn't seem to be a way to extinguish them. They spread like wildfire.

There was even some talk after Judge Morgan passed away to retry Mr. Colton. But Carla said she would do everything in her power to fight the gossip. As she shared about her own loss and sorrow — all caused by her own gossiping tongue — she'd even shed a few tears.

The cool cloth on Lillian's face and neck helped to refresh her, but there was so much to consider. It was a disturbing situation. After hearing Carla's passionate words, Lillian knew she trusted the older woman. Especially after she scolded men, women, and children for spreading the hearsay. Anyone willing to stand up to bullies was all right in her book.

But then there was the little nagging in the back of her mind. What if Mr. Colton truly was a dangerous man? And he had just fooled the entire community all those years? It did seem that he only had one advocate she knew of in the entire town: Mrs. Clark. Was *she* blinded by her own need of redemption from the sin of a malicious tongue?

"Lillian?"

"Hmm?" She rinsed out the rag one more time and ran it over her face.

"Are you all right, dear?" Carla reached out for Lillian's hand.

"Oh yes. I'm so sorry. I'm just exhausted from the trip."

The sweet lady walked around Lillian, straightening her clothes and dusting them off a bit more. "You're a bit wrinkled, but I don't think we can do much about that. We need to get you out there, because it will be quite a drive to the Colton farm. I'm sure little Jimmy will want to meet you tonight before he heads off to bed. Here's your lovely hat." She eyed the fetching piece that so perfectly matched Lillian's suit. "We need to get you a sunbonnet. Once you're out on the farm, you'll need one. Oh, and probably a different one for traveling back and forth. I'm guessin' you traveled mostly in enclosed carriages." She smiled at Lillian. "Pardon me for sayin', but you look to come from wealth. I don't figure you have any sunbonnets."

"You're correct in your assumption, Carla. I would appreciate your help. I had some very lovely walking-out bonnets, but failed to bring any of them with me. I did, however, bring a straw riding bonnet, so perhaps that will suffice for now." Lillian pinned her hat into place, then tucked her reticule into her traveling bag so she wouldn't have to bother with it on the ride to the Colton place.

"There." Lillian picked up the bag and smiled. "I'm ready." She followed Carla out of the small storeroom into the main area.

A large man sat in the seat she had occupied earlier in the day. As she approached, he stood — goodness, he was tall — and removed his hat to greet her. "I must apologize, Miss Porter, for being so late. My wagon had trouble, and I had to do the repairs on the road. I had hoped to arrive in town before you."

She examined his deep brown eyes. He seemed sincere in his apology and didn't look like a murderer. Not that she'd ever met one. "It's quite all right. Thank you for coming." His dark brown hair touched his collar in the back but wasn't untamed. And even though he wasn't spotless, she imagined that if she had to fix a wagon in the middle of the road, she wouldn't be clean, either.

He nodded to her. "I hate to rush, but we do have quite a bit of a drive. I'm sure Mrs. Goodman will have something for us to eat when we get home." He bowed a bit to her. Hesitant and humble, despite his imposing size. The poor man. What had these people done to him? And after he'd lost so much.

"Woody, it's good to see ya again so soon. You need to come back more often. Especially now that Miss Porter's here." Carla walked forward, patted the man's arm, and tucked a creamy package of cloth into Lillian's bag.

"Good to see you, too, Carla. I'm sorry for all the trouble."

"Like I said before, they're good people. Just give 'em time." She turned to Lillian. "Now, if you need anything, you let me know, all right?"

For some odd reason, tears sprang to Lillian's eyes. She thought her world had turned upside down when Grandfather said he never wanted to see her again. Well, the events of the past few hours had done quite a bit of emotional upheaval, as well. Add that to her tired state and she was quite a mess. "I will. Thank you so much for all your help today, Mrs. Clar— oh, sorry, Carla."

"You're most welcome." The soft, plump woman reached out and hugged Lillian. Not one of those simpering ninny hugs where they barely touched and pretended to kiss each other's cheek. No, this woman knew how to hug. She squeezed and made sure the recipient knew she meant it.

Lillian could use a hug like that every day. She hugged her new friend back and then followed Mr. Colton out the door.

She watched as several people along the street stopped and stared. No matter. She straightened her shoulders and stood proudly beside the wagon as Mr. Colton loaded her things. It wouldn't do any good for her to doubt her new employer. She'd followed the good Lord and her dreams here, and this was the only option she had. Going home was out of the question.

One thing was certain, Woodward Colton was a large man. He stood almost a foot above her, and she wasn't short for a woman. His broad shoulders accentuated his height, and the way his muscles bulged against his shirt as he lifted the trunks left no doubt he was strong. For a moment, she could imagine how the rumors had taken root. His size could be a bit intimidating. But he didn't seem at all like a killer. At least from what she knew of him so far. And from what Carla had told her.

"Are you ready, Miss Porter?" He stood in front of her with his hat in his hand.

She blinked several times. How long had she been staring? "Why, yes, of course."

He climbed into the wagon and reached down for her.

"Um . . ." Lifting her skirt, she realized she hadn't been watching *how* he'd climbed into the wagon. Heat crept up her cheeks. "Is there a step?"

His deep chuckle was warm. "I do apologize. I'm guessing you've never ridden in a farm wagon before?"

She shook her head and tried not to laugh at herself. "I've only ridden in carriages, and there's always a little step."

"Well, let's remedy that." He hopped down from the wagon and pulled an empty wooden crate from the back. "Mrs. Goodman uses this." He turned it upside down.

"You can step on this, then the hub, and then the top of the wheel. You have to keep moving once you start. Otherwise, you could find yourself in trouble if the horses move. After a time, you won't need the crate and can just step up on the hub."

Lillian eyed the situation with a bit of skepticism. This was her new life, and she'd best learn quick. Woody went to hold the horses while Lillian worked up her courage. The traveling suit was difficult to maneuver in and quite heavy, but nevertheless she was determined. Lillian drew a deep breath, whispered a prayer, and then followed Woody's directions.

Reaching the driver's boot, she turned and beamed a smile at Woody. "I did it!"

He chuckled and released the horses' harness. "That you did." He retrieved the crate, and once he'd reloaded it in the back, he hopped up to the wagon seat as if it were no big feat. "I promise it'll get easier."

Lillian relaxed and drew a long, deep breath. It had been more of a hike to climb up into the wagon than she was used to, but she'd made it on the first try. Which brought a flood of relief. Her imagination had conjured up unladylike images of her sprawled in the street. As she settled onto the hard wagon seat, she thought about all the luxuries she'd taken for granted grow-ing up in an affluent family. In fact, every-one she knew — even at church — was from the same walk of life. How many times had she missed a need because she'd been sur-rounded by people who lacked for nothing? When Grandmother was still alive, she'd been involved in multiple charities, but Lil-lian had never been allowed to attend any of the meetings or go to any of the places they served. Instead, she was to remain at home, deep in her studies with a variety of tutors.

The horses moved forward, and Mr. Colton cleared his voice. "I am very sorry I was late today. The reach broke . . . uh, that's the piece that connects the front and rear axles. I had the part to repair it, but it's time-consuming. I hope it wasn't a terrible inconvenience for you."

The wagon seat was narrow, but she tried to keep a few inches between them. Chanc-ing a look at her employer, she pasted on a smile and tried not to think about the gos-sip. "The Clarks were very gracious to me. It wasn't a problem at all."

His jaw twitched a little. "I'm glad to hear it. But I do hope you will forgive me."

"Of course." The intensity of his gaze

made her want to cry. What had gotten into her?

"Look . . ." A long sigh accentuated his words. "I know you must have heard some awful things in town."

Lillian looked away to her right. What could she say? His close proximity made her nervous, and she reminded herself that a judge had cleared him.

"You've just met me, and I can well imagine what you think of me, especially if you heard the rumors."

She bit her lip and turned toward him again. Searching his eyes for the truth.

He held her gaze for several moments, then looked ahead again. "Rebecca and I came here to farm. Olives and possibly other fruit. But after a few short years, our olive grove became very prosperous, and it was all we could do to keep up with the orders for table olives and olive oil. We were busy, but we were happy." He took a deep breath, as if bracing himself for his next words. "My wife was murdered, and I don't know who did it or why. She was the most incredible woman I'd ever known." He clamped his mouth shut and his jaw clenched.

Lillian watched him for several moments, hoping he would continue. He didn't have to tell her what happened, but he'd been honest with her anyway. Baring his soul to a stranger. She admired him for that, but she was completely uncertain what she should say. *"I'm so sorry for your loss"* didn't seem the least bit useful at a time like this.

"I can't say it's been easy. The grief just about ate me up. And I got pretty angry at God. Especially when the townspeople turned against me." Another sigh. "I'm sure you've heard that they blame me — think I did it. Thankfully, Judge Morgan didn't listen to rumors. I wasn't even home when it happened. I didn't kill my wife, Miss Porter." Kind eyes, deep and brown, stared back at her. This man couldn't be a killer. Wounded, yes. Grieving, yes. But not a killer.

All she could do was nod. What if her judgment was wrong? How often had she actually been around people?

"I've got to look forward. I've got a boy who needs me and needs to heal, and a farm to look after." He looked down at her. "I'm very thankful you answered my advertisement. I had several applicants, but you were the only one who seemed qualified."

Qualified? Her? She'd never even been a nanny. "Thank you. I sincerely want to help, but I don't know how qualified I am."

"You're the only one I felt peaceful about. Thus, you're the only one I responded to."

His words penetrated a deep place in her heart. The need to be wanted. To be a vital part of a family. But as she took a moment to gather her thoughts, weariness took over. It had all been a bit too much. And as much as she wanted to like this man beside her, she couldn't forget the words of all the townspeople.

Then her throat constricted with conviction. Carla's passionate pleas about the dangers of gossip came back to Lillian. If all the folks in town had allowed their opinions to be shaped by hearsay, they were wrong. And that made Lillian wrong for listening to them. *Oh, Lord, help me to trust, and help me to discern the truth.*

"Did I say anything to upset you?" Mr. Colton leaned an inch toward her.

Catching his gaze again, she smiled. A real one this time. "No. Not at all. I appreciate your honesty. I'm just weary."

"I'm sure the trip was exhausting. Mrs. Goodman will have your room all ready for you when we get there, and you can have a day or two to get settled and rest."

"Thank you."

He leaned forward then and placed his elbows on his knees as he drove the wagon.

The gesture to give her a bit of space was nice, or maybe he just needed to stretch out his back. Either way, she appreciated the quiet. They both seemed content to ride along in silence.

As the wagon moved down the rough road, Lillian tried to focus on the luscious, green rolling hills, the scrub oak and other trees that dotted the landscape. Wild flowers dotted the side of the road in hues of orange and yellow. The sky was turning a pretty pink and purple as the sun began to set behind them. Maybe if she just shut her eyes for a moment and relaxed . . .

She could wait till tomorrow to think about all that had transpired today.

CHAPTER SEVEN

"Don't you hurt my mama!"

Jimmy bolted up in bed, his limbs shaking with the memory of the dream. With tentative movements, he placed his feet on the floor and headed to Papa's room, but he wasn't in there. That's right, he'd gone to town to pick up someone.

Heading to the kitchen instead, the smell of cookies drew him and reminded him of good memories and settled his nervous stomach. Mrs. Goodman made the best cookies. His favorites were when she broke up little pieces of chocolate and added them to the dough.

He pulled out a chair, the scraping noise making their housekeeper turn around.

"Couldn't sleep, huh?" She poured him a glass of milk. "Nightmare?"

Jimmy nodded.

"Wanna talk about it?"

He shook his head hard.

She looked at him and nodded. "I admire the strong, silent type. And I think I've got a cure for those bad dreams. How about a fresh cookie or two to go with your milk?"

He nodded again. Mrs. Goodman was old with glasses on her nose and white hair. Like a grandma. But she always understood. Even without his words.

She placed a plate of cookies in front of him and turned back to the stove. "I'm sure your pa will be back soon. Then you'll get to meet Miss Porter. She's coming just for you, Jimmy, and she sounds like such a nice lady."

He reached for a cookie as a shiver traveled up his spine. It only meant there was one more person the bad man could hurt. Jimmy hadn't seen him since that day, but he knew the dirty killer would come back. 'Cause he'd been looking for something and said he would stop at nothing to find it. Another tremor made him slosh his milk against the plate of cookies. He ducked his head. If only he were bigger. Stronger.

Mrs. Goodman didn't scold him. She didn't even say a word, just cleaned up the milk with the towel from her shoulder.

Tears burned his eyes. He wanted to cry. More than that, he wanted his mama. She would hold him as he cried and tell him it would all be good.

Maybe he should tell Papa everything. He didn't know how much longer he could hold it in. The nightmares came every night. He tried to hide it from Papa and Mrs. Goodman, but they knew.

He took another cookie. The sweet chocolate melted on his tongue.

But if he went to Papa, what would happen?

Jimmy swallowed the cookie and drank his milk. As he wiped his mouth with his sleeve, he knew he could never talk.

The bad man had warned him. Not one word.

Or everyone would die. Just like his mama.

Darkness surrounded him as Woody steered the team under the arch that welcomed him home. Memories washed over him of better, happier days. He shook his head. Forward. He needed to look forward.

He shifted in his seat and focused on the house, trying not to disturb Miss Porter. The dead weight of her head on his shoulder made his arm go numb, while something on her fancy hat poked him in the neck. She'd fallen asleep a good while earlier; he wasn't sure when. But she'd almost fallen off the wagon, and he'd pulled her back. He'd been caught up in his own thoughts. Wondering what she thought of him, and if she was scared half out of her wits to be working for him.

Thoughts of little Jimmy crossed his mind. A smile tugged at his lips. This was what his son needed. He would talk again, and they could heal. He pulled up in front of the massive porch, set the brake, and then tapped Miss Porter on the shoulder.

She didn't budge.

He leaned his head down. "Miss Porter?" and tapped again.

"Yes?" She jerked up straight, her hat askew. "I'm sorry. Are we here?"

With a nod, Woody climbed down and reached up to assist her. Mrs. Goodman and Jimmy walked out the front door. Jimmy's hair stood up on end, and he was in his nightclothes. Woody's heart clenched a little tighter.

"Miss Porter, are you up for introductions?" He spoke in a hushed tone to make sure she was fully awake, since she wobbled a bit once her feet hit the ground.

"Yes. Please." She smoothed her hair, pushing errant pieces back under her hat, and stepped forward.

"This is Mrs. Goodman, my housekeeper, and my son, Jimmy."

"Nice to meet you, Miss Porter." His housekeeper smiled.

"Thank you. It's nice to meet you, too."

"Come here, Jimmy." Woody held out his hand.

But the boy didn't move.

"Jimmy, son, I told you to come here." He waved him forward with his hand.

His son shook his head.

"James Colton, you are being rude to Miss Porter. Now . . . come here." He hadn't meant for his words to be so harsh or so loud. But that's how they tumbled out.

Jimmy looked down and ducked behind Mrs. Goodman's skirt.

"Give the boy some time, Mr. Colton." The new nanny touched his arm. "It's late, and I'm sure this is a bit overwhelming."

Embarrassed and discouraged that Jimmy didn't respond as he'd hoped, Woody turned. "Miss Porter, might I remind you that you have been hired by *me*. And this is *my* son. This is *my* farm and *I* am in charge here. If I ask my son to come forward, I expect him to come forward." As soon as the words were out, he wondered where they came from. Had he really spoken such atrocities before he'd thought them through?

The smile left Miss Porter's face. She

glanced back to the wagon, and for a moment Woody wondered if she was contemplating her return to town.

What had gotten into him? He walked up the steps to the porch and knelt in front of Jimmy. "Son, I'm sorry. I never should have spoken to you that way. I've had a rough day, but that's no excuse for my actions. Will you forgive me?"

His son nodded, came forward, and reached for him.

Woody took his little frame into his arms and walked back down the steps. "Miss Porter, I also need to apologize to you. I'm sorry." A burning sensation started in his throat as Jimmy wrapped his arms around Woody's neck. "I'd like to introduce you to my son, James. We call him Jimmy. And I promise that an episode like that will not happen again."

She hesitated a moment, then nodded. She stepped toward them and gave Jimmy a soft smile. "Hello, Jimmy. I'm Lillian."

Jimmy laid his head on Woody's shoulder but lifted his small hand in a short wave. That would have to be good enough for now.

"Please, again, forgive me." Woody hoped he hadn't ruined everything. Had he really been in such a foul temper ever since Rebecca died? No wonder Mrs. Goodman often gave him that motherly look that made him want to hide in his office.

Miss Porter gave him a slight smile. "I do. Maybe if we all get a good night's sleep, tomorrow we'll be able to start over. I know I often get out of sorts and don't act like myself when I haven't had enough rest."

Start over. If only he could start the whole last year over.

Lillian had been deeply touched by Woody's honesty on their ride out to the farm, but when he'd knelt to apologize to his son, she'd wanted to cry. She'd never seen or heard a man apologize before.

Mrs. Goodman approached her. "Let's get you settled, Miss Porter."

Lillian glanced around.

"It's just us, dearie. Woody went to tuck in Jimmy for the night, and then he'll fetch your bags and take them to your room. Meanwhile, let me show you around a bit so you'll know where things are."

"Oh. Thank you." She followed the housekeeper up the steps and into the massive home. It wasn't at all what she'd expected of a farmhouse. But then, she hadn't known what to expect.

The beautiful hand-carved door opened

107

into a spacious foyer. It housed a grand staircase beyond what looked like a parlor on the left. To the right, the foyer opened up into a smaller sitting room. Mrs. Goodman detailed the building of the home by Woody just a few years prior and what the land was like before the Coltons arrived, but Lillian found herself caught up in the pictures on the walls and the homey touches that made her feel welcome and accepted. Rebecca Colton must have been a wonderful woman. A pang hit Lillian's chest. She wished she could have known the lady of the house.

"This is the music room." Mrs. Goodman opened a door just off the small sitting room. She picked up a lighted lamp by the door and stepped into the room. "Nobody goes into it anymore. Rebecca was the only one who played the piano. She had started to show Jimmy how, but then . . . well . . . you know the rest."

Lillian moved across the room to touch the beautiful mahogany wood. "I play. In fact, it is something I feared I would miss coming to California. Do you suppose Mr. Colton would mind if I played it and even used it to teach Jimmy?"

"I can't say for sure, but I know Woody to be a fair man. Just ask him and see what he says. Could be if it grieves him too much, he'll still allow you to use it when he's away. Now, come along. There's more house to see."

They moved back through the house, with Mrs. Goodman commenting all the while. Finally they reached a large room with a lace-covered table and six chairs. To one side was a beautiful china hutch.

"These are Brown-Westhead Moore dishes, if I'm not mistaken." Lillian smiled at the sight of the china. "My grandmother had a complete table service of these. She ordered them from Spaulding in Chicago."

"They were Rebecca's favorite." Mrs. Goodman came alongside Lillian. "She thought them quite smart."

"Oh, they are. I love that they have the white base, but then the gold and burgundy leafing around the edges with the pink roses and green leaves make them absolutely charming. I ate many a meal on dishes just like these." She looked up and smiled. "I'm sorry, I didn't mean to delay you."

"It's no trouble. As you can see, this is the dining room." Mrs. Goodman continued on through the butler's pantry. "And, of course, here on the other side is the kitchen." She went to the stove. "You must be starved. I've got a couple of plates warming here.

Take a seat. With just the three of us, we usually eat here."

Lillian almost collapsed into a chair, not even sure she had the strength to lift a spoon. But when the plate was set in front of her with roast beef, mashed potatoes and gravy, and green beans, her stomach growled loudly enough to echo off the walls.

Mrs. Goodman laughed. "Eat up, child. I know you're about to fall over from exhaustion. I can see it in your face." She turned but spoke over her shoulder. "We'll get you all settled in your room after you've had your fill."

Lillian pulled off her hat and gloves. "Thank you." She scooped mashed potatoes into her mouth. It wasn't very ladylike, but no one was watching, and the smell was about to drive her mad. The potatoes were a creamy, buttery goodness on her tongue, and she almost groaned in delight. This must be what heaven tasted like.

Lillian sat up straight and reprimanded herself for her irreverent thoughts. Goodness, first her manners, and then her thoughts . . . what would her grandmother say? A little giggle escaped as she placed her fork into the roast beef. As it melted in her mouth, she knew she had to learn to cook like this. Swallowing, she wiped her mouth with a napkin. "Mrs. Goodman, this is by far the best meal I've ever had."

The older woman turned and smiled at her. "Thank you, dear."

"Do you think you could teach me?"

"To do what?"

"To cook, like this." Lillian closed her eyes as she indulged in another forkful.

The housekeeper dried her hands on a towel and sat across from her at the small worktable. "You don't know how to cook?"

Lillian shook her head. "I'm sorry to say, I don't. At the manor — my grandparents' home — we had an entire kitchen staff, and I was always shooed out."

Mrs. Goodman studied her for a moment. "Of course I'll teach you. Every woman needs to know how to cook. Every man, for that matter." She chuckled. "I'm a bit surprised, though."

"Why?" The last bite tasted just as good as the first, and Lillian was sorry to be finished.

"Well, I noticed your clothes and trunks and such, and I wondered why you would be in need of work?"

A shiver ran up her spine, but Lillian shook it off and breathed deep. It was best to be honest up front. "My mother was an only child. She and my father died when I was a baby. While it's true my grandfather is a very wealthy man, I've longed to live my own life. To find purpose and follow my parents' dreams." She looked away. "He — my grandfather — disowned me when I left."

"Gracious, child. That's terrible."

Lillian leaned forward. "Please keep this to yourself, Mrs. Goodman. My grandfather doesn't wish to speak to me or hear from me, and I'd rather just move on with my life from here." Tears pricked her eyes.

"Of course, Miss Porter." The woman leaned forward and squeezed her hand. "But I can't help wondering, if you're his only family —"

Lillian held up a hand. "I know. And I will try to reach out to him . . . in time, but my grandfather is a stubborn man. As stubborn as they come."

"Then we'll just have to be your family now." The older woman nodded. "Mr. Goodman — God rest his soul — and I were never blessed with children, and the Coltons have become my family."

The tears threatened to spill. "Thank you, Mrs. Goodman. I don't have anyone else. I've been pretty sheltered most of my life. I've had a proper education and was trained in what my grandparents thought important, but I doubt arranging flowers and speaking French are of very much value here."

Mrs. Goodman sniffed and wiped the corners of her eyes with her apron. "Well, aren't we a pair? Let's get you to your room. I'm sure that a good night's sleep will be just the thing for you." She hopped out of the chair like someone half her age. "Leave the dishes. I'll get them later."

Picking up her things, Lillian followed Mrs. Goodman, and they took another hall toward the back of the house.

"This is the library — where Mr. Colton does most of his office work for the farm. If you can't find him anywhere else, he's most likely in there. I'll show you the upstairs tomorrow. There are four more bedrooms and a sitting area." She kept walking. "And this hallway leads to our wing. Your room is there on the left, and my room is on the right. The room at the end of the hall is our own private bathroom and water closet."

Lillian opened the door to her room. Her luggage sat at the foot of the bed. A beautiful mahogany bed with matching dresser were the main pieces in the room, but there was also a comfortable sitting area, an armoire, and bookcase. The room was papered in a light blue rose pattern with all the trim painted in white. A quilt in all shades of blue covered the bed, and deep navy-blue cushions adorned the bed and the small couch. It took her breath away. And the tears started in earnest. Smiling through them, she turned to the older woman. "Mrs. Goodman . . . I . . . I . . ."

"I'm glad you like it, dear. Now, you get to bed. If you need anything during the night, I'm just across the hall." And for the second time that day, Lillian found herself wrapped in a warm hug.

CHAPTER EIGHT

A clock somewhere in the house chimed midnight. Lillian was weary to the bone, and yet she couldn't sleep. So she'd unpacked her small bag and found a lovely cream sunbonnet that Carla must have tucked in there among her things. How sweet of her — if only everyone would treat each other with such kindness. It made tears well up in Lillian's eyes. Swiping at the tears on her cheeks, she went back to unpacking and decided she might as well tackle the trunks.

When the last item was tucked away, she lay in bed again, only to toss and turn. All the details that had skittered through her mind on the trip were now in front of her. All the adjustments. No staff to press garments or help her dress. And her hair! Goodness, she could manage a bun and a braid on her own, but she'd had someone arranging her hair since before she could remember.

Fiddlesticks. She was thinking like a selfish child, all worried about such petty things. She was here to work, and work she would. All the trappings of her former life were just that. Trappings. It was time to focus on what the Coltons needed. What Jimmy needed. The past was the past. Lillian would look forward, not back.

Her mind swept in a hundred different directions. Excitement and nervousness flowed through her. But oh, how she needed rest. Getting up again, she reached for her robe and then wrapped it around her. Maybe a glass of water would serve to cool her nerves and help her to relax. All the tension of the past few weeks pressed in on every part of her body. She headed to the kitchen and prayed for sleep.

As she passed the library, a shaft of light shot out into the hallway. Mr. Colton must still be awake. Maybe if she kept her steps light, he wouldn't notice her.

But the sound of his voice stopped her in her tracks. Only a foot from the door, she debated turning around and heading back to her room until she heard her name.

"— Miss Porter. Lord, I'm so ashamed of my behavior toward her tonight. But we need her so desperately. Please . . ." His words became muffled.

Lillian stepped closer and peered around the door. Mr. Colton had his head in his hands, elbows on the desk. His lips were still moving, but she couldn't make out the words. Then he shook, almost as if he were crying. His shoulders lifted as he inhaled, and Lillian felt like an intruder. She stopped looking and turned back toward her room.

"Oh, God. Please help me. I need to find a way to help my son. I feel him slipping away, and I'm afraid. I can't lose him, too. . . ."

Woodward Colton's words reached her ears as she walked back to her room. New determination surged through her. That broken man crying out to God couldn't be a murderer. She wrapped her arms around herself and returned to her room.

There was a little boy who needed her.

God had brought her to this olive farm for a purpose. And she would do everything in her power to fulfill it.

The morning came sooner than Woody would have liked, but the smells of breakfast wafting from the kitchen made his stomach growl. Today was a new day. He splashed cold water on his face and dressed. Maybe Miss Porter would be able to break down

Jimmy's invisible walls. Hopefully she'd had enough rest and would at least feel up to meeting with Woody about his expectations for her job.

As he headed to the dining room, he heard voices. Jimmy? Could it be?

His heart leapt and he tried to muffle his steps and listen. A childish giggle came from the dining room. Unable to contain his excitement, Woody rushed to the dining room and pushed the swinging door open.

Jimmy sat at the table laughing. The baby bunny they'd rescued tickled Jimmy's chin with its nose. The tiny animal sat ensconced in some sort of sling around his son's neck. Another giggle came from the boy. It wasn't words, but it was something.

Lillian bustled in from the kitchen with a tray of biscuits in her hand. Her dark brown hair hung in a long braid, and her green eyes glistened with merriment. As she set the biscuits down on the table, she smiled at Woody. "Good morning, Mr. Colton."

He swallowed and found his tongue. "Good morning." How long had it been since he'd heard his precious child laugh?

She turned and headed back to the kitchen as Woody looked on. Her yellow dress was beautiful and sunny, but far too fancy for a nanny on a farm. Another giggle from

Jimmy tore his gaze from the door. The bunny was now rubbing his ears up against the boy's neck.

Lillian returned with Mrs. Goodman and they both carried platters of steaming food. They set them down, wiped their hands on their aprons, and took their seats.

"Aren't you going to sit, Woody?" Mrs. Goodman placed a linen napkin in her lap as if nothing were awry and this was an average, ordinary, everyday kind of meal.

He blinked several times. All heads turned to him. He'd been standing in the same spot since he'd entered. He took a deep breath. "I'm sorry. Of course." If they could all pretend this was normal, so could he.

Jimmy reached a finger up to pet the head of the bunny.

"Son —"

"Don't you worry about a thing, Mr. Colton," Miss Porter expertly interrupted, "we gave the rabbit a good scrubbing this morning, didn't we, Jimmy?" She widened her eyes at Woody, nodded, and put on a stiff smile as if to say, *"Keep your mouth shut, Colton."*

Mrs. Goodman also smiled and nodded.

Remembering the unfortunate incident the evening before with his harsh words, Woody realized he needed to slow down and

119

think before speaking. Of course she hadn't audibly said the words — he could well imagine them — but how had the astute Miss Porter known he was about to scold the boy?

"We fashioned the sling for him this morning to help keep the bunny warm. And this way, Jimmy can keep a close eye on him." She slathered butter and preserves onto her biscuit as if nothing were amiss.

"That's a wonderful idea." At least he hoped it was. What did he know about baby brush rabbits? Other than they were a nuisance to the vegetable gardens. But watching Jimmy smile was enough for him. "Why don't we thank the Lord?" He reached out his hands, to Miss Porter on the left and to Jimmy on the right.

"Don't forget to mention Mr. Whiskers," Miss Porter leaned in and whispered.

"Mr. Whiskers?"

"The bunny."

"Oh. Yes, Mr. Whiskers." He looked over to Jimmy and gained a smile from his son. Bowing his head, Woody found himself already baffled by the morning's events. Was he dreaming this? "Thank You, Lord, for this beautiful day and the bounty that is set before us. May we always be truly thankful, and may we serve You with our energy and time today." He cleared his throat. Exactly what did one say to the good Lord about a bunny? "Thank You, Father, for helping Jimmy to save Mr. Whiskers. May he thrive in our care. In Jesus' name we pray these things. Amen."

He took a bite of bacon and placed his elbows on the table as he chewed, steepling his fingers. "Miss Porter, I wonder if —"

"Mr. Colton, forgive me for interrupting, but if you don't mind, I would prefer it if you would call me Lillian. At least around the farm. Miss Porter is such a mouthful." She picked up her biscuit again. "I've told Jimmy that he may call me Miss Lillian."

If his son ever spoke again. Woody pushed the negative thought aside. "Of course —"

"Mrs. Goodman has shown me all around the house and kitchen, so I've asked Jimmy to show me his favorite places around the farm today, if that's all right with you."

"That's fine." He finished his piece of bacon and reached for another, unsure whether she was finished.

"I'll need to sit down with you at some point and discuss where he is with his lessons. Mrs. Goodman has already told me that the school is too far of a walk for Jimmy right now."

"Yes —"

"And then possibly sometime in the coming weeks, you could start teaching us about the olive farm. Jimmy and I need to learn all we can to help." She finally stopped long enough to take a bite out of the biscuit she'd held aloft for the last few minutes.

Mrs. Goodman looked at him from across the table. She gave him a very slight nod as she sipped her coffee.

So, no. He hadn't imagined the craziness of this morning. Something was up, and Mrs. Goodman and Miss Porter were in on it together. With a glance to Jimmy, he nodded back and played along. "Yes, of course."

Mrs. Goodman and Miss Porter chattered about recipes and the fluffy biscuits while Woody watched his son. For the first time in a long time, he saw a bit of color in the boy's cheeks. How that happened overnight, he had no idea, but he wouldn't complain.

"You'd better eat, Jimmy." Miss Porter smiled and winked at his son. "I hear there's a fishing hole around here, and I need someone to teach me how to fish."

Jimmy's eyes grew and he nodded his head, but he still hadn't touched his food, just kept petting the bunny. Certainly the woman could see how thin his son was. Ah, but maybe that was her tactic. Just treat him as though nothing were wrong. Treat him just like she would any other child.

Woody glanced at Miss Porter and saw her unspoken request of help. "Oh yes." He jumped in, even though he wasn't sure he knew the rules of this new game. "We've got a great fishing hole. Jimmy knows all about it. But it's quite a ways from the house, so you'll need your energy."

"And sturdy boots," Mrs. Goodman added.

"Oh, I'm glad you mentioned that. I'd better find some appropriate shoes." Miss Porter gave a slight nod. "So what do you say, Jimmy? Will you teach me how to fish?"

Jimmy's mouth opened, then closed just as quickly. He looked to his father, and Woody smiled. His son nodded at Miss Porter.

"Wonderful!" She clapped her hands together. "But you have to finish your breakfast if we're going to go. In fact, I think I'll need another biscuit myself." His new nanny made a big show out of grabbing another biscuit.

Jimmy glanced around the table, and to Woody's great surprise, the boy began to eat. He looked back to Lillian Porter and watched her finish her biscuit and then proceed to lick her fingers.

The woman hadn't even been there a full

day, and yet she'd turned their world around.

Mrs. Goodman stood beside him an hour later as they waved to Jimmy and Lillian from the porch. Armed with fishing poles, worms, a picnic, and a baby rabbit, the two had set off for the pond. As soon as they were out of earshot, Woody turned to his housekeeper and crossed his arms. "All right, Mrs. Goodman. What exactly happened in there today? I almost didn't think I was in my own home." The events at the breakfast table flashed through his mind. "Did you see Jimmy? He actually looked as if he might answer her when she asked about fishing."

Mrs. Goodman laughed a hearty laugh and sat down in one of the rocking chairs. "You know, Woody, I'm not even sure what's going on myself, but you found yourself a winner in that nanny of yours. She came into the kitchen this morning before I'd even gone to fetch the eggs, telling me that she'd been up half the night with ideas and questions. So I told her to follow me to the chicken house and we could talk as we worked. I taught her how to collect eggs. She might not know anything about farm chores and household duties, but she's got a willingness to learn. She's cheered my spirits considerably."

The older woman began a slow rock in her chair and gazed off into the distance. "I never thought the grief of losing Rebecca would ease much for any of us. It's just been too hard. But that Lillian. Whew. She's bursting at the seams. It's almost like a ray of sunshine has finally broken through the clouds. And you know what?" She looked back at Woody. "The more she talked this morning, and the more questions she asked, the more I realized that God sent us exactly what we needed. I mean, you saw Jimmy smile today. He ate all of his breakfast, and for goodness' sake, the boy even laughed!" Wiping a tear from the corner of her eye, she sighed heavily. "So when that gal told me she had a plan, I wholeheartedly agreed."

Woody chuckled and leaned against one of the porch posts.

"I'm just glad you picked up on it as soon as you did."

"If she hadn't given me that look and you that nod, I might not have." He looked toward the pond. "I have to admit, I was a bit confused — even thought I was dreaming at one point."

Mrs. Goodman stood and came over to where he stood. She patted his shoulder. "Sorry we didn't have time to fill you in, but I think Lillian's right. We need to move forward and be as normal and positive as possible. I'm not getting any younger. I might be good at cooking and cleaning, but even though I've been working for you all these years, I had no idea what would help Jimmy come out of his stupor."

Woody could only nod.

She patted his arm this time. "You're going to make it, Woody. We all are. With God's help."

And Lillian's. But he left that part unspoken.

CHAPTER NINE

A sound almost like tinkling bells floated on the breeze. Harry Longstreet walked to the top of the bluff to see where it came from. Hiding behind a tree, he peeked around it and saw the pond that sat on Pa's property.

He'd always liked that pond. It was pretty, and Mama had taught him about wild flowers there.

A lady in a yellow dress and a little boy chased something fluffy. It kind of bounced along. The lady laughed. So that's what sounded like bells. Harry liked it. A lot.

He sat down by the tree and picked at the grass at his feet while he watched. The lady in yellow caught the ball of fur and walked over to a blanket laid out on the grass. The little boy followed, and she tucked the fluffy animal into a red pouch around the boy's neck.

They sat down and looked like they were eating. Harry's stomach growled. Watching them eat, he wondered how it tasted. He licked his lips.

The thought of food pulled him. Without even thinking, he got to his feet and walked toward the pond. Maybe they would share. They looked like nice people. He'd met some nice people when his ma was alive.

As he got closer, the little boy pointed at him.

The lady in the yellow dress turned toward him. She stood up and put her hand on the boy's shoulder.

"Hello." She brushed the front of her skirt and stood in front of the boy. She looked a little afraid. "Are you one of Mr. Colton's workers?"

Harry took his hat off like his ma taught him. "Hi. I'm Harry."

"Harry." The lady nodded but still looked like she was worried. "I'm Miss Porter. Do you work on the farm?"

"No. I'm just Harry." He tried to bow like Ma said men were supposed to, but he dropped his hat and then tripped when he tried to pick it up.

"Here, let me help you." The yellow-dress-lady-Miss-Porter held out a hand to him.

Harry bit his lip. His knee hurt as he stood up. Tears burned his eyes.

"Did you hurt yourself?" She didn't look

afraid anymore.

He nodded.

The little boy peeked from behind the lady. He waved his hand.

Harry waved back. His knee wasn't so bad.

A little nose poked out of the red pouch. The boy petted it and tucked it back in.

Harry moved forward. He really wanted to see the fluffy thing. "Can I see it? I saw you chasing it earlier."

The boy nodded.

Miss Porter in her yellow dress laughed. "Yes, Mr. Whiskers escaped, and we had to chase him. He's too little, and we didn't want him to get hurt. He's just a baby."

The boy with the red pouch held out the animal in his little hands.

Harry gasped, "It's a bunny rabbit! I love bunny rabbits!" He jumped up and down. "They hop all over the place and like carrots. And they're fast, fast, fast." He smiled at Miss Porter. She smiled back and watched him with a strange look on her face. Harry hoped that didn't mean she wouldn't like him. A lot of times people had looked at him like that and then got mean.

Her strange look went away. "Yes, they are." Miss Porter's yellow skirt fluttered in the breeze like butterfly wings. Her laughter made his heart happy.

Harry reached out to touch the baby bunny. Its little nose tickled his hand. He leaned his head to the side and held his hands next to the boy's. "You have little hands. Look how big mine are."

The boy nodded.

"It's okay. You can talk to me. I'm nice. My name is Harry." He waved at the boy again. Just to show how nice he was. And he smiled. Real big.

Miss Porter in the yellow dress touched his arm. "This is Jimmy. He doesn't talk right now."

"Oh." Harry scratched his head. "Why don't he talk?"

"I don't know, Harry. But it's all right that he doesn't talk right now. Maybe one day we'll be able to help him talk again. Do you understand?"

Harry nodded. "Uh-huh." He turned to the little boy Jimmy. "I'll still be your friend whether you talk or don't."

Jimmy smiled at him.

"Are you all alone, Harry?" Miss Porter looked behind him.

"Yep." He swallowed. "I mean, yes, ma'am. My ma always told me I better have good manners. And I try, I really do, but sometimes I forget. Sometimes I use the word *ain't,* too, and Ma never liked it."

"Where's your ma now?" She looked over his shoulder again. He looked back to the hill he'd come down earlier.

"She died. So she's in heaven. With God. And Jesus, too. And my grandma. And —"

"I'm so sorry, Harry."

"It's okay. She died a long time ago. I can't really remember her face anymore. But I remember what she taught me, and I remember her voice. She sang to me, too. Only she didn't tell me I'd have to live with my uncle. I didn't like that."

"So is your uncle around?" She looked happy to hear him talk. No one really listened to him anymore.

He shook his head really hard. "No, no, no. I don't live with him no more. He's mean, mean, mean." Brother warned him to never mention any names, or the fact that Pa had once owned this land. And Harry didn't mind. He never wanted to say Uncle John out loud ever again. He couldn't remember why he wasn't supposed to, but there were lots of things he forgot lately. His cousins had hurt his head a lot. Since then, things were sometimes fuzzy.

"I'm sorry." Miss Porter in the yellow dress looked sad, but then she smiled again. "Why don't we talk about happier things? We could play a game." She turned to the little boy who didn't talk. "Jimmy, would you like to play a game?"

His little head bobbed and he smiled.

Harry liked these people. They *were* nice.

"All right, then" — Miss Porter put a finger to her lips — "what should we play?"

Harry's stomach growled a lot louder than before. He felt heat race up his neck, and he grabbed his belly.

Miss Porter smiled at him. "Are you hungry, Harry? We have this great big picnic and we haven't finished yet. We have plenty to share."

"I don't want to miss the game. I like games." He was torn between hunger and his new friends. He hadn't played a game in a long, long, long time.

She laid a hand on his and tugged him toward the blanket. "Don't you worry, Harry. We can eat *and* still play a game."

Little Jimmy put his hand on Harry's other arm and beamed up at him. Harry didn't think he'd ever been happier.

Lillian watched Harry walk back up the bluff. She'd uncovered very little about the young man as the afternoon progressed. His ma and pa were dead, he had a mean uncle he didn't live with anymore, and he was twenty years old. So where did he live? Was he all on his own? Even though he was an imposing figure and an adult in years, it was apparent that his mind was on the same level as Jimmy's. This made Lillian's heart ache. Who took care of him? Where did he get food? What would happen to him?

There was a young man named George that Reverend Owens had taken in back in Indianapolis. People said he was simple. Lillian had never known anyone more generous or kind. "Pure of heart" is what Reverend Owens used to say. Lillian always thought how refreshing and encouraging George was every time she spoke with him. She'd had that same feeling today.

Within an hour of their meeting, Harry and Jimmy were the best of friends. Jimmy never spoke, but Harry always understood the boy immediately. It was uncanny. Almost like they were having a conversation. When they went to pick flowers by the pond, Lillian had listened and watched closely.

Jimmy pointed to a patch of yellow flowers with what looked like bright red smiles on one side of the flower's face. Harry spoke up. "My ma said those are monkey flowers. See, it's like they have a big red mouth. I bet Miss Lillian likes them, too. Some monkey flowers are just yellow, and some are purple." He frowned. "I think there are other colors, too."

Jimmy pointed to another flower, and Harry nodded and picked one. "These purple ones are pretty, too. These are lupine. My mama liked flowers. They were her favorite." He held one out toward the rabbit. "Mr. Whiskers, do you like those? Okay. We'll pick some of those, too."

"Harry, you seem to know a lot about flowers."

He nodded with great enthusiasm. "I do. My ma taught me. She loved to plant flowers, and she showed me how and taught me their names." He frowned. "Some I forget."

Lillian shrugged. "I learned a lot of things that I've forgotten, too." Her reply seemed to make Harry relax.

And the afternoon had been filled with Harry's childlike voice and Jimmy's smiles.

But the true highlight had been when they'd played together. Jimmy's laughter echoed through her mind. Such a beautiful sound. Mrs. Goodman had told her just that morning that Jimmy hadn't spoken since his mother's death, had eaten very little, and hadn't laughed at all. So when he'd come down the stairs and stared at the baby rabbit in the box, Lillian knew exactly what to do. The baby bunny wasn't thriving all by itself, and neither was Jimmy.

She'd carefully bathed the little rabbit while Jimmy watched. She'd then fashioned that ridiculous sling out of a bandana Mrs. Goodman said was Mr. Colton's and told Jimmy that it was special-made for baby bunnies. He believed her, and his eyes lit up to have the rabbit so close. As he poured himself into his little furry friend, Lillian and Mrs. Goodman almost cried together over the biscuit dough. An instantaneous transformation had taken place.

The same thing happened during their picnic lunch. Mrs. Goodman had packed five sandwiches, saying that fishing and picnicking always made her hungry. And at the picnic, Lillian's little charge ate two whole sandwiches. She wasn't sure if he was trying to keep up with Harry or if he was just that hungry — but either way, it pleased her like nothing else could.

As Harry crested the hill to return to wherever he'd come from, she looked back at Jimmy. The little guy had fallen asleep leaning up against the tree. Apparently, playing in the sunshine took all his energy. But she didn't mind. She'd let him sleep while she cleaned up their picnic, and then she'd walk him home. She spied the fishing poles lying in the grass. They never did get around to fishing today, but that was all right. There were plenty of days ahead.

After she packed everything back up in the basket, Lillian folded the blanket and stared at Jimmy's little form. No wonder Mr. Colton had been worried. The little guy was way too small for his age. And if he hadn't been eating, it was a wonder he hadn't gotten seriously ill.

Lord, help me to know what to do to help this child. You've brought me this far. Thank You.

Her heart swelled with love for her little charge. The first day of her new job hadn't even finished yet, but she knew that God had given her love for Jimmy Colton.

Sunday morning Lillian dressed with great care for church. She wanted to make a good impression on the people of Angels Camp, if for no other reason than to prove to them that she was healthy and happy. She took up her hand mirror and made certain her hair looked all right. She'd had to work quite a bit to style it as the maid had back in Indianapolis. It wasn't even close to the elaborate looks her maid had achieved, but it would do. She smiled, feeling reassured. It looked just fine.

She left her hat and gloves on the bed and headed to the kitchen to work with Mrs.

Goodman. The older woman never shooed her out and seemed to enjoy Lillian's company. For the first time since her grandmother had passed, she felt like she belonged.

Mrs. Goodman stood over the stove frying bacon.

"Good morning." Lillian grabbed an apron.

"Good morning, dear." Mrs. Goodman turned and smiled and looked up and down at her dress. "Well, isn't that lovely?"

Lillian gave a quick turn, letting the layers of pale pink silk gauze over a darker pink taffeta swirl around her. "I wanted to look a little nicer for church today."

Mrs. Goodman's face fell. "Mr. Colton doesn't go to church right now. Not since his wife . . . well, you know . . . all the rumors."

"Well, do you go to church? I could ride with you."

"No, I'm afraid not, dearie. I almost slapped Mrs. Francis last time I went."

"What?" Lillian laughed. "You almost slapped someone? I can hardly believe it."

But Mrs. Goodman was very serious. "Oh, you'd believe it if you heard what they were saying."

Lillian furrowed her brow and placed her

hands on her hips. "Let me guess. They were saying that Mr. Colton murdered his wife. That he was a despicable human being, and that he shouldn't be allowed around women and children."

Mrs. Goodman gasped. "You've heard?"

"From more than one squawking hen, if you'll pardon my expression." It angered her more each day she spent on the Colton farm. "How could anyone ever think that?"

The older woman removed the bacon from the pan and sat down at the table. "Sit down, Lillian. Please."

"Of course." Whatever was bothering the older woman was about to come out. And it was serious.

"Mr. Colton said that you knew about the rumors and about how his wife died, but he didn't tell me that you'd heard it all first-hand from town."

Lillian nodded. "He was late to pick me up because he had to repair the wagon. I had the lovely experience of waiting inside the general store. And while Mrs. Clark is a wonderful woman, I can't say much about the rest of the town that I had the chance to meet."

"I can well imagine." Mrs. Goodman got up and poured herself a cup of coffee.

"Would you like one? This might take a while."

Lillian nodded again and accepted the cup.

"While there are a few people who refuse to believe the rumors about Woody, they don't have much say. The loudest and gossipiest ones get all the attention. And I don't mean to say that all the people are bad. They're not. They've just bought into the lie. Relying on rumors and hearsay to color their judgment. Thankfully Judge Morgan was a fair and wise man. It's been about a year and a half since it happened.

"The day Rebecca was murdered, I was out helping Woody with the olive trees. It was January, and he'd fallen a few weeks earlier and had injured his shoulder, right after he'd started pruning the trees. And Woody kept saying, 'When it's time to prune the trees, it's time to prune the trees.' He'd gotten sorely behind with his injury, his workers were gone for the time, and a storm was coming. You could feel it in the air. And it was a big one. With the wind blowing, and all that was left to do, I offered to help Woody, knowing that serious damage to the trees could ruin the crop for the year. Rebecca hadn't been feeling well for a few days, and Woody told her to rest and watch over Jimmy.

"And as the good Lord allowed, we were as far from the house as we could possibly be when she was murdered. When we returned for lunch, Rebecca was dead at the bottom of the stairs. We found Jimmy in the closet, crying. It was the most horrible thing I'd ever seen." She used her apron to wipe her eyes. "So you see, I was with Woody the whole time. He didn't kill his wife. Someone else came into this house. A thief, most likely . . . tore the place up." She sighed. "There was an investigation, and I testified to the judge. There were never any formal charges against Woody. But the people in town were suspicious. Oh, there's always been problems with gangs attacking the stages, especially if they know they're carrying gold — this is gold country, you know — but no one had done it on a farm before. At least not in our little community. Someone then said that maybe *I* couldn't be trusted, that I made up my statement to save Woody from jail."

"That's terrible." Lillian reached forward and grabbed the woman's hand. "People can be so cruel with their words. Did no one stand up for Woody?"

"Pastor Seymour tried to. He and Woody were good friends once, and the pastor knew Woody wasn't capable of hurting anyone — especially his beloved wife. Pastor came around to see Woody nearly every day, but Woody pushed him away and finally demanded he stay away."

"And he was the only one?" Lillian shook her head, feeling close to tears.

"There were a couple of other men, but I think they were afraid. I heard there were some threats made toward them."

"How could people act that way?"

"They were scared. Everyone was — especially since it was a woman who was killed. In her own home." Mrs. Goodman stood back up. "All of the furniture had been sliced with knives, the curtains torn down, so Woody took it all out and burned it. But when Woody started taking everything down off the walls, Jimmy stopped him. With tears in his eyes, the little boy just shook his head. The house was quite empty for a while. With exception to the piano, everything downstairs is less than a year old. Woody told me later that he was glad Jimmy stopped him. For a long while it was hard to see remembrances of Rebecca, but later we all needed those remembrances. We clung to them. Loved them. I don't know if we'll ever get beyond the grief."

She choked on her words. "I'm sorry. I

don't think I want to say any more. It's just too hard right now. But I will say one last thing: I think you can understand now why we don't go to church. The people who said they were our friends no longer trust us. They turned their backs on us in our time of great need. And so we don't want anything to do with them."

CHAPTER TEN

Woody saddled his two best horses, Alexander and Sunflower, in preparation for showing Miss Porter — Lillian — around the farm. More than two weeks had passed since his nanny arrived, and he'd admittedly been absent on purpose. A lot.

After the first day when she dived right in, Woody dealt with a whole new wave of grief. Grief and hope all at the same time. But somehow, it didn't seem right to allow hope entrance. That meant he was really moving beyond Rebecca's death. And he wasn't sure he was ready. Or even wanted to.

Yes, he wanted his son to speak again. He longed for the boy to heal. But the stark realization hit him square in the face. To hope — to heal — meant to move forward. And moving forward meant letting go. As much as he wanted to hope, he didn't want to let go. Thus the war began in his heart and mind. Miss Porter was very capable. She'd done an amazing job with Jimmy from the moment she came down to breakfast that first morning. His boy was eating and had color in his cheeks. His little legs were filling out, and Woody often heard laughter come from him. So why did he feel like he was betraying Rebecca?

She'd been everything to him. Their marriage had been almost perfect. Deep down inside, he knew she'd want him to be happy. To move on. When Rebecca gave birth to Jimmy, she'd fallen so ill that the doctor wasn't even sure she'd make it through. She made Woody promise that if she died, he'd find another wife to love him and the baby. He'd promised, but even then he'd known he didn't really mean it. He wasn't sure then or now that he wanted to go on living — if it meant living without her.

There. He'd admitted it. And he was ashamed.

Lord, You've given me so much. It's been devastating to lose Rebecca — You know that better than anyone — but I'm stuck. I'm not ready to move on, and yet my son needs me. Please, help me to get past this muddy bog I seem to be mired in.

As he led the horses out of the barn, Woody found himself craving the Word again. It had been a long time, but he needed it. Longed for it. Maybe that was the key to getting past the ugliness and sorrow.

Miss Porter headed toward him from the house, wearing a very smart blue riding outfit complete with a split skirt. It still amazed him that God would send him a nanny with no experience who seemed to lack for nothing materially and yet was as down-to-earth as Mrs. Goodman. But here she was. And she was perfect for the job.

Her dark hair was arranged in a bun at the nape of her neck with a wide-brimmed straw hat resting just over it. Blue ribbons secured the hat in place. Sophisticated and carefree. The two words blended together to make up Lillian Porter. He'd also add *stubborn,* and *strong-willed* from what he'd seen, and he had to admit *pretty.* But he didn't want to think too long on that.

"Good morning." She waved to him.

"Mornin'." He tipped his hat.

As she climbed his makeshift stairs to mount her horse, she nodded in his direction. "Thank you, Mr. Colton. This worked perfectly." She settled astride atop the animal.

"Well, I recall you asking for a step." He chuckled. "And just call me Woody. You were right. Around the farm, we might as well call each other by our given names. Although if I started calling Mrs. Goodman 'Harriet,' she might toss me out with the dishwater."

Lillian laughed. "I know. She told me she hated her name. That's why she calls everyone 'dear' or 'dearie.' Apparently her husband called her 'sweetheart.' " She sighed.

Great. She was probably a hopeless romantic. "Was Mrs. Goodman all right with you leaving?"

She laughed again, seeming quite amused with herself. "I think she was relieved. I burned a batch of cookies and dropped a mixing bowl. It shattered into a million pieces." She shook her head. "I have a lot to learn."

He smiled. "Well, I was asking more along the lines of you leaving Jimmy."

"Oh, of course." She blushed. "Mrs. Goodman told me she has no problem keeping an eye on Jimmy, but I'd rather not take too long. I know that she had quite the list to accomplish today. Which reminds me" — she pulled out a small leather-bound book and a tiny pencil — "I want to take copious notes, and I have quite a few questions."

"All right, then. I'm assuming you're an

experienced rider?"

"Yes, sir." She sat straighter and tucked the book away. "As I told you, I've ridden both sidesaddle and astride, but I prefer the latter, no matter how shocking it might seem. Honestly, I think women have put far too many restrictions upon themselves. After all, it is nearly the nineteen hundreds."

He laughed and leaned down from his mount to open the gate. He let Lillian pass through first and then moved his gelding to follow. "I know you've been down to the pond, but have you seen the olive groves yet?"

"No, I haven't. Well, I've seen them, but not up close."

They kept a steady pace to the groves while Woody pointed out the flower gardens around the house, the large vegetable gardens, and, beyond the pond, the tender fruit orchard whose little saplings would hopefully bloom with fruit in the coming years. The barns by the house had been pretty self-explanatory, but then there were two larger barns out by the groves. "These buildings are for my equipment to tend the trees and where we brine the table olives and press the other olives for oil. And the smaller building in the rear is the housing for my workers. They have their own rooms and a kitchen to cook for themselves."

"Oh, that's lovely. I was wondering about the men." She tilted her head. "Back to the olives — I'm curious — is that why there are two groves? One for table olives and the other for olive oil?"

"Yes."

"Two different kinds of olives for the two different purposes?"

"Yes." She caught on quick. "Producing table olives here in California is new. Rebecca and I had wanted to be the first really prosperous farm to supply all the grocers with table olives."

"I thought the trees looked just a tad different. I'm fascinated with table olives. They are my absolute favorite, but I know they have been hard to come by."

"Well, the process is relatively new to keep them preserved, but ancient in that olives have always been a delicacy."

She nodded. "What other equipment do you need?"

Her observation skills were impressive. "Well, we need barrels for brining the olives. Granite wheels for the pressing. Barrels for the oil. Ladders. Trimming blades. There's quite a list."

While they stopped, she pulled out her little book and started writing, then looked up again. "How often do you trim the trees?"

"We prefer to call it pruning. We prune them every other year in the winter months. Olives tend to produce in high yields one year and then less the next. In the off year we prune, and that gives us an even better crop the next year. We try not to let them get over twenty feet. It's pretty difficult to harvest if we let them get out of control."

She nodded and wrote some more. "When is harvest?"

"September through November most of the time. Sometimes even into December. It takes us a while to get to all the trees. The olives we use for olive oil are shaken out of the trees with special wooden rakes onto large sheets of cotton. It takes a while since there can be over a thousand olives per tree. But we have twice as many olive oil trees as we do table olives. Those trees have to be picked by hand so there are no bruises on the fruit."

She raised her eyebrows and her mouth formed an *o* as she wrote. "How many workers do you have?"

"Only five. I normally give them the months of January and February off. Since not all of them are from around here, they like to go visit their families." He frowned.

"I can't always get workers from around here."

"Well, I think it's quite kind of you to let them leave to see their loved ones."

He shrugged. "They deserve the break. Harvest season can be grueling. We have the pickers and then we also have to get all the olives cleaned. Then prepped for whichever direction they go, whether it be oil or to the table."

She scribbled in the book faster than he thought possible. "When will Jimmy start to help?"

Woody looked the other direction. Why did such a simple question squeeze his heart like a vise? "Well . . . he'd been helping in the groves since he was little. Rebecca often strapped him in a contraption on her back. Then, when he was a little bigger, he helped me pick the leaves out of the olive bins as they were being washed. But then Rebecca died . . ."

"And he hasn't spoken since."

Woody nodded. "I don't know what he remembers about the olive groves. And I don't know what he saw or heard the day his mother died. Then he started withering away." He turned toward her again. "We're all just a little hesitant to move on with life."

"That's understandable." She tucked her

book back into her skirt. "He loves you, you know."

His heart clenched as he nodded.

"Would you be okay with us helping every now and then? So he can learn what his papa does and how he provides for his family?"

"That's a good idea." No, it wasn't, his heart wanted to shout. Rebecca was supposed to be here. Teaching Jimmy alongside Woody. He shook his head of the negative thoughts. How long was he going to allow this dark cloud to reign over him? He drew in a deep breath and let it go. One step at a time. One day at a time.

"So what else can I learn? How many acres do you have, and how many trees?"

Woody pushed his horse forward and stopped for a moment as another wave of regret washed over him. Let go, Colton. Let go.

"Woody?"

"I'm sorry." He cleared his throat. "Fifty acres for the olive groves. Fifty for the orchard that you saw but will take many years to establish, and two hundred in surrounding land. Right now we have five hundred trees producing for the table olives and a thousand trees for olive oil. But I've planted a lot more — almost twice as many

151

on each side. You've probably seen the little saplings. The problem will be at harvesttime. I'll have to hire additional workers once those trees start to produce."

"My goodness. Well, they are beautiful, Woody." She pulled her horse even with his, seeming content to just look at the beauty of the groves.

"You should see it in spring — around April and May when the trees begin to bloom and are covered in white flowers."

"I bet it's breathtaking."

He nodded. Then turned his horse back toward the house. "We better get back for lunch so Mrs. Goodman doesn't worry. Is there anything else you'd like to see? Any other questions?"

"This has been very helpful, thank you. I know if I'm to do my best by Jimmy, then I need to be well acquainted with the farm and what we do here."

"You're doing just fine, Lillian."

"I noticed the flower beds needed attention." She bit her lip. "That's something Jimmy and I can tend to and incorporate learning at the same time. I've not cared for a garden myself, but I've watched it done enough that I feel confident I can manage."

Another of Rebecca's loves. Her flowers. Would the ache ever go away? He cleared his throat. "Well, I suppose that would be fine." As heartbreaking as it felt to have someone else — another woman, no less — tending to Rebecca's flowers, maybe it would help his son in some small way.

She nodded and exhaled a large breath. "I have a lot to learn, but I do believe that everything we do should be done to the very best of our ability for the glory of the Lord. This is a wonderful place, Woody. Thank you for being patient and explaining. I'll work hard and learn everything I can."

"No doubt, Lillian. Don't fret over it." If he could just take his own advice.

God had provided in miraculous ways. He understood grief was a process, but he hadn't expected so much to get churned up as he healed.

Turning back to glance at Lillian, he watched her face go from a smile to a concerned expression. "Are you sure you don't have any other questions?"

She scrunched up her nose. "Well, not about the farm. But I do have a question about a young man."

"A young man?"

"Yes, his name is Harry." She flicked a bug away from her face. "Do you know him? Have you met him before?"

"No, I can't say that I have." Woody

looked over at her. Her brow was furrowed. "Has he bothered you?"

"Oh, heavens, no." She shook her head. "But I've been worried about him ever since we met him."

"We?"

"Yes, Jimmy and I — we met him on our first picnic. Poor thing was half starved to death. He said that he's twenty years old, but he's just a child, really. I've met someone like him before — our minister had taken him in — back in Indianapolis. They're not dumb by any means, but they never seem to really mature all the way. Harry seems to be on about the same level as Jimmy mentally. Back east they called them simple-minded, but I didn't like that terminology at all."

Her sympathy for the young man was clear. But after what had happened to Rebecca, Woody felt a pang of caution. "Did he have a weapon? Did he seem at all dangerous?"

She laughed and shook her head. "Goodness, Woody, no. Not at all. He was gentler than Mrs. Goodman. He might be large in stature, but that boy seems to have a heart of gold. I was just hoping you knew something about him. Maybe how we could help him. I can't help wondering how he's taking care of himself. He said he was all alone."

"Still . . ." Woody frowned and tried not to sound too stern, considering he'd given her a bad first impression already. "You should be cautious just in case. We still don't know who killed my wife."

Lillian reached across from her horse and patted his arm. Her touch seemed to burn through the fabric. It'd been so long since anyone had touched him. "I'm so sorry, Woody, I wasn't thinking. I understand where your fears come from, but there's no way Harry could have hurt your wife. Why, the boy stepped on a flower and cried when he crushed it." She shook her head. "The only thing that stopped his sobbing was Jimmy bringing him another one. And personally, I think he's good for Jimmy and Jimmy's good for him. Those two communicated that day like nothing I have ever seen or heard. Maybe Harry can help Jimmy heal."

"But you don't know where he lives?"

"No. That's why I was asking you about him."

"I'll keep my eyes and ears open."

"Thank you, Woody." She sighed. "I just know the good Lord would want us to help Harry. And maybe in turn, Harry will help us."

For a moment she was silent, but just when Woody figured all her concerns were addressed, she started in again. "There is one more thing. I hope you won't think me too forward."

"What is it?"

She looked away for a moment, and Woody thought she might have decided against posing her question. Finally she straightened and looked back at him. "I wondered if . . . if I might . . . play your piano."

Woody hadn't expected such a question and couldn't keep the surprise from his face. Lillian waved a gloved hand. "If it's too soon, I understand. It's just that I love to play. Music has always been such a comfort to me, and Mrs. Goodman said that your wife had just started to teach Jimmy. I thought it might be a way to connect him with his memories of her in a good way. Of course, I do understand if that isn't what you want and the memories of your wife are too difficult. I will respect your wishes, but —"

Now it was Woody's turn to raise his hand as if in surrender. "If you'll stop long enough to draw breath, I'll give you an answer."

She looked at him and blushed. "I do

apologize."

He forced a smile. First the flowers, now the piano. Why not just rip the scab right off his heart and let him bleed to death? But his own words betrayed him. "It's quite all right. I would be happy for you to use the piano. I closed that room off not because I didn't want to remember my wife, but because nobody else plays. I'm sure Jimmy would be glad for the opportunity to learn."

He turned his horse back toward the house and this time didn't wait for any other questions. Even though his chest felt like it was being crushed, he knew his answer was the best.

If he could survive it.

CHAPTER ELEVEN

Darwin swiped a hand down his clean-shaven face. He hadn't been without a beard or mustache since he could grow facial hair. Ma wouldn't even recognize him.

It was about time to head into Copperopolis. He needed supplies and liquor — and the only way to find out if his trick worked would be to hang out and keep his ear to the ground. Angels Camp would be too close, and there might be bounty hunters hanging around.

Saddling his horse, he looked around for Harry. Dagnabbit, that fool boy was never around. If he got them caught, Darwin would have to shoot the kid himself — promise or no promise to Ma. He was *not* his brother's keeper.

Blast. A stream of curses flew out of his mouth. The boy must've wandered off ex-plorin' again. Well, Darwin would just have to give his kid brother a talkin' to when he got back.

Kicking his horse into a gallop, Darwin could almost taste the whiskey waiting for him in town. It had been too long.

The long ride did nothing but sour his mood. He should be riding in style. Not eating dust and having to do his own dirty work. He ought to own his father's property, but instead that Colton fellow did, and he'd planted olives. Olives of all things. Darwin couldn't stand them.

By the time he reached the edge of Copperopolis, he was ready to beat somebody up. His blood boiled at the injustice of it all. Here he was. A man of means. With lots of gold. And someone else was standin' in his way.

He flipped a coin to a kid at the livery and dismounted. "Clean him up for me. I got business in town."

"Yes, sir." The kid turned the coin over and over in his grubby hands.

Darwin sauntered into town in Saul's duds. His disgusting cousin had always liked things a bit too fancy for Darwin's taste, but if he wanted people to believe he was dead and his cousin still alive, he'd have to play the part.

He nodded his head to some ladies on the boardwalk and smiled at the children. See?

He could be a good guy. Fit in. Just like everyone else. He just needed his gold.

Stopping in the general store, he watched the people around him. No one seemed to be scared of him or even recognize him. In fact, two women even batted their eyelashes at him as he held the door. Maybe he should've cleaned up years ago. Time to take the next step.

As he went farther down the street, he found a saloon. One of his favorite places to visit. Many times. He walked in and stood at the polished pine bar. Not a peep from the barkeep. Several men looked his way and then went right back to what they were doing.

Chuck, the regular barkeep, dried a glass and placed it in front of him. "What'll ya have?"

"Whiskey."

Chuck served it up and Darwin drank. The old-timer didn't recognize him, either.

He stood there for a good thirty minutes just listening and drinking. He should've killed Saul a long time ago. This was too easy.

Curly Jones and Gus Parker entered from the back of the saloon. Gus hiked up his pants and then took his stance at the end of the bar. Curly wobbled his way over to join him. The two were always there — same place, same scowling expressions.

Now things would get interesting. If Darwin could fool these two, he could fool anyone.

Chuck poured them drinks and they lifted their glasses and looked straight at him. But neither one did anything other than nod and drink.

"I need another, Chuck." Gus spoke a little too loudly. It was apparent he'd already had a start.

Curly just laughed as Chuck poured another round.

"Hey, Chuck, did you hear about the body they found on the way to Stockton?"

Darwin's ears perked up at the conversation, but he kept his head focused on his drink. He hadn't seen either of the men in years, but that didn't mean they wouldn't figure out who he was.

"Nope. Can't say that I have." Chuck went back to washing and drying glasses. "One of your pals?"

"No pal to us." Curly swigged another.

Gus chuckled. "Nope. No friend of ours. They think it's that no-good Darwin Longstreet."

"I heard he was wanted, but I always keep my mouth closed when it comes to the

161

customers. Even mean ones like Longstreet." Chuck's towel circled the glass again. "He wasn't my favorite customer, that's for sure. And he had a nasty temper. Don't surprise me at all that he finally got his comeuppance." He set the glass down. "They sure it's him?"

Gus squared his shoulders and pushed out his chest. Tucking his thumbs in his suspenders, he narrowed his eyes. "I just heard the marshal say they had incriminatin' evidence on the body. But the body wasn't recognizable no more. He'd been dead awhile." He lifted his glass for more. "And beat up real bad before that."

Chuck obliged and filled the glass again. "Well, I guess they'll have to let his kin know, huh?"

"Yup. Not that his cousins and uncle are much better. I've always been glad they live over Manteca way. Keeps 'em from venturing over here too much." Gus reached an arm over and clasped Curly's shoulder. "You know, I didn't much care for Darwin, but maybe we should drink to him."

Curly guffawed. "Sure, Gus." He raised his glass.

Darwin turned and threw a coin on the counter, headed for the door.

"To Darwin!"

"To Darwin." Curly echoed. "Good riddance."

"May he burn in the lowest pits of —"

The voices faded behind him. He didn't need to hear the rest. Who cared what those drunks thought anyway? A smile stretched across his face.

His little trick had worked. Darwin Longstreet was dead.

Lillian dipped her pen once more and continued her lengthy letter to the staff at Fletcher Manor. So much had happened in such a short amount of time. Each week she wrote an update. She'd have to make sure she sent them soon. Her stack would definitely grow after tonight. Had she really been in California almost three weeks? What a thrill it was to share it with her friends back home. This letter would be fat indeed. Already seven pages! She glanced aside at the one-page missive she'd penned to her grandfather. Would he read it? No doubt Stanton would give it to him, but stubborn Adam Fletcher might very well throw it into the fire.

The thought saddened her. Here she was, following in her parents' footsteps and finding what she'd discovered were her own dreams. She was making a difference and felt that God truly was using her service. It invigorated her each and every day. How had she lived so long and not experienced this true joy?

The lamp on her desk flickered and her thoughts traveled to Jimmy. The little boy captured her heart. He still wouldn't speak, but she didn't mind. He was eating and had become very curious and adventurous. Each day he worked on drawing letters and numbers on the slate with her. He seemed eager to learn and eager to please her. If she could teach him enough reading and writing, he'd finally be able to communicate with her — with all of them.

Tomorrow they would take another picnic to the pond and she would practice her fishing skills. The last trip had been a disaster. Jimmy laughed and laughed. All because she wouldn't bait her own hook with the still wiggling and very-much-living worm. Well, she would have to show him tomorrow that she was made of sterner stuff. Secretly she hoped that Harry would show up again. After her talk with Woody, she was even more convinced that the boy needed help. And now that she'd finally gotten a taste of living a life that mattered, she longed to do more.

She laid her pages out to dry and extinguished the lamp. Tomorrow would be a glorious day.

The next morning, rain poured from the sky. Mrs. Goodman had already told Lillian that summer rains were rare, but given they were suffering drought, this was no doubt welcome relief. As Lillian entered the kitchen, she immediately spotted Jimmy by the screen door. Gone was the scrawny boy from a few weeks ago. He was still thin and small, but he finally had a healthier glow about him. But this morning, the sheen of tears in his eyes was almost Lillian's undoing. Rain wasn't a welcome relief for Jimmy.

She crouched next to him and placed her hand on his shoulder. "I'm betting the sun will come out in a few hours and we'll still make our fishing trip. And we need to remember to be thankful for the rain. It's been a very dry summer, and that's not good for the olives."

He sniffed and looked at her, a glint of hope in his eyes.

"I'm not even averse to trying my hand at fishing in the rain. I read in a book that the fish like to bite when it's raining." She winked at him. "So we'd better get to our breakfast and studies."

Jimmy nodded, but his disappointment was clear that the weather had not co-operated with their plans. He turned toward her and put his arms around her neck.

Lillian felt her eyes grow wide, and she wrapped her arms around the boy. She looked up and caught Mrs. Goodman wiping a tear away. Lillian felt like crying herself.

It had been a tough couple of weeks. Woody had informed her that he would be working long hours and absent from Jimmy a lot. It was time for the table olives to come out of the brine, and they had to hand-wash all the barrels of olives multiple times and give them enough time in the fresh air to turn their lovely black color. Then the canning process would take place. He assured her that it would only be two to three weeks, but it had taken its toll on his son.

When Jimmy pulled back just a smidge, Lillian loosened her hold but kept her arms around him. What a delight this child was to her soul. *Thank You, Lord, that I can be here for him. I know this has to be hard on both father and son.*

Jimmy touched her locket with his fingers and then leaned his forehead against hers. He pulled back again and looked at her with questioning eyes.

"Yes, you may open it." She nodded and smiled.

His little fingers fumbled with the clasp, but he got it open. For several moments, he just stared.

"It's my mother and father. They died when I was very young." She watched his expression, knowing the grief this poor boy experienced. "I miss them very much. But this way I carry them with me always, and I know they loved me, and I love them." Lillian took a moment to look up at Mrs. Goodman again, wary of moving too fast. "Do you have your very own picture of your mother?"

Jimmy shook his head. A single tear slipped down his cheek.

"Would you like one?"

He nodded.

"Let me talk to your father and I'll see what I can do, all right?"

A tiny smile lit his face.

"Your father told me that your mother used to play the piano."

Jimmy nodded.

"And that she was teaching you to play."

Again he nodded.

Lillian continued. "Well, it just so happens that I play, as well, and would love to teach you — if you like."

Jimmy's eyes widened, and he nodded with greater enthusiasm.

"Wonderful. We'll have lots of fun with the pianoforte."

Mrs. Goodman placed a huge plate of pancakes on the table.

"Yum. Do you smell that? Mrs. Goodman has made my favorite — pancakes! I'm starving, how about you?" She tickled his tummy.

He nodded and giggled.

Over her short time on the farm, she'd learned to interact with Jimmy and ask him questions that were easy for him to communicate an answer without speaking. If she tried to draw too much out of him, he got aggravated and would shut down. But if she asked mainly yes or no questions, he was very responsive. For whatever reason, Jimmy Colton refused to speak. Only time would tell if she could get to the root of the problem, but he didn't need to feel pressured to speak, of that she was certain.

Having been uninformed of the extent of the situation before her arrival, Lillian had assumed that the boy was in shock. But on her very first day when she'd heard him laugh, she began to puzzle over his condition. According to Woody and Mrs. Goodman, he hadn't done much since his mother died. They had found him lethargic most of the time, and he would gaze at nothing. He preferred to be alone. After his initial burst of trust and openness with Lillian, she, too, found that there were a few times he reverted to an almost dreamlike state, where he just stared off into space and didn't even move.

Mr. Whiskers was definitely beneficial, and Lillian found herself thanking God daily for the bunny. She didn't know how the rabbit had come to be part of the family, but she was thankful that the animal seemed to be just what Jimmy needed. He not only needed to be nurtured, but he needed to nurture something in return.

By the time they were finishing their pancakes, Lillian was happy to see the sun poking through the clouds. "Looks like we better hurry up with our lessons so we can get to the pond."

Jimmy nodded and hopped out of his chair. He handed his plate to Mrs. Goodman and went to Mr. Whiskers's box to get him in his sling.

"Wash your hands first, please." Lillian smiled around a bite of pancake. "We don't want to get sticky syrup all over our slate."

He raced to the basin and cleaned his hands and then went back to fetch the bunny. In record time he was in his chair in the dining room where they did their lessons.

After he'd drawn all twenty-six letters twice and the numbers one through ten twice, Lillian decided she couldn't wait any longer and they should just head to the pond. The ground was sure to be wet, but then again, they'd had so little moisture, the ground might have soaked it all up already.

Her little student sat with his tongue hanging out one side of his mouth as he made another eight.

"Good job, Jimmy." She took the chalk and drew a smiling face and a star. "But I think I hear the fishies calling my name. Are you ready to help me catch some dinner?"

He jumped up and smiled.

That was all the encouragement she needed. They put their things up on the shelf and headed to the kitchen. "Be ready, Mrs. Goodman. We're planning on catching enough fish for dinner."

"Oh, really, now." The older lady placed her hands on her hips. "Well, I'd just love me some fish, so you better catch a bunch." She tapped Jimmy on the nose and he giggled.

They grabbed their poles and the picnic basket. Lillian had prepared for the day by wearing her oldest dress and boots. She had no doubt that they would return to the house filthy and smelling of fish, but it would be worth it. If it put Jimmy at ease and made him happy, it might make it possible for him to speak. Lillian would skewer worms on hooks all day if it brought about those results.

As they half walked, half ran to the pond, Lillian prayed the whole way that not only would she be able to murder a worm by squishing it onto the hook, but that Harry would show up. She wasn't above asking for divine intervention even in the smallest things.

When they crested the last hill before the pond, she knew at least one part of her prayer had been answered affirmatively because Harry sat on the opposite hill. It was apparent he had spotted them because he waved and then skipped his way down the bluff toward them.

The rest of the morning flew by in a flurry of what Harry termed "fish, fish, fish." Not only did she become an expert at threading her worm onto the hook, but she caught eight of their twenty fish.

Harry babbled all morning to Jimmy about Mr. Whiskers and flowers and catching fish. Lillian rather enjoyed listening and

171

watching. But when she pulled out the picnic basket for their lunch, she hoped it was the right time to ask some questions.

"So, Harry, where do you live?"

He sighed. "Way, way, way over there." He pointed to the direction he'd come down the hill.

Bother. That didn't help her much. "Did it take you a long time to walk over here? Because if it didn't, we'd love to see you more often."

"It's a good long ways, but I don't mind walking. I've walked a couple times all the way to the big trees all by myself."

The big trees? "You mean the redwoods? The giant trees?"

He nodded, never taking his eyes off the last sandwich in his hand. "They're so big, you could build a house inside them."

Jimmy's eyes grew wide.

"I mean it. It took me fifty big steps to walk around one of them, and I've got big feet." Harry took a bite and kept nodding to Jimmy.

"I've always wanted to see the redwoods, but they're a long ways from here. That must have been quite a walk." Lillian couldn't believe this young man had gone all that way.

"Yep. Ma told me about them a long,

long, long time ago. When she died, I went to see them. It gave me a happy memory of her. She said God grew them big and strong like me."

What innocence and beauty. Simple-minded indeed. How many people missed out on knowing kind souls because someone else labeled them as simpleminded? She frowned. Or unsafe, as they had labeled Woody.

Lillian shook her head at the thought. What a sad world they lived in. Harry was one of the sweetest human beings she'd ever met, and Woody had a gentleness to him that made her ever more convinced that he could never hurt anyone.

"There's all kinds of neat explorin' things to do around here. There's lots of forests and places to climb, and water — lots of water falling from the mountains. It's real pretty. But sometimes I get lost or go too far. It takes me a while to get back home."

"It's not safe to go off by yourself, Harry. There are all kinds of dangers out there." She had read of the new national park, Yosemite, being established just the year before. It wasn't all that far from Angels Camp, but it was noted for having high cliffs and perilous settings.

"It's not dangerous. It's just a long way to walk."

"From the sounds of it you must be describing Yosemite National Park. I've read about it, and it does sound quite beautiful."

Harry nodded. "It's my special place."

Lillian wondered exactly how far away it was and how Harry could ever manage on his own. He was a strong young man, but she feared there might come a danger that he couldn't surmount. She'd have to encourage him to stick closer to the farm for his own good.

". . . Hey, Jimmy, have you ever seen a gold mine? There's lots of them around here 'cause we're in gold country. Isn't it wonderful that God grows gold in the ground?"

Lillian gasped and realized she hadn't been listening like she should.

Harry continued on for several more sentences without taking a breath.

"Harry!" She finally got a word in edgewise. "I think it's fascinating that you know so much about gold mines, but those are not safe places to be."

"Oh, but I live in one, Miss Lillian. I explore them all the time and never have problems."

Oh, goodness. How could she get out of this one? Jimmy's eyes were glued to Harry, eating up every word he said about gold and mines and quartz. And to find out that the poor young man was living in a mine! Glory be. Time to change the subject. She'd have to address this later. "Harry, why don't we have a little contest to see who can catch the most fish this afternoon?" She reached into her pocket. "I happen to have a shiny new penny that will go to the winner."

Both boys jumped up and scrambled to the pond.

Her shoulders shook for a moment. Harry lived in a mine. Alone. The ramifications of his situation hit her in the stomach as if someone had physically struck her. It was a good thing she found out about it now. Maybe there was something she could do.

First things first. She'd have to take the long way home with Jimmy so she could explain to him that mines were dangerous places and that he should *never* go into a mine. Never.

Chapter Twelve

Jimmy stared at the ceiling and wondered how Mr. Whiskers was doing by the stove. Papa told him that once his bunny got a little bigger, he could bring the box upstairs to his room. He couldn't wait for that day. Then maybe he wouldn't feel so alone and scared at night. Maybe the nightmares would go away for good.

Miss Lillian didn't know how bad the nightmares were. Papa was still the one to come comfort him, which he liked. But he really liked Miss Lillian, too. She seemed to understand. And he trusted her.

She was nice, pretty, and smart. She made him laugh. Especially the funny face she made when she put a worm on her fishing hook.

Jimmy fidgeted with the edge of his blanket. But what was really special about her was that she was new. She didn't carry around the sadness and the memories of

Mama. But she did know what sadness was. She'd lost her own Ma and Pa a long time ago.

He wanted to talk to her. But the ugly face of the bad man came back to his mind. No. He wouldn't do it. But that didn't stop him from wanting to. At least she understood.

Maybe the bad man was gone. He could've done something else real bad and got himself killed.

If that had happened, then Jimmy knew he could talk again. But how would he find out? He'd just have to wait. His stomach swirled. The bad man was still out there. He knew it. And he often felt like those mean black eyes were watching him. All the time.

Jimmy shivered and pulled the blankets up higher. Time to think of something else. He needed good thoughts or he'd never be able to go to sleep. Maybe he could go climb into Papa's bed. He always felt safe there.

Papa. He'd been working so hard lately. Jimmy missed seeing him. But Miss Lillian had been teaching him all about their olive farm. And she promised that as soon as the canning process was over, they would be able to help more often.

Jimmy wanted to help. His father loved

this farm, and his mother had loved it, too. So he'd decided when Miss Lillian came that he would grow big and strong and help out with the olives. Even if he never spoke again, he wanted to work at his pa's side.

Maybe that way he could keep the bad man from ever coming back and hurting the people he loved.

Every bone and muscle in Woody's body ached, but the canning process was complete. Finally. He dusted off his pants with his hat as he walked in the back door and then took off his boots. God sent Miss Porter at just the right time. Otherwise, poor Jimmy would be even worse off now. Woody knew his absence was hard on the boy. Rebecca had died and immediately there was all the trouble with the law and people's accusations. Time was consumed by having to answer to those allegations. Time that took him away from Jimmy. Then even after the judge cleared him, there was the farm to contend with and workers who were apprehensive about what had happened. Consequently, Woody neglected Jimmy, leaving him in Mrs. Goodman's care. A part of him hated doing so, feeling that he was abandoning Jimmy at a time when he needed his father most. Another part of him couldn't bear to see what had happened to his son. Jimmy's silence was just one more painful reminder of the loss they endured.

Woody's stomach growled as he got a whiff of his dinner plate warming on the stove. Removing the towel, he prayed on the way to the chair so he could dig in as soon as he sat down. *Sorry, Lord.* His abbreviated prayer made him all the more mindful of the way he'd neglected his walk with God.

When Rebecca had been alive they had a complete list of goals they'd hoped to accomplish. The olive farm, a large family, and enough money to help anyone in need at any given time. Those were the physical — tangible — goals. There had been spiritual ones, as well. Both he and Rebecca were determined to know God better and to raise their family to fear the Lord. They attended church, read their Bibles, and prayed together. He smiled at the memory of teaching Jimmy how to pray.

"Why do we put our hands together when we pray?" Jimmy had asked him. The question surprised Woody, and he had no real answer.

"I guess," he'd told Jimmy, "because we were taught to do it that way by other folks."

"But God will listen to us even if we don't put our hands together, won't he?" Jimmy pressed to understand.

"Of course," Woody replied. "God will listen to us always, no matter where our hands are. He doesn't really look at the outward appearance, but at the heart. He wants our hearts to be fixed on Him." It seemed so simple back then.

"I've done a poor job of that, Lord." Woody shook his head at the realization. He tried to maintain a strong faith, but his pain always seemed to get in the way. "I want to do better. I *will* do better. Show me what it is I need to do."

By the time he was halfway done with his plate, his hunger had abated and he realized that Mrs. Goodman and Lillian were nowhere to be seen. Surely they hadn't retired so early, had they? He'd fully expected his son to be asleep, but not the ladies. They seemed to enjoy each other's company in the evenings. He started to reach for the latest copy of the *Mountain Echo* newspaper from Angels Camp, but the silence of the house stirred concern. What if something had happened to them? What if something had happened to Jimmy? Thoughts of finding Rebecca dead and Jimmy terror stricken flooded his mind, and Woody jumped to his feet, newspaper still in hand. The need to find them took precedence over his exhaustion.

He pushed the swinging door into the dining room and came to an abrupt halt. Mrs. Goodman and Miss Porter were sitting at the dining room table, both with their heads buried in their Bibles. Several other books lay open at their fingertips.

The sight caught him by surprise, but it also made him breathe a sigh of relief. After several moments he realized they hadn't heard him come in, so he cleared his throat and rattled the newspaper.

Lillian looked up at him. "Well, good evening, Woody." Her smile did something unusual to his insides.

"Evening. What are you two fine ladies up to tonight?"

Mrs. Goodman finally looked up from her reading. Peering over the edge of her spectacles, she laughed and pointed at her table mate. "This here young woman thought we needed to be doing some studying together, seeing as how we aren't in church right now. But heavens, I didn't think she'd start with the last book in the Bible. I know I'm ornery, but there's a reason I've left this one alone all this time." She leaned back in her chair and shook her head. "I'm com-

181

pletely perplexed."

Woody laughed and smiled at Lillian. "You chose to start with Revelation? That's mighty ambitious." He took a seat across from her.

Her brow furrowed as her cheeks turned a lovely shade of pink. "Pardon me for being blunt, Woody, but I'm tired of being told that certain books of the Bible are too 'ambitious' or too 'difficult' for me. Isn't God's Word for all of us?"

He'd embarrassed her rather than encouraging her. What a dolt. He prayed for the Lord to give him the right words so he could smooth it over. "Forgive me, Lillian, that's not at all what I meant. I *admire* the fact that you want to study Revelation. I was just thinking it was ambitious because of all the men I've heard argue about its meaning."

Mrs. Goodman nodded. "He's right. About ten years ago, our pastor had several men riled up about it. It was a disaster, and the church split."

"Goodness. I wasn't trying to incite any quarrels." Lillian laid her hand on the book she'd been writing in and bit her lip.

Mrs. Goodman reached across the table and patted Lillian's hand. "It's all right, dearie. It's been a while, but there were many years that Woody spent poring over the Word. If I remember correctly, he loves to study." The older woman winked at him. "I think he'd be willing to share his knowledge with you."

Woody chuckled. Leave it to Mrs. Goodman to make sure he got the hint. He'd been admonished and praised all at the same time. "I'd love to help."

Lillian sat up straighter and beamed at him. "Really?"

"Yes, ma'am." He set the newspaper down and leaned his arms on the table. "Now that the canning is done, I'll be back home earlier in the evenings. I don't like being away from Jimmy that long anyway, and to be honest, I've been longing to get back into the Word, as well. I've" — he reached back and rubbed his neck — "had a . . . difficult time since Rebecca died, but the good Lord showed me a while back that it's time to move past it." But where was he to move on to?

"So will you study with us?" Lillian's smile could light up a room. He noticed how very pretty Miss Porter was. Her green dress set off her green eyes, which sparkled with delight as she waited for his answer.

"I'd love to."

"And is it all right if I have a lot of questions?"

"Of course."

"Truly? You don't mind?"

"Not at all. But I can't guarantee I'll have the correct answer. That's what we'll have to ask the Lord to show us as we study."

Lillian jumped from her chair, and before he knew it, she'd leaned over the back of his chair and hugged him. The physical touch was a healing balm, but she pulled back immediately and went to hug his housekeeper. He was certain she didn't mean anything improper by it, but the remembrance of her arms around his neck would stay with him.

Mrs. Goodman rubbed her hands together. "I think I'm almost as excited as she is." She hooked her thumb toward Lillian.

"Me too." Woody laughed. And he was. Excited to dig back into the Word and excited that his heart no longer felt broken in two. *Show me what it is I need to do,* he'd prayed only moments ago. This was one time God had certainly answered quickly.

Later that night after the house was quiet and everyone was asleep, Woody went to his desk in the library and sank into the padded chair. He pulled open a drawer on the left and pulled out a leather-bound journal. Opening the book, he thumbed through the few pieces of newsprint and then looked over the pages of notes he'd written there.

This was his account of Rebecca's murder and all that had happened to him afterward, as well as all that he had done to try to find the real killer. He'd listed every clue, every detail of that day and the days that followed in the hope of helping the law enforcement people find the murderer. But Sheriff Stanley Hobart wouldn't even consider his findings. Hobart had been convinced, as had many of the other people in town, that Woody was the true culprit.

"If you wouldn't have been so blinded by your certainty that I killed Rebecca, we might have found her killer by now." He shook his head and turned another page in the book.

He'd written down the time he and Mrs. Goodman had discovered the murder, as well as the temperature and weather of the day. He'd noted the clothes worn not only by Rebecca and Jimmy, but also the ones he and Mrs. Goodman had worn. He'd noted who was working for him and lengthy details about each man — their families — their habits and reputations.

Woody tried his best to figure out anything that would point him in the right direction. At one point, after the judge had cleared him, Woody left Jimmy with Mrs. Goodman so he could try to investigate what few clues he did have. That had turned out to be a waste of time. There just wasn't enough information, and the only physical evidence available to him was a dead wife and mute son.

He closed the journal and started to put it back in the drawer when he spied something shiny. Dropping the book back atop his desk, he picked up the brass button. This was the only other physical evidence. A button. A single brass-colored button. It wasn't anything special, but Woody knew immediately that it belonged to the killer. First of all, it didn't match anything owned by the family or Mrs. Goodman. It didn't even match anything his crew wore. Second, it had been tightly grasped in Rebecca's right hand. She'd obviously pulled it off her killer's coat.

He'd looked everywhere for a man wearing a coat with just such buttons. No matter where he went, his eyes were open to that detail. But he never saw anything even remotely similar.

Turning the button in his hand, Woody

clenched his jaw. His only connection to the killer. The one tangible thing he had to identify the man. Even holding it now brought up an anger inside that Woody knew was best left buried.

He threw the button back into the drawer and slammed the journal in on top of it. Maybe it was all just a waste of time. The sheriff would never consider his evidence, and Woody would probably never know who killed his wife and forever changed his life.

CHAPTER THIRTEEN

Harry walked to town in the wee hours of the morning. The leather bag his ma had made was strapped across his chest. He wanted to do something special for Miss Lillian and Jimmy. His new friends weren't mean at all. They treated him like Ma used to treat him. And that made him feel good inside. Maybe one day he could live with a nice family like that.

It wasn't that he didn't love his brother. He did. It's just that Brother wasn't always nice.

Harry shook his head. He should never think bad thoughts about his brother. Mama had told him many times that Darwin had problems that were heavy to bear. That made Harry sad.

Darwin could be good. In fact, he even gave Harry some money the other day so he could get food. Brother said he was gonna be out of town for a while. But since Miss

Lillian had given Harry some extra food, he'd had money left over. So he was gonna use the money to buy them something nice.

The morning sun was over the horizon when he arrived in Angels Camp. The Stickle brothers owned the general mercantile, and he liked it better than the Clarks' general store. Mrs. Clark was always nice to Harry, but Mr. Clark didn't like him and shooed him away whenever she wasn't looking. He decided to go to the Stickle brothers' store.

Inside, he picked up a sugar stick for Jimmy and a wooden whistle. He counted his coins and realized he had plenty left, so he found some pretty ribbons for Miss Lillian. Green. Just like her eyes.

Too many people had come into the store now, and it made him nervous. He dropped a couple coins and fell down when he tried to pick them up. A boy in the corner laughed at him.

"It's all right, Harry. I remember you." Mr. Stickle — Harry couldn't remember which one — waved him toward the counter. "Come over here." The man sized him up. "Why, I haven't seen you in years. Looks like you grew another foot."

Harry shook his head and looked down at his feet. "Nope. I still have just two."

Mr. Stickle laughed, but it was a good kind of laugh. "Well, let me see what you have."

Harry paid for his things and Mr. Stickle wrapped them in brown paper. Harry was glad the man hadn't asked him anything. Darwin would be so mad if he knew Harry had come to town.

"Thank you." Harry tried not to look at the boy in the corner. He could hear him saying mean things about the man who was an idiot. He tucked his package in his leather bag.

Harry's bottom lip quivered. He wished Ma were here.

"You're always welcome, Harry," Mr. Stickle whispered. "You head on out. I'll take care of those youngsters. They just need their mouths washed out with soap."

As he left the store, he felt sad. Why did people have to be so mean? He wasn't an idiot. No. No. No.

On the outskirts of town, he realized he still held the change in his hand. Opening his fist, he found a note. He couldn't read it, but he would bring it to Miss Lillian. So he tucked the note in his bag, as well. The thought of seeing his friends brought a new smile to his face. He counted his coins again and tried to think of another surprise. Mrs. Rolleri!

He raced back to the Hotel Calaveras and knocked on the back door to the kitchen.

Mrs. Rolleri answered it and smiled at him. "Why, Harry, I haven't seen you in ages. I'm so sorry about your mama."

"She's in heaven."

"I do believe she is, Harry." She hugged him. "Now, what can I do for you? I'm making some ravioli right now. Would you like the first ones?"

He nodded. A lot. "I want to do something nice for my new friends. Do you have enough I could share with them? I've got money." He held out his coins.

"You put your money away, young man. This is a gift from me. I've thought of you many times wondering what I could do to help you after your mama passed. Let me do this for you, yes?"

"Yes. Yes. Yes." He nodded again and smiled as he tucked the money back in his pocket.

"You wait here, and I will be just a moment." She went back into the kitchen.

Harry sat down on the steps and wondered what the note said. Miss Lillian would read it to him, he knew she would.

Mrs. Rolleri returned with a bucket. Harry

stood up and peered inside. It was *full* of ravioli. Mrs. Rolleri was famous for her ravioli, and Harry's mouth started to water.

"Oh, thank you, thank you, Mrs. Rolleri!" Harry jumped up and down. It would be a perfect gift.

"Here's a note on how to finish them. And here's a jar of my sauce." She tucked the jar and note into his bag since his hands were full with the bucket. She covered the bucket with a towel. "You come back and see me again, yes?"

"Yes."

She kissed his cheek and said good-bye.

Then he ran down the street, he was so excited.

But a big, hairy man stumbled out of one of the saloons and almost knocked Harry down. "Hey, watch it! You dumb or somethin'?"

Harry backed up and checked the bucket.

"Hey! I was talkin' to you. Get outta my way."

"I'm sorry. I'm not in your way." He shook his head. Harry couldn't understand why the man was mad.

"Idiots like you are always in the way." The man shoved Harry and made him fall down on his backside. "Get outta town, you big oaf. Nobody wants you here." The man's words slurred like Uncle John's when he'd gone drinking.

Harry sat on the ground, hugging his bucket and bag. He wasn't an idiot. Why did people call him one?

He peeked under the towel and found all the ravioli were still okay. Looking at the ground around him, he sighed. He hadn't spilled any. Knowing how hard Mrs. Rolleri worked to make all the ravioli by hand, he didn't want to see anything happen to them.

A wagon pulled up beside him and stopped.

Harry crawled away and cowered until he looked up. Relief flooded through him. "Mr. Stickle!"

"You all right, Harry?" The man frowned.

"Uh-huh." He hopped up.

Mr. Stickle looked behind him. "Harry" — he blew out a big breath — "some people are mean just to be mean. I'm sorry for what that man did to you."

Not all people were mean. And Mr. Stickle's kindness made Harry feel good. He smiled up at the man.

"I need to make a few deliveries. Which way you headed?"

"That way." Harry pointed with his elbow.

Mr. Stickle chuckled. "Can I offer you a ride . . . that way?"

"Thank you, yes! It's a long way to walk, and Mrs. Rolleri gave me ravioli." He held up the bucket for inspection.

"I see that." Mr. Stickle took the bucket while Harry climbed into the wagon.

"You're a nice man, Mr. Stickle."

"You are too, Harry. The world needs more people like you."

The nice comment made Harry want to sit taller and puff out his chest. As he took the bucket back and cradled it in his arms, he wondered if Ma was watching from heaven.

"No, not quite. That note is a *D,* not a *C.* Can you find all the rest of the *C*s?" Lillian smiled at her little charge, his face focused and determined.

After a moment of thinking, he nodded and played the correct note, looking to her for approval.

She clapped. "Yes, good job! *C* is always on the left of two black keys. The pattern is always the same. Now play the rest."

As the rest of the notes resonated from the beautiful grand piano, Lillian patted his back and smiled some more. "You've got it. Now let's find all the *D*s. Where would all the *D*s be?"

Jimmy stuck out his tongue and squinted.

Pointing to the correct key, he looked up again for approval.

"Very good. Now play the rest of them." She glanced out the window and found the sky a brilliant blue. After they finished up at the piano, it would be a good time for a spell spent outside in the fresh air.

When Jimmy had successfully played all the notes in a row, Lillian was satisfied they were making grand progress. "All right, young man, you are doing brilliantly." She hugged him. "Now, I think it's time to go outside. What do you think?"

He hopped off the bench and nodded.

"You go see Mrs. Goodman for a snack and then meet me on the porch in a few minutes, all right?"

He turned on his heels and ran to the kitchen.

Lillian hurried to her room and grabbed her bonnet and her book *Guide to the Study of Insects* by A. S. Packard, Jr. She hoped her enthusiasm for learning about bugs as a child would be equaled in her young charge.

As soon as she sat on the front steps, she opened the book to the page that showcased *Plate 8*. The sketches of moths and larvae in all different stages sent a little thrill of excitement through her. She had loved bugs growing up. Grandmother encouraged her learning and curiosity until Lillian left a jar of her collection open in the parlor one day. After a disastrous afternoon tea with the Ladies' Auxiliary, Grandmother stopped the actual bug gathering and shifted the focus to books about bugs.

Lillian giggled with the memory. Always a spirited child, she pondered how much work it must have been for her dear grandparents. The thought sent a pang through her chest. If only Grandfather would respond to her letters.

Jimmy sidled close to her and pointed to the page.

Her attention quickly back on task, she wrapped an arm around his shoulders. "Do you like bugs?"

He nodded and pointed to the words at the bottom of the page.

"It says, 'Transformations of Moths.' " She placed a finger under each letter. *"T. R. A. N. S . . ."* and then sounded it out for him. "See the *m?* You have two of them in *Jimmy.*" She took the slate and wrote his name.

He nodded again and leaned into her a little more.

Oh, the things this child could do to her heart. How incredible to be loved and trusted so unconditionally. She explained what she knew about each picture, and he traced the drawings with his fingers.

A movement down the lane caught her attention, and Lillian squinted into the distance. "Why, look, it's Harry."

Jimmy needed no further encouragement. He got up and ran to meet his friend. Lillian set the book aside and stood to wave. She walked down to join them near a bed of various rose bushes. Just the day before she and Jimmy had weeded this particular bed, and she'd very much enjoyed the sweet scent of the blossoms.

"Harry, it's so good to see you."

"It's good to see you, too." He smiled and looked down at the flowers. "You took out the weeds."

Lillian was surprised by his knowledge. "Jimmy and I did it yesterday. Do you like roses?"

He nodded. "I do. My ma planted them."

"She planted roses?" Lillian smiled as Harry nodded. "I'll bet they were beautiful."

Harry nodded again and then held out a bucket. "I brought a surprise." His eyes twinkled with merriment.

But Lillian found herself hesitant to look. Surely, big, sweet Harry wouldn't put a snake or anything else slithering in a bucket to give her, right?

"It's okay. It's a good surprise."

"Thank you. That's very kind of you." Lillian accepted the gift and lifted the towel. "Ravioli — my goodness — how . . . where . . . ?"

Harry clapped his hands together. "Mrs. Rolleri is famous for her ravioli, and she made them herself just a little bit ago." He reached into his bag. "And here's a note on how to fix 'em and her special sauce, too."

Words seemed stuck in her throat as emotion welled up. "But how did you . . . ? Did you walk all this way?"

He looked down at the ground and put his hands behind his back. Toeing the dirt with his boot, he peered up through his hair in the front and then looked back down. "Oh, it was nothin', Miss Lillian. I got up real early and walked to town and then Mr. Stickle gave me a ride in his wagon for most of the way out here."

"Come on with us up to the house, Harry. You must be ready for a rest. What time did you leave this morning?"

"A couple hours afore the sun came up."

And here it was almost noon. Lillian blinked back the tears. What an amazing young man. But she didn't want to embarrass him, so she acted like everything was normal.

"I have a favor to ask." Harry stopped and dug around in his bag.

"Of course, what can I do?"

"Could you read me this note?" His hand shook as he held out a crumpled piece of paper.

Lillian smiled up at him. "Sure." She took the paper. "It reads: 'Harry, you are a good man. Don't ever let anyone tell you otherwise. George Stickle.'" She wanted to cry. Someone else had seen the beauty inside this young man. If George Stickle was in front of her right now, she'd give him a kiss on the cheek.

Harry beamed and held out his hand for the note. He closed his eyes and tried to repeat the note. "Harry, you are a good man. Don't ever let no one tell you otherwise."

"Anyone," she inserted.

"Anyone," he repeated. "Thank you. Ya think you could teach me how ta read, Miss Lillian? My ma used to help me make letters and numbers."

"I'd love to! And maybe you could teach us about flowers." She looked down at Jimmy. "We could work on some lessons together, couldn't we?"

Jimmy's little head bobbed as he smiled up at Harry and reached for his hand.

"It's time for our noon meal. Why don't we eat some of this yummy ravioli Harry brought us?" She took hold of Jimmy's other hand. "Wasn't that a wonderful surprise?" Lillian felt like she could float to the house.

"Wait, wait, wait, Miss Lillian." Harry stopped and dug in his bag again. "I almost forgot. I've got more surprises." He pulled out a brown package and handed it to Jimmy. "You'll have to open it together, since Mr. Stickle wrapped it together. I wanted to bring presents to my nice new friends."

If her heart could have melted any more for him, it would have in that instant. "Harry, your friendship is present enough."

He beamed. "I like being your friend."

"We like being yours." They reached the steps of the porch and she set the bucket down.

Jimmy stared up at her.

"Go ahead. You untie it." She placed her hands under the brown paper just to make sure nothing fell out.

Jimmy gasped and ran over to hug his older friend, a sugar stick in one hand and the whistle in the other.

Lillian couldn't help the tears this time and allowed them to slip down her cheeks. He'd bought her ribbons. Green ribbons. She walked over and joined the hug.

"What've we got here?" Mrs. Goodman's voice came from the porch. "Can I get in on that hug?"

The two boys walked up the steps and hugged the older woman.

"Mrs. Goodman, I'd like to introduce you to Harry. Harry, this is Mrs. Goodman."

The housekeeper received another hug and then patted her hair. "Well, land sakes, dearie. I figured this was our Harry I've heard so much about. Welcome." She smiled at their guest.

Jimmy picked up the large bucket and tried to hold it aloft for Mrs. Goodman's inspection.

"What's this?" She peeked under the towel. "Do I smell Olivia's famous ravioli?"

Harry nodded. "Yes, yes, yes. All for us."

She inhaled deep and closed her eyes. "She makes the best, and that will definitely beat the sandwiches I was going to make. Let's get to it, then. I'm practically starved."

Lillian stood back and watched the trio walk inside, her heart bursting at the seams. She started in after them, then remembered her book. She turned to pick up the volume, but then a tingling chill raced up her spine. For a moment she froze. She clutched the book close and drew a deep breath. Was someone watching her? She glanced around the front yard and beyond to some of the outbuildings. Perhaps it was just Woody passing by, but surely he would have called out in greeting.

Laughter erupted from inside the house, and she shook her head. Must be her wild imagination. But movement beyond the large oak tree at the end of the lane made her look back a second time. Someone *was* there.

And they'd been watching.

Darwin watched the farmhouse from behind a large oak, certain that no one would spot him. When the pretty lady came out on the porch, he'd moved a little closer to get a better look. Had that Mr. Colton taken another wife?

He froze in place. The woman looked straight at him. Could she see him? Darwin didn't so much as breathe. He supposed if she called out to him, he could make a run for it. But he sure didn't want to create a scene and stir up trouble for himself. It was bad enough that he'd seen someone going into the house who looked an awful lot like

Harry. But that was silly. Harry knew better than to come back here. He'd warned him enough times, and Harry was generally obedient.

The woman went back into the house, and Darwin let out the breath he'd been holding. He needed to figure out how he could go snooping around the place without getting caught. He'd been watching to see what kind of routine they kept, but it seemed no one, save Mr. Colton, did things on a regular basis. They didn't even go to church on Sunday, which was pretty unusual. Of course, Darwin had heard rumors about Colton being blamed for his wife's death. That thought made him smile. It was nice to see somebody else get blamed for bad things besides himself.

He moved off in the brush and trees and skirted around the property until he had a clear sightline to some of the outbuildings. From his perch he could see there were four or five men working to load and unload barrels and crates. From time to time he'd catch sight of Colton himself.

"It oughta be me running that place, not you," he muttered.

He thought of what Harry had said about relocating the gold. Stupid kid thought he was doing the right thing, but Darwin felt certain no one would have found the gold he'd hidden. Of course, Harry had found it, but he'd no doubt been watching Darwin bury it.

Darwin squatted down and picked a long blade of grass. In time Harry would remember, but time was something Darwin didn't have a lot of. If he couldn't get Harry to tell him soon, it was going to be too late, and Darwin wasn't about to let all of that gold slip through his fingers. Even if it cost that pretty lady her life — he would get his gold.

CHAPTER FOURTEEN

After a trip up to Stockton, Darwin was even more convinced that his trick had worked. They declared the body of Saul Longstreet to be Darwin Longstreet, buried him in a pitiful grave behind the jail, and said they'd send someone to notify the next of kin.

That should give him a few weeks — maybe even a month or two — to help Harry remember where he hid the bags, go get them, and hightail it outta town before Uncle John got suspicious.

He rubbed his hands together by his campfire. If he could find a home for his simpleminded brother, he'd pay to make sure the dumb boy was taken care of — and fulfill his promise to Ma. Then he'd be free to do whatever he wanted. Mexico still had a nice ring to it. Once Uncle John figured out Saul wasn't coming back, he might suspect what Darwin had done. Hopefully he'd just think that Darwin had killed Saul and then someone else had killed Darwin. It seemed reasonable to him. After all, the body was long buried by now. Even if Uncle John realized what Darwin had done, he wouldn't be able to find him in Mexico. Not even the law could come get him in another country. At least he didn't think so. Things were looking up. And he wouldn't lose this time. Not ever again.

Once he got back, he'd watch Pa's old place on a regular basis. He had to figure out when he could search, and he'd have to make sure that Colton kid didn't see him. On the other hand, he might be as blind as everyone else to Darwin's true identity. It might be possible Darwin could just waltz in there on some pretense — maybe ask for a job. He'd heard that Colton often hired workers to help with the olives. If Darwin could get himself hired, it might allow him to look around in his free time. Still, there was Harry to consider, and also the risk that the Colton brat would recognize him. He could ruin everything for sure.

But then Darwin remembered his threat. The kid was scared. And he wasn't talking. All of Angels Camp knew the kid hadn't spoken since his ma died.

He sneered. He'd only figured to scare

the boy into saying nothing about the death of his mother. Darwin hadn't imagined it possible for a child to stop speaking altogether. Harry sure never shut up. Of course, Harry was too stupid to know if he should be afraid. Jimmy Colton had no trouble realizing the dangers that saying too much could bring. Still, if the boy needed a little encouragement to keep his mouth shut, Darwin could supply it in spades.

That gold was calling his name.

Lillian finished setting the table in the dining room and pulled out her Bible and the letter she'd tucked in it from Stanton. Mrs. Goodman had given it to her earlier, but she wanted to read it in private, hoping there would be something from her grandfather inside, but dreading the words all at the same time. Perhaps after their evening Bible study, she would share with them all if it was good news.

Since Jimmy was occupied practicing his piano lesson, Lillian decided to slip away to her room to read the letter. Surely she had a few minutes to herself, and she couldn't wait any longer. As she slid her finger under the flap of the envelope, she breathed a prayer.

The envelope held six pages neatly penned

in Stanton's elegant script. But nothing from Grandfather.

With a sigh, she sat on her bed. At least she had news from home. Grandfather was probably just being his ornery, stubborn self. And she'd resigned herself to being cut off for good.

But she wouldn't let that discourage her. She had this letter here and now and it acted like a balm to her wounded heart. It didn't take long to read through the missive, and after sharing all the news regarding the staff, Stanton finally mentioned her grandfather.

I'm sad to report that your grandfather refuses to read your letters, but I fear his health is not good. He won't admit to it, but his summer cold last week has caused him to decline. I'm praying he will come to his senses soon enough. Rest assured, we are all praying for him to reconcile with you. Maybe the good Lord above has afflicted him to get his attention. You asked me to be honest with you, and I am dedicated to it, Miss Lillian. Please be in prayer for your grandfather. We greatly anticipate your next collection of letters.

All will be well, as our Lord is in

control. We greet you with love and prayers,

Stanton

Folding the letter, Lillian prayed for Adam Fletcher. She loved the old man so dearly. Only God could get ahold of him now and do a mighty work in him. She sighed. There had been a time when her grandfather faithfully sought God's guidance. How could the loss of a spouse cause a man to so completely put God aside? An image of Woody came to mind. Even though Woody was much kinder and gentler than Grandfather, the same grief and anguish was in his eyes. Apparently such things were not unusual. Mrs. Goodman had told her that Woody had been faithful to attend church and read his Bible before his wife was killed. Did Grandfather and Woody blame God for their losses? Was their diminished faith a sort of punishment they were meting out to the Almighty? Or was it to punish themselves for not having been able to save their loved ones from death?

Losing Grandmother had only caused Lillian to grow closer to God. She'd had no one else to turn to. Her grandmother was gone, and in so many ways, she'd also lost her grandfather.

"And now he's lost me, as well." She hadn't meant to speak the words aloud. The thought caused Lillian a sense of guilt. Here she was all caught up in her misery, but even though it came at his own hand in some ways, Grandfather also suffered loss.

"And he pushed God away."

She shook her head. He truly was all alone. It was a terrible thing to ponder. What an utterly hopeless feeling to have no one to turn to.

A knock at the door drew Lillian's attention upward, and she tucked the letters in her pocket. "Come in."

Jimmy burst into the room, beaming a smile. He hurried over to her and grabbed Lillian's hand.

"Is it time for dinner?"

He nodded. Lillian smiled and got to her feet. "Then we should be on our way." She let the boy escort her down the hall, thinking all the while how much he'd changed since her arrival. It was nothing short of a miracle, and she felt certain he would talk again.

As they entered the dining room, Woody looked on with a smile. "There's my boy."

Jimmy ran around the table to him and leapt into his father's arms. It was so good to see him filling out and smiling. Watching father and son brought another twinge to her heart. Even though she had been loved as a child, the absence of parents still grieved her. But this wasn't about her — she was here for Jimmy. Lillian shot a quick prayer heavenward for complete healing for the boy. Whatever horror had kept him from talking, God had already conquered.

To Lillian's surprise, Woody whispered something to Jimmy and the boy nodded enthusiastically. She cocked her head to one side. "Are we keeping secrets?"

Jimmy beamed her a smile while Woody laughed. "I simply told him, Miss Nosey, that you were like a beautiful ray of. sunshine. And he agreed."

Lillian felt her face grow hot and her heart flutter. Woody was, after all, a very handsome man, and she wasn't used to being paid such sincere compliments by men. At least she hoped it was a sincere compliment.

"I suppose," she said, going to her place at the table, "that sometimes it's best to not know everything."

Woody laughed and set his boy down, and they all took their places at the table and bowed their heads. His voice resonated in the wood-paneled room. "Father, we come before You again, grateful. Thank You for all that You have provided. Thank You for sending Your Son as a sacrifice for us. And thank You for this food. In Jesus' name we pray, Amen."

Mrs. Goodman passed the platters of fried chicken and roasted potatoes.

"So what have you all been up to today?" Woody directed the question to Jimmy.

The boy just smiled at his father and took a bite of chicken.

Lillian laughed. "We had a visit from Harry today."

"Did you, now?" Woody's brow furrowed a bit. "How did it go?"

"He brought ribbons for Miss Lillian that match her eyes," Mrs. Goodman chattered, "and a sugar stick and whistle for our little man here, *and* . . . he brought some of Olivia Rolleri's ravioli." She *mmmm*ed to herself. "Such a generous young man."

Woody's brows rose. "Do tell."

Lillian jumped in, having recovered from her embarrassment. "Yes, he said that he wanted to bring presents for his nice friends. Isn't that just the sweetest?" She knew Woody didn't know Harry yet, but hoped he wouldn't have a problem with the young man. While she felt she knew Woody fairly well, she wasn't sure what he thought about those who were slow like Harry.

Jimmy nodded and pulled half a sugar

212

stick covered in fuzz out of his pocket.

Woody chuckled. "Looks like it picked up a little lint there."

Mrs. Goodman reached across the table. "Here, let me wash that off for you." She took the candy to the kitchen.

Woody cleared his throat. "So I'm sorry I stayed out in the groves all afternoon and missed the ravioli." He looked at his plate. "Mrs. Rolleri does indeed make the best."

Was that irritation in his voice? Jealousy? Lillian couldn't decipher it. "I apologize we didn't save you any." She laid her fork down and looked straight at his head, willing him to look at her. "Should we have fetched you? We didn't know exactly where you'd be working, but perhaps we should have tried to find you. It honestly didn't dawn on me. I didn't mean to upset you."

"I'm not upset." He stood and laid his napkin on the table. As he walked to his son's chair, he reached down and tousled the boy's hair. "Perhaps a bit cautious about things since Rebecca, and it just concerned me." He gave her a look over Jimmy's head.

Ah, that was it. He didn't wish to discuss it in front of the boy. She'd wait until after dinner when Jimmy was in bed. Woody and Mrs. Goodman and little Jimmy had become very dear to her. It wasn't until that moment that she realized just how much. It caused her pain to even think of offending her boss.

He nodded and sat back down as Mrs. Goodman returned with the candy stick, clean and shiny. As they finished their meal, Woody asked his son yes or no questions, and Mrs. Goodman piped in with her jovial comments about the day.

"Sam brought the mail from town," Mrs. Goodman said. "I put it on your desk in the library after I sorted through it to give Lillian her letter."

"You've had a letter from home?" Woody questioned.

Lillian stiffened. She hadn't exactly been open and forthright with Woody about her grandfather. She felt it was a matter that was best left unspoken. "From a friend." It wasn't really a lie.

Woody picked up a piece of chicken. "It's good to have friends." His voice betrayed a sadness that Lillian quickly understood. Mrs. Goodman had told her how most of the Coltons' friends had deserted Woody and Jimmy after the murder.

"There were also some newspapers," Mrs. Goodman continued. "I happened to take a look at a copy of *The Morning Call* out of San Francisco. Seems there were some bad storms back east of us — cyclones. Caused the death of some folks."

"Where?" Lillian tried to keep the worry from her voice. "Not Indiana."

"No, seems like it was Minnesota and North Dakota. Sure glad we don't have storms like that here. Although the rain would be a relief."

Lillian nodded and picked up her water glass. "Cyclones are fearful things. I've gone through more than my share of storms. The winds are fiercer than you can imagine — even if you're not hit directly." She shuddered. "We had a portion of our roof ripped right off the house one year. I thought the entire house might collapse around us." She happened to notice Jimmy's eyes had gone wide. "You are very blessed not to have to worry about such things out here." She smiled and the boy seemed to relax.

"There's been flooding in Colorado," Mrs. Goodman added. "Easy to see where all our rain has gone. Oh, and the paper mentioned that a wanted man who used to live in this area was finally found. Darwin Longstreet. I'm not sure exactly where he lived or who his people were. It just said the Angels Camp area."

Woody seemed momentarily perplexed. "Longstreet? That name sounds familiar.

What was he wanted for?"

"I don't recall that it said," Mrs. Goodman answered. "I suppose you can read the article for yourself when you have time." She got to her feet. "But for now, I believe it's time for dessert."

Jimmy pushed his empty plate back and nodded with great enthusiasm. Lillian laughed. It was certain that Jimmy was excited about the prospects. When Mrs. Goodman returned with a tray of individual desserts, Jimmy clapped his hands.

"He loves your blackberry shortcake," Woody said. He looked to Lillian. "You're in for a real treat. Mrs. Goodman makes some of the finest blackberry preserves and sauces. She even makes a syrup for pancakes."

"They look delicious." Lillian took the portion Mrs. Goodman offered her. Thick dollops of whipped cream topped the berries and cake. She waited until everyone had theirs and Mrs. Goodman had reclaimed her seat before digging in. The flavors were most incredible.

Lillian hated to stop eating long enough to praise the dish, but she could see that Mrs. Goodman was waiting for her reaction. "This is so good. I don't know when I've ever had anything so amazing."

"I told you so," Woody said with a forkful midway to his mouth. "I'd bet anything if she'd enter these in the county fair, she'd win all of the blue ribbons."

"Oh, go on with you, now," Mrs. Goodman countered. "You're prejudiced."

Lillian sat back and enjoyed the easy banter. What a difference a few weeks had made. Gone was the cloud of grief that had resided over each one in the household. God had been so faithful. Leading her to a family that needed her. Giving her the wings to soar.

"Perhaps you can teach me." Lillian threw the older woman a grin. "I know I have the tendency to burn things and well, apparently, I'm given to mixing up sugar for salt, but I'd love to try."

Mrs. Goodman chuckled. "Yes, it would be vital to know your sugar from your salt, but I think you could manage it. You're truly doing quite well in the kitchen."

Lillian laughed. "Now, if I could also master cutting out a pattern." She looked at Woody, seeing his confused expression. "Mrs. Goodman was teaching me about cutting material for a new shirt by taking apart an older shirt to use as a pattern. I'm afraid I somehow managed to make a mess of things."

Again the older woman laughed. "Now, dearie, I told you these things take time. I've been sewing since I was a wee girl."

"Yes, but I imagine that even when you were a wee girl, you never cut out three sleeves for the same shirt."

Woody laughed and Jimmy snickered while Lillian could only shrug. "If we happen upon a three-armed man, the shirt would work nicely."

Woody stopped laughing. "Since I'm the only man in the house, I presume it was my shirt you were making."

For a moment Lillian thought he might be offended. Perhaps he didn't like the idea of anyone but Mrs. Goodman sewing his clothes. But just as quickly as the anxious thoughts came, Lillian was relieved to hear him continue.

"In that case — just put the third sleeve aside for later. I'm sure to tear up one or both of the other sleeves in time. This way we'll just have a spare."

"There, you see," Mrs. Goodman said, nodding, "it's just as I suggested."

They refocused on the food at hand, and Lillian felt a sense of ease that she'd not known before coming to this house. No one seemed to mind overmuch that she lacked a variety of skills that most young ladies would have been taught. It was a sense of family. Of belonging.

With dessert devoured, Mrs. Goodman began to clear dishes, and Jimmy hopped up to help.

Woody leaned his elbows on the table and drank his coffee. "Are you ready to study more of Revelation tonight?"

Lillian's heart jumped at the intense look in his eyes. This man had much more depth than she ever imagined. She loved their discussions in the evening because she'd often get a glimpse of a different side of him. And she really liked that man. Not that Woody wasn't a good man to begin with, but he was so guarded. Probably because he'd been hurt, he'd lost his wife, and people had turned on him.

"Lillian?"

She jumped. She'd done it again. Lost in her own thoughts. "I'm sorry, yes. I'm really looking forward to it. Shall I go get our Bibles?"

"I've got mine right here. You go fetch yours and Mrs. Goodman's, and I'll tuck in Jimmy for the night." He touched her shoulder as he walked past.

For a moment, she could still feel the warmth of his hand there. It was unlike anything she'd ever felt. Of course, she'd never had the attention of any young man. Once Grandmother died, her grandfather kept her pretty much secluded, except for church, and no young man dared to approach the old grouch to ask about calling. Lillian's desire to live her life and make her mark somewhere had always included the dream of a family, but she'd never been one to fantasize about love. Maybe because she'd never had the chance. Amazing how one little touch could awaken her senses to it.

After nearly two hours of study and discussion, Lillian stretched and yawned. The clock down the hall chimed the hour as the pendulum kept time. How different Woody was from Reverend Owens. She'd had such respect for the good shepherd of her church at home until she'd gone to him with her questions. He'd patted her arm and treated her like a child. *"Why don't you let the men handle the heavy thinking passages. It's much too burdensome for the weaker gender. . . ."*

But not Woody. He'd answered every question he could, but only if he could back it up with Scripture.

Lillian leaned back in her chair. She wanted to keep studying but knew her mind was tired, as well as her physical body.

Mrs. Goodman stood and tucked her

Bible under her arm. "I believe I'll retire to my room and spend some time on verse five and 'remember therefore from whence thou art fallen, and repent, and do the first works . . .' " She wiped away a tear and sniffed. "Good night to you both."

"Good night, Mrs. Goodman." Woody's voice was soft and reflective.

Lillian stood and hugged the woman who had become so dear to her. No words were necessary.

Woody also stood as the older woman left. "These verses have done a lot to get me to thinking, as well. I think I will retire to the library."

"Woody, please wait. . . ." She'd been debating whether to refrain from telling him the truth of what she'd seen earlier, but she realized that Jimmy's safety was far more important than her silly fears of being embarrassed. "I know this may sound silly, and you might think me overly cautious, but . . . well . . . I think I saw someone watching us today."

CHAPTER FIFTEEN

There was a fire in the mine tonight. The glow of it bounced along the walls. That meant Darwin must be back. Harry ran up the hill to the entrance, singing, "Brother, Brother, Brother!"

"Shut your trap, Harry." Brother wasn't in a very good mood. "This place is cold as ice. You should have had a fire going." Darwin put another log on the fire, then pulled his coat up around his neck. He fumbled with the only two remaining brass buttons. "You know I don't like the cold. Where've you been?"

"Around." Harry toed his boot into the dirt. He didn't want to tell the truth.

"You need to stop running around without me. You might get hurt."

"But you told me that nobody could see me with you."

"That's right." Darwin stepped real close to him and squinted. "That means you should stay here."

"Inside the mine? All day?" Harry shook his head. "No. No. No. I can't do that. I can't stay inside the mine all day." He grabbed the sides of his head. "No. No. No! Don't keep Harry in the dark mine. No. No. No." He felt like he couldn't breathe and started pulling on his hair. Tears burned his eyes and he couldn't see. He stumbled backward to the entrance. "No. No. *No!*"

Darwin tackled him and covered his mouth with a dirty hand. "Be quiet, you idiot!"

Harry bit his brother and yelled, "I am not an idiot. I am not!" He kicked and punched and kicked some more.

Darwin backed away, his eyes a fiery red. "Harry, it's time for you to be quiet. Don't make me hurt you."

Harry pulled his legs up to his chest and curled into a ball. Why was Brother being so mean? "Don't hurt me. Don't hurt me. Don't hurt me," he chanted.

A curse word echoed off the walls. "Oh, stop it. I'm not gonna hurt you. I need your help, remember?"

Harry nodded and relaxed just a bit.

"Just don't go into town around people, got it?"

"I won't go, I promise. There was a mean

man there and he pushed me into the ground." Harry decided not to tell Darwin about his nice friends. After he helped Brother find his stuff, maybe Brother would go to Mexico by himself.

"A mean man? Was he following you?"

Another nod.

"Was he watching you?"

Again a vigorous nod.

"When did you go to town, Harry?"

He shrugged his shoulders. "It was a long time ago." Harry didn't know if Darwin believed him or not.

"Doggonit, Harry. I bet he's after our gold." Darwin paced the front of the mine where they'd made camp. He pointed at Harry. "Do not go back into town for any reason."

"I won't."

"Not ever."

"Okay." Harry crossed his fingers behind his back. He wouldn't ever tell Brother about his nice friends. They didn't live in town, so it wasn't a lie. "Okay. Okay."

"I think we need to speed up our plan a bit. . . ." His brother mumbled some more and came closer and patted his shoulder. "I'm sorry I yelled at you. Let's get you some food. And maybe you can remember where you moved my stuff."

Brother was being really nice again. Harry liked it when he was nice. It helped him feel good and safe. "Okay. I remember moving it."

"Good. Good."

But a lot of stuff was fuzzy in his mind. What would Darwin do if Harry couldn't find it?

A shudder shook him.

He put a hand to his head. The sooner he remembered, maybe the sooner Darwin would leave and Harry could be with the nice people.

Harry watched Darwin open a can of beans and set the can in the fire to warm. He thought again of Mrs. Rolleri's ravioli and how nice she'd been to him. Mrs. Rolleri had a whole lot of children, but she was always so nice. She reminded him of Ma. Ma had always been nice. Smelled good, too. Harry missed that. Darwin never smelled good.

Miss Lillian smelled good, but she smelled different than Ma. Ma smelled like flowers. She loved flowers, and she constantly grew them and taught Harry about them. The memory made him smile. Ma loved roses, and now Miss Lillian and Jimmy took care of the roses.

Memories of his mother made Harry feel

225

better. Ma never yelled at him or called him stupid. She was ever so happy when he remembered the names of her flowers. Miss Lillian was going to teach him to read, and he was going to teach her the names of the flowers. He smiled to himself. He liked it when he could help people.

"What's got you lookin' all happy?" Darwin asked.

Harry knew he couldn't tell Darwin, so he shrugged. "Just like bein' happy."

His brother looked at him for a minute, then pulled out a tin of crackers. "We won't have to live like this for much longer, Harry. As soon as you can remember where you put the gold, I can get us a place where we can eat proper meals."

"At a table with real dishes. Like we had when Ma was here."

"I suppose," Darwin replied. "Ma did set a nice table."

Harry nodded, pleased that Darwin didn't seem quite as angry as he had been earlier. "I think about Ma a lot. She was good."

Darwin handed Harry some crackers. "She was good. She sure didn't deserve what she got out of life."

"She was happy." Harry ate one of the crackers and tried to remember his mother's smile. "Do you remember her?"

Darwin looked at him like he might start calling Harry names again, but after a minute or so he shrugged. "Hard not to remember Ma. She had a hard life. Pa and me . . . we were no good. Never were any good. Her kin weren't any good, either. But Ma was a lady." Darwin's gaze went to the fire. "She never had much, but she did her best with what she had."

"She liked flowers."

Brother's face looked sad. "Yes, she liked flowers."

"I like flowers, too."

Darwin checked the beans and pulled them off the fire. "Men don't bother with flowers, Harry. That's somethin' only women do." He drew a deep breath and shook his head. "I don't want you talkin' about it anymore. Ma's dead and gone. There's no sense in talkin' about the dead."

Harry frowned, confused by his brother's words. "But she wasn't always dead."

"That's a stupid thing to say. Of course she wasn't always dead." Darwin began to eat his share of beans from the can.

Harry knew that when his brother had eaten half, he'd give the can over to him to finish. It hurt to have Darwin tell him that what he said was stupid. The nice people didn't mind when he talked, but Darwin and the other people . . . mean people . . . they always made him feel bad.

"I like remembering Ma." Harry looked at Darwin and then popped a cracker into his mouth.

Later Darwin watched Harry as he slept. Sometimes he felt like his father had — that Harry should have died at birth. He'd almost died a couple of times when he was a baby, but Ma caught on real fast that there were things Harry couldn't do like other babies. She made sure he was safe and kept him at her side almost constantly.

It was hard to admit, but Darwin wondered even now if it wouldn't be better for Harry to die. There was no place for Harry in this world. He couldn't work a decent job, and he certainly didn't have a cunning mind to steal or cheat for his living. No woman would ever marry him, and no man would want him for a friend.

Darwin had made Ma a promise to take care of Harry.

The reminder flickered through his mind but was quickly followed up with another thought. If he ended Harry's life — he would be taking care of Harry. No one would ever be able to hurt Harry again. Better still, if heaven was a real place like Ma thought, then Harry would get to be with her again. He'd be happy.

The fire was dying out, so Darwin threw another log on. The damp chill of the mine seemed to seep into his bones. Harry never seemed to notice. He'd been so happy to get away from Uncle John that he never grumbled.

Darwin shook his head. Harry wasn't such a bad sort, but he was completely useless. There would never be anything Harry could do that would benefit Darwin, and that alone gave credence to his thoughts of murder.

It wouldn't really be murder, would it? It was more like putting a sick animal out of its misery. Or better yet, killing the runt of a litter because you knew it would never survive. Harry would never survive without him, so it was more like a mercy that Darwin would end his life and set him free from the pain of this world. A world that would never accept Harry as he was.

Sliding into his bedroll, Darwin couldn't shake the thought from his mind. Always before, he'd thought of paying someone to take Harry off his hands, but in truth this would be the better way. He would get Harry to figure out where he'd put the gold, and then he'd see to it that Harry had an easy death — something without fear or pain. After all, Harry was his brother.

The heat of August was upon them and things were drying out. Too much. They hadn't had any significant rain since April, just a sporadic shower here and there, but never enough to make a difference. Woody lifted his Stetson to look at the grove. They'd been hand-watering, but it was a tedious job on top of everything else. Especially since Lillian's announcement a week ago. He'd tried to remain calm and assure her that everything was fine. Encouraged her that she'd done the right thing in telling him, but there was nothing to worry about.

But there *was* a reason to worry. His wife had been murdered and they still didn't know who did it or why. And Lillian *had* seen someone.

He'd had his men check the entire farm, taking precious time away from their duties. The men were thorough and just as concerned as Woody, but all they found was one suspicious boot print and a cigar butt near the main road. Nothing else. But nothing else was really needed. Woody didn't smoke cigars, and his workers couldn't afford them. Someone had been there, just as

Lillian had suspected, and they needed to be careful. That someone could be the same man who killed Rebecca.

Woody tried not to appear worried about the matter. He didn't want to get Mrs. Goodman and Lillian worked up when none of them could be sure that the observer was definite trouble. Most of all, he didn't want to scare Jimmy. The boy had endured far more than he should ever have had to, and Woody was now convinced it was fear that kept Jimmy mute.

He spoke to his crew and was glad when one of the men brought up the idea of posting a guard. At first Woody had his men taking turns to be on watch twenty-four hours a day, but with the drought so fierce, he needed every man to help haul water. And even with their help, things were starting to look bad.

Lord, we need rain. And we need protection. I'm trying not to fear, but I do feel caution. Lillian was correct, someone has been watching the place. I feel it. The men feel it. We know that You are the real Protector. Please give me the strength to do what needs to be done and to face whatever comes.

His open communication with the Lord was coming with greater ease now. And the burden of grief that had weighed down his

231

chest for all this time was at least lifting. Well, maybe *changing* was a better term. The sadness over losing Rebecca had somehow transformed into a determination to find her killer. Woody owed her that much, especially given that no one else seemed compelled to learn the truth. No, everyone else believed *he* was the killer, and they didn't care about the truth or the pain they'd caused.

At least Lillian believed him.

Thoughts of his son's nanny brought warmth to his middle. Her green eyes were so expressive. Her smile so pleasant — her nature so kind. For the first time since losing Rebecca, Woody actually found himself longing for a companion. Always before, grief and guilt had kept him from even considering such things, but Lillian brought new life to him and to Jimmy. Especially Jimmy. Earlier she had asked Woody if he had a photograph of Jimmy's mother that he could give his son. She expressed how precious her locket photos of her parents were and how Jimmy needed something that he could hold close to remind him of his mother. Woody marveled at her insight and genuine concern for Jimmy. She didn't approach her position there as just a job but firmly positioned herself as part of the family. Her enthusiasm for life had begun to chip away at the wall Woody had put in place, and her gentle kindness was healing their wounds.

Lillian's intellect was also amazing. It especially came to light when they were studying the Scriptures together. He enjoyed hearing her thoughts on the passages they read. There was a smart brain in that pretty head. He smiled. Lillian was quite pretty, and he found himself thinking about her more and more. Sometimes he couldn't even remember clearly just how bad things had been before she'd come. What did that mean?

He shook his head. It didn't mean anything. It couldn't mean anything. She worked for him, and that was that. But something deep inside Woody protested that thought most adamantly.

"Mr. Colton!" Sam, his crew boss, bolted through the trees. "There's a problem by the brining barn."

"What's happened?"

"One of the horses stepped in a hole and went down. I think he's all right, but I'm gonna watch that leg for signs of swelling. But the fact is, that hole wasn't there before today. We got to looking around and there were quite a few holes, and they're not made by animals. At least no animal I know of."

"How can you be sure?"

" 'Cause someone's been digging big holes and covering them back up. At least most of them were filled back in. Animal ain't gonna do that."

"Not a four-legged one." Woody met the other man's worried face. "But what about a two-legged varmint?"

Woody went with Sam and together they searched for holes and filled them back in as they went. There were at least a dozen. It was a wonder none of the horses had broken legs. But there was no rhyme or reason for it. Why would someone be digging holes on his property? And then filling them back in. Why go to all the trouble?

A brief memory crossed his mind. There had been unexplained digging on his property another time. When was that? It seemed quite a long time ago — maybe right before or after they built the new house. But hadn't that turned out to be raccoons or badgers? He shook his head, wishing he could remember.

"Mr. Colton!"

Great. What now? He and Sam both looked up to find Miguel, another of the workers.

"What is it?"

The man looked at Sam and then back at Woody. "I'm sorry, sir. I looked around like Sam told me — to make sure nothing else was out of place, but . . ." His man looked down at the ground. "Two barrels of olive oil were destroyed."

"What?!" That was one hundred gallons. And a big chunk of income. He shook his head as he and Sam followed Miguel to the mess. Absolutely nothing could be done. Someone had taken an axe to the barrels. But why only these two, he had no idea. He noted the marks from the tops of the barrels. They were identical, so that meant they were from the same row — row *H* — but nothing else jumped out at him. He stood with his hands on his hips for several minutes. What a waste.

"We'll clean it up, Mr. Colton," Miguel assured. "But I wanted you to see that there are footprints, and they don't match any of us."

Woody knelt down where the tracks were clearly visible. "No, this fella has really big feet." He frowned. Hadn't Lillian said that Harry fella was a big guy?

"So someone is sneaking around with the intention of causing damage to the place — and possibly to the people living here."

Woody rose and shook his head. "I had hoped we were done with things like this, but it looks like I was wrong."

"You want one of us to ride for the sheriff?"

Woody gave a bitter laugh. "Hobart won't care. He'll just think I did it."

Sam was clearly upset. "Well, don't worry. Me and the boys will take turns keepin' an eye out."

"I appreciate that, but you all need your sleep, too. We have way too much work to do to see that big order filled for the folks in Fresno."

"We can figure it out — take shifts." Sam's expression was one of determination. "I'm sure sorry, Mr. Colton."

Woody nodded. He looked at the sky. He'd already missed suppertime. What a day.

As he trekked back to the house, his frustration and worry set in again with a vengeance. Exhaustion washed over him, slowing his step. He needed food and a good night's rest. Tomorrow would be another day, and things were bound to make more sense after he got some sleep.

Lillian sat at the dinner table with Jimmy on her lap. She was reading to him from the book of Genesis. About Noah. For a moment, his heart nearly stopped. For a moment he saw Rebecca. She had often held Jimmy and read to him. Not just the Bible, either, but all sorts of wonderful stories. He let go a heavy breath. Was it wrong of him to have these memories, but also think with great fondness toward Lillian? Lillian was filling the empty place left by Jimmy's mother. He needed that. Woody needed it, too.

"And so you see, when God tells us to do something, Jimmy," Lillian explained, "we need to obey and get the job done. Otherwise we might find ourselves in a flood of other problems." She closed the Bible and hugged him close.

Woody's heart warmed for a moment, then guilt and a little anger surged through him. His life should be so different from the way it was, but instead he had to worry about someone watching them and damaging his goods for whatever reason. He had to isolate himself out here on his property to avoid the townspeople, who were certain he was a killer. Nothing was going the way he'd planned it to. And added to this, he'd missed time with his son tonight. All because of this mess. His relationship with Jimmy was a mess, his olive grove was a mess. He was a mess.

Mrs. Goodman entered. "Woody! Well, I'm so glad you made it in. I've got a plate warmin' on the stove for you. Let me get it." She went back toward the swinging door.

"Don't bother. I'll take care of it myself," he grumbled. Not meaning for his words to sound so harsh, he softened his tone. "I need to wash up anyway, so I'll grab it while I'm in there."

His housekeeper raised her eyebrows but didn't say a word as she headed to a chair next to Lillian.

All eyes were on him as he went to the kitchen, no doubt wondering what had gotten into him. He took his time washing up and said a little prayer to help him not be such a disagreeable grouch. There was something going on inside him that Woody needed to figure out. He knew he needed to spend more time with Jimmy. Again the regret and guilt threatened to eat him alive. It was true enough that he had work to do and that such work took time away from his son. It had taken time away from him and Rebecca as well. Reality hit him hard. Rebecca had been killed because he was away, busy with the olives.

But a silent reminder rebuked him. Rebecca died because a madman beat her and threw her down the stairs. It had nothing to do with the trees or Woody's busy schedule. So then, why did he feel so guilty? So angry? And furthermore, how did it all relate to his listening for God's voice?

When he made it back to the dining room with his food, he was resolved to put such thoughts behind him. He could always ponder these things later — when he was alone. He sat down at the table and found the ladies in a lively discussion. He forced a smile, silently prayed, and then dug into the food. He felt half starved after this day.

"But don't you think it's time to go back?" Lillian still held his son. The boy looked asleep on her shoulder as she rubbed his back.

Mrs. Goodman flashed a look at him. "I don't know if that's a good idea, dearie."

"What's not a good idea?" Woody took another bite.

His nanny shifted her weight and turned toward him. "We've had such a wonderful time studying the Bible together, I was wondering why we couldn't go to church."

"Miss Porter . . ." The frustration rose in a huge wave — so much for not being a grouch. "I've already told you that we will not be returning to church. The answer is no. Those people —"

"Woody, I know they've hurt you. I know

you haven't been in a while. But the Good Book tells us not to forsake the gathering together and fellowship with other believers." She offered him a smile. "I just thought —"

"I said the answer is no." He felt the heat rise in his neck.

She fell silent, and for a moment Woody thought that would be the end of it.

"Well, I am asking you to reconsider and discuss this with me."

She looked at him with such hope that Woody felt all the more guilty. But instead of trying to explain, he just put up his defenses. "You are quite pushy, aren't you?" Those words definitely came out harsher than he intended, but she deserved it. She had no idea what he'd been through today. "There will be no discussion."

Her face registered a bit of hurt and then shock. She straightened her back and narrowed her eyes. "No wonder people in this town are so suspicious of you." She stood with Jimmy in her arms. "Maybe I shouldn't have . . ." She snapped her mouth closed.

"Shouldn't have *what*?" Woody stood, his anger in full force now. "Go ahead. Finish what you were about to say."

Mrs. Goodman picked up his plate, no doubt trying to get his attention off the discussion at hand. "I'm going to go wash this up. Would you like anything else?"

"Please excuse us, Mrs. Goodman."

The older woman nodded but gave him a pointed stare.

He saw the warning but didn't take heed. He wasn't going to be reprimanded like a child. Not in his own house. Not in front of his son.

Lillian shook her head as tears pooled at the corners of her eyes. "I'm sorry. I didn't think before I spoke."

"You're right. You didn't. You have no idea, Miss Porter, what this family has endured from the people of Angels Camp. No idea. And just because you had one opportunity, one afternoon, to listen to their gossip and lies doesn't make you an expert on what it feels like to be ostracized. What it feels like to lose everything."

She stood her ground. "But you *didn't* lose everything, Woody. You are still here. Your precious son is still here. Your farm is still here. God's got this under control."

"Like He did the day Rebecca died?" His anger only increased. "Do not presume to tell me how I should feel or choose my words for me." He stalked around the table. "We are in a drought. We had one disaster after another today, and I've had just about enough."

She stepped back, her hand on Jimmy's head. "I was just asking about going to church, Woody. We don't even go into town. I don't know anyone." She was so calm.

Which only angered him more. And why, he didn't know. "The answer is no."

"You know what?" A new spark lit in her eyes. "I think you're afraid. And you know what else? I think I will go to church by myself. And I will go to town by myself. Why? Because I'm tired of people telling me what I can and cannot do and keeping me locked up like a prisoner."

"You feel like a prisoner?" he roared. "Fine. Then why don't you just pack your bags. You are free to go, Miss Porter." He yanked his sleeping son out of her arms, which roused the boy.

Her mouth dropped open. Tears streaked down her cheeks. Her hands fisted at her sides. "You want me to leave. Fine, I'll leave. If you aren't too caught up in your rancorous attitude, you might remember that you haven't ever paid me my wages. I'll need that money to buy a stage ticket." She turned, but then whipped right back around and pointed her finger. "You're going to turn out just like my grandfather. Bitter, angry, and all alone." She whirled back around and left him standing there.

Jimmy wiggled out of his arms. When his feet reached the floor, he gave Woody a sad, teary-eyed look. And then ran out of the room and up the stairs.

Mrs. Goodman returned and crossed her arms.

"Don't say it."

"Don't say what? I wasn't going to say anything." She started to leave and threw over her shoulder, "But I *will* go check on Jimmy, if you have no objections." She shook her head. "No, I don't even care if you have objections."

Woody was left standing in his dining room assessing the damage. What had he just done?

CHAPTER SIXTEEN

Jimmy ran as fast as his legs would carry him. Why would Papa be so mean to Miss Lillian? He yelled at her just like that bad man had yelled at Mama. Jimmy burst into his room. Fear built up inside him. He looked frantically around the room. He didn't want to see his papa act that way. He loved Papa. But now, he was also afraid of him.

He grabbed his pillow and yanked off the pillowcase. Miss Lillian was a good person. Jimmy liked her. A lot. But Papa told her to go pack her bags. That meant she was leaving.

It didn't make sense.

Papa liked Miss Lillian. Said she did a good job. When he tucked Jimmy in at night, he often talked about how she was good for them.

Jimmy shook his head. He couldn't understand why they had to fight. He didn't want to see them fight ever again, and he didn't want Miss Lillian to go. Tears threatened to spill as he grabbed his slingshot, some toy soldiers, and his comb. Mama had always told him to comb his hair first thing every morning. Last of all, he grabbed Mr. Whiskers. Jimmy didn't have time to secure the sling around his neck, so he tucked Mr. Whiskers inside his shirt.

He was certain if he ran away, Miss Lillian would stay. She'd be worried about him. Jimmy was sure of it. She'd be worried, and she'd come to find him. Jimmy slipped down the back stairs, stopping to listen in case Mrs. Goodman was in the kitchen. She wasn't. He hurried out the back door and only then realized it was dark. He hated the dark. Clutching the pillowcase to his chest, Jimmy wondered if maybe this was a bad idea. What if that bad man was out there somewhere? He hesitated, wondering what he should do. And then it came to him. He'd go to the pond. Miss Lillian knew he loved it there, and there was a big tree where he could climb up and sleep if they didn't find him until morning.

Maybe Harry would come to the pond tomorrow, and then they could all fish together and go back to how things were before Papa got mad.

Jimmy hurried past the barn and along the path to the garden. The glow of the house light faded more and more the farther he went. Past the garden it got more difficult to see. He tripped and fell over a tree root. It had gotten really dark. He worried that he might have hurt Mr. Whiskers and made a quick assessment. The rabbit seemed fine, so Jimmy tucked him back inside the shirt.

A noise to his right made him stop. Was it a wild animal? Was it the bad man?

Fear spurred his little legs into action. He ran blindly through the trees, hoping that he'd soon reach the pond. Hoping that if the bad man was out there, he wouldn't know where to find him.

The killer's voice sounded in his head. *"You better not say a word about me to anyone, you hear me? I'll kill your pa and your little housekeeper, and I'll kill everyone in town if you say one word."*

He wouldn't say a word. He wouldn't. But the voice from his nightmares followed him all the way to the pond and up the tree.

Miss Lillian had told him to talk to God when he was afraid. *"What time I am afraid, I will trust in thee . . ."* She said it was from Psalms. But did talking to God count?

246

Would the bad man find out? Wait, Miss Lillian said he could talk to God in his head and that God would understand. Then nobody would ever know.

God, I'm afraid. Please don't let the bad man come back. And please don't let Miss Lillian leave.

He shivered and wrapped his little jacket around himself and Mr. Whiskers. Maybe he could sleep for a bit while he waited for Miss Lillian to find him.

"Woody! *Woody!!*" Mrs. Goodman's voice echoed down the stairs.

The panic Woody heard in the older woman's voice reminded him too much of that day . . . when Rebecca . . .

No. His thoughts couldn't go there. He took the stairs two at a time. "Mrs. Goodman, where are you?"

"Jimmy's room."

He raced to his son's room and found the woman crying by the bed.

But his son wasn't there. What was going on? "Mrs. Goodman?"

"He's gone. I've searched the entire upstairs. Every nook and cranny." She pointed to the head of the bed. "Look. His pillowcase is gone from the pillow. And . . . Mr. Whiskers . . ."

The horror hit him like he'd been punched. The way Jimmy had wrestled out of his arms earlier. The look the boy had given him. His son had run away. But to where? It was pitch black out and a new moon.

Lillian. Lillian would know.

He raced down the stairs to her room and nearly crashed into the wall when he came around the corner so fast. He banged on her door.

"If you are here to tell me to hurry it up, I'm almost done, Mr. Colton."

Exasperating woman. She was just as stubborn as he was. "I'm not here about that. Please let me in. It's an emergency."

He heard her shuffling around and then the door opened. Her red-rimmed eyes told him the true state of her emotions. "Yes?"

"It's Jimmy. He's run away."

She grabbed her shawl without even waiting for him and wiped a hand down her face. "When?"

He sighed. "Right after I told you to pack your bags, I'm sorry to say. He gave me a look and raced to his room. I thought he was still there, but Mrs. Goodman went to check on him and he's gone. With Mr. Whiskers."

"Well, we've got to go after him, right

now! He's out there all alone and it's dark and he's so small —"

He grabbed her shoulders to cease her from working herself up any further. "I know. That's why I came to you. I thought you might know where he would have gone."

She bit her lip and her brow furrowed. Then her eyes widened. "The pond! He loves the pond. But that's such a long ways!" She wiggled out of his grasp and ran back in her room. "I need my boots. Where are my boots?"

He hadn't noticed that she was in her stocking feet. "I'm going to run out there. Please ask Mrs. Goodman to stay here, and if you could bring a lantern when you come, I would really appreciate it."

She nodded and kept looking for her shoes.

Woody didn't have time to lose. His son was so small. Anything could happen at night out on the farm. One of his workers had mentioned seeing mountain lion tracks only last week. What if that animal was around here now? Woody's mind jumped from one horrible thought to another. What if Jimmy had fallen in the pond? He couldn't swim yet. Then the worst of all came to mind. There had been a stranger lurking around — possibly the same man who'd killed Rebecca. What if he found Jimmy first? Woody thought about rounding up his crew to help look for the boy, but there just wasn't time. Knowing Lillian, she would think of just such a thing. She had a way with figuring out all the necessary details.

As thoughts rampaged in his mind of everything that could possibly happen, Woody ran faster and faster. How could he have been so stupid? This was all his fault. And now his son was out there all alone.

His eyes gradually adjusted to the night, but without the light of the moon, it was difficult going. Twice he almost ran into a tree. "Jimmy! Jimmy! Where are you?"

With his son not speaking, Woody was afraid that even if he was near, he wouldn't receive a response.

His lungs burned, but he had to press on. He had to find his son. He'd lost Rebecca; he couldn't lose his precious son, too. It would be too much. *God, I can't handle it. You know I can't. I'm so sorry for my anger and my treatment of Miss Porter. I'm so sorry for all the doubt and worry and fear that drove me to it today. I'm sorely lacking in my faith, Lord. Please strengthen me, and please help me find my son.*

How much time had passed since his little

boy left? What if Lillian was wrong and he was searching in the wrong direction? Doubts raced through him again and he had to mentally push them aside. He couldn't do that anymore.

The pond had to be getting close. He could smell the water, but with the trees on this side it was even darker and slower going.

Up ahead he heard the snap of branches. Woody stopped and listened.

"Now, come on. It's not safe." Whose voice was that? Did someone have his son?

Woody pressed up against a tree and leaned around it, trying to get a look. In the darkness he could make out a dark moving form. A large man had ahold of a small boy and was dragging him by the arm. Jimmy! He bolted out from the tree. "Stop! Let go of my son!" Woody moved forward.

The man stopped and didn't move. The smaller form, no doubt Jimmy, wiggled in the man's grasp.

More scrambling sounded behind him. "Did you find him?" The voice was female and out of breath. The glow of lantern light revealed Lillian's worried expression.

How did she get here so fast? That woman would never cease to amaze him.

"Shh. He's over there. Some man has

ahold of him." Woody kept going. "Please let my son go. Don't hurt him."

Lillian followed him, holding the lantern high. The man moved and Jimmy kicked and squirmed.

"Stop! Please! He's just a little boy." Woody swallowed the tears threatening to choke him.

The man released Jimmy and took off running. Jimmy ran too, but instead of running toward his father, he ran a circle right around him.

"Jimmy! Harry!" Lillian cried.

"Jimmy!" Woody shouted at the same moment, wondering why his son would run away from him.

"You scared him." Lillian ran off in the *other* direction, holding up the lantern. "Harry, wait! It's all right, he didn't know who you were. . . . Haaaaaarrrrrrrryyyyy!" She grabbed her side and stopped. Great big huffs came from her, and the lantern bounced up and down. And then Jimmy plowed into her and held on for dear life.

Woody had never felt more confused or wounded in all of his days. Watching the two embrace, he wasn't sure how to dig himself out of this hole.

Lillian held his son's face between her two hands. "You all right?" She glanced over at

Woody and grabbed Jimmy's hand. "Let's go talk to your papa, okay? He's been mighty worried."

Jimmy scowled at Woody and then looked back to where the man had run.

"We'll find Harry tomorrow. Your father just scared him."

And that made Woody feel about two inches tall. He took a step forward to meet them. "That was Harry?"

She nodded.

If ever he wished he could start a day over, it would be now. He met Lillian's eyes. "I'm sorry. I saw him dragging Jimmy" — he looked at his boy — "and I thought he was hurting you."

Jimmy stomped his foot.

"He wasn't hurting you?"

His son crossed his arms and shook his head.

"Let me guess, he was bringing you back home?"

This time a nod and deep scowl accompanied the stomp.

"Ah . . . and you didn't want to come because you were mad at me?" Woody crouched on one knee in front of his son and watched the anger flash across Jimmy's face. "Look, I'm sorry. To you both . . . I never should have opened my mouth earlier.

It was wrong." He looked up at his former nanny, who would hopefully reconsider. "I don't want you to go. I had a horrible day and took it out on you. We need you."

Jimmy jumped into his arms and started crying. Woody held on tight. "You scared me, son. I love you so much, and I can't bear to lose you. Don't you ever run away again, all right?" He felt a nod. "I know you were upset that I told Miss Lillian to leave, but you need to promise me that instead of running next time, you'll come to me and we'll work it out." Another nod. "I love you, Jimmy."

His son squeezed his arms around him, but then he pulled back. Woody frowned as Jimmy began to squirm. He dropped his pillowcase as he struggled. But just as Woody feared the worst, Jimmy pulled Mr. Whiskers from inside his shirt. With a smile, Jimmy once again relaxed in his father's arms.

"I'm certainly glad Mr. Whiskers came through all of this unscathed," Lillian declared, picking up Jimmy's pillowcase. She handed it back to the boy.

Woody stood, lifting his son and Mr. Whiskers. He looked at Lillian, hoping she would know how sorry he was for all he'd said. "Please forgive me, Miss Porter . . . Lillian. I am ashamed by my behavior. Will you please stay?" With his right arm wrapped around his son, he reached his left arm out to her.

She stood still for too long.

Oh, Lord. Please help me not to have ruined everything.

Jimmy sucked in a breath.

Lillian reached out toward him and placed her hand in his. "I'm sorry, too. I don't know what's gotten into me lately." She took a deep breath. "And to answer your question, yes, I'll stay. However, be warned. I'll probably speak my mind again — at one turn or another."

Woody chuckled. "I like your spirit." They started walking back to the house, and she didn't remove her hand from his, even while holding the lantern out to light their way. Woody felt the warmth all the way up his arm, and it had nothing to do with the lamp.

"I hope that's true, but I've held it in for so long, I'm afraid I probably don't control it the way I should." A long sigh escaped. "I haven't been completely honest with you, Mr. Colton . . . Woody. I lashed out at you earlier and compared you to my grandfather, which was a horrid thing to do. I'm sorry."

He had wondered about her family, but she'd been very distant about them. Mrs.

Goodman told him that she received mail from Indiana but that Lillian would have to share the details when she felt the time was right. "Would you like to tell me about him?"

Another sigh. "It's rather a long and sad story, but yes, I want you to know it all."

As they walked Lillian shared the events of her life. Woody listened without interrupting, hoping she would feel free to talk about whatever came to mind. He found that suddenly he wanted to know everything about her. Every single detail.

". . . and Grandfather disowned me when I announced that I was leaving. I'm sorry I hid that from you."

"It's all right. I understand — not why he disowned you, but why you kept it to yourself. That's a very private matter." He paused and swallowed, unwilling to break their connection, but he had to ask, "So how are things with your grandfather now?"

"Unchanged, I'm sorry to say. Stanton — he's my dear friend and Grandfather's butler — and I write back and forth. But Grandfather refuses to even read any of my letters."

He squeezed her hand again. "Give it time. Maybe that will change. You never know what the Lord can do in someone's life."

Lillian reached up to smooth Jimmy's hair. "He's asleep, isn't he?"

Woody chuckled again. "Yes, he's like a deadweight on this shoulder. I haven't been able to feel my arm for a good while. I'm glad he thought to put Mr. Whiskers back in his shirt. I'd never forgive myself if something happened to him."

"I think that's something of a habit with you."

He said nothing. What could he say? She was right. He hadn't been able to forgive himself for not keeping Rebecca and Jimmy safe.

Her silence washed over him, and they continued their walk back. Words weren't really necessary. But he was thankful that she had accepted his apology and would stay.

Several minutes passed where the only sounds were their boots on the crunchy grass. Woody tried not to think about how the drought would affect his crop. The olives were already showing signs of withering. He shook his head. Worry and doubt had gotten him into the horrible predicament today. He couldn't afford to do that again. God was in control. He knew that and would have to rest in that.

The house came into view and Lillian removed her hand from his. "I think I'll run on ahead to let Mrs. Goodman know that we found him. That way we can get a hot water bottle in his bed and warm it up for him, and warm up Mr. Whiskers's box, too." Without waiting for a response, she took off at a fast pace.

Was she running from him? The last half hour had been wonderful and Woody felt whole again. Holding his son, listening to Lillian, and holding her hand. It had seemed . . . right.

"That you, Mr. Colton?" Sam came from the direction of the barn.

"Shhh. It's me."

The man approached and gave a nod. "I see you found Jimmy. I'll let the men know."

"How did you know he was gone?"

Sam chuckled. "That Miss Porter came flying into our quarters. She wasn't there but long enough to tell us to be looking for Jimmy — that he was lost outside some-where."

Woody shook his head. When had she even had time?

"That Miss Porter is really something." Sam turned away. "I'll let the men know you found your son."

Miss Porter really *was* something. Something very special. A new wave of emotions spilled over him as he continued the trek home. For the first time, when he thought of the future, his heart didn't ache. And the image in his mind included a dark-haired, green-eyed spitfire of a woman by his side.

Despite a happy outcome to the traumatic events of the evening, Woody found sleep impossible. He tossed and turned for a long time, trying to force it to come, but his mind and spirit were troubled. Finally, he got up and went to the open window. Gazing out into the darkness, he thought again of all he'd said and done that day.

Thoughts returned of how he'd not listened for God's direction in a long time. It dawned on him that perhaps Lillian's request for them to go to church was God trying to work through Woody's stubbornness.

"Lord, I know I've got a lot to figure out, but I just don't feel like facing those people any more than I have to. They're harsh and judgmental. They don't care about the pain they've caused."

Forgive them.

Those two words seemed to be murmured

on the gentle breeze that touched Woody's face.

"How can I forgive them when I can't forgive myself? How can I not blame them for my pain, just as I blame myself?"

And blame God.

The thought hit him hard. Did he really blame God for all that had happened? Woody let go a heavy breath. He'd tried so hard to be stoic — strong for Mrs. Goodman and Jimmy. He'd tried to maintain his faith, but always there had been something that just seemed to distance him from God.

Tears came to his eyes. "I never meant to blame You, Lord. But if I'm honest, I guess that hard question of 'why' keeps coming to mind. Why did this happen to my family? Rebecca loved You even more than she loved me and Jimmy. You could have kept her from harm. You could have kept her safe. But You didn't." It was true. He blamed God.

The silence around him was deafening.

Woody fell to his knees. "I'm so sorry, Father." He didn't try to keep his tears from falling. His heart was broken at the way he'd put a wall between himself and God. "I never meant to let that happen. I never saw it before now. Probably because I couldn't bear to. Please forgive me." Woody buried his face in his hands. "Please help me to forgive those who've wronged me. Help me to forgive myself."

CHAPTER SEVENTEEN

Warmth from the sun's rays on her face awoke Lillian on Sunday morning. Another scorcher of a day to be sure. As she sat up and stretched in bed, she prayed for the right words to ask Woody if she could go to church. She didn't want to put any more division between them. After their scare last night, she felt they were on a tenuous footing. She knew how to ride a horse but had no clue how to drive a wagon. And she wanted to take Jimmy with her. The little boy needed to be in church. They could always walk, although that would be quite a hike.

Am I stepping out of bounds, Lord? I feel certain You want us in church, but maybe I've gone about it all wrong. Please show me what to do.

She got out of bed and picked out a dress, the same one she'd chosen on that first Sunday when she thought they would all go to church together.

A knock sounded on her door.

"Who is it?"

"Lillian, it's me." Woody's deep voice resonated through the wood. "I just wanted you to know that I have a horse saddled for you if you'd still like to go to church this morning."

She smiled heavenward. *Thank You, Lord.* "Thank you."

She heard him walk away and hurried to put the dress away and retrieve her riding costume. She dressed quickly, humming happily to herself. Now all she had to do was get permission to take Jimmy with her.

As she entered the kitchen a few minutes later, Lillian donned an apron to help Mrs. Goodman.

The older woman turned, spoon in hand, and smiled. "I was just starting the oatmeal. I hear you're going to church this morning."

The comment made her stand a little straighter. "I am." She gasped. "Goodness, I didn't even think to ask if you would like to come. I'm so sorry. . . ."

"Think nothing of it, dearie. If you recall, I'm not real keen on people in town right now. Causin' so much hurt to us." Mrs. Goodman shook her head. "But after all our studyin' and talkin', I must say I'm thinking on returnin' myself."

Lillian wrapped her arms around the woman's shoulders and let out a little squeal. "Truly?"

"Yes. Maybe next week." The morning just kept getting better and better. One step at a time. She just needed to breathe and relax.

Lillian stepped back and took the large spoon from Mrs. Goodman's hand. "I'm so happy I think I can even make the oatmeal without burning it."

The family gathered at the dining room table, and Woody led them in prayer.

After several bites of breakfast, Lillian gathered up her courage. She looked first at Jimmy and then to his father. "Woody, I was wondering if it would be all right to take Jimmy to church with me this morning?"

His face showed no sign of what he was thinking as he chewed, and he remained silent. Jimmy's face held a clear indication that he liked the idea. He nodded most enthusiastically, but still Woody said nothing.

Oh, dear. Maybe she should've waited another week? Maybe she shouldn't have asked in front of Jimmy.

Then Woody cleared his throat and laid his fork down. "As much as I am uncomfortable with the situation, I know that things need to change. He should be able to go to church, if he wants to." He went back to eating.

"So is that a yes?"

He didn't smile, but he nodded.

Lillian clapped her hands and Jimmy bounced in his seat at the news. Maybe it hadn't been the best idea to address it at the breakfast table in front of the boy, but she needed the buffer. "Thank you, Woody. Again. For everything."

"I'll be praying for you." He lifted his coffee cup to his lips. "I don't want to judge those people the same way they've judged me, so I'll keep my mouth shut. But know that I'm praying all goes well."

She nodded and took in the solemnness of his statement. So much hurt and heartache. She'd experienced only a tiny bit of the censure of the town, and it had hurt her deeply. What if they said something horrid in front of Jimmy? Surely no one would do that in front of a child. She caught Mrs. Goodman's smile of approval and felt the doubts slip away.

"I'll write out directions for you so you'll know the way. We had been attending the community church, but there's also the Methodist church and the Catholic church."

"I'd like to go where you had been going. The community church is fine."

"Good, good."

Their conversation died off and Lillian could feel the tension, subtle though it was. This was a big step for Woody Colton. Hopefully, it would lead to more healing steps along the journey.

Half an hour later, Jimmy sat in front of Lillian on the horse. She held him with her left arm and marveled at the way God had answered her prayers. On the way to town she sang every hymn she could remember, hoping it would ease her nervousness. Her deepest desire was that the community would see not only that she was no worse for her stay in the Colton household, but that Jimmy was doing so much better. She hoped that their appearance in church would signal to the congregation that they needed to rethink their prejudicial and judgmental attitudes.

She glanced heavenward. *Please, Lord, let them be kind to Jimmy. I can take most anything they say or do, but he's still so wounded.*

She turned onto Main Street. The town looked all but deserted. For the first time she really took in the sight of it. It seemed a very pleasant little town with brick and stone buildings. There was a variety of businesses, surely enough to suit the needs of the population. Up ahead she saw the church. There were buggies parked out front, as well as several saddled horses tied to the hitching post.

Now that she saw the church in front of her, her stomach was all aflutter, but she knew she needed to stay strong for Jimmy. She directed her mount toward the hitching post, praying all the while that God would go before her.

She dismounted, helped Jimmy down, and tied up the horse. Figuring how to get back on the horse would be interesting without her step, but she had confidence she could find a way. All that mattered now was that she was at church. After two long months of not attending, she prayed the fellowship with other believers would be sweet.

Squeezing Jimmy's hand, she led him up the steps and through the door. Almost all the seats were taken, so she had to walk all the way to the front with her little charge and could feel the stares on her back. But thankfully, right as she walked into the row, the pastor stood at the front and told everyone to stand and open their songbooks.

Lillian smiled as she realized the selection. How perfect for her heart today: "Blest Be the Tie That Binds."

As the people sang the lyrics together, Lillian's heart lifted with encouragement.

Blest be the tie that binds
Our hearts in Christian love;
The fellowship of kindred minds
Is like to that above.

Oh, Lord, how I would love for there to be fellowship and kindred minds that look favorably on the Colton family. Lillian glanced around for a moment. If only there was a way to help these people understand just how wrong they were about Woody. About everything.

She noticed several faces had turned to stare at her. With a bravery that didn't quite reach her heart, Lillian smiled, gave a nod, and then turned back to the words in the hymnal.

From sorrow, toil, and pain,
And sin we shall be free;
And perfect love and friendship reign
Through all eternity.

The organ fell silent and the hymnals closed. Lillian felt her eyes well up with tears. Oh, how she had missed this fellowship — this joining together in worship of God. The tears trickled down her cheeks. What a beautiful gift God had given her this morning.

Jimmy tugged on her arm, and she smiled down at him. As they sat back down, she pulled him onto her lap. He touched her wet cheek and looked at her as if to question. Lillian hugged him tight, whispering into his ear, "These are happy tears."

She wiped her face with her hankie and tucked it back into her sleeve. The pastor asked them all to turn in their Bibles to the book of James, chapter three.

Lillian pulled her small Bible out of her handbag and set Jimmy back down beside her. She pointed to the verses for Jimmy as the pastor read them. When he reached verse eight, her heart skipped.

"But the tongue can no man tame; it is an unruly evil, full of deadly poison. . . ."

She felt her cheeks heat up. Had he known they were coming to church this morning? Surely these people were listening, right?

The pastor continued reading, "Out of the same mouth proceedeth blessing and cursing. My brethren, these things ought not so to be. . . . Can the fig tree, my brethren, bear olive berries? Either a vine, figs? So can no fountain both yield salt water and fresh. . . ."

As he finished the passage, Lillian was overjoyed at the *amens* that echoed throughout the small building. Maybe the Lord had already done a mighty work in the people here. Maybe that's why He made sure she was there this morning. Hope sprang up like a fountain in her soul.

"My brethren" — the pastor walked to the side of the pulpit — "do you heed these words? Our tongues are the most brutal weapon we can wield. And I am sad to say that gossip is rampant in this community. Yes, I know, I know, you would argue that it is rampant everywhere" — he held up a hand and gave them a fatherly smile — "but that is no excuse for us allowing it here. I feel at fault for not encouraging it to come to an end sooner. After all, it is my job to help guide you in righteousness.

"Of course, I'm a sinner just as you are. I've made my share of mistakes and want to start this day out by first seeking your forgiveness." There was murmuring throughout the church. "I have not directed you as I should have. I have, in fact, failed quite miserably this last year."

Lillian heard some shifting in seats, but all was quiet. No *amen* this time.

"Our beautiful little town of Angels Camp has grown to more than two thousand people. Now, I realize we aren't anywhere near so big as, say, Stockton or other towns, but there are two thousand souls whom the Lord loves right here in our community, yet only a handful who venture to church each Sunday.

"Of course, everyone has their reason for not attending, but of late I've been convicted to visit more and more homes to better know the people and invite them to join us in worship." He paused for a moment and let go a heavy sigh.

"I know this is not going to be easy to hear, but as the shepherd of this flock, I must speak difficult truths without wavering."

Lillian all but held her breath.

"And I stand up here ashamed to say that there are many, *many* people in this town who refuse to go to church anywhere because of the gossip from our lips. Yes, I said, *our.* Meaning those of us who call ourselves Christians. Because we are all guilty of it." The pastor stood tall and rigid. He took a deep breath. "I was asked this last week to go visit a man who had been injured in one of the gold mines. He was dying. When I talked to him about Jesus and salvation and that all he had to do was believe, he laughed in my face. And you know why?"

Lillian shook her head and almost asked "why" out loud as she waited for the minister to go on.

"Because his sister had come with him to California. A beautiful young woman. Within the first few weeks of their arrival, a young man started paying her attention. A wealthy young man from a good, upstanding, churchgoing family. He eventually compromised her in a brutal way and left her for dead. Those of you who have been around for thirty years probably know the story well. Or, at least, whatever version you've chosen to believe. The young woman lived, but the damage had been done. When the young man found out she'd lived through the ordeal, he told his family a lie. That lie got spread about and shared from person to person. They were good society people, so why wouldn't the story be true? Right?"

Not a sound came from anywhere in the room.

"After months of gossip and lies being spread about this beautiful young woman who'd had her whole life ahead of her and had her innocence taken away by a greedy young man, she ran away. But the lies had gone before her. No one believed her. When she ran out of money, there was nowhere else to go. She was forced into the life of a harlot."

A few murmurs echoed around the room.

"When her brother found out where she was, he went to get her. But it was too late. She'd died in the brothel." His voice broke with emotion.

More murmurs.

"Do you understand what this poor woman had endured? Did you know that she loved the Lord and had hoped to marry a minister one day? She was precious in the eyes of the Lord. Special to Him and yet . . . like His Son . . . despised and rejected of men."

A few gasps floated to Lillian's ears. But she couldn't care less what the people around her were thinking. She wanted — no needed — to know the end of the story.

The pastor moved forward again and gazed around the room. "My dear people, I'd heard the story and the rumors of this young woman before. But what I had been told wasn't even a shred of the truth. And yet, it has been what was believed." He sighed. "The brother of this poor young woman was devastated. And angry. He wanted revenge. So he went after the young man. Went to his large home in Sacramento to confront him. But the young man wasn't there. He'd traveled here to find the brother. When he found out that the brother was gone, he wrote a long letter, saying he couldn't live with himself any longer for what he'd done. He confessed and asked for forgiveness. And then he hanged himself."

More gasps and whispers.

The pastor pulled a letter out of his Bible. "This . . ." he choked. "This is the letter of confession, anguish, and regret that the brother held on to for all those years. Oh, he could have come into town and shown it to everyone and belittled the man and his family. He could have sought retribution in any number of ways. He could have spread his own story to squelch all the rumors and prove to this town that his sister was innocent. But when he found the young man, the loss of both young lives broke the brother. He realized that he didn't want to have anything to do with anyone who called themselves Christian. Because this . . . *this* is what Christians did."

He stopped and put the letter inside his coat. His tone became more stern — that of a rebuking father. "This man, on his deathbed, had lived a life as a recluse because he didn't want to ever have to deal with the pain that Christians caused. I spent an hour with this man as he breathed his last, trying to give him the hope that is only in Christ. And yet, how hard it is for one to believe when the example we set before them is so poor.

"I don't know if the man ever believed. That is not for me to say, because only God knows the heart. But I pray that God drew this man to himself in that last hour. Shame on us all for allowing this sort of thing to happen.

"In closing, I would like us all to bow our heads and think about people we have hurt with our words. And I would hope to challenge you all with the words of James, chapter one, verse twenty-six: 'If any man among you seem to be religious, and bridleth not his tongue, but deceiveth his own heart, this man's religion is vain.' "

As the pastor closed in prayer, Lillian felt hollowed out. The gut-wrenching story had torn at every corner of her heart. Gone were the thoughts of the others and if they had been listening. Her own heart was convicted and tender. *Lord, help me to bridle my tongue and use it only to glorify You.*

The pastor dismissed the congregation, and there wasn't a word said as they shuffled out. Not even in greeting to him as they exited. It seemed people couldn't get away fast enough. Lillian held back with Jimmy and waited until they were last.

Reaching the pastor, she shook his hand. "Good morning, Reverend. My name is Lillian Porter."

"I'm glad to meet you, Miss Porter. I'm Pastor Seymour. How is it you have come to share our fellowship today?"

"I'm this handsome young man's nanny." She looked at Jimmy and smiled. "This is Jimmy Colton."

"Yes, I thought I recognized him. It's been a long time, Jimmy. Do you remember me? I used to be good friends with your father and mother."

Lillian felt Jimmy take a step back and move closer to her side. She knew he felt uncomfortable with strangers, but she'd hoped he might remember the pastor. Instead of making an ordeal of the situation, Lillian hurried to continue her thoughts.

"It was Jimmy's father who suggested this church. I'm glad he did." Just then an older woman came to join them.

"I'd like you to meet my wife," the pastor said, putting his arm around the woman. "My dear, this is Miss Porter. She's Jimmy

Colton's nanny."

The woman smiled and nodded. "I'm so glad to meet you and see Jimmy again."

Lillian realized that time was getting away from her and didn't want to give Woody and Mrs. Goodman any reason to worry about them. "It was wonderful to meet you both. Thank you for the sermon today, Pastor Seymour. I am sure I will be thinking on it for a long time."

He smiled back at her. "Thank you, Miss Porter. I'm so glad you all came today. I hope you will return."

"We will." She squeezed Jimmy's hand. "We definitely will." She turned to go.

"Oh, and Miss Porter . . ."

Lillian paused. "Yes?"

"Please tell Woody I send . . . no, *we* send our love."

Lillian smiled. "I will, Mrs. Seymour. I'm sure it will mean a lot to him."

Chapter Eighteen

Darwin paced the mine. Why did his dim-witted brother have to get involved? Of course, if Harry hadn't moved the gold, someone else probably would have it. So in a way he should be grateful, but his no-good uncle and cousins had obviously beat Harry's head a few too many times, because the kid couldn't remember anything.

Harry was crouched up against the wall, chewing on his fingernails. "I'm sorry, Brother, I really am. I'm tryin' real hard to 'member."

Darwin leaned up against the wall and beat his head against the stone a few times. It infuriated him. His gold. And he couldn't even find it! The entire world was against him. It always had been. He'd never got an easy deal even once in his life.

Moans came from his brother. "I don't mean to make you mad, Darwin. I'm sorry. I'm really sorry, really sorry, really sorry."

The big guy cowered and covered his head with his arm.

Darwin sighed. He didn't have patience for this. But every time he raised his voice or got angry, Harry got even more worked up and couldn't remember. If Darwin could keep himself calm for a little bit and talk to Harry the way Ma did, then maybe that would help the kid conjure up where he'd hidden the sacks.

So he crouched down in front of his kid brother and put on the sweetest tone he could muster. "It's all right, Harry. I know you're trying. I just need to find it because mean Uncle John told the constable a lie about me, and he's trying to find us."

Harry frowned. "Uncle John is very, very mean. I don't want him to find us."

"I know, little brother. So we don't have a lot of time. I just don't want them to hurt you anymore."

"You know that they hurt me?" Harry jumped up. "No, no, no. How did you find out? They told me if I ever told you, they would kill me and you, too."

Darwin almost laughed. Kind of like the threat he'd given the Colton kid. But he had to calm Harry down. So he placed his hands on his brother's shoulders. "They won't get to you, Harry. I promise. I found

279

out because I'm your brother. That's why we went away, so I could protect you."

"And I could help you." Harry smiled.

"Yes, so you could help me." He had to work at keeping his voice soothing. "All we need to do is help you remember, right?"

"Right." Harry seemed to have forgotten about everything else and paced the open area of the mine like Darwin had been doing. He furrowed his brow and clasped his hands behind his back.

Darwin waited, but nothing happened. So he slid down the wall and covered his face with his hat. Maybe he could shut his eyes for just a few minutes. . . .

"Brother, Brother!" The singsong voice was back.

Darwin opened his eyes and lifted his hat.

"I remember!" His brother walked around clapping. "Well, I remember a few things. How many bags were there?"

"Ten."

"Well, I 'member five for sure. There was one biggest one, right? And another big one?"

Darwin nodded.

"Those're in the well."

"Okay." He leaned forward and tried to remain calm.

"There's another one in the attic of the

big new house. Under the floorboards. I snuck in there and hid it when they were building the house 'cause they dug up where I hid it first and I was afraid they'd find it."

"Go on."

Harry squeezed his eyes shut tight and chewed on his lip. "Oh, oh, I had another one. . . ." He pointed to his head and his eyes popped open. "In Ma's rose garden. Under the chicken. Two are there."

"Huh? What chicken?"

"The chicken you killed when you got angry. You were mean to it and Ma said you hurt it so bad we couldn't even eat it. So we buried it under a stone in the rose garden."

"I don't remember killin' no chicken." Darwin realized he'd raised his voice again, but at least the kid had remembered something. And something was better than nothing.

"Oh, I do." Harry nodded. "And it's a reminder to not lose our tempers."

Yeah. Sure. A chicken as a reminder to not lose his temper? Poor, innocent Harry. If he thought the worst thing Darwin had ever done was kill a chicken, then the kid was dumber than he thought. But if keeping calm would keep Harry remembering, then Darwin would put his best foot forward. After that, he'd have his gold, and his brother . . . well . . . his brother could have a good, long rest.

The sun beat down on Woody as he gazed out at the olive grove. When he'd checked the trees earlier, they were sorely in need of water. And a lot of it. Even with all his men, they couldn't keep up with the hand-watering. They just couldn't do it. *Lord, we need some rain. In a bad way.*

Some of the olives were showing the signs of the drought. If he didn't do something and soon, he might even lose a good portion of the crop. The only way to get water to all the trees would be to dig an irrigation ditch. If they could get water directly from the spring-fed pond to the grove, then they could water all the trees at once. It might be worth the time and effort. And it might be the only way to save the farm if the drought continued.

Gathering his men together, he laid out the plan. They'd need more shovels, and if he could find some trenching spades in town, that would be even better. The men would set out to start digging the trench at the pond, and Woody would go into town for supplies.

As he walked back to the house, he decided he wanted to ask Lillian to go with him. He'd been encouraged by her words about church on Sunday and Pastor Seymour's prudent message. But even more than that, he wanted to spend more time with her.

He took the steps up the porch two at a time and swung open the screen door. The most beautiful music rose up to greet him. Following the sounds, Woody momentarily forgot his mission. He stood in the open entryway to the music room and watched Lillian as she played the piano. Jimmy sat beside her on the bench. He watched her hands the entire time.

"She's quite accomplished, isn't she?" Mrs. Goodman whispered, coming up behind him.

Woody nodded and continued to listen until Lillian finished. Jimmy clapped his hands, so Woody thought it only appropriate that he clap, as well.

Lillian looked over her shoulder, then jumped to her feet. "I was just showing Jimmy how the simple song I've been teaching him will one day sound when he learns more about the piano and how to play."

"Well, it was beautiful. I seem to remember Rebecca playing that same song." Woody waited for a painful memory of his wife to come and put a damper on his mood. When it didn't, he breathed a sigh of relief.

"I need to go into town for some supplies. I was wondering, Mrs. Goodman, if you had a list you could give Lillian and if you'd watch Jimmy for the afternoon so that Lillian could go with me."

"I'd be happy to. I have a list started in the kitchen." Mrs. Goodman scurried off and called over her shoulder, "I'll be back in a jiffy."

A smile split Miss Porter's lips. "I'd love to go. Thank you for thinking of me. In fact, I have a stack of letters I've been wanting to post." She bent down to Jimmy, who was all smiles. "I want you to finish your piano practice and then work real hard on your letters and numbers this afternoon, all right?"

His son nodded.

Woody winked at him over Lillian's head.

Mrs. Goodman returned with the list and handed it to Lillian. "Why don't you look it over real quick and make sure you understand my scrawl." The older woman laughed.

"Looks good to me." Lillian patted her hair. "Let me run to my room, and I'll be ready to go."

Woody nodded and watched her race

down the hallway. "I'll go get the wagon."

The drive to town started off quiet. But it could've just been the heat. Woody felt the sweat dripping off of him, and he could see Lillian fanning herself out of the corner of his eye. He had lots on his mind to keep him occupied, but for some reason, the female next to him kept distracting him.

He felt her shift in her seat.

As she turned to face him a little more, he felt part of a breeze from her fan. The wagon wheel hit a rut, causing Lillian to bounce against him, and he reached out to steady her. "Sorry about that."

She laid a hand on his arm to straighten herself and fanned even faster. "Goodness, this heat is quite oppressive today, isn't it?"

As the warmth from her hand seared his arm, he couldn't agree more. "Yep. We're in a drought, and it's had me more than a little bit concerned."

She whipped around to face him again. "Oh, goodness, I hadn't even thought about how this might truly affect the crop. I mean, I knew you were hand-watering and all, but . . . oh, Woody, I'm so sorry I hadn't asked about that. Jimmy and I can come and help. We've been watering the flowers and vegetable gardens."

"Don't worry about it. I know you've had

your hands full, as well, and I haven't wanted anyone to worry. But that's the reason we're headed into town today. The men and I came up with a plan. We're going to dig an irrigation ditch from the pond to the olive trees."

"Goodness! That's a long ways. Will it save the crop?"

"I surely hope so. I have a big order to fill, and it will mean the difference between us getting through to next year or . . ." He let the words go unsaid. "We're a bunch of hard workers, so I'm hopeful we can get it done. We can always dam up the irrigation ditch if we don't need it, and then have it to use the next time the rains fail to come."

"It's a blessing your pond is fed by the spring then, isn't it?"

He nodded. "It was one of the reasons I bought this place."

"Who lived there prior to you?"

Woody shrugged. "I never knew. The bank owned the property, and that's who I bought it from. I'd heard there was a family who lived there until the death of the mother. Seems they headed out after that, and the bank took possession. I had an inheritance and the cash to buy it outright."

"How nice for you, but sad for the other family." Lillian shook her head. "I suppose it was the mother who planted all those lovely flower beds. Mrs. Goodman told me they were here when she came to work for you all those years ago."

"Yes. I think the flower beds convinced Rebecca to live there, too."

"I have to admit I'm anxious to see what it all looks like come spring. Mrs. Goodman told me there were a great many flowers that only bloomed in March and April. She said it gets prettier every year, and last spring it was an absolute riot of color."

Had it been? Woody didn't recall. He had been so lost in grief that he'd barely remembered to tend to the trees.

Lillian continued. "I'm especially amazed at the roses. There are a great many varieties. We had roses back in Indiana, and I'm more or less familiar with them. I wasn't allowed to tend them myself, but I was often in the company of those who did and asked a great many questions."

Woody laughed. "I'll just bet you did."

"Well, if you don't ask, you won't learn."

"So what other questions are you burning to ask?"

Lillian cocked her head to one side. "Well, let me think. I did notice that the pond was lower this time of year. Will that affect your plan for the irrigation ditch?"

"Nah, I don't think so. There's still a lot of water there, and it is fed by the spring. I've never known it to get much lower than it is. But we will keep an eye on things."

As he laid out the whole plan to her, excitement built in his gut. They could do this. The good Lord had given him the men and the strength to do it. This life wouldn't be without hardship, but he could carry on in faith.

They approached town, and Woody steeled himself. Even if Pastor Seymour had given a sermon on gossip that had reached into the hearts of everyone there, the wagging tongues wouldn't have stopped in just a matter of days. It would take a long time to get rid of well over a year's worth of rumors and lies.

This time, he headed to Stickle Bros. mercantile. He parked the wagon in front and helped Lillian down. "Look, I know what you said about the sermon, but I wouldn't be too hopeful that folks have changed their thinking." He nodded toward the store. "I remember you said I hadn't paid you." He gave her a sheepish grin. "I apologize for that. I plan to get you some money from the bank, but in the meanwhile you can pick out anything you need in the store and I'll pay for it."

She smiled. "I only said that to get back at you. I wasn't feeling too kind at that moment."

"Maybe not, but you were right. I hadn't been very considerate of your needs." He offered Lillian his arm and tried not to act like a giddy schoolboy when she took it.

George Stickle greeted him at the door. "Woody. Good to see you. It's been a long time."

"Sure has, George. And I'm sorry for that."

"I'm sorry, too, Woody. For that and a lot of other things." The two men exchanged a glance. Woody wasn't sure what to say.

"Ah . . . I'm in need of some sharp spades. I need to dig a long irrigation ditch." He remembered Lillian beside him. "George, I'm sorry, this is Miss Porter."

George held out his hand. "Nice to meet you, Miss Porter. I'd . . . uh . . . heard talk about you, and I believe I saw you in church on Sunday with little Jimmy."

"You are correct." Lillian smiled at him and then turned to Woody and touched his arm. "I'm going to see to Mrs. Goodman's needs for the house." She walked away and Woody couldn't help but watch her.

George smiled at him. "She's a pretty little thing."

Woody felt his face grow hotter than it had been in the sun. He nodded. "She's been real good with my son." He couldn't bring himself to look George in the eye for fear he'd see that Woody's interest in Lillian was for more than Jimmy's sake.

George didn't seem at all concerned. "Let's go see about those shovels."

The next hour passed in a blur as Woody worked with George on his list of tools and supplies. Seeing the time was close to noon, Woody took off his kerchief and wiped his face.

"If you don't mind, just stack the stuff up for me. I'll be back in a few minutes, but I need to get to the bank before they close for the lunch hour."

"It's not a problem, Woody. You might even want to escort Miss Porter to lunch."

Woody hadn't thought that Lillian might be hungry. He frowned, knowing that he probably wouldn't be accepted in any of the little cafes. At least not without a scene.

"Maybe I'll just pick up a few things from you before we leave." He could see Lillian at the far end of the store looking through some bolts of cloth. "If she wonders where I've gone, just let her know I had bank business, would you?"

"Sure thing, Woody." George smiled.

"Take your time. I'll see that Miss Porter finds everything she needs."

Woody made his way to the bank in quick, long strides. He didn't look left or right but simply focused on the brick building ahead of him. He was glad to see that the bank was empty when he entered. The teller was curt but conducted business in a civil manner. After watching the man count out his money, Woody stuffed it in his pocket and headed back to finish loading his wagon.

Passing by one of the stores that specialized in women's gewgaws, Woody notice a light blue parasol. He wondered if Lillian had thought to bring any with her from Indiana. She must not have, or surely she would have brought one for their drive to town. He thought about buying it for her, but the lady clerks inside would probably want nothing to do with him.

Maybe he'd mention it to Lillian before they left town. So far things had gone pretty smooth, but just as he approached the wagon, Woody saw that once again word must've gotten out that he was in town, because a small crowd had formed. George was loading the wagon with the feed that Woody had ordered for the horses, while Lillian was apparently still shopping. Woody followed George into the store and picked up one of the grain sacks while his friend got the other. Then Woody led the way out to the wagon.

No one had said anything to his face yet, but he could hear the insults and the crude remarks. Louder and louder. People wanted to make sure he knew what they thought of him. Woody just wanted to do whatever it took to get his supplies and get out of town without incident.

George leaned toward him, the sack balanced on his shoulder. "It's hard to keep turning the other cheek, isn't it? I don't see how you do it." As he dropped his heavy load into the back of the wagon, George shook his head.

Woody wanted to tell him that he was biting his tongue until it nearly bled, but what good would that do? They only had one more load to carry. He went back inside the store and got Lillian as she finished up. She would unfortunately hear it all as they left, but it couldn't be helped.

Woody took the packages from Lillian, not even daring to look at her. If she wondered about his brusque manner, she'd know soon enough what was wrong. He put the packages in back with the other purchases, then helped her up to the wagon seat. But instead of sitting down, she just stood there. So

Woody went around to the other side and climbed up. He took the reins, hoping that would signal her. Was she in shock? What was going on?

"You plannin' on killin' her like you done killed your wife, Colton?" One voice rose above the others.

He thought of a hundred different heated retorts he could throw out, but Woody held his tongue.

George Stickle stepped up to the porch in front of his store and crossed his arms. "Go home. All of ya."

"You gonna stand up for this man, Stickle? Are ya? What if we stopped buying supplies from you because you're friends with a murderer?"

"Yeah!"

"Yeah!" The crowd was rowdy today.

The wagon shook with quite a force as Lillian stomped her feet. "I've had just about enough. You should all be ashamed of yourselves!" Her voice resonated well beyond the crowd and even caused people down the street to stop and stare.

Where the power had come from, he had no idea, but Woody was shocked at the force of her voice.

"Why, I saw you" — she pointed — "and you" — she pointed again — "and you, and you, and you" — she didn't spare anyone her gaze or her finger — "and you, and you in church on Sunday morning. Did you not hear a word of what the preacher said? How dare you malign this man and bear false witness against him when you don't know the truth! You're a bunch of judging gossips, and I'm ashamed for you. I'm ashamed that you call yourselves Christians."

The crowd quieted, but many looked on with arms crossed and deep frowns.

"How many of you have even bothered to ask how little Jimmy is doing? Well? How many have asked how Mr. Colton is doing? Can you imagine how devastating it would be to come home and find your wife murdered? No. You can't. Because you'd rather believe the worst and spread rumors because they make you feel better about yourself. Well, I'm here to tell you right now that I've had enough of this garbage. If Jesus himself were here, I'm afraid He'd have to call you a bunch of hypocrites."

She sat down on the bench seat of the wagon and huffed. Woody found it impossible to move. He'd never heard anyone defend him with such passion.

Silence reigned for a moment. Then several men went and joined George on the porch. And then a few more. Within moments, there were twelve gathered on the porch, and one moved forward. Woody had known this man quite well at one time. "We'll stand alongside you, Woody. And I'm sad that it has taken us this long to do it. We're sick of the gossip in this town tearing folks apart." His words were like balm on a wound.

The rest of the people on the ground erupted in heated debate with those on the porch. How had this happened? What had gotten into people?

Sin. That's what. And they were all guilty of it.

Woody lowered his head. He didn't know how they could ever overcome the ugliness.

Lillian stood again, and Woody's head shot up. Her face was a deep shade of crimson. "Keep thy tongue from evil, and thy lips from speaking guile! Psalm thirty-four, thirteen. Were any of you there the day that Rebecca Colton was murdered?"

The crowd silenced once again.

"Did any of you witness her death?"

No response.

"Then I suggest you keep your mouths shut."

"And why should we listen to you, missy? You weren't there, either. We've heard from plenty of people what this man is capable of." The voices erupted again.

Woody touched Lillian's elbow. Rage radiated off of her in waves. He couldn't do anything to make this better.

"Settle down!" Sheriff Hobart arrived on his horse and looked down at the people.

But they just kept arguing and squabbling. The cries of "retrial" were heard several times.

"I said, settle down!" the sheriff hollered louder. "And if you don't settle down, I'm gonna haul all of ya down to the jail and lock you up."

The crowd quieted again.

"Now," the sheriff continued, "get out of the middle of the street and go about your business afore I lose my temper." He rode his horse closer to Woody and leaned in. "That means it's time for you to leave, Colton. I've had just about enough of you causing trouble in this town." His eyes narrowed. "And as soon as the new judge comes through, I just might sit down with him and have a chat about retrying you."

"Well, at least maybe a new judge would want to see all the evidence and know all the facts instead of just the ones he wants to know." Woody lifted the reins and signaled the horses to move forward.

As soon as they were away from the town,

Lillian started crying. "I'm so sorry for losing my temper. I've never been so mad. What is wrong with those people?" She pulled out a handkerchief from her reticule.

He couldn't help but laugh at the sad situation. "It's called a sin nature. Thanks for standing up for me back there. Nobody's ever done it . . . quite so . . . firmly." He looked at her and grinned. "I really appreciate it."

She obviously didn't find it as funny as he did, because she scowled and took out her fan again. She wiped her eyes with one hand and fanned with the other. It was several minutes before she spoke again. "It was wrong of me to yell at them."

He grinned. He didn't mind having her on his side. "Hey, I've seen you with your dander up. Maybe not to that extent. All the same, I'm glad it wasn't directed at me."

"I'm ashamed that I could have such an outburst. Sometimes I think that I've just held things inside me for all my life. I guess I'm feeling it's time to let it go."

He gave her a sidelong glance and his grin widened. "Just as long as it's not aimed at me, I think I can handle it."

She finally relaxed a little at his comment. "Those people were so ugly. There was hatred in their eyes. I'd heard some of them raise their protests when I first came to town, but at least they were somewhat civil." Lillian let out a long sigh. "So this is what it's been like for you all this time?"

He nodded.

"How can you stand it?"

"I don't. I've avoided those people at all costs."

There went the fan again. Whipping back and forth faster than a jackrabbit across the field. "Well, I think it's time to face those people head on."

"What do you think we just did, Lillian?"

"I know, I know. But the problem is, they know that they've got you cornered. And since you don't go into town often, that just fuels their fire."

He hadn't thought of it that way. And he wasn't sure he liked where she was headed.

"Since I'm being blunt anyway, I think I'll just give you my opinion." She paused and turned to him. "I think you've been hiding and grumbling too long, and it's time to show the people of Angels Camp the real Woody Colton."

It irritated him just a bit that she thought he'd been hiding and grumbling. Even if it was true. "They had the opportunity to see the real me. All those years before Rebecca died. Some of those men were ones I

counted as good friends. They knew me —
knew what I stood for — and they turned
on me anyway."

"Yes, they did, but at least some of them
have turned back. If they can see the error
of their ways, then others can, too. With the
good Lord's strength, we can do this,
Woody." She closed the fan and grabbed his
forearm with both of her hands. "You saw
all those men who joined Mr. Stickle in
defense of you. There's bound to be more,
especially once those twelve start working
on the others. Now that they've made a
stand, they won't be quite so afraid to voice
their opinions."

He thought about that for a moment.
He'd almost forgotten that people had come
to stand up for him. He'd had good friends,
and they'd tried to help him through his
loss, but Woody had made it almost impossible. He'd pushed them away — all of
them. It had been easier all these months to
hide. And blame it all on the fact that they
hated him and gossiped about him.

"I think you should join me in church on
Sunday."

"Whoa, that's taking it a bit fast, don't
you think? Did you see how many people
hated my being there today? Even the sheriff
doesn't believe in me."

"Well, we'll just have to change their minds then, won't we?" Her smile lit up the whole valley.

His heart skipped a beat. At least that's what it felt like. He was acting like a school-boy with a crush on the teacher. If Lillian knew he was thinking once again of how attractive she was and how much he had come to enjoy her company, she might climb down from the wagon and walk home. He drew in a deep breath and tried to steady his nerves before he finally replied, "I'll think about it."

That night after supper, Lillian graced them with her piano playing. Jimmy sat beside Woody the entire time, watching his nanny's every move. Woody remembered the way Rebecca would play for them sometimes. Jimmy always seemed fixated on the music. With these thoughts in mind, Woody remembered Lillian's request for Jimmy.

"He needs a picture of his mother — something he can keep with him," she had told him. *"He saw my locket, and I told him how special it was to me to have pictures of my mother and father."*

Woody got up and went to the small desk in the sitting room. Lillian began to play

300

another song, this one Woody recognized as from the *Pirates of Penzance.* He and Rebecca had attended the comical opera in San Francisco years ago. They had laughed and laughed at the Major-General song that Lillian now played.

He couldn't help but hum along as he opened the desk drawer and rummaged to the very back. There he pulled out a small tintype photo of his wife. She looked rather impish, despite the photographer having told her not to smile or move. Woody grinned. Rebecca had been just as stubborn as Lillian.

Mrs. Goodman sat tapping her toes to the beat of the music while Jimmy bounced up and down when Woody returned. He took his place once again beside Jimmy and handed him the tintype.

"Miss Lillian said you'd like a picture of your mother. I thought you could have this one."

Jimmy stopped bouncing and took the tintype in hand. He looked at it for several moments, then hugged it close and smiled up at Woody. The moment belonged just to them. Mrs. Goodman still tapped and Lillian still played, but just for those few precious seconds, Woody and Jimmy were connected in a way that had been absent since Rebecca's death.

Jimmy got up on his knees and kissed Woody's cheek. After that he wrapped his arms tight around Woody's neck. Woody put his arm around the boy and held him close. It was the first time since losing Rebecca that Woody felt everything would be all right.

CHAPTER NINETEEN

Saturday morning, Lillian stood at the pond with Jimmy, fishing pole in hand. They hadn't seen Harry in over a week — well, since Woody had scared him off — and it worried her. She knew the young man was probably afraid and pretty fragile. He needed to be loved just like everyone else. Sometimes she felt certain someone was watching them and hoped if so, it was Harry. She wanted him to know that he could come back to them — that things were better now.

But with the men furiously digging the trench from the pond all the way to the olive grove, she knew Harry was probably afraid to come back.

Jimmy looked up at her, that same question in his eyes.

"We'll see him soon. I'm sure of it. Don't worry. I think Harry can take care of himself." She walked to the tree and tied another ribbon-laced package. They'd taken to drawing pictures for Harry since she'd found out he couldn't read, and they'd fold them up with goodies and tie them to the tree. Each time the pictures had been taken, so Lillian hoped and prayed that meant Harry was coming to get them.

She looked down at her little charge again. Jimmy had become much more than her student or ward. She loved him as if he were her own. This family had woven itself into her heart without her even realizing what happened. She kissed the top of his head. "Let's head back to the house. We've got lots of baking to do today, and we need to get ready for church tomorrow."

He held her hand as they made the long walk back to the house. She often hummed or sang to him as they walked, but today her thoughts kept returning to a letter from Indiana. Stanton told her that her grandfather still refused to hear about her notes home. And to make matters worse, he was sick. Stanton promised to be honest with her, but she felt that maybe he was holding back a little. If her grandfather hadn't left his bed in a couple weeks, that meant he was *very* sick.

Lillian pondered the silence around her. Sweet little Jimmy still refused to speak.

And he might not ever. Grandfather refused to acknowledge her or respond. Would they ever get beyond the silence?

The next morning, armed with cookies for the pastor and his family and a picnic lunch, the entire Colton family headed into town for church. Woody, Jimmy, Mrs. Goodman, and Lillian. She'd insisted that Mrs. Goodman sit up on the seat with Woody while she and Jimmy made themselves a comfortable couch out of blankets and cushions in the bed of the wagon.

The thought of all of them attending church together had kept her up most of the night. And now her stomach was all aflutter. *Please, Lord.* She didn't know what else to pray. But God knew.

A poke to her shoulder brought her awake, and she realized they had reached the church. Jimmy stared at her. Apparently she'd fallen asleep in the wagon. Fiddlesticks. She reached up to adjust her straw bonnet. Hopefully her hair wasn't a mess. But at least it was better falling asleep here rather than during the sermon. That would be embarrassing. She'd have to make sure to get enough sleep before church from now on.

Woody helped her down from the wagon and she saw the hesitation in his eyes. This couldn't be easy for him. Especially after the other day. But at least they were here.

The church was pretty quiet as they entered and took seats in the back. Pastor Seymour got up and led them in a song, but Lillian couldn't focus on the hymn. She felt the stares of people and hated how it made her feel. How she longed to keep Woody and Jimmy from feeling any more hurt and pain.

The minister launched into his sermon on James, chapter four, and Lillian tried so hard to stay attentive. But the lack of sleep the night before kept haunting her. And then she'd get distracted by every little movement and hope it wasn't someone coming to say something ugly to her family. Yes, she had to admit it. They were just as much her family as those back in Indiana. And she would protect them just like she would family.

Toward the end of the service, the reverend asked them all to look again at verse seventeen of chapter four. She looked down at her Bible and read the words along with him, "Therefore to him that knoweth to do good, and doeth it not, to him it is sin."

Pastor Seymour closed his Bible and

looked down at the congregation. "If you know to do good and not harm and you don't do it, you are in sin. You are just as guilty as . . ." He paused and looked around the room before adding, ". . . a murderer."

He waited another few moments before continuing in a gentle, fatherly manner. "Sin is sin. There aren't little sins and big sins. There are sins that are more acceptable than others and still other sins that bear greater consequences in the world. But God can't abide it in any form." Despite the gentleness of his tone, he fixed them with the stern expression of a father reprimanding his children.

Lillian noted a great many people bowed their heads as if the intensity of the pastor's gaze was too much to bear. Good. Let them feel guilty for how they'd acted. Let them be the ones to be uncomfortable instead of Woody. She didn't suppose those were the thoughts of a good Christian woman, but she was angry. Angry that people could be so cruel. Angry that it had gone so long unchecked. Perhaps with Woody absent from their lives, people figured they could just hide their ugliness and pretend they were in the right. Well, there was no pretending that now.

Pastor Seymour finally smiled. "We're

blessed, though, because Jesus said He'd pay the price for our sins. Isn't that a wonder? He didn't do anything wrong, but people condemned Him. He didn't do anything wrong, but He willingly took on our sins and died. Better still, He rose again and lives.

"Folks, I know it's easy to be caught up in sin. Especially lies. Satan works it in such a way that it seems logical to accept lies as truth. But you need to remember something as you point your finger to accuse one another. Satan . . . is the accuser of the brethren. I think you need to ask yourself exactly who you're siding with. Who stands to benefit? Let's pray."

Outside the church, several men approached the Colton wagon, and Lillian braced herself for the worst. Jimmy tightened his hold on her hand and leaned closer to hide his face against her sleeve.

A man Lillian heard the pastor call Stan Van Dyke spoke first. "Colton, we need to apologize to you. We believed the worst, when we all knew what kind of man you were. We'd witnessed it firsthand, and yet we took hearsay and rumors above it." The man who led the group held out his hand. "I hope you'll forgive me."

"Me too." Another held out his hand.

Lillian walked Jimmy a few paces away to allow the men some time. Woody needed this. God alone knew how much pain these men had heaped upon Woody in the past, but now it was time for them to apply a soothing salve and let the healing begin.

Mrs. Goodman walked toward her. "Two ladies just apologized to me, Lillian. Two! Can you believe it? Apparently the good minister's sermons have been convicting the people."

Lillian let go of Jimmy to hug her friend. "That's wonderful news. Truly."

"I hear that you made quite an impression on the town, as well. Standin' up as you did for your boss." The older woman nudged her.

Lillian looked back to where Woody conversed with the men. "He's a good man. People just needed to be reminded of that. Why is it that we allow fear to overrule everything else?"

"I don't know, dearie, but it sure is sad." Mrs. Goodman shook her head. "I can't say that I ever thought I'd see the day when people would be apologizing for their words and for listening to the gossip. You've been a healing balm to this town. All we needed was for a stranger to come in and clean up the mess everyone else felt was perfectly acceptable."

Lillian shook her head. "All they needed was to take their eyes off Woody and his situation and put them back on Jesus."

Woody walked over to them then. Lillian thought she saw a glimmer of tears in his eyes. His gaze held hers for just a moment, but in that moment they seemed to share so much. He was precious to her — so much a part of her heart. How it all happened, she hadn't a clue. But she thanked the Lord for making her path straight to Angels Camp.

"You all ready to head out for our picnic?" He glanced toward Mrs. Goodman and smiled.

"Sounds lovely, young man. I haven't been on a picnic in years." Mrs. Goodman winked at them both.

"Where's Jimmy?" He looked around.

Lillian's heart plummeted. "He was just here." She glanced around, as well.

"Let's split up. We'll find him faster that way." Woody took off toward the west side of the churchyard, and Lillian went the other way. Mrs. Goodman headed toward the street and town.

Lillian called out for the little boy but couldn't see him anywhere. Maybe he'd followed a rabbit somewhere? Or needed to use the outhouse? She checked back inside the church, but everyone was gone. Then she went back around the church again. The cemetery stood off in the distance, and she noticed two figures.

Father and son.

She took her time walking over there, trying to slow the rapid pace of her heart. Jimmy must be visiting his mother's grave. Why hadn't she thought to bring him here before now? The poor child. He'd endured so much and still grieved the loss of his mother. Feeling guilty for neglecting such an important thing for Jimmy, she slowly walked up.

Woody's back was to her as he crouched by his son. He wrapped the boy in his strong arms.

As Lillian neared she heard Jimmy's soft sobs and Woody's words of comfort. She turned to go, to give them privacy, but stopped when she heard Woody's pleas.

"Son, please, talk to me. I can't help you if you don't share with me what's going on in that head of yours. I know you miss your mother. I do too. More than you know. But I want to help you."

Lillian couldn't help it. She turned back around to watch and listen.

Jimmy shook his head over and over again. Tears streamed down his little cheeks.

"Did you see what happened to your mother, son? Did you?"

Jimmy's sobs turned into wails, and he just kept shaking his head.

Woody picked him up and wrapped him in a tight hug again. "I'm so sorry, Jimmy. I'm so sorry I wasn't there to protect you."

Darwin awakened early that Sunday morning. He'd waited an entire week for all of the people on the farm to leave at the same time. He had been nearly ready to march in there and hold them all at gunpoint in order to get his gold. Desperation and hunger made a man do crazy things. But then on Saturday when he'd been watching them from the coverage of the trees, Darwin overheard them mention attending church the next day. They were all going to go — even the workmen. This was the opportunity he'd been waiting for.

He crept around, being as quiet as possible. He didn't want to wake Harry. Harry was such a big guy that he ate his weight in food almost daily. However, they'd run out of food, and Harry had begun acting like a five-year-old, demanding something to eat. Darwin tried to explain it to Harry, even encourage him, that the sooner he was able to remember where he'd hid all of the gold, the sooner they'd be able to buy food. But it did little good, and Harry just continued to complain. It was one more justification for ending Harry's life. Darwin's gold wouldn't last long if he had to keep up with his brother's voracious appetite, and no one was going to take in a big oaf who'd eat them out of house and home.

Darwin all but tiptoed to the narrow shaft where he'd hobbled his horse. The shaft looked to have been one that someone started and then abandoned. It was perfect for keeping his horse hidden out of sight. He saddled the gelding, then led him out of the mine. His plan was to approach the farm from the north and leave the horse grazing there out of sight. Then he'd sneak down past the outbuildings, avoiding the one that housed the crew. Hopefully they'd all gone to church, as well, but Darwin wasn't going to take any chances.

He'd just mounted his horse and started down the trail when he heard the unmistakable sound of Harry lumbering after him. Great. That was just what he needed. Now he had to deal with the constant babbling of his simpleminded brother.

"Are we going to get the gold, Brother?" Harry asked as he caught up to the horse.

"Yes, but we have to be very quiet. We

don't want to wake up anyone if they're sleeping."

Harry put his finger to his lips. "Shhhh."

Darwin nodded. "Exactly."

"I'll be very quiet," Harry promised.

Darwin doubted it was even possible but had no choice but to let Harry follow. After all, he might very well remember where he'd hidden some of the other bags.

As they got closer to the farm, Harry poked him. "Brother, Brother. I remember more."

Just what Darwin hoped. "Tell me, Harry. What do you remember?"

"I took some of the bags to my special place, so that no one would ever find it. I ran out of places to hide it at the house."

"Where's your special place?"

"Oh, it's a long, long, long, long, long, long ways from here. It took me two days to walk there."

"Two days? What were you thinking?"

Harry frowned. "I was thinking that I had to keep your stuff safe, Brother. I was thinking hard."

"Well, we can take horses to get there. That is, if you remember how to get there."

"I remember. It has all sorts of caves to hide in, and there's water, and it falls down from the mountain. It's beautiful. Miss Lillian called it a new park."

Darwin looked at him for a moment. "Are you talkin' about that new national park? Yosemite?"

Harry nodded and clapped his hands. "Yes. Yes. Yes. That's it. Miss Lillian called it that."

Great. That was a long ways. He and some friends had hidden out there years ago when the law was bearing down on them for a little bank robbery they'd pulled. There were enough canyons and gullies and caves in there to keep them looking for the next hundred years. Darwin shook his head. He'd have to worry about that later. After he got the gold off the Colton property. Property that should've been his.

First things first. He'd have to look in the first place he'd buried the gold and make sure that Harry hadn't left any. Then he'd have to look by the well. That would be a challenge.

As they neared his original hiding place, Darwin glanced around. "Harry, you keep an eye out. If you see anyone, and I mean anyone or anything comin' this way, you let me know."

"Okay, Brother. You can count on me. I'll be the lookout."

Darwin dug by their ma's favorite tree. It

315

took him a long time just to get a foot down.

"Want me to dig for a while?"

"Sure." Might as well let that big oaf do some of the hard work. Darwin watched the surroundings.

A loud clink reached his ears. Harry jumped up and down. "I hit something!"

Sure enough. When Darwin jumped in the hole with his brother, he pulled up a leather sack. They dug some more with their hands, and he pulled up one more bag. Convinced there weren't any more, Darwin looked at Harry. "Fill the hole back in. Nice and packed." He looked at the sky. The sun was well into the west, past high noon. That meant they were running out of time. "We gotta be quick, Harry."

"I can be fast."

"You better be."

Darwin raced to the top of the hill. In the distance, he spotted the wagon. That meant they only had about ten minutes to get out of sight. He ran back down the hill and grabbed the sacks. But carrying more than one would be too much for him for long. Gold was heavy.

He heaved one over his shoulder and headed back toward the mine. "I'm gonna get this one over that hill and then come back for the other."

"Uh-huh," Harry grunted. He was almost done filling in the hole.

"Hurry up. They're coming."

By the time Darwin made it back, his brother was done and had grabbed the other leather sack. They made it to the bluff just in time. Harry kept on running, but Darwin turned and wanted to watch. He'd heard about the well-to-do new nanny that Colton had hired. Had the boy opened his trap yet?

He heard laughter drift toward him from the house, and Darwin looked on. It was the boy. And he was laughing. The ladies went inside the house, and Colton rode the wagon to the barn while the boy chased a rabbit in the yard. "Come this way." Darwin willed the child to come closer. He hadn't come this far to see the sniveling little brat ruin it all.

The kid caught the rabbit and tucked him into something wrapped around his shoulder but kept coming toward the tree that Darwin hid behind. When he could hear the boy's footsteps, Darwin checked to make sure no one else was around and ventured out into plain sight. He wasn't sure the child would recognize him, since he was clean-shaven.

The boy stopped in his tracks and stared. His face went white.

317

Darwin couldn't help but give him a smug smile. Now was his chance to get rid of the one and only witness to the Colton murder. But if he took the boy now, more people would come out to investigate. And he couldn't deal with that. Not until he'd gotten all his gold back. Darwin wanted the kid dead. But he wanted his gold more.

The kid stood there shaking.

"Not one word, kid. You hear me? Not a word. Or you're all dead, including that pretty little lady that's come to live with you." The boy's eyes widened even more.

Movement at the house caught his eye, and Darwin slunk behind the tree again.

"Jimmy . . . come on in and wash up." The new nanny's voice floated from the porch where she stood with her hand at her brow line to shade her eyes. She was a pretty thing. Hopefully she hadn't spotted him.

Darwin stayed behind the tree until he heard the boy's footsteps running the other way. He could only hope that the kid would be scared enough to keep his mouth shut.

Until Darwin could shut it permanently.

CHAPTER TWENTY

By Wednesday at lunch, Lillian was worried. They'd had so much fun at their picnic on Sunday — it had been a joy to hear Jimmy's laughter. But that evening he wouldn't eat his dinner, and he went to bed early. Monday morning he wouldn't cooperate with anything. Just sat in a chair by the window in his room petting Mr. Whiskers. He refused to come downstairs. Refused to eat. And wouldn't even look at her.

Thinking that he was just getting back at her for scolding him to clean up his room Sunday afternoon, she didn't pay too much mind. But when dinner came and went and the child still hadn't moved, she began to get concerned. She'd hoped his mood might be different on Monday. Mrs. Goodman even tried to cajole him out of his stupor with some of her famous cookies with chunks of chocolate. Still Jimmy sat in complete silence, not looking at either of them. Lillian tucked him into bed Monday night because Woody had been out late digging the irrigation ditch. She knelt by his bed and prayed aloud.

"Lord, please help Jimmy with whatever it is that is bothering him. Help him to know how much he is loved by his father and Mrs. Goodman . . . and me. He's so special to me, Lord, and I want him to know that no matter what, he can always talk to me."

Later she discussed it with Mrs. Goodman. The woman had shrugged her shoulders and said that sometimes little ones pitched a fit. It could even be that the heat was getting to him. Lillian thought to ask Woody about them taking a dip in the pond, but she didn't know if that would cause problems for the irrigation ditch, so she said nothing.

Tuesday rolled around and the same thing happened. Mrs. Goodman voiced her concern, as well, and said they should give it one more day. The boy had bags under his eyes and had only drunk a little water all day long.

Wednesday morning Lillian went to check on him and found him still in bed. But this time he wasn't just sullen or depressed looking. The boy seemed sick. He wouldn't respond to any of the questions the two women asked and stared off into space. The thing that really set Lillian to worrying was the fact that Mr. Whiskers was still in his box.

She and Mrs. Goodman stood at the door as Lillian pulled it closed. "We've got to do something. I'm going to go look for Woody. Will you keep an eye on Jimmy?"

"Sure thing, dearie."

Lillian raced out of the house and headed to the pond. The men had made good headway with the trench but were now digging it deeper at the source. At least that's what she remembered Woody saying. The man had looked like he practically fell into bed each night and was gone well before she made it to the chicken coop each morning.

The heat was draining, and in her corset and long skirts, she had to walk half the way rather than run. By the time she reached the pond, perspiration soaked her blouse. She looked around to see where Woody might be working but only found two of his men. "Where is Mr. Colton?"

"He took a horse to town, miss. Two of the spades broke, and we need to finish to save the trees."

She nodded and headed back to the

house. She'd just have to wait until he returned.

But as soon as she reached the back door, Mrs. Goodman met her with wide, teary eyes. "He's now running a fever, Lillian. And it's high. He's tossing and squirming and his breathing doesn't sound right."

Lillian raced up the stairs. One look at Jimmy and she knew she had to get him to the doctor. "Mrs. Goodman, please find one of the men, ring the bell, holler, do whatever you can, and get them to hitch up the wagon. I've got to get him to the doctor."

She heard the woman rustle out of the room.

Lillian put her hand on the boy's brow. It was terribly hot. "Oh, my sweet Jimmy. I'm so sorry, but we're going to get you to the doctor just as quick as we can. I need you to fight, little one. Fight for all you're worth so that we can go fishing and have picnics the rest of the summer."

Grabbing the wash basin, she dipped a clean shirt in it and bathed him with the tepid water.

She changed him out of his sweat-soaked clothes and put a clean nightshirt on him. Wrapping him in a sheet, she carried him down the stairs. It had to be cooler down there anyway.

Within a few minutes she heard the wheels of the wagon. *Thank You, Lord!*

Mrs. Goodman waited at the wagon with a few blankets and made a bed for the boy as Lillian carried him out.

Once he was settled into the wagon, Lillian turned to Mrs. Goodman. "Please let Mr. Colton know as soon as he returns that we've gone to the doctor. Hopefully I'll pass him on the road, but I don't know."

Sam, the man who'd gotten the wagon ready, piped up. "He probably won't come that way, Miss Lillian. He was in an all-fired hurry to get back here, so he'll probably take the shortcut from the pass."

Mrs. Goodman must've sensed her worry. "Don't worry, dearie. I'll let him know. You just get our little Jimmy boy to town. I'll go out and let the other men know, too."

Lillian climb up into the wagon as if she'd been doing it all her life. Sam held the horses and gave her a nod as Lillian picked up the reins. Now was not the time to tell them that she'd never driven a wagon before. She could do this. Jimmy needed her.

She slapped the reins to the horses' backs and they took off at a fast trot. Each hole, bump, and jostle to the wagon sent her gaze to the back to check on her little guy. She tried to sing for the first mile or so but kept choking on her tears. Maybe prayer would be better. "Lord, please, I need help getting to town. I don't even know if I remember how to get there, and I sure don't know where the doctor is. Please heal Jimmy. Please. I love him so much. And please help Mrs. Goodman find Woody. His son needs him. I need him. I can't do this alone, Lord, I can't. I need his strength." She poured her heart out to the Lord and cried until she could hardly see. Thankfully, the horses knew where they were going and kept up a steady pace.

At the edge of town, Lillian glanced back again. Jimmy's face was so flushed. His body limp.

Unsure where to go, she headed for the church, and if she couldn't find the pastor, then she would head to Mr. Stickle's store. She knew she could get him to help her.

As luck would have it — if she believed in luck — Pastor Seymour was in the cemetery tending the graves. Lillian called out to him as soon as she was close enough.

"Pastor Seymour, please help me!"

The man raced toward the wagon. "Is everything all right?"

Lillian pulled back on the reins to stop the horses. "I need the doctor, and I don't know where he is."

The minister looked in the back of the wagon and didn't hesitate to climb up on the wagon seat. "Let me take you there." He grabbed the lines and steered the team down the street.

"Thank you." Lillian took a moment to wipe her face. She was sure it was a mess and tear-stained, but she didn't care. All she cared about was getting Jimmy to the doctor.

They made it to the little clinic within moments, and the reverend made quick work of tying up the team and helping Lillian down. The doctor came out the door and helped to carry Jimmy in. "His fever is high. How long has he been like this?"

"A few hours." Lillian gulped down her emotions. "But he hasn't eaten much at all in several days."

"Fluids?" The doctor stared at her. "Has he had anything to drink?"

"A little water, but I'm afraid that's it."

"Let's get him back to the table and I'll examine him."

After they laid Jimmy down, Lillian couldn't stop the tears. His little body looked so frail. She reached out to brush his light brown hair off his forehead. "He's so hot, doctor."

The doctor nodded to Pastor Seymour, and the reverend wrapped an arm around her shoulders and guided her from the room.

Please don't let him die, Lord. Please . . .

Now was his chance. They'd loaded up the kid in the wagon — he looked like he was dead — and that nanny lady took off toward town. He'd seen Colton ride off earlier, as well, and the men were all back at the pond digging some stupid trench.

He watched a few more minutes and saw the housekeeper hightail it out the other direction.

Perfect. His luck had changed. Darwin dashed down the hill, staying low and close to the trees. When he reached the house, he ran upstairs and up to the attic. It might take him a while to find which floorboard it was under. Harry had been sure it was in the corner, but he couldn't remember which one. Darwin came close to smacking Harry upside the head. It was infuriating to be at his brother's mercy. Nevertheless, Darwin was determined to find that gold — his gold. He'd rip up every single floorboard in the attic if he had to.

Three corners and ten boards later, he reached under it and felt leather. Yes! He'd found it. He pulled out the sack and decided to rip up the rest of the boards just in case his fool brother had hidden more than one bag up here.

"Woody, is that you up there?"

Blast. That old housekeeper was back.

Darwin grabbed his sack and the bar he'd used to pry up the boards. Maybe the old hag wouldn't see him. He came down the attic stairs and waited.

"Woody?"

He peered around the corner, hoping to head down the other flight of stairs to the main level, but she turned and spotted him. Dagnabbit, the old woman was fast.

"Who are you? What are you doing here?" She narrowed her eyes.

Darwin cursed his luck, knowing that now he was going to have to kill again. But he didn't want these fool people finding his gold. It was his. And he was going to get it. He lunged at her with the bag held aloft. He dropped the pry bar but managed to knock the old woman off her feet.

But she was quick. She grabbed the bar and struck him in the shin.

"Owwwww!" he howled. "You fool of an old woman." He raised the bag again. "It's time to say good-bye."

CHAPTER TWENTY-ONE

The doctor came out of the little room in the back. Lillian jumped to her feet. "What is it, doctor? Is he going to be all right?"

The man's sleeves were rolled up to his elbows, and he removed his glasses. "He's got quinsy, miss. I'm afraid he needs an operation to remove his tonsils."

She sat back down. "An operation?" Her hand quivered as she covered her mouth. Poor little Jimmy.

"It's quite routine, I assure you. I can perform the operation right here."

The news helped restore a little blood to her brain. "So he'll recover?"

"Oh yes. Most boys his age are up and running into mischief in just a few days. He'll be chattering your ears off by Saturday, just you wait and see."

Well, she wasn't sure about the chattering, but she would take the running, even into mischief. Lillian stood again. "May I see him?"

"Of course. While you're talking with him, I'll get everything prepared for the surgery. You might let him know what's going to happen so he won't be overly afraid. Tell him that I'll help him go to sleep, and when he wakes up, he'll have a very sore throat, but that it will get better."

Lillian allowed the good reverend to lead the way. When they reached the room, she saw that Jimmy's eyes were open. They were a bit glazed, but he was looking at her.

"Oh, my sweet boy." She kissed his forehead and leaned over him to talk to him. "There's nothing to be afraid of. The doctor can make you all better. He's going to help you sleep, and then while you're sleeping he'll fix your throat. I'm sure it's already sore, but the doctor said it would be a little worse when you wake up. But it will heal quickly." She kissed him again.

Jimmy reached for her hand, and it melted her heart.

She squeezed his hand. "Jesus will be with you the whole time. And the reverend and I will be waiting right out there." She leaned in to hug him and found herself enveloped in a fierce hug from the boy. "I love you, Jimmy. When it's all over, I'll be right here. All right?"

He clung to her, but finally he pulled away and nodded.

"Don't forget, I love you. And your pa loves you." She smiled. "And don't forget, Mrs. Goodman and Mr. Whiskers love you, too."

A slight smile tipped the boy's lips.

The quiet pastor came forward and said a prayer over the surgery and Jimmy. Lillian found herself squeezing Jimmy's hand with every word the man said.

The doctor came back in. "Are we all ready?"

"Yes." She let go of Jimmy's hand and smiled. And prayed it was convincing.

Woody slowed his horse as he reached the part of the trench where he'd been digging. As he dismounted, he grabbed one of the new spades and looked at the sky. He had a few hours of light to dig in. If they didn't hurry up and get this trench finished, there'd be no hope for this year's crop. Between the drought and the extreme heat, they couldn't keep the olives from shriveling up for too much longer.

Sam ran to him waving his arms. "Mr. Colton, Mr. Colton!"

"What is it?" Woody knew by the look on his foreman's face that something wasn't right. Hopefully nothing else had broken.

"We've been waiting for you. It's your son." The man bent over to catch his breath. "Miss Lillian took him into town to the doctor. He had a really high fever."

"Is Mrs. Goodman with them?"

"No, sir. She stayed at the house in case you came back."

Woody fought with all the doubts flooding him. He could lose his son. He could lose his crop. *Lord, why are You doing this?*

"I can take care of things here, Mr. Colton. The men and I will continue to work hard."

"Thank you, Sam." He unloaded the other tools out of his saddlebags. "I'm going to stop by the house to let Mrs. Goodman know I made it back, and I'm riding into town. I'm sure she'll be able to help you with anything you need in case I need to stay in town."

"Yes, sir."

Woody turned his horse and raced for the house. He'd have to get a fresh horse, too. This one was spent.

He practically flew into the barn and unsaddled the bay gelding. He got Chestnut ready to go and tied him up to the post by the house. But something wasn't right. The front door stood wide open. He raced up the steps to the porch and into the foyer.

His heart raced in his chest. "Mrs. Goodman?" As his gaze went up the stairs, he saw her arm hanging over the edge. "Mrs. Goodman!"

Memories flashed back of the day they'd found Rebecca. A guttural cry escaped his throat. *"No!"* Taking the stairs three at a time, he reached the top and knelt down beside his beloved housekeeper. This woman and her husband had been by his side for so many years until James Goodman — Jim to his friends — had died of a heart attack. Little Jimmy was named after the strong man who'd been like a father to Woody.

He reached down and touched her face. It was still warm, but there was bruising on the left side of her face. He put his ear by her mouth and heard a ragged breath. She remained unconscious, and Woody tried to figure out what had happened. Had she fainted from the heat? He reached out to undo the buttons at her neck and he saw the unmistakable marks. Someone had tried to strangle her. He all but collapsed on the step and saw the pry bar and the blood. Woody hadn't noticed blood on his housekeeper, but when he lifted her head and shoulders up, the back of her dress was blood soaked. No!

Gingerly, he lifted the woman into his arms and then took the steps slowly. He'd have to hitch up the wagon and get her into town.

Jimmy! His son was at the doctor right now, and that meant that Lillian had taken the wagon. Woody would have to race to the brining barn and get the other wagon. *Lord, I could use some help here.*

He made it out to the porch and laid his faithful housekeeper down. "Hang in there, *dearie.*" His voice cracked at the use of her beloved endearment. "We're going to get you help."

Without a second to lose, Woody rang the bell by the porch. Hopefully one of the men would come running.

Miguel rounded the corner before Woody let go of the rope. Thank God for answered prayer.

"Boss?" The man spied Mrs. Goodman.

"I need you to run as fast as you can to the brining barn and get the old wagon hitched up. I've got to get Mrs. Goodman to town. She's hurt pretty bad."

Miguel ran off without another word.

Woody went inside and wet down a towel to lay over Mrs. Goodman's face. He found a few blankets in the closet and would use those to cushion her in the wagon. As he ministered to the older woman, his gut clenched. As soon as he brought Mrs. Goodman in, he knew what conclusion the people would come to. And it wouldn't be pretty.

The older woman moaned. Her eyelids fluttered.

"Mrs. Goodman . . . Mrs. Goodman . . . can you hear me?"

She mumbled something and then winced and cried out in pain.

"Who did this to you?" His heart broke. Who would do such a thing? And why? Twice he'd failed to protect those he loved. The sound of horses brought his head back up.

Miguel made it back in record time with the wagon. He set the brake, then jumped down and held the bridle strap of one of the horses while Woody tossed the blankets to him and then carried Mrs. Goodman down. He carefully placed her on the blankets.

He turned then to Miguel. "Please tell the men what happened. We'll need someone to guard the house. Someone broke in and attacked Mrs. Goodman." Woody noticed the blood on his hands and wiped them against his pants.

"What about the irrigation, sir?"

Woody climbed into the driver's seat and picked up the reins. "Right now all I care about is getting Mrs. Goodman to the doctor. Tell Sam he's in charge and to do whatever he can. I'm going to need all of you working." He shook his head. "No, I'm going to need a miracle." Woody released the brake and slapped the lines against the horses' backs.

"*Sí.*" Miguel nodded, his expression most somber. "We'll take care of everything, Mr. Colton."

The long road ahead of him was a bumpy one, but Woody pushed on. He couldn't allow anyone else to die because he hadn't been there.

But as the light waned and Mrs. Goodman's moans increased, he wondered if he would make it to town in time.

And would he ever get to see his son again? Or would the townspeople just string Woody up from the nearest tree?

Chapter Twenty-Two

Someone kept patting his face. "Jimmy . . . wake up, Jimmy."

It wasn't his father. And it wasn't the reverend. But another man was telling him to wake up. He didn't want to. The bed was warm and his throat hurt. He was tired of his throat hurting.

"Miss Porter, maybe if you came over here and spoke with him. He doesn't want to wake up for me, but his eyes keep fluttering." The man's voice stopped.

Then he felt a kiss on his forehead. "Hey, sleepyhead. It's time to wake up." Miss Lillian's voice washed over him. He tried to open his eyes.

Everything was blurry at first, but when the haze cleared, there she was. Right above him. Smiling.

"There's my big guy." Her smile got even bigger. "The operation is all done. And the doctor said you did great. So in a few days, you'll be feeling all better."

He nodded.

She leaned in and hugged him. "I love you so much, Jimmy."

That made him smile. She loved him and hugged him just like Mama used to.

The man came back — he must be the doctor. "How are you feeling?"

Jimmy looked to Miss Lillian.

The doctor chuckled. "It's okay. You can just whisper. I don't want you talking too much the next few days, but it won't hurt you."

Jimmy shook his head.

Miss Lillian touched the doctor on the arm and whispered, "He hasn't spoken aloud since his mother died."

The doctor nodded and looked back at Jimmy. "That's all right. You just rest, and I'll make sure that Miss Porter knows exactly what you need." The man took Miss Lillian by the arm and walked her out of the room.

"I'll be back in just a minute," she called over her shoulder.

Jimmy wanted her to stay. He didn't like being alone. All the happenings of the past few days came back to him. Church, visiting Mama's grave, their picnic, and then the bad man coming back. Jimmy shivered and closed his eyes. He had hoped so much that the bad man was dead.

"Is something bothering you, son?" Pastor Seymour's voice came from the corner.

Jimmy opened his eyes and saw him.

The reverend stood and came to his side. "I'm here if you need me, son." The man grabbed his hand and squeezed. "Why don't we pray?"

For several minutes the nice minister prayed for Jimmy to heal and for everything to go well so that he could go home and be with his family right away. But Jimmy prayed a little differently. God was the only One who knew the truth. The only One who could protect them all from the bad man.

God knew the words that Jimmy couldn't say and why he couldn't say them.

Lillian stood outside the doctor's office and breathed in the fresh evening air. The heat had been so intense for weeks, it was nice to feel a cool breeze tonight. The sun had long set, but there was still light to enjoy the evening. Lots of people were out and about in town, and she found the noise and ruckus made her long for the quiet of the farm. But the doctor assured her that after a night or two she'd be able to bring Jimmy home to finish his recovery. His fever had already diminished, and he'd had several sips of water before falling back asleep.

She stretched her limbs one more time and prayed that Woody would make it back into town soon. As she turned to go back into the clinic, the reverend was coming out.

"If you don't mind, I think I'll head on home now. My wife is used to me disappearing, but she'll start to worry if I don't show up for supper."

"Thank you, pastor. I can't tell you how much it meant to have you here today."

"If you need me, just send someone for me." He tipped his hat to her. "I'll keep praying."

"Thank you."

The man left, and as she watched him walk away, a wagon came barreling down the street. Reverend Seymour stopped.

Lillian raced down the stairs. "Woody!"

He climbed down from the wagon and caught her as she jumped into his arms and hugged him tight. "I'm so glad you made it!" Her words rushed out. "He's going to be fine. Just fine. He had quinsy and had to have an operation to have his tonsils removed, but he's already made it through the surgery just fine and he woke up and —"

Woody's hand came over her mouth. His

339

mouth formed a grim line. "It's Mrs. Goodman, Lillian. It's not good." He gently lowered her until her feet touched the ground again.

Looking into his deep brown eyes, she shivered. Something shook her to the core. "What's wrong?" She followed his gaze to the back of the wagon.

Reverend Seymour looked over the side to where the older woman lay unnaturally still. "What happened?"

Woody lowered his eyes to hers again. "I don't know. I had come into town for tools and went back to the irrigation ditch to dig when John told me what had happened with Jimmy. I raced back to the house to get a fresh horse and to let Mrs. Goodman know that I had heard and was headed into town. When I got to the front door, it was standing wide open and she was collapsed at the top of the stairs."

"Oh no." Lillian went to her friend. "Oh no. Mrs. Goodman . . ." Tears shook her frame. "Who would do this to you?"

"I'll tell you who did this!" The sheriff's loud voice boomed across the street. He stomped toward them. "The same man who murdered his wife. I'd heard tell the Colton boy was in the clinic, and I came to see why. This is even worse than I thought!" Several

340

men came to join them from across the street.

The reverend came forward with his hands up. "Now, wait just a minute, sheriff. Mr. Colton did not kill his wife. And why would he bring Mrs. Goodman to the doctor for help if he was the one who did this to her?"

"I don't rightly know, *reverend*," Hobart sneered, "but I don't have the mind of a murderer. It's all too clear what has happened here." The man waved at the woman lying in the wagon. "Look at her bruised face! I'll wager she's been beaten just like Rebecca Colton, and by the same man."

The men behind him murmured as yet more people began to gather.

The sheriff seemed to feed off the growing crowd. "What?" He got in Woody's face. "Did you throw this one down the stairs, too? What'd you do to your boy?"

Lillian pushed forward and stood between the sheriff and Woody. "How dare you? You don't even have any proof! Mr. Colton had been in town buying tools needed for the farm when Jimmy got really sick. I brought Jimmy into town and Mrs. Goodman stayed to let Mr. Colton know what had happened."

"Exactly." The sheriff nodded. "You

341

weren't there, so how would you know? Your testimony means nothing."

Woody seemed to be at his wits' end. He pointed his finger right into the middle of the sheriff's chest. "I didn't hurt Mrs. Goodman, nor did I kill my wife." He glanced around at the growing crowd. "I'm pretty much sick and tired of being accused of something I had no part in."

"Once again a woman in your household is beaten — maybe she'll even die," Hobart countered. "That seems too much for coincidence."

"It does, doesn't it?" Woody all but growled. "I think you probably hit the nail on the head when you said the same man who murdered my wife did Mrs. Goodman this harm. But I'm not that man." He leaned closer to the sheriff. "Do you hear me?"

"I hear you just fine, but I don't believe you." Calls of support for the sheriff came from the crowd.

Lillian couldn't help but wonder where Woody's friends were. Why was no one there to lend him support?

"I don't much care what you believe," Woody said. "I didn't do anything to hurt either woman."

"Do you have witnesses who can defend

your innocence?" The sheriff crossed his arms and narrowed his eyes. "Well?"

Lillian couldn't take any more. "What about the men who work for Mr. Colton? Have you talked to them? What if they saw something? They were there waiting to let Woody know about his sick son. Who just had surgery, I might add." She placed her hands on her hips. Standing up to bullies seemed to be her new calling in life. "I won't stand for you accusing a man falsely. And when Mrs. Goodman — who needs medical attention immediately — wakes up, I'm sure she will be able to clear it all up."

"It's all right, Lillian. You don't have to fight this battle for me." Woody looked at her for a long moment and then turned back to the sheriff. "Now, I suggest you get out of my way so I can get Mrs. Goodman the help she needs."

The sheriff didn't move. "Or what? You gonna beat me up, too?" Someone in the crowd had the audacity to laugh out loud. Others just encouraged the sheriff to arrest Woody right then and there.

The doctor came out of the clinic. "What is going on here?" He spotted the wagon and Mrs. Goodman. "Good grief, men! Get this woman inside." He turned to the sheriff. "I suggest you get rid of this crowd now,

Sheriff Hobart."

The lawman turned to Woody. "We're not finished yet."

The crowd roared in approval.

Lillian stood her ground and stared the man down. "We'll be in the clinic, sheriff. I suggest you do your job and go find who almost killed my friend!"

The hours passed in a slow torture of waiting. Woody watched his son sleep and prayed for Mrs. Goodman. The woman had been there for him for years. She was family. How did this happen? *Again!* Whoever beat Mrs. Goodman must've been the one who killed Rebecca. Woody didn't know how to prove it, but in his gut he knew it was true.

He clenched and unclenched his fists. If he didn't get ahold of his anger, who knew what he would do? And that wouldn't be good. Jimmy needed him. The farm needed him. Lillian and Mrs. Goodman needed him. If only that rat of a sheriff would do his job and find the real criminal. Why were the men of this town allowing someone to terrorize their women?

Lillian paced the floor across the room, her hands folded in front of her face and her lips moving but no words coming out.

She must be praying, too.

He stood and was drawn to her. Touching her shoulder, he waited for her to open her eyes. "Why don't we pray together?"

Tears streaked down her cheeks. She nodded, "I'd like that very much."

Beside Jimmy's bed, Woody took Lillian's hands in his. His heart lurched and his stomach churned as he fought the anger and the grief. "Father, right now we come to You a mess. Lord, You know I'm dealing with my anger, and I need Your help. Thank You for bringing Jimmy through surgery and for Lillian having the wisdom to bring him in to the doctor when she did." He swallowed back the tears. "Thank You for my boy, Lord. Help him to heal completely. But right now we are hurting and grieving for Mrs. Goodman, too. She looked really hurt. Please help the doctor to know what to do and Lord . . . please . . ." — he sniffed — "please heal her. She means so much to this family, and she's just an innocent woman caught in the middle of something awful. I ask, Lord, no, I'm pleading with You, that You would bring the truth to light. I ask all these things in Jesus' name."

Lillian's soft voice washed over him then. "Father, thank You so much for bringing Jimmy this far. Please heal him totally. I pray that You would also help him talk again. We don't know what's holding him back, but, Lord, You do. I also come to You now, Lord, on behalf of Woody. He's had to bear so much heartache and shame and lies and gossip because of all this. Please help this town and everyone around here and especially the sheriff to see the truth. We need to find the killer, Lord. And that man needs You. Because we know we'd all be in the same boat if it weren't for You. I pray that You would heal Mrs. Goodman and that You would turn this town around for Your glory. In Jesus' name I pray. Amen."

When he opened his eyes, she was staring at him with her big green eyes. Her long dark hair had come loose from the pins, and even though it was disheveled, it was natural and beautiful. She didn't release his hands, and he was glad. Something in that moment cracked the shell around his heart. He felt closer to God, and he felt drawn to Lillian. And it didn't hurt to feel drawn to her. There was no guilt and no heartache. Only joy and hope.

The doctor cleared his throat at the doorway. "I'd like to speak to you both about Mrs. Goodman."

Lillian didn't jump back in shock or pull away from him in fear. Instead, she held on to one of his hands, and they followed the doctor down the hall together. When they reached another room, he held out his hand for them to enter.

He followed them in and sat down. "Woody, I'm glad you got her here when you did. The poor woman has six broken ribs, and one was perilously close to puncturing her lung. In fact, it's a miracle that both her lungs weren't punctured from these injuries."

"Will she make it?" He felt his voice crack on the question.

The older man rubbed his neck. "I can't say for certain, but the chances are good." He looked down at his hands. "Once we get past the first few days. She's got the broken ribs, a broken leg, and a broken arm and collarbone. The bruising is substantial over her whole body, and there are lacerations on her back, but miraculously there seems to be no head trauma other than that bruise on her cheek. The attacker probably slapped her."

"It looked like he tried to strangle her, too," Woody added. "I saw marks on her neck."

The doctor nodded. "I saw them, too, but it doesn't appear the man caused much damage. He didn't crush the windpipe.

Maybe he heard someone coming and stopped. Hopefully she wasn't long without air. We should know in a few days. I'm giving her some medicine to see that she rests without pain."

"But we need for her to tell us who did this." Lillian stepped forward. "I don't want her to hurt, but neither do I want them to take Woody to jail for something he didn't do."

The doctor looked at her and then turned his focus to Woody. "I believe you when you say you had nothing to do with this, but Mrs. Goodman is in no shape to be questioned. It's going to have to wait. I'll let the sheriff know that, too."

Woody ran his hand through his hair. "Is there anything we can do?"

The doctor shrugged. "She will be in a great deal of pain for several weeks. That will be the hardest. And then the lack of mobility will frustrate her, I'm sure. As long as there hasn't been any major internal bleeding, I think she will recover. But again, it will take a great deal of time."

Woody leaned in and touched his housekeeper's hand. "She's a fighter. I know that. Do whatever it takes. I'll pay you whatever it costs."

The doctor shook his head. "I'm not worried about money right now. For the time, our challenge will be to get her past these first few days."

Woody looked back to the doctor. "You said, once we get past the first few days. Exactly what did you mean?"

The doctor sighed and his brow furrowed. "There's so much we don't know about the brain. As I said, I couldn't find any apparent trauma to the head, but she appears to be comatose — whether that is from the intense amount of pain she is enduring or from the physical trauma to her body, I don't know. As I mentioned, I will keep her medicated to keep her from as much pain as possible, but we also want her to regain consciousness. That is very important. If she doesn't wake up in the next few days, I will be less optimistic about the outcome."

Lillian put a hand to her mouth and sobbed.

Woody pulled her into his arms and looked at the doctor. "Thank you, doctor. I'm so sorry we had to meet under these circumstances."

The man nodded.

Woody nodded as well. "And thank you for all you've done for my son and for Mrs. Goodman. She's an important part of our family."

The doctor rubbed his neck. "If you'll excuse me, I am going to try to get some rest. My quarters are just upstairs, so please ring the bell if you see that either of the patients needs anything. I would ask that someone stays with each of them, as these next few hours are crucial."

Lillian took a deep breath and faced the doctor. "Thank you, sir. We can trade off. I'd like to stay with Mrs. Goodman for a bit if that's all right."

The doctor touched her shoulder. "Keep talking to her. It might help her wake up."

She nodded and the doctor left.

Woody still had his arm draped around her shoulders and didn't want to leave her, but he knew it was what they needed to do. "Will you be all right?"

She sniffed and wiped at her cheeks. "Yes. I just need to pull myself together. I was so worked up over Jimmy earlier and now Mrs. Goodman. I think my emotions are catching up with me."

"That's understandable." He squeezed her shoulder again. "I'll be right down the hall if you need me."

Woody dreaded leaving her, but he ached to see his son again. The morning, he feared, would bring his toughest day yet. The sheriff wanted to blame him not only for beating Mrs. Goodman but also for killing his wife. And the townspeople seemed riled up enough to become a lynch mob.

As he sat beside his son's bed, he brushed the light brown hair off the boy's forehead. God had given him so much. There was a time, even recently, when Woody was too tired to fight. He'd been ready to give up. His grief and burdens too much to bear. But things were different now.

He didn't know how God would do it, but Woody knew that He could. The storm might be coming, but if he could weather it, there just might be something beautiful on the other side.

He hoped and prayed that it would be so.

Glancing out the window, he saw the sun coming up. *Lord, the only way I'm going to make it through this is with Your strength. I don't have it. Please help us all. . . .*

CHAPTER TWENTY-THREE

Banging in the distance brought Lillian out of a deep sleep. Who was knocking? Where was she? As she sat up, the events of the past day collided with her brain. She stretched and looked at Mrs. Goodman. The woman hadn't moved at all.

Lillian leaned in and kissed the older woman's cheek. "I love you, dearie. I'll be right back."

She attempted to smooth her dress, but it was a rumpled mess after the last day and night, and she really didn't care. But the closer she got to the door, the more noise she heard. And it wasn't a pleasant sound.

The doctor was already there. With his hands out. "Now what seems to be the problem? I've got patients in here who need their rest to recover, and your ruckus is not helping the situation."

Lillian came up behind him and watched the sheriff strut up the steps. "I'm here to arrest Mr. Woody Colton."

She burst forward. "On what charges?"

"Attempted murder and murder!"

The crowd roared with voices and cheers.

She shook her head and crossed her arms. "This is ridiculous, sheriff, and you know it."

"I know no such thing, young lady. Now, I did what you suggested and interviewed Mr. Colton's men." He waved his arm.

Lillian watched as Sam, Miguel, and the others came forward. "Good."

"And with their testimony, I'm here to arrest Mr. Colton."

"What?" She couldn't believe this man. She wanted to wring his neck but knew that wasn't a very Christian thought.

The doctor turned to her. "Go get Mr. Colton. I'll keep everyone outside."

She nodded and hurried down the hallway. When she got to Jimmy's room, the boy's eyes were open and he was smiling at his pa. But Woody was fast asleep in the chair, his head leaned back against the wall. She went to Jimmy and kissed his forehead. "I need your father, and then I'll be right back, all right?"

The little boy nodded and closed his eyes.

Lillian tapped Woody's shoulder, but he didn't budge. "Woody," she half whispered.

"Woody. Wake up!"

Still nothing.

So she got closer and ran her hand down his face and patted his cheek. "Woody." Inches from him, she was startled when he opened his eyes. Those chocolate-brown eyes drew her in, and she wanted to sob in his arms. But now wasn't the time. She had to be strong.

"The sheriff is here." She backed away and waited for him at the door.

The soft look that had been in his eyes as he awakened slowly turned hard. "I'm afraid this isn't going to be pretty, Lillian. I need you to watch over Jimmy and Mrs. Goodman for me until it's all cleared up."

Having already heard the sheriff's intentions, she nodded. "I'll be by your side, Woody."

"I appreciate that."

He looked down at Jimmy. "I had been waiting for you to wake up." He smiled. "You are one tough little guy. I know your throat is sore, but the doctor tells me that's going to pass in a few days. Then we'll get you home to Mr. Whiskers." Jimmy reached out and squeezed Woody's hand and returned his father's smile.

Woody's joy faded, however, as he glanced at Lillian and then sighed. "Son, things are

354

going to get kind of rough for a little while. Some of the people out there think I'm to blame for hurting your mama and Mrs. Goodman."

Jimmy's face scrunched, and he shook his head and looked at Lillian as if for answers. She came to his side. "Someone hurt Mrs. Goodman, but she's all right." Tears came to the boy's eyes and his lip quivered.

Woody reached out and gently turned Jimmy's face toward his. "Son, I need you to be strong and pray. Miss Lillian will take care of you and Mrs. Goodman until I can be back with you." He leaned down and kissed the boy's forehead. "I love you."

Jimmy nodded, but remained mute.

Woody took Lillian's elbow and led her toward the door.

As they reached the front, Lillian knew he'd heard what people were saying out in the street. They walked out onto the porch together. The doctor closed the door behind them, giving Lillian a sad smile. She grabbed on to Woody's arm.

The sheriff came forward again. "You're under arrest, Colton."

"And what are the charges?" This came from George Stickle. He and a group of Woody's supporters came forward.

She felt Woody's arm flex under her

fingers. But he remained calm, his face an emotionless mask.

"Attempted murder and murder. What did you think?" The lawman spat on the ground.

George shook his head. "We heard what happened, and we think you're jumpin' the gun here."

The crowd supporting Hobart moved closer.

"Your men are here, Woody," Lillian whispered to him.

Woody spoke up. "What did my men have to say, sheriff? Didn't you get their testimonies?"

"I shore did, Colton. Two of them hadn't seen you for hours, and while Sam's story corroborates yours, it still doesn't prove you didn't beat Mrs. Goodman." The sheriff smiled and pulled Miguel toward him. "But see, it's Miguel's testimony that really turned things around."

The sweet man who'd worked for Woody for years held his arms out and looked as if he wanted to cry. "I didn't say anything against Mr. Colton, sheriff. He's a good man."

The sheriff laughed. "Ah, but what you did say clinched it for me."

Lillian didn't like this man. How could he be a man of the law and be so horrible?

"What exactly did Miguel say?" She knew the worker would never tell a lie against his boss.

"He told me that he saw Mr. Colton carry Mrs. Goodman out of the house, and her blood was on his hands."

The sheriff's supporters went wild with questions and accusations and horrible words for Woody. Lillian gasped, shaking her head. "But he was carrying Mrs. Goodman. She was bleeding, so of course Woody had blood on his hands! Miguel was coming in answer to the bell. He didn't just happen to see Woody sneaking off with Mrs. Goodman's unconscious body. Why would Woody bother to ring the bell for help if he wanted Mrs. Goodman dead?" She'd heard the whole story from Woody the night before.

"To cover his own tracks!" The sheriff hurled himself forward and grabbed Woody's arms.

As Woody's arm was yanked from her grasp, Lillian watched his eyes. She didn't know how, but somehow he was remaining calm. Even as the sheriff handcuffed him.

She moved forward and put her hands on Woody's chest. "I'll be here for you, Woody. I know you didn't do it. I know it! I'll do everything I can. I'll hire a lawyer. I'll —"

He cut off her words by kissing her forehead. His actions so stunned her that all
Lillian could do was stare in wonder. "Take
care of Jimmy and Mrs. Goodman. The men
will take care of the farm. It's time to leave
this in the good Lord's hands."

She nodded.

He gave her a sad smile. "Thank you for
believing in me."

"Always." The tears streamed down her
face, and she bit her lower lip to keep from
sobbing. She wasn't going to give this horrible crowd the satisfaction of seeing her fall
apart.

Then the sheriff dragged Woody away
from her, and most of the crowd followed.
She had to get to the truth before this crazy
town took matters into its own hands.

Woody's men came up to her, along with
George and the others who supported
Woody. Sam held out his hat. "We're so
sorry, Miss Lillian. We had no idea the
sheriff was going to twist our words. We
know Mr. Colton is innocent."

"Thank you, Sam." She looked each man
in the eye. "And all of you. Thank you."

"What can we do?" Miguel looked awful.
"We have to do something."

She nodded. "First, we have to pray for
the truth to be revealed. Second, we can't

let the olive crop fail. Not now. So the best thing you can do for Woody is to get that irrigation ditch finished and help the crop survive. You know far more about olives than I do."

Sam shook his head. "It won't be easy. Mr. Colton does the work of ten men. With him gone and the time we've lost, I don't even know if it's possible to save the trees."

"But we must," Lillian insisted.

George Stickle nodded toward the other men. "Maybe we can think of something."

Sam nodded. "We'll do our best!" He looked at the other men. "Water is the key. We should get right back to the farm."

A deputy came running back toward them and shouted at the men. "You fellas can't go anywhere. The sheriff sent me back here to get ya. You'll have to testify as soon as the judge gets here — and he's on his way — so he doesn't want ya goin' anywhere."

Lillian's shoulders fell. How would they be able to save the crop now? It was as if the sheriff was deliberately trying to ruin Woody. She put her hands on her hips and narrowed her eyes. Well, she wasn't about to let that happen.

Not to the man she loved.

Loved?

She watched Woody's men as the deputy

led them away. This sudden revelation kept her from further protest. She was in love with Woody. She'd never been in love before. When had this happened? How had it happened? Did Woody feel the same way? After all, he had kissed her forehead. For a moment the realization panicked her. She was in love with a man the town of Angels Camp planned to hang.

Lillian shook her head. "I don't know what to do." She glanced heavenward. "I don't know what to do."

George Stickle patted her shoulder. "Try not to worry, Miss Porter. We'll figure something out. There're more folks here who believe in Woody than you'd think. We'll just put our heads together and figure out something."

"He's going to need a lawyer." Lillian looked at George, tears blurring her vision.

"I'll take care of that." Stan Van Dyke stepped forward. "My brother is a lawyer over in Modesto. I'll go wire for him right now."

Lillian smiled in gratitude. "Thank you. Thanks to all of you, just for showing up and proving to Woody that somebody cares."

Woody sat on the hard cot in the cell and smiled. What had come over him? It was

360

like an instant peace flooded him, and he knew exactly where it had come from.

God.

He'd finally given his burdens over to the Lord, and his heavenly Father made sure he knew that everything would be okay. It was an experience Woody never had before. Even with all the fear banging at the door to his heart, he knew he could trust God for the outcome. And even if that outcome meant he went home to be with the Lord, Woody was okay with that. Always before he'd worried about Jimmy's well-being, but now with Lillian, he knew Jimmy would be just fine. She and Mrs. Goodman would see to it.

If Mrs. Goodman survived. The thought of his housekeeper and friend dying caused his heart to ache, but even at that Woody knew God's hand was upon them and he was at peace.

He shook his head. It didn't make any sense.

But it didn't have to make sense. Tomorrow he might be flat on his face in worry and doubt . . . today even. But right now he would rest in the Lord.

Woody thought of his son and the love they shared. Earlier Jimmy had squeezed his hand and smiled. So much to be thankful for, and Woody wanted to focus on the good things.

And then there was Lillian. From the moment she'd seen him drive up and jumped into his arms, Woody knew. He loved her. He knew she would never have the slightest doubt about him. Lillian would never believe him capable of hurting Mrs. Goodman, and she would fight for him and for his son. If anything happened to Woody, Lillian would take care of Jimmy and save the farm for him.

Footsteps sounded down the hall. The skinny deputy looked at him. "You've got a visitor. That reverend you asked for wants to see ya." He unlocked the door and let the minister in. "But I'm only allowed to give you fifteen minutes. That's it."

Woody nodded and the deputy walked off.

Pastor Seymour looked at him. "I know this is awful hard, Woody. Just so you know, I'm behind you, and there's a lot of other folks who are, too."

"Thank you, pastor. But that's not why I asked you to come down here."

"Certainly. Why don't we pray?" The pastor removed his hat.

Woody reached out and touched the minister's hand. "While I definitely want to pray with you before you go, I need you to help me with something else."

"All right. What do you need?"

"I need help with some documents. I need to dictate my will to you today and make sure that it will be legal . . . just in case . . ." He paused and let go a heavy breath. "In case I die."

CHAPTER TWENTY-FOUR

The doctor checked Jimmy over, and Lillian watched from the corner of the room and tapped a finger to her chin. Two days had passed since they'd taken Woody away. They wouldn't let her see him, and Mrs. Goodman hadn't woken up yet. All of Woody's men had been shut up in the hotel so that they couldn't leave before giving their testimonies. That smelled a bit fishy to her, but no one asked her opinion.

The doctor said something to Jimmy, and the boy's giggled response resonated in Lillian's heart.

The older man came over to her and took hold of her elbow. "Miss Lillian, if I might have a word with you, please?"

"Sure." She pasted on a smile. "I'll be right back, Jimmy."

The little boy nodded.

The doctor led her outside the door and stopped. "Miss Porter, I'm afraid Jimmy won't be able to leave the clinic as soon as I'd hoped."

She put a hand to her throat. "Why? Is he okay?"

He patted her shoulder and walked with her down the hall. "It's nothing to be too worried about, but I'm afraid he's weak. You'd told me that he refused to eat or drink hardly anything since Sunday before he got sick. Well, since he didn't have nourishment for those few days and he's so little, his body is taking a while to recover." He folded his hands behind his back. "I'm sure he will have a full recovery; it will just take a little longer. I've ordered some hearty meals for the child starting tomorrow — of course they will be soft, but more substantial than we would normally recommend — because he needs to build up his strength. But today he will have lots of broth and liquids.

"I'm going to have food brought for you, as well. You don't look any too good at this point, and I won't have you collapsing on my watch." He looked her up and down with a most serious expression. "Also, I am going to have a cot brought in. You'll need somewhere to sleep while you're in town. It's not much, but I'm guessing it will be better than a chair."

"Thank you, doctor."

"My pleasure." He took her hand. "I figure with you acting as my nurse, it's the least I can do." He gave her hand a squeeze. "I am very sorry for all that you are having to go through right now. Rest assured I will be praying for you all."

The kind doctor released her to walk toward Mrs. Goodman's room. Lillian pondered what to do next.

The farm needed tending and there were no men to tend it. So far the sheriff hadn't let Woody's workers go, and to make matters worse, he declared Woody's place the scene of a crime and forbid anyone to go out there. Mrs. Goodman hadn't woken up, but she would need help as soon as she did. Jimmy couldn't go home yet until he built up his strength, and Woody needed a lawyer and a miracle.

Pacing the hall, Lillian prayed for divine guidance. She couldn't be in all these places at once. So the question was, what did they need the most? She didn't care about what the sheriff said regarding the house. She needed clothes and a few other things. Not only that, but she had to do what she could to save the trees.

"But what can someone like me do?" she

muttered, shaking her head. "Lord, I need help."

Mrs. Seymour came through the outside door at that moment and waved at Lillian in the hall. "I thought I'd come over and see what I could do to help you."

Lillian lifted her eyes toward the ceiling. *Thank You, Lord.*

An hour later, Lillian slapped the reins on the horses' rumps and got the wagon moving down the road at a quick pace. She'd heard that the sheriff had ridden out to check the theft of a pig on one of the nearby farms. If she got home quickly enough, she could dig on the trench for a couple of hours and make it back to town to try to visit Woody before she went back to be with Jimmy and Mrs. Goodman for the night. Mrs. Seymour had agreed to watch both patients for her for the rest of the day.

As long as she had breath, Lillian would work herself to the bone to do all she could to save the farm and Woody. Mr. Van Dyke's brother was due in at any time, so he would handle the legalities involved with Woody's arrest. Soon he'd have Woody out of jail. At least she hoped he would.

If Mrs. Goodman could just wake up, she

would clear Woody's name for sure, but there was no guarantee of that happening before the judge came. And they had an olive crop that would die without enough water.

She didn't bother to unhitch the horses when she made it to the house. It would be faster if she could get the wagon out to the site of the trench anyway. So she ran inside to change into something suitable to wear while digging. She'd never even held a shovel, but she could do this. Mrs. Goodman had taught her to make biscuits and pie, so surely she could learn how to handle digging a trench. After all, Woody needed her. Her family needed her.

She found an old riding skirt she thought might work, but the problem was the skirt part. If only she could wear a pair of denims like the men.

Woody was much bigger than she, but with a good belt, Lillian felt certain she could make a pair of his pants work. She went upstairs, pausing at the sight of dried blood where Mrs. Goodman had no doubt fallen. She made a mental note to clean it up before leaving. But if she did that, then the sheriff would know she'd gone against his demand that no one set foot on the farm.

"I'll worry about that later."

Lillian made her way to Woody's room and paused a moment at the unforgettable scent of his cologne. It was a simple room, but there were still the womanly touches that Rebecca Colton had no doubt applied. A man wouldn't have concerned himself with putting hand-crocheted doilies on the nightstands. Not only that, but the draperies and quilt were decidedly feminine. On top of the dresser Lillian spied a photograph and drew closer to inspect. It was a wedding photo of a much younger and carefree Woody and a lovely light-haired woman.

For a moment Lillian considered Rebecca Colton, waiting for some pang of jealousy to surface. There was none. The woman was beautiful, and from what Lillian knew, she had been a wonderful wife and mother. The love she held for her husband radiated from her face.

"I love him, too," Lillian whispered, touching her finger to Rebecca's face. "I love your son, as well. I promise to do for them whatever I can." Was Woody even ready to love again? She sighed and put the picture aside to go in search of trousers.

Feeling much more comfortable and ready to work, Lillian jumped up into the wagon with ease. It amazed her what a difference clothing could make. She felt at least twenty pounds lighter. Now if she could just manage to get the wagon out to the pond.

Last thing she knew, they were widening the trench at the pond to prepare it for enough flow to all the olive groves. The men had staked out the area to show the graduated width, and then Woody had told her that there were only a few more feeder trenches to dig.

It required more maneuvering than time to reach the pond. The path wasn't very wide, and the horses were rather agitated to be navigating through the brush. But once there, the clearing met with their approval. Thanks to the pond, there was some green vegetation to munch on and water to drink, and that seemed to assuage their anxiousness.

Lillian hopped down and surveyed what needed to be done. She could do this. She could. She pulled on a pair of Woody's work gloves. They, like the pants, were too large but would have to suffice. Grabbing a spade, she tried it out on the ground. It looked a lot easier when the men were doing it. The ground was hard and dry.

Within minutes, sweat drenched her neck and back. Women's corsets were not meant for this kind of work. But the thoughts of Woody in jail and Mrs. Goodman wounded and comatose pressed her forward. With each sharp thrust of the spade into the ground, she thought of the lies and gossip that had been spread. And as she pushed the tool through the crusty ground, she thought of how the truth would set things right. As she tossed the dirt behind her, she thought of how they could all start fresh.

And what would that look like? Well, Lillian could hope. As soon as the revelation had hit her at the clinic, she couldn't get the thought out of her mind. She did *love* Woody Colton.

She loved everything about him. His stubbornness. His quiet strength. His loyalty. His love for studying the Word. Even his brusqueness, his moodiness, and his temper. Every part of him was endearing to her. Maybe that's how God intended love to be. She didn't even know how or when it happened. But now she couldn't get his brown eyes out of her mind. The way he looked at her and made her feel important. The way he strode across the olive grove. The way he knelt in front of his son.

The way he prayed.

The way he'd held her in his arms as she cried.

Tears streamed down her face, mixing with the sweat and the dirt. She couldn't imagine life without him. It was definitely love.

Lord, we desperately need Your help. Woody needs to be released. Jimmy needs strength and healing. That poor boy has had more than his share of horrific moments. Mrs. Goodman needs healing and to come awake. And we need a miracle out here for the olives. Please don't let Woody lose his crop. Could You please send some rain? Or at least some help to keep digging? Thank You, God.

The shoveling was tedious and slow going. But she had lots to pray about and lots to think about. Her muscles would surely protest tomorrow, but if she kept going, she might be able to help save the crop. And that was worth every ache and pain.

After an hour, she'd made it about a foot. Rather than get discouraged, she started singing hymns. And if she had to go through every one she could remember and then start over again, she would. Drenched from head to toe in her own sweat, her clothing started to chafe with each shovelful she threw, but she refused to quit.

On the chorus to "Blessed Be the Name," Lillian heard a voice join hers. It startled her so much that she flung the shovel along with the dirt. But off in the distance was the answer to one of her prayers.

Harry.

He was half running, half skipping down the hill to the pond. When he reached her, they finished the chorus together, and Lillian gave him a kiss on the cheek and hugged him close.

"Harry, I'm so glad to see you." She pulled away. "You are a godsend."

He ducked his head. "Aw, thank you, Miss Lillian. I'm glad to see you, too. Why are you out here digging, and why are you wearing men's britches?"

Laughter bubbled up out of her. She must be quite the sight. "I'll tell you that in just a minute, but first tell me how you are — and where have you been? I was so worried about you that night when you ran off. Jimmy's father didn't mean to scare you like that."

He kept his head down. "I ran away because I thought he was mad at me. I would never ever, ever, ever hurt Jimmy. Ever. Never ever." He shook his head. "But I've been coming back and watching. When you sang today, I wanted to come. So I did."

"I'm so glad you did!" Tears sprang to her eyes again.

"What's wrong, Miss Lillian?"

"Jimmy got sick and had to have surgery, so I had to race him in to town to the doctor, and then someone attacked Mrs. Goodman at the house, and she's really hurt. And they've arrested Woody for it. And now all of Woody's workers are in town to testify, and if this trench doesn't get dug, then we won't be able to get the water to the trees, and we could lose the entire olive crop." She sat down on the ground, exhausted.

"Will Jimmy be okay? And Mrs. Goodman?"

She nodded. "Jimmy is getting stronger all the time. The surgery went well. But Mrs. Goodman still hasn't woken up, so we need to pray for her to wake up, okay?"

"Why did they put Mr. Woody in jail?"

"They think he hurt Mrs. Goodman, and they think he killed his wife."

"Oh. That's bad." Harry shook his head. "But he didn't do it?"

"No, Harry. Woody didn't do it."

"I can dig, Miss Lillian. I can dig fast. Can I help?"

"Do you understand what needs to be done?"

"No, but you can show me, right?"

She smiled and nodded. Tears threatened again. This big giant of a boy was so tenderhearted and sweet.

He reached down and helped her up. "We

can do this, Miss Lillian. We can. Let me help."

"All right." She spent the next half hour showing Harry everything she understood for the project. Hopefully Woody would be free and the men could come back soon. The next time she looked up, she knew she needed to get back to town. "Harry, you sure you're okay out here?"

"Uh-huh. I'll keep digging. Don't you worry."

"I'm not worried about the job, Harry. I know you'll do well. But I am worried about you as a person. I want to make sure you are okay." She reached up and brushed the hair off his forehead like she did Jimmy's.

He smiled down at her. "I'm good. I'm a hard worker."

"Yes, you are." She climbed back up in the wagon. "I've got to get back to town to check on everyone. I'll tell Jimmy I saw you and that you can't wait to go fishing again." She paused and wondered if she should warn Harry about the sheriff. "Harry, there's one other thing. The sheriff said nobody was to be out here on the property. If anybody comes, you should probably hide. Can you do that?"

He laughed. "I hide really good, Miss Lillian. Nobody can find me if I don't want them to."

Lillian nodded. "I know it might seem like we're breaking the law, and maybe we are, but this time the law is wrong." A confused look crossed Harry's face. "Don't worry about it, Harry. I'll explain it later."

He waved and smiled. "Okay. I'll go work."

"Thank you, Harry."

She drove the wagon back to the house and got a fresh change of clothes. It wouldn't do to go into town all filthy and dressed in men's trousers. She paused again at the scene of Mrs. Goodman's collapse and decided against cleaning it. If there was evidence, it could only help Woody — not hurt him. He didn't do this terrible thing, but someone had, and they deserved to be caught.

Lillian washed up and slipped into her clean clothes. While she was changing it dawned on her that she should pack a few things for Woody, Jimmy, and Mrs. Goodman. Then, as she was about to leave, a thought came that could only have been sent by the Lord for the care of one of His creatures. Mr. Whiskers needed someone to watch out for him. She found Mr. Whiskers in his box. He looked no worse for the wear, but Lillian knew he must be hungry and thirsty. She put a bit of water into a shallow bowl and then spied some leafy beet greens that Mrs. Goodman must have been working on before the attack.

"This ought to hold you." She left a few of the greens next to the water bowl.

Even though it would take extra time, she went in search of Harry once more. Harry eagerly agreed to check up on the rabbit every day and to give him water and fresh lettuce from the garden. Lillian thanked him.

"If you're hungry, I know Mrs. Goodman wouldn't mind if you looked around in the kitchen. I think the cookie jar is full, and I know there are other things in the cupboards."

Harry smiled and patted his stomach. "I get hungry a lot."

Lillian nodded and returned his smile. "I'm sure you do."

With everything tended, Lillian hurried back to the house. In her mind she went over everything she could think of that might need attention. The garden needed water like everything else, but there simply wasn't time. The only livestock were the horses, and they had been used for the wagons. Woody's were still in town. She sighed. There was so much to remember. She looked back to the house as she climbed up into the wagon again. Something unsettled her, but she didn't know what.

Lord, we need Your protection. Thank You for sending Harry.

As she drove back to town, she continued praying. There were too many difficulties in her life right now. Grandfather was sick and wouldn't speak to her. Woody was in jail, and Jimmy and Mrs. Goodman were in their sickbeds. She couldn't do this on her own.

When she reached the doctor's house, Mrs. Seymour came out to meet her. "Jimmy is getting a bit restless, but he's gotten a lot of nourishment today, and the doctor is happy about that."

"What about Mrs. Goodman?"

"No change. At least not yet. But we will keep praying."

"Thank you, Mrs. Seymour."

"I'll come back tomorrow." The pastor's wife smiled. "In the meanwhile, what do you plan to do about the team?"

Lillian looked at the horses and shook her head. "I figured I'd have them stabled. I don't even know where Woody's team is." She glanced around the street for some sign of them.

Mrs. Seymour nodded. "Joseph took them home. I'll have him come get your team, as well."

"Joseph?" She tried to remember who that might be.

"My husband," Mrs. Seymour replied. "I'll send him to tend to your team. Just come to the parsonage if you need them."

"Thank you again." Lillian shook her head, feeling the weariness of the day settle over her. "I honestly don't know what I would have done without you."

Lillian rushed in the door and went straight to Jimmy's room. He sat up in bed looking at a book.

"Look at you, young man. You look like you're feeling better." Lillian kissed his forehead.

Jimmy nodded and grinned at her.

"Do you like this book?"

Another nod.

"I hear you did very well this afternoon." She sat on the bed and snuggled up beside him. "Guess what I did?"

His brow lowered as though he were going to try to guess, but he just waited.

"I used a shovel for the first time today and dug part of the irrigation trench. Whew! It was hard work." She lifted her arm and flexed. "See? Don't my muscles look bigger already?"

Jimmy giggled.

Oh, how she loved that sound.

"Oh, and I checked on Mr. Whiskers. He's doing very well. Harry has agreed to watch over him for you."

Jimmy nodded and smiled. Lillian could see this news met with his approval.

"Well, while you keep looking at your book, I need to check on Mrs. Goodman and then go visit your pa, all right?"

He nodded again, then reached over to the side table. Picking up a piece of paper, he thrust it at her.

"You want me to bring this to him?"

Another nod.

"That I can do. Now you behave yourself and stay in bed. I'll be back in just a little bit."

She closed his door and ran into the doctor in the hallway. "Oh, I'm sorry."

"It's quite all right. I was hoping to be able to speak with you." The kindly man didn't look at all happy.

"What about?"

"I've heard news that the judge will be here next week."

"Goodness. The wheels of justice move pretty quickly."

"Well, they certainly do when you are a close family friend of the sheriff."

All air whooshed out of her. "Oh."

"I wanted you to be aware. Mr. Colton's

lawyer stopped by earlier to get my assessment of Mrs. Goodman and asked if I would give my testimony, as well. Rest assured I will do everything in my power to help."

She wrung her hands together. "Is there any sign that she might awaken soon?"

He shook his head and shrugged. "These things are difficult to predict. But I am hopeful."

"I am too." Lillian made herself take a deep breath and worked to calm her thoughts. "Would you mind keeping an eye on Jimmy while I see Mrs. Goodman for myself? And then I need to take a few things to Mr. Colton."

"Certainly. I can spare a half hour or so until you return, unless I have an emergency that comes in."

"Thank you. I think I'll go see Woody first and then come back to spend time with Mrs. Goodman. That way, I'll be able to hear Jimmy if he needs me."

She raced out the door of the clinic to the wagon and found Pastor Seymour just about to climb up and take the reins.

"Has there been any change?" He waited to mount the wagon.

"Jimmy is much better, but Mrs. Goodman remains unconscious." She reached into the back of the wagon for the things she'd brought. "I'm glad I caught you before you left. I almost forgot about these things." Tears pricked her eyes for the hundredth time that day, but she pasted on a smile. She couldn't allow for it all to overwhelm her. No matter what.

His expression grew quite serious. "I heard that the judge is coming in next week."

She nodded and bit the inside of her cheek. If she didn't leave soon, she'd certainly bawl like a baby in front of the man. "The doctor just told me. They certainly are anxious to string Woody up."

"Well, I feel confident that God has other plans. Woody has good friends and, from what I hear, a good lawyer."

Lillian wanted more than anything to take courage in that. She met the older man's gaze. "I hope — no, I pray that you're right. I've come to care quite deeply for him — for all of them."

The pastor smiled. "I know you have. Now don't let me keep you any longer. I have a feeling the best medicine for you will be to see Woody and know that he's all right."

Lillian nodded and turned on her heel. Exhaustion stumbled her steps, but she marched her way to the jail anyway.

She wouldn't let anything stand in the way of seeing the man she loved.

But to her disappointment, her determination couldn't get her past the sheriff. Ornery man. He adamantly refused her admittance, telling her women weren't allowed in the jail. Nevertheless, she wasn't going to give up.

Every day, for five days, Lillian returned and demanded to be allowed to see Woody.

On the sixth day, she went with an entourage of friends, including lawyer Van Dyke, who rattled off all sorts of legal jargon and threatened Sheriff Hobart with some kind of personal lawsuit.

"Fine. I'll let her in." The sheriff voiced his displeasure. "But you haven't heard the end of this. I'll take it up with the judge tomorrow."

The lawyer patted Lillian on the back. "That's quite all right, sheriff. We have a few things to take up with him, as well."

Hobart narrowed his eyes and waved at the gathering of people outside his jail. "Go on with you now. I'll let her see her precious Mr. Colton."

The others dispersed while the lawyer

gave Lillian some last bits of advice. He leaned close and whispered, "I'll be just down the street at the hotel where Woody's men are being held. That's another matter that isn't going to bode well for Sheriff Hobart. That's illegal detainment, and he'll answer for it."

Lillian nodded. She waited until Mr. Van Dyke was a few steps away before she turned to face Sheriff Hobart.

"I'm ready to see Mr. Colton."

The sheriff opened the door to the jail, but the scowl never left his face. "That confounded city lawyer said I have to let you in, but I don't have to let you stay very long."

CHAPTER TWENTY-FIVE

Woody heard Lillian before he saw her. She was giving the sheriff a piece of her mind — that was for certain — and it didn't sound like she was backing down.

He chuckled to himself. She was a lady, but she was a spitfire. Resilient. Stubborn. And he loved her. That realization had encouraged him throughout the day.

"Colton!" the sheriff yelled down the hallway, none too happy it seemed. "You've got a visitor." The rotund lawman stomped his way toward Woody's cell, with Lillian behind him. "Your fancy lawyer said I have to let her see you, but I can't let her in there, 'cause that ain't appropriate, and I don't trust you. You've got two minutes. That's it." The man stormed off.

Lillian smiled at Woody and held out his Bible. "I brought this for you. Thought it might bring you comfort and help fill the time."

He reached through the bars and took the Bible and laid it on his bed. "Thank you." He reached through the bars again and held out his hands.

She took them in hers and winced. Woody looked down at her hands. There were open but dry wounds — from the looks of it, blisters that had popped. "What in the world have you been doing?"

She blushed. "Ah . . . well . . . driving the wagon." She lowered her voice. "I drove back to the farm, only don't tell Sheriff Hobart." Lillian shrugged. "Forgot my gloves."

He nodded and tried to be gentler as he kept hold of her. "There's something I need to tell you, Lillian."

"I need to tell you something, too."

His heart did a little flip. "You go ahead. Ladies first."

"The judge is coming tomorrow, and he's an old family friend of the sheriff. Mr. Van Dyke says that indeed all the evidence against you is circumstantial and not very good at that. Jimmy is doing much better, but he will have to stay in the clinic until his strength returns and he's had enough nourishment. Mrs. Goodman still hasn't awoken." She bit her lip. "I think that's it. Oh, wait! The sheriff still hasn't allowed

Sam and the men to go back to the farm. Mr. Van Dyke said he's going to sue the sheriff and the town for false imprisonment and illegal detainment. There, I think that's it." She gave him a sad look and a sigh. "Okay, your turn."

"Lillian . . ." He wasn't as good at spilling information out. How could he tell her? "I've been doing a lot of thinking. And I need to tell you —"

"Time's up!" the sheriff bellowed.

Woody grabbed on to her hands tighter. Blasted Hobart.

Footsteps headed toward them.

No time to say all he'd planned. Instead, he blurted, "Lillian, I love you."

Her eyes rounded and she gasped.

The sheriff grabbed her shoulders and pulled her away from the cell and headed her down the hall. Poor woman. A glazed, shocked look covered her face. Woody sure messed that up.

But not more than a dozen steps down the hall, Lillian pulled away from her captor and raced back to Woody's cell. The sheriff huffed and marched after her. "Now, look here —"

But she was quick. Lillian leaned in toward the bars and smiled — mere inches from his face. "I love you, too." She turned on her heel and dashed back toward the stunned sheriff. "Thank you for your generous amount of time, Sheriff Hobart. I'll be certain to let everyone know about your gracious treatment." With an impish grin, she walked out the door.

Woody couldn't help but smile. Goodness, that woman did things to his heart.

As soon as the sun broke through the cave entrance, Darwin was ready to set out. He'd laid low long enough — nearly a week. The day before, he'd been determined to get some information on Colton and his housekeeper. Lucky for him, he'd managed to meet up with a group of miners who were headed to Angels Camp for supplies. He slipped in with them, heard all the gossip, then slipped out again. No one the wiser.

Colton was in jail, and his housekeeper and son were in the hospital. Better still, he'd learned that the sheriff wouldn't let any of Colton's men return to the farm. In fact, he wouldn't let anyone go to the farm. He wished he'd known sooner. He could have spent the last few days retrieving the rest of his gold. But there was no use moaning about it now. Fact was, nobody was looking for him, and nobody would be able to interfere with his task.

Life couldn't go better. It was almost as if he'd planned it this way.

He dragged Harry out of bed. "Come on. We've got to go get the rest of my gold today. And you need to show me where it is."

Harry's wide almond eyes seemed to light up as he nodded. He hurried to dress. "And then you're going to Mexico?"

Darwin stopped in his steps. "How'd you know that?"

"I heard you talking to yourself the other night."

This couldn't be good. If Harry thought Darwin was leaving him, he might not help find the gold. "I'm gonna take care of you first, Harry. Don't you worry about that. I'll make sure you don't have a thing to worry about." He patted his brother's shoulder, hoping that would seem brotherly.

Harry came around and hugged him. "I know. I know. I know. You talked about that, too." He danced around the mine's entrance. "Let's go get your gold. Then I can work." Darwin frowned, having no idea what the big oaf meant, but one thing was for certain. He'd have to refrain from talking to himself anymore.

Harry sang stupid songs all the way to the Colton place and every so often called out the name of random flowers. It annoyed Darwin, but he couldn't say anything. Ma had said Harry was special, but to Darwin he was just a dim-witted nuisance. Only one more day of this. One. More. Day. He could handle a day.

When they reached the house, Harry kept walking toward the olive groves and then to the barns. "I had to keep reburying it 'cause I didn't want no one to find it."

After a couple hours of digging, they'd pulled up three more bags. Harry was sure that he'd also carried a couple out to the Yosemite area, but they were small, and Darwin decided they weren't worth the trouble. Harry annoyed him too much.

That left two. The largest ones.

"Where's the rest, Harry?"

"Follow me. I'll show ya. I remembered real good."

They trekked back toward the house. The heat of the day was upon them at this point, and Darwin was sweating under the weight of the bags. One. More. Day. Then he'd be free to go on his way.

Harry stopped at the well.

"Why'd you stop?" Darwin looked around him.

"I put the big bags here."

"Where?" He looked around.

"There." The big galoot pointed straight down the well.

"You did what?!" Darwin dropped the sacks.

"I put 'em down the well." He toed the ground and tucked his hands behind him. "I told you that, 'member."

"No, I don't remember!" Darwin lost all patience and hit Harry with his hat. *Down* the well. Not *by* it.

Harry flinched but only shook his head. "Was that bad?"

Darwin threw his hat on the ground and let go a stream of curses. "How are we supposed to get them out?"

"I dunno." His brother wouldn't look at him now.

"Of all the stupid, idiotic things to do, Harry! I can't climb down there, and you definitely can't climb down there. There's no way to get my stinkin' gold!" He lunged for his brother and shook him by the shoulders. "We are not leaving without that gold, you understand me?" He shook him even harder. "So you better figure out how we're going to get it! And you better figure it out fast."

He picked up his hat, then stormed off toward the house. Who cared if the kid was scared of him now? He'd told him where the gold was — he just couldn't get to it.

Darwin's temper needed something to hit. When he climbed the porch, he picked up a rocking chair and smashed one of the front windows. That felt good. The Colton fellow didn't deserve to have this property. *Smash. Smash. Smash.*

Once the front windows were all broken, he threw down the chair and stood on the porch, catching his breath. This land belonged to his family. Colton might've built this nice house, but that didn't matter. His mother had planted the gardens and flowers, and his father had . . . well, his father had been good for nothing but robbing others of their wealth. Still, this had been their home, and it wasn't right that the bank could just up and take it. Darwin had half a mind to burn it to the ground. He smiled. Maybe that was the answer. He'd get Harry in the house, knock him unconscious, and then set the whole place on fire. That would take care of two birds with one stone. But first, there was the not-so-small task of getting his gold out of the well. Especially since he'd have to go without the other bags. Stupid Harry. How could he take it off the property? He'd never remember where he hid it.

Darwin eyed the well again. That gold was

his. And he intended to get it.
No matter what it took.

CHAPTER TWENTY-SIX

They needed a miracle. A really big one.
Lillian walked into Mrs. Goodman's room.
"Hello, my friend." She sat on the edge of
the bed and squeezed the older woman's
hand. "The judge just met with the sheriff,
Woody, Mr. Van Dyke, and the witnesses
and decided that there is enough to move
Woody's case to trial. I can't believe this is
happening." She took in a shaky breath.

"We've all been praying and crying out to
the Lord. But we need you, Mrs. Goodman.
We need you to wake up." Lillian squeezed
the woman's hand a bit harder and pulled it
to her chest. "We need you back in our lives.
We need you well. We need you to bake
cookies, and sing silly songs with us, and
call us all 'dearie.' " Big fat tears rolled
down her cheeks. The doctor had seen signs
that the older woman was coming out of
her coma, but to Lillian she looked the
same.

"Please, Mrs. Goodman. Please, please wake up. You're the only one who can clear Woody." The sobs overtook her then. "I love him. And I know you do, too."

After a good cry, she touched her friend's face. "You've got a bit more color today. Oh, how I long to see your smile again." Lillian laid the woman's hand back down by her side. "Jimmy is doing better. The doctor hopes he'll be able to go home tomorrow. But I don't know what we'll be going home to. Oh, this is such a mess."

Rubbing her head with one hand, Lillian placed the other on her hip. The judge's ruling today wasn't what she'd hoped to hear, but she shouldn't have gotten her hopes up. Still, Woody would get a fair trial. At least, she prayed it would be a fair trial. Mr. Van Dyke said that if they couldn't get twelve impartial men together for the jury, he would move to have the venue changed, and that meant they'd take Woody to another town.

The one good thing that had happened today was that the judge allowed Woody's men to go back to the farm. He warned them not to go anywhere else because he would need their testimony for the trial. But at least they could tend to the olive trees. If there were any trees left to be tended.

She'd tried to explain to them what she'd gotten done and how Harry was probably still out there helping, but warned them he would probably run away if he saw them. Lillian begged them not to chase the young man or yell at him. The men assured her they would do everything in their power to save the crop.

But had she done enough? Why did it feel like her world was crashing around her?

Closing her eyes, she clung to the tiny thread of hope she had left. Woody loved her. God hadn't brought them this far to abandon them. Whatever came, she would stand by his side.

Turning back to the bed, she watched Mrs. Goodman. The poor woman had been through so much.

A moan escaped the older woman's lips.

Lillian dashed back to the bed. "Mrs. Goodman? Mrs. Goodman? Can you hear me?"

Another moan. This time longer and louder.

Where was the bell? She looked all over and then ran back to Jimmy's room and started ringing the bell as she ran. "Doctor!"

As she ran back in her friend's room, she saw Mrs. Goodman's eyelids flutter. She was waking up! Praise God!

The doctor bolted into the room and rushed to his patient's side. "It's okay. We've been waiting for you to wake up. Go ahead. Open your eyes if you can."

Lillian stood back and watched. "Please, Mrs. Goodman, wake up. Please."

"Lil . . ." Her eyelids fluttered again.

"Yes, I'm here. I'm here. Talk to me." Lillian grabbed the woman's hand.

The doctor pulled out an instrument and listened to his patient's heart. "She's got a nice strong rhythm. I think she's going to fully wake up. Keep talking to her."

Mrs. Goodman's eyes popped open. "Ouch, dearie. You don't have to squeeze my hand so hard!"

Tears raced down her cheeks as Lillian laughed out loud. "You're awake!"

"Well, of course I'm awake. I'm talkin' to ya, aren't I?" She tried to lift her head.

"Whoa." The doctor held his hand up. "Not so fast. You have a lot of injuries and several broken bones."

"Is that why I feel like I've been run over by a herd of cows?"

"Yes, ma'am. I'm sorry to say." The doctor looked at Mrs. Goodman's eyes. "They look clear. Can you see me all right?"

She nodded.

Lillian interrupted. "Do you remember what happened?"

Mrs. Goodman closed her eyes. "Remember what?"

Lillian paced the hall. Mrs. Goodman had been awake for two days, and she couldn't remember the attack. But bits and pieces were coming back to her, so they all prayed for a full restoration of her memory — even as difficult as it was.

The judge wanted to start the trial immediately, but Mr. Van Dyke managed to get a stay in order that Mrs. Goodman might recover enough to give testimony. Van Dyke knew the law, and the judge agreed to the delay. Mr. Van Dyke also told her that the judge seemed to be a fair man, not as prejudiced as they'd feared. For that, Lillian was quite grateful.

"You're going to wear a hole in the floor." The doctor came from Mrs. Goodman's room. "Come here and join us."

Lillian followed. "Please tell me she remembers more." She'd gone to sleep the night before praying in desperation that God might clear away the confusion in Mrs. Goodman's mind. Each day she knew a little more, but the doctor insisted she not push herself, and while Lillian agreed, she feared for Woody. Now, after being busy with Jimmy all morning and waiting for the doctor to finish his exam of Mrs. Goodman, Lillian was desperate to know the news.

"Now, don't rush her," the doctor commanded.

Mrs. Goodman scrunched up her face and then frowned. "Nobody's rushing me. Lillian, you look like you haven't slept in a week."

"I've slept." Lillian came to the older woman's side. "I'm just desperate for you to remember what happened at the farm and who did this."

"Well, I can remember enough. The doctor said the town is blaming Woody. I can't believe it. Just let me go to the judge and set things straight."

"So you know who did this?" Lillian wanted to shout for joy. "Oh, dear Mrs. Goodman, please tell me his name."

"I don't have a name, dearie, but it wasn't Woody. Of course, you know that."

"Can you identify him?"

"I sure can. I'll never forget that evil face. Had eyes like the devil himself."

Lillian almost asked how the older woman knew what the devil's eyes looked like but decided against it. What was important was that they get Woody set free. "I'm going to fetch the lawyer. Oh, and the sheriff . . . and the judge. Goodness, I'll make the entire town come."

Lillian had all three men there in record time. Word spread quickly that Mrs. Goodman was giving an account of her attack, causing others to gather outside the doctor's place. Lillian could hear people talking outside the open windows and prayed the truth would be known once and for all.

"So you're certain, Mrs. Goodman, that your employer, Mr. Colton, was not the one who attacked you?" the judge asked in a gentle voice.

"I'm quite sure. Not only that, but you need to know something that fella said when he was hitting me."

Everyone in the room waited for what she was about to say. Lillian all but held her breath.

"Go ahead, Mrs. Goodman," the judge encouraged.

"He said he was going to kill me . . . just like he had Rebecca Colton."

Lillian thought she might faint. She leaned back against the wall. The truth. The truth of what had happened to Woody's wife was finally out.

"Are you sure he said that?" Sheriff Hobart asked, skepticism written all over his face. "Did he say why? What's his motive?"

"Of course I'm sure. We've only been telling you it wasn't Woody since it happened, but you had to get your nose set in one direction, and that left a killer out running around to strike again." Mrs. Goodman's response showed her mind was nearly restored to her original snappiness. "I caught the man sneaking out of the attic with a big bag in his hand."

The judge stared the sheriff down.

Lillian looked back and forth between the two men. Was this enough to set Woody free? It had to be. She chewed her lip and waited.

"Well . . . I guess . . . I was wrong." Sheriff Hobart gave a sheepish shrug. "I didn't mean to accuse an innocent man, but you have to admit it didn't look good."

"Neither has it looked good for you and most of this town to condemn Woody," Mrs. Goodman replied. "But I suppose we have to allow for ignorance and stupidity."

Lillian wanted to cheer. In fact, she couldn't suppress a giggle accompanied by tears of joy. She wanted to dance and sing and praise God all at once, and had the room not been full of people, she just might have done exactly that.

After hearing Mrs. Goodman's description and full account of what had happened, the judge admonished the sheriff to release Woody immediately. "And, Hobart," the judge added with a shake of his finger, "you'd do well to get out there and find this killer."

The sheriff nodded. "Yes, judge. I will. I'm going right now."

Lillian leaned down and gently kissed Mrs. Goodman's forehead. "You have saved the day, dearie."

The older woman smiled. "No, God did that. He just used a battered old woman to see it done."

Wiping a tear from her eye, Lillian smiled. "That He did, and for that I'm so very grateful. I know Woody and Jimmy will be, as well."

The doctor entered with Jimmy in his arms. "I was thinking, you could use another visitor to this celebration." He set the boy down on Mrs. Goodman's bed. "Now, neither one of you needs to get very excited, but I think this calls for a little lenience. Jimmy, you mustn't jostle Mrs. Goodman around, because she has several broken bones. But I think from the smile on her face that just having you nearby is going to hurry her healing along."

Jimmy smiled but looked hesitant as he

reached out for Mrs. Goodman's hand. Lillian placed her hand over Jimmy's. "We've got more good news, Jimmy. Your pa is going to be with us shortly. Mrs. Goodman was able to tell the sheriff that he didn't hurt her. Mrs. Goodman saw the man who hurt her. He's the same man who killed your mama, and now the sheriff will be able to hunt him down."

Instead of the smile she expected, Jimmy frowned. Lillian couldn't begin to understand all that the boy had gone through, but she wanted him to be happy. "Now, don't you worry. Mrs. Goodman is going to be just fine, and your pa will be, too. The most important thing is that God has let the truth be known, and He's brought Mrs. Goodman back to us."

A commotion in the hallway drew their attention to the door as Woody burst into the room. The look on his face was one of pure elation. "Mrs. Goodman!"

Jimmy jumped off the bed and wrapped himself around his father. Woody lifted the boy in the air and hugged him close for a moment. Then he reached out and motioned Lillian to join them. Without hesitation Lillian stepped into his arms. It was the one place she truly felt she belonged.

"Where's my hug, young man?" Mrs.

Goodman teased.

He laughed and handed Jimmy to Lillian before he stepped closer to the bed. He leaned over his dear housekeeper to kiss her cheek. "I think this will have to suffice for right now. You've got too many bruises and broken bones."

"Well, I suppose you're right at that, but when I'm recovered I'll expect my due."

"And you will get it," Woody replied.

"Oh, this is the best of days." Lillian put Jimmy down and pulled a handkerchief from her pocket. "I'm sorry for the tears, but I'm just so happy."

"Then let's add to that happiness." Woody fixed her with a broad smile.

Before Lillian could ask about the comment, Pastor Seymour entered the room with his wife. Woody nodded and then went to Jimmy and whispered something in his ear. The boy nodded enthusiastically and clapped his hands.

"What's this all about?" Lillian looked to Jimmy and then Woody before setting her sights on the pastor and his wife. "Do you know?"

Pastor Seymour laughed. "I do indeed, but I figure it's Woody's place to make the announcement."

Lillian looked to Woody, who crossed the

room to come to her side. "All right, so what did you and Jimmy just conspire?"

Woody's eyes seemed to darken as his expression turned sober. "I asked him if he would like to have a new mother."

Lillian couldn't have been more surprised. Her mouth opened, but no words came out. This only served to make Woody laugh.

"Miss Porter, I've never known you to be without an opinion. Perhaps you feel I should give you a formal proposal." He dropped to one knee and took hold of her hand. "Lillian, you have turned my world from dark to light. You've brought joy not only to me, but to my son."

"Don't forget me," Mrs. Goodman threw out.

Woody nodded. "And you've made Mrs. Goodman very happy." He looked to the older woman, who nodded in approval, and then back to Lillian. "I think we are all madly in love with you, and so it seems only appropriate that you would join our family."

He got to his feet and continued. "I know this is short notice, although I've had this planned for days with Pastor Seymour. And I figure you probably wanted to have a fancy church wedding and a lot of friends and family in attendance, but I thought maybe Pastor Seymour could just marry us here and now. If that wouldn't be too much of a disappointment, I promise we can have a big church wedding later if you want, but I can't risk losing you. I don't want another day to pass without the assurance that we'll spend the rest of our days together."

Lillian felt the tears slip down her cheeks but did nothing to keep them in check. She swallowed the lump in her throat and fixed her gaze on Woody's face. "I would be honored to marry you, Mr. Colton. Furthermore, I cannot think of a better place for our wedding. We're here with our dearest friends and loved ones. I don't need anything more."

Woody pulled her into his arms and kissed her in a long, sweet kiss that Lillian hoped might go on and on.

"You're jumpin' the gun and puttin' the cart before the horse, son." Pastor Seymour put his hand on Lillian's shoulder and pried them apart. "We haven't said the *I do*'s just yet."

Mrs. Goodman laughed, which was followed by a small moan. "Oh dear, I keep forgetting about those ribs. But, if you'll remember, pastor, Woody was always one for rushing ahead."

Woody put his hand to his chest in surprise. "Me? Why, I've always been one to

406

think things out quite clearly. When I know what I want — I go after it. And what I want right this minute is to marry this beautiful woman."

Chapter Twenty-Seven

"Woody. Woody, wake up."

The sound of Lillian's voice broke through his deep sleep and he sat up and stretched. Every muscle ached from sleeping in a chair all night long. "I'm awake."

She laughed. "You don't look awake."

"I was dreaming of this beautiful woman."

She raised a brow. "Oh, really? Then maybe I should just let you go on sleeping instead of giving you this cup of coffee along with some really incredible news."

He laughed and sat up straight. Careful of the steaming mug, Woody took the coffee and set it aside. Then he pulled Lillian onto his lap and wrapped her in his arms.

"You are the only beautiful woman I'll be dreaming of. And as for incredible news, you'd have to go a long ways to top our wedding. I still marvel that you would marry me and then spend your wedding night in a clinic tending to my housekeeper and son.

You are a most amazing woman, Miss . . . no, Mrs. Colton."

Lillian blushed and raised her hand to his cheek. "You need a shave and a clean shirt. I happen to have the shirt ready for you, but you'll have to tend to the shaving yourself."

He rubbed his bristled jaw against her cheek. "You sure you don't want me to grow a beard?"

"Where you're concerned, I'm only sure of one thing," Lillian replied. "I love you, and I pray that I'll make you a good wife."

"I cannot imagine you as anything other than perfect." He sensed her embarrassment and released her.

She patted her hair and gave him a flirtatious smile. "Let's just keep it that way, Mr. Colton. I don't want to disappoint my husband."

How he wished circumstances were different at the moment. But they were still in the hospital, newlyweds or not. "Now, what's this incredible news?"

"A crowd gathered at seven this morning outside the town hall, since your trial was supposed to start today. But instead of a trial, they were treated to a speech by the sheriff and also from the judge. In front of all those people, Woody, the sheriff told them what happened and that they all needed to be wary and on the lookout for Mrs. Goodman's attacker. He even went so far as to tell them that the same man was responsible for Rebecca's death. He gave them a description of the man Mrs. Goodman encountered, and he apologized and told the people how wrong he had been — about everything, including blaming you for what happened to Rebecca. It was like God finally opened the eyes of the people. It was wonderful." She clasped her hands together underneath her chin. "Then the judge spoke. He was very imposing and firm, even when a few in the crowd tried to argue and debate. He threatened to have all the naysayers arrested if they didn't shape up. Pastor Seymour then got up and said if anyone wanted to join him, they would have a prayer meeting at the church right now for your . . . our family. At least a hundred people followed him down the street to the church."

Her words struck his heart, but he found himself hesitant to believe it. Would people really change after all this time? There was bound to be gossip continuing until the culprit was caught. And Woody wasn't sure when or how they would accomplish that.

Lillian grabbed his hand. "You don't

believe it will do any good, do you?" She cocked her head to one side. "I know this has been extremely hard on you, Woody, but you've got to have faith that God will work this for His good."

"I know. My faith has just taken some bruising and battering from these folks, and I've got to overcome the habit I've developed of hardening myself." He looked down at Jimmy. "I need to keep my priorities straight."

He let go of Lillian's hand and sat on the side of Jimmy's bed. "You doing all right, son?"

A giant smile answered his question.

"I won't leave you if you don't want me to, but I do need to check on the olive trees. Would that be all right? I'll run down to the farm and be back to stay with you again tonight?"

The smile continued, this time accompanied by a nod.

Lillian went to the other side of his son's bed. "And I'll be here all day. We'll go to Mrs. Goodman's room when she wakes up and visit with her for a little while. Maybe we can even read her a book." Her face lit up, and she looked down at him with love.

A warmth rushed through Woody. She really cared for his son, and she cared for him. How had he gotten so lucky to be blessed by this woman? There was no reason she should have ever considered being his nanny, much less his wife.

She loves you, a voice seemed to speak to his heart. Woody nodded. Love changed everything. It could heal wounds, soothe anguished hearts, and give strength to the weak.

Woody reached over to touch his son's chin. "Well, then, that sounds like a fun day. If you don't mind, I'll head out to the farm and I'll be back. You take care of your new mama for me." Jimmy smiled and took hold of Lillian's hand and nodded with great enthusiasm.

"We'll make sure to find some supper for you." Her smile lit up the room. He found himself more anxious to leave so he could get back. "Oh, and Woody — the horses and wagons are at Pastor Seymour's place."

He laughed. "I guess that's helpful information."

Waving at Jimmy and nodding at Lillian, Woody put his hat on his head and headed to fetch his wagon and team. While his heart soared with feelings of love and family, relief and gratefulness, the weight of responsibility pressed in again on his shoulders. There was a man out there who thought nothing of beating an old woman half to death. There was a man out there who thought nothing of killing a helpless mother with a young son. The farm he loved no longer felt safe, and he worried that bringing his family home again might prove dangerous. Not only that, but if his trees didn't get water, they would die. And if Woody couldn't save them, he might well face a financial blow from which he'd never recover.

Where do you put your trust?

The silent prodding came from deep in his heart and made him straighten in the seat and smile. Woody determined to push the doubts and worry aside. It didn't matter. The Lord giveth and the Lord taketh away. He would bless the name of the Lord. He had Jimmy, Mrs. Goodman, and Lillian. If the worst thing happened and he lost the farm, well, he would keep on. His trust wasn't in the farm. His trust was in the Lord.

Woody pushed the horses as hard as he dared to the farm. The irrigation ditch would take a lot more work, and the last two weeks had been scorchers.

Instead of stopping at the house, he drove the wagon to the pond. To his surprise, the men were nowhere in sight, and a beautiful stream of water flowed through the fully completed irrigation ditch. How had this happened?

He set the brake and hopped down from the wagon. Marveling at the water flowing from the pond, he stared at the ditch and followed the stream with his eyes. Off in the distance, the grove was getting water. Not only was the main ditch dug, but feeder lines went off of it to extend into areas deeper in the grove.

"Mr. Colton!" Sam's voice drifted on the hot breeze.

Woody turned and saw his crew boss running toward him.

Sam waved and ran the rest of the way. "Did you see? It's a miracle!"

Woody laughed. He couldn't contain the joy. "I see it, Sam! It's a miracle indeed. How did you all finish this? You fellas must have been digging night and day since they let you go."

"No, sir." Sam beamed at him. "It really is a miracle. When we got here, the ditch was finished, and not just the main. Water was already flowing throughout the groves. The trees are in good shape."

"You mean, *you* didn't finish the ditch?"

"No, sir."

"None of the men knew about this?"

"No, sir. Although Miss Lillian had been

414

out here, and she mentioned someone named Harry."

Lillian's blisters. Woody scratched his head. It made a little more sense now. Harry must've helped a lot. He glanced heavenward and knew that no matter who had done the actual work, the miracle had come from God alone. He pulled his hat from his head and bowed in prayer.

Thank You. Not just for this, but for everything. The bad. The good. The times of confusion and pain, as well as those of contentment and pleasure. I never thought I could pray such a prayer, but Lord, I think I finally understand about those verses in Philippians and learning to be content no matter my circumstances.

He looked back at the ditch of water — water that would provide new life to his trees. Lillian had blessed him and Jimmy with new love, and God was blessing him with new hope. The old was truly passing away and all things were new.

"Boss, I don't want to interrupt, but I suppose you saw the house when you passed by."

Woody looked at Sam and shook his head. "I wasn't paying any attention. My mind was all about this water and the trees."

"You'd better let me ride back with you, then."

Frowning, Woody felt the hair on his neck prickle. "What happened?"

"I don't rightly know. When we got here we found quite a mess."

Chapter Twenty-Eight

Lillian wiped her neck with her handkerchief. She'd love nothing more than a dip in a cool stream at the moment. This heat was insufferable.

Mrs. Goodman had fallen asleep again, but she was clearly feeling more like herself. The doctor was pleased, which made Lillian pleased. It would be days, maybe even weeks, before she could go home, but it couldn't come soon enough.

Jimmy padded into the room in his stocking feet, his hair all tousled.

"Well, look who's awake from his nap?" She picked him up for a hug. "My goodness, you're getting very heavy. You must be eating well, huh?" She tickled his tummy.

He smiled sleepily and laid his head on her shoulder. While he had improved by leaps and bounds, the boy still had a lot of healing and catching up to do. An entire year of mourning his mother's death had taken its toll on him, as well as his recent bout of quinsy.

"Why don't we go back to your room and read your book again?"

He nodded.

With a quiet click, Lillian shut the door to Mrs. Goodman's room and headed down the hall. She set Jimmy down halfway there. "You really are getting heavy. You must be growing."

This elicited a bigger smile, and Jimmy stretched his neck and stood on his tiptoes.

"Lillian, I'm so glad I caught you," Mrs. Seymour's voice echoed down the hallway. "I have a telegram for you. They brought it to our house, and I promised to get it to you."

The pastor's wife handed over the paper, and Lillian put a hand to her throat. What could be so important that a telegram had to be sent? Grandfather? Fear and guilt gripped her, but she pasted on a smile and helped Jimmy up onto his bed.

She found her voice. "Would you mind reading to Jimmy for a few minutes while I check this?"

"Not at all." Her friend smiled at her. "Take all the time you need."

Lillian walked out of the room and closed the door. She leaned against the wall and opened the telegram.

LILLIAN PORTER, ANGELS CAMP,
CALIFORNIA
YOUR GRANDFATHER IS
GRAVELY ILL.
REFUSES TO CORRESPOND OR
SEE YOU.

BUT I REQUEST YOUR PRESENCE
AS SOON AS POSSIBLE BEFORE IT
IS TOO LATE.

STANTON

She clutched the paper to her chest and let out a little sob. Grandfather. That stubborn man. But this time, his stubbornness couldn't save him. Stanton wouldn't have resorted to a telegram unless it was dire. Her grandfather must be dying.

But she couldn't leave. Not now. She and Woody had just married. Not only that, there was a killer on the loose, and Jimmy and Mrs. Goodman needed her.

Oh, what to do?

Several moments passed as she pondered the situation. Turning back to the room, she opened the door. "Mrs. Seymour, I need to send a reply, if you could stay for a few more minutes?"

"Certainly." The two went back to the book they were reading.

Lillian grabbed her bonnet and headed to the telegraph office. She would ask Stanton to keep her abreast of the situation, but she wouldn't be able to leave just yet. Oh, but she longed to see her grandfather one more time. But would he refuse? So would traveling out there even be worth it? Maybe the old man's stubborn disposition would keep him alive a little longer. But how could she be in two places at once?

Lord, I don't know what to do. Woody needs me. Mrs. Goodman and Jimmy need me. And Grandfather is sick. I don't know how bad it is, but You know. Please help me to make the correct decisions. And please heal Grandfather. Even if it's just his heart You heal so he can go home to You in peace.

The house was still intact, but someone had made sure to leave a mess. Was it some sort of message?

Woody stood on the porch and slapped his hat against his thigh. All the windows on the main floor were smashed in, and four rocking chairs were mangled and lying on their sides on the covered porch.

Sam sighed beside him. "I'm sorry, boss. I didn't notice it right away. We were all so worried about getting water to the trees that I don't think any one of us gave it a thought. We tried to start cleaning up, but we didn't get all that far."

"It's all right, Sam. Frankly, it doesn't surprise me." He glanced at the second floor and then to the tiny windows of the attic. "Come with me."

Woody raced up the stairs to the second floor and then up the stairs to the attic. Sure enough, as soon as he reached the top, he found all the floorboards torn up. Someone had been up here looking for something. So the man who'd hurt Mrs. Goodman must've hidden something — something very important or valuable — up here.

"The man who killed my wife hid something up here. He was here to find it when Mrs. Goodman interrupted him."

Sam gasped behind him. "Whoa. Why would he have hidden something in your attic, boss?"

"I don't know, Sam." Woody shook his head. Now if he could just fit the rest of the pieces of this puzzle together. "Let's head back downstairs. I probably need to let the sheriff look at all this." Woody remembered his journal of evidence, as well as the button. "He needs to see some other stuff, as well."

■ ■ ■ ■

Bone weary, Woody headed back into town after he and the other men boarded up the open windows. Sam promised they'd focus on cleaning up the mess, since it was evident that the trees were in good shape. He'd need to order new windows and other repair provisions in the morning.

Woody left his horse once again in Pastor Seymour's barn and went straight to the jail, only to find the sheriff gone. The deputy promised to send him by but figured it would be morning before he'd return. Woody was touched when the deputy offered an apology for his previous behavior and attitude toward Woody.

"I guess it was easy to judge you wrong when everybody else was," the deputy told him. "Don't make it right, though, and I'm heartily ashamed."

Woody thanked him and headed out for the clinic. It felt so good to be free of suspicion — at least by most of the population. He entered the clinic and immediately heard Lillian's laughter from Mrs. Goodman's room. It drew him like a moth to the flame. As he opened the door, he heard Mrs. Goodman laughing, as well. It helped him to push aside his worries.

"Oh, dearie, don't make me laugh anymore. It hurts these ol' broken ribs of mine." But the woman kept laughing anyway.

Jimmy sat on the end of the older woman's bed and bounced.

Lillian reached for his son. "You better stop your bouncing, too, young man. We want Mrs. Goodman to be able to come home as soon as possible, don't we?" She looked down at him but then caught Woody's eye. "Woody! You're back." She set Jimmy on the floor, and they both scurried over.

With his son's arms wrapped around his legs and Lillian's arms around his shoulders, Woody couldn't think of a better ending to a day. He kissed Lillian with all the energy he could muster. They were married. The weight of the thought thudded all the way down to his toes and then lifted him back up again.

Lillian pulled back with another blush. "And you look like you could fall asleep standing there." She placed her hands on her hips. "I asked for Pastor Seymour to find another cot, and he did, so there's one in Jimmy's room for you to sleep on tonight. It looks like you need to head there right now." She pushed him to the door but stopped a moment and threw over her shoulder, "Mrs. Goodman, I'll be back in a few minutes. Let me fetch Woody's plate for him and get these two to bed."

"That's fine with me, dearie." His housekeeper lifted a hand in a wave. "Good to see you, Woody. Get some rest, and we'll catch up in the morning."

He winked at her and allowed Lillian to keep pushing him out the door. "Good night, Mrs. Goodman."

Lillian fussed and hovered until Jimmy was ensconced in covers and pillows on the bed and Woody had a plate of steaming food in front of him. "The doctor said that Jimmy could go home as soon as we wished. Mrs. Goodman still needs time to heal, but she's doing very well." She plumped another pillow for the cot. Woody couldn't help but watch her.

"Not much of a honeymoon, eh?" He grinned as she blushed. He picked up his fork and speared a chunk of potato. "But I promise I'll make it up to you. Once this is all settled and Mrs. Goodman is back in one piece, I'll take you away for a proper wedding trip."

Lillian said nothing, but the way she worried her bottom lip made Woody wonder if she regretted having married him so quickly. He didn't like to think she'd changed her mind — after all, it was a bit late for that.

"You know," Lillian finally spoke, "I don't really need a wedding trip. However, I might have some ideas for one if you insist." She looked like she might say something more, then turned back to check on Jimmy. "He's already asleep."

The warm food hit the spot and stopped the gnawing in his stomach. "I asked the sheriff to stop by."

She looked at him oddly. "Is something wrong?" She sat on the cot across from his chair.

He glanced at Jimmy and lowered his voice just in case. "Well, there was some ransacking done to the house. Windows broken and such. I found floorboards in the attic torn up. That must've happened the day Mrs. Goodman found the intruder." Woody finished his plate. "But the windows hadn't been broken when I found her, so someone's been back."

She covered her mouth with her hand. "Goodness. Is it safe to return home?"

He loved hearing the word *home* out of her mouth. "That's what I want to talk to the sheriff about. I'd like him to see the torn-up floorboards, too. Maybe there's some kind of clue. Maybe there are tracks he can follow."

"I'm sure the sheriff will be able to help. Especially now that he knows the truth about you." She reached forward and touched his knee.

It was true. Now that Sheriff Hobart wasn't blaming Woody anymore, he would truly look for the killer, wouldn't he?

"I'm sure the sheriff will figure all this out real soon, and we'll get it all behind us." Lillian's touch on his leg seemed almost electrified. Woody realized just how much he longed to hold her. He pushed aside his growing desire and smiled. "Hey, guess what? We had a miracle out on the farm."

Lillian stood and came up beside him. "Really? A miracle?"

"Yep, I went back today to work on the irrigation ditch, and it was already flowing. Not just the main line, either. There were lines off of the main and out into the groves. The men didn't finish it and don't know who did. But we were able to water all the trees today. All of them! I think, in fact, the trees are going to be fine — the crop, too."

Lillian lowered her head, then glanced up at him through her long lashes.

He leaned forward. "So is there something you'd like to tell me?"

She fiddled with her handkerchief.

"Maybe about how you got those blisters on your hands?"

She looked up at him. "I *did* drive without my gloves . . . so don't go thinking that I lied to you. I just left out the part about learning how to use a shovel." She straightened her spine and raised her eyebrows as if she dared him to scold her.

Woody laughed and shook his head.

"I went there with the intention to do anything I could to help, especially since the sheriff wouldn't let your men leave town. I was worried. So I went against his command that no one set foot on the property. I was determined to see that ditch dug. But after donning a pair of your trousers and trying to figure out a shovel for the first time in my life, I found out that an hour's worth of my sweat made little more than a few inches of progress." She laughed along with him. "You should've seen it. I was a mess."

He grinned, imagining her dressed in his trousers. "I would have liked to have seen that."

His comment brought a flush to Lillian's cheeks. She hurried on. "But the real miracle came in the form of our friend, Harry. That young man dug like there was a cyclone after him. He was the one who finished it. I'm certain of it."

CHAPTER TWENTY-NINE

Jimmy tugged at the loose thread on the bottom of his shirt. The sheriff had been with them for over an hour already. The bad man was still alive. He'd hurt Mrs. Goodman. Almost killed her — just like Mama.

But now, he and Mrs. Goodman had both seen him, and it didn't matter that the sheriff had a name to call the man. What mattered was the man was still able to hurt the people Jimmy loved.

Miss Lillian sat on the edge of Mrs. Goodman's bed with Jimmy in her lap. She stroked his hair as the sheriff talked.

"We're pretty certain that the man we're after is indeed Darwin Longstreet. I got to looking through all of Woody's notes on the evidence, and then checked out some old records and realized that Longstreet's family once lived on your property."

Papa shook his head. "Longstreet. It's all beginning to fit together. Mrs. Goodman had mentioned reading about his death several weeks ago, and I knew the name sounded familiar. Could be the bank manager mentioned it when we bought the place."

"Yeah, it belonged to Longstreet's father, a no-good bum. He died and left a widow and two sons, one of which was Longstreet."

Papa looked upset, and that made Jimmy more than a little afraid. "So you're saying Longstreet's actually alive and my farm had once been his father's?"

The sheriff nodded. "Apparently Longstreet staged it all. They thought the body was his — but too many things weren't adding up. When John and David — Darwin's uncle and other cousin — showed up to report David's brother Saul missing, the authorities did some more digging. The dead man turned out to be Saul and not Darwin Longstreet. That's why I was gone all day yesterday. I went up to Stockton. Found out everything I needed to know. Darwin is dark-haired, wiry, and mean. Apparently he didn't get along with any of his kin and hated the fact that you now own the land that he believes should be his. They're pretty sure he had killed more than once before. He was convicted once of murder already and escaped from jail. And his kin were pretty sure he'd killed not only his cousin Saul but his kid brother, too."

Miss Lillian gasped. "That's awful."

The sheriff nodded. "Beat his cousin beyond recognition so the law would figure it was him. Sorry to be so blunt, Miss Porter."

"She's Mrs. Colton now," Papa told the man, and Jimmy couldn't help but tighten his hold on his new mother's arm. He was so afraid that the bad man would come and take her away like he had his other mother.

"Congratulations," the sheriff offered. "Anyway, you all need to be aware of the danger. It was always rumored that Longstreet had hidden a large amount of gold on the farm, but apparently no one could ever find anything and figured it was just a rumor. Now, however, with all that's happened, I'm of a mind that there is something there that Longstreet is after. Probably what he was after when he killed your wife."

Jimmy buried his face. He knew the bad man wanted treasure. That's what he'd asked for when Jimmy had surprised him.

"My guess is that he still hasn't found what he wanted or he wouldn't have tore up your house. If we could come up with a plan to trap him . . ."

"What if he already got it all? And that's

why he hurt Mrs. Goodman. She said he hit her with a sack of rocks or what felt like that. It was probably the gold he was looking for." Miss Lillian hugged him tighter. Even though Jimmy felt safe in her arms, his heart still beat faster knowing the bad man was still alive.

"I don't think he would have bothered to show back up and trash the house if he had what he wanted. Seems to me those are the actions of a frustrated and angry man." The sheriff looked stern.

Jimmy tuned out the adults. If the sheriff knew who the bad man was, then maybe they'd catch him soon. Maybe he could tell his papa what he knew.

But no. If the bad man was that close, he'd know. Just like he'd known where Jimmy was that day on the hill. Before he got sick.

He'd kill everyone before the sheriff could catch him. He'd already hurt Mrs. Goodman, and Jimmy couldn't bear it if he hurt his pa or Miss Lillian . . . Mama. What if he thought Jimmy had talked? He'd come after them all for sure.

Jimmy turned into Lillian's arms and closed his eyes tight. No matter how hard he tried, he couldn't get Darwin Longstreet's face out of his mind. Taunting him.

■ ■ ■ ■

Lillian turned in the wagon and waved at the doctor and Pastor Seymour and his wife. A niggle of fear resided in her gut, but she tried her best to squelch it. Fear wasn't from the Lord.

But there was a killer on the loose. He'd killed Rebecca Colton. Had done something horrible to little Jimmy. Killed who knows how many others, including his own kin, and had hurt Mrs. Goodman.

He had to be stopped.

Woody and the sheriff had argued all morning about the choices they had. It was finally agreed upon that Mrs. Goodman was still too fragile to be moved and would remain in the clinic. The rest of them would return to the house, letting it be known in town that they were back in residence. The sheriff and his deputies would work with Woody and his men to lay a trap for Darwin Longstreet. The sheriff felt certain that Longstreet would show up again once he felt that it was safe enough to do so. If Woody and his family acted like everything was back to normal and word got around that everyone was certain Longstreet was long gone, the brute might just feel safe enough to reshow his face. And when he did — they'd be ready. But Lillian wasn't at all sure that was the right answer, and neither was Woody.

As they pulled out of Angels Camp, Lillian turned to look at Woody and then to the little boy sandwiched between them. *Please, God, let this be the right answer.* Those two had stolen her heart, and she couldn't bear to think of anything happening to either of them. What must they have felt to lose Rebecca? What must they feel now — with her murder brought back to the forefront of everyone's mind and her murderer on the loose?

A shiver raced up her spine. She wanted to cry.

Lillian couldn't help but notice that Woody watched the surrounding area with an eagle eye. He'd been serious and quiet ever since they'd met with the sheriff. Was this the way their life would be until Longstreet was caught? What if he was never caught? She steadied her nerves. She needed to be strong for Jimmy. It was clear that the boy was still afraid. Maybe more so since hearing the sheriff's conversation.

"Looks like it may rain, and I hope it will." Woody looked at the accumulating clouds overhead. "I just hope it will hold off until

434

we get home. But even if it's pouring when we reach the house, I want you two to wait until I have the men go through it and make sure no one is inside." Woody's words were hushed and stern. Long gone were the traces of a man in love. Maybe it really had been too good to be true. How could Woody truly love her when he was still obviously in love with his first wife? He couldn't let Rebecca go. As soon as the sheriff had discussed the details with them, Woody had focused in on one thing — justice for his wife.

"Did you hear me? Wait until we've checked to make sure it's safe."

Lillian nodded but said nothing. They'd already discussed all of this, and she figured he was just reiterating due to anxiety.

When the house finally did come into view, Lillian couldn't help noticing the boarded-up windows. Woody had told her about it, but seeing it brought tears to her eyes. She quickly wiped them away and gave Jimmy a smile.

"It's good to be home." She squeezed his shoulders, but he didn't acknowledge her in any way.

Her heart clenched. Maybe she'd come to call this home too soon. Gotten too attached. The Colton men would never love her the way they had Rebecca. Doubts poured through her mind. What had she done? Had she made everything worse? Why had Woody even asked her to be his wife?

Sam and the others appeared and did as Woody asked. While they searched through the house, Woody stood guard with the rifle he'd bought in town. Once Sam reappeared at the front door, Lillian climbed down from the wagon and reached up for Jimmy. He didn't move for a moment, but just stared at the house.

"They've checked it all out, Jimmy, and it's safe." She hoped her voice sounded more convincing than she felt.

"I still think you should have stayed in town." Woody shook his head. "I'm not comfortable with this."

Lillian threw him a look. "I'm sure it will be all right. Come on, Jimmy. I need your help to make something for us to eat." Finally he stood and moved to where she could help him down.

Woody came alongside them. "I want you to stay inside and lock the door. I'm going to help Sam check the immediate area, and then I'll come join you."

Lillian nodded and ushered Jimmy into the house. The torment in Woody's eyes made her want to cry. All her selfish thoughts tumbled back in — how could she even think about herself at a time like this? God had brought her here. She'd agreed to marry Woody because she loved him. She loved his son. So she would do the very best she could to help them both, for the rest of her life.

A rumble of thunder drew her attention back to the sky. It appeared a storm was working its way toward them. "I think we should go and check on Mr. Whiskers. You know I asked Harry to watch over him, but I don't know if he's had a chance these last couple of days given the situation."

Jimmy took off at a run for the kitchen, and Lillian followed close behind, praying that the little rabbit was still alive. Mr. Whiskers proved to be just fine. Jimmy picked him up and held him close while Lillian began to search the cupboards for something she might prepare. Much of the food items they'd had prior to Mrs. Goodman's attack were gone. She smiled. No doubt Harry had helped himself as she'd suggested, but there was no sign of him otherwise. A horrible thought crossed her mind. What if this Longstreet fellow had hurt him? After all, the sheriff had said the man killed his cousin and brother. She shuddered. All she could do was pray for Harry's protection.

CHAPTER THIRTY

The rain poured down on Harry as he watched Jimmy's pa from the trees. He and his men moved around the farm grounds. They acted like they were looking for something, but he didn't know what it was.

As Harry turned his head, the bruises on his neck and face hurt. Darwin had gotten mad at him and hit him, even though he showed his brother where the bags were. Harry didn't understand. Why was his brother so mean?

It scared him.

It also scared him that he'd overheard Darwin say that he wanted Colton and the kid dead.

Colton was Jimmy's pa. So that must mean the kid was Jimmy. Harry couldn't let Darwin hurt them. But he didn't know how to stop it.

"Aren't you Harry?"

Harry startled. He hadn't been paying attention and somehow Mr. Colton managed to sneak up on him. Brother told him not to talk to anyone or be seen by anyone. But Harry knew it was too late to run away. Besides, Miss Lillian said that Mr. Colton was a really nice man.

Slowly standing up with the rain dripping from his hat, Harry looked behind him. Darwin hadn't followed him this time, so maybe he didn't know where Harry had gone.

"I'm Harry." He looked at the man, then lowered his head just a bit. "You're Mr. Colton. Jimmy's pa."

The man smiled, but it was almost a sad smile. "Yes." He stuck out his hand. "I wanted to shake your hand, Harry. I think we got off on the wrong foot."

Harry looked at his raggedy boots. He'd never thought of one of his feet being wrong.

"I know that night you were just trying to get Jimmy to come back home, but I frightened you, and I'm sorry. I'm grateful that you helped Jimmy that night."

Harry perked up at this. "Jimmy's my friend."

The man nodded. "I know, and I'm glad. Jimmy needs a good friend like you." He smiled. "Harry, I also need to thank you for all you did to finish the irrigation ditch. That was a lot of hard work, and I'd like to pay you for your time."

Harry reached out and shook Jimmy's pa's hand. "Oh, no, no, no. You don't have to pay me. I did it as a friend to help. Miss Lillian was out here digging, and I just wanted to be nice because she's been so nice to me."

Mr. Colton laughed. "I bet that was a sight, watching Miss Lillian try to dig."

The tension was gone and Harry giggled. "Oh, she looked really funny. She was wearin' . . . pants." He whispered the last word, then spoke up once again. "But she really tried. She's just not as strong as me."

"I can imagine." The man put his hand on Harry's shoulder. "You helped save my olive crop, Harry. I mean it. We wouldn't have made it without you. Thank you."

"You are very welcome, Mr. Colton. Yep, yep, yep."

Mr. Colton frowned and Harry stepped back. Had he done something wrong?

"Harry, why don't you come to the house and get out of the rain? I'm sure Jimmy would love to see you."

"I . . . I . . ." Harry looked around, still anxious that Darwin would know where he was. "I can't."

"All right. But since you've been around

here, maybe you can help me. Somebody broke into my house and hurt Mrs. Goodman. She's in the hospital now." Lightning flashed across the sky, but Mr. Colton acted like nothing was wrong.

"Who would hurt Mrs. Goodman? She gave me a hug!" Harry had a bad feeling in his stomach.

"Someone beat her pretty bad after they dug around in our attic. That same person broke my windows. They were looking for something — a treasure that they'd hidden in my house."

Harry thought he might get sick and squatted down. Oh no, no, no. That meant . . .

Mr. Colton crouched down next to Harry. "Have you seen anything, Harry?"

He squeezed his eyes shut. He wanted to help his nice friends. In fact, he was hoping to live with nice people like them after Brother left. They might let him live in the barn, and that would be so much better than the dark cave. Maybe he could tell them the truth. Maybe it would help them. Maybe Darwin could go away for good. "I don't know for sure, Mr. Colton." Rain mingled with tears to blur his vision.

"It's okay. You can trust me. Just tell me what you do know."

"But I promised."

"Sometimes you have to break a promise to tell the truth. Is that what you need to do?"

Harry nodded and bit his lip. Mr. Colton was right. It was a bad promise he'd made to Darwin. Because it wasn't the truth. He stood up, and Mr. Colton did, too. "My brother must be the one who hurt Mrs. Goodman and broke your windows."

Mr. Colton's face turned really white, and when the lightning flashed, it made him look mad. "Is your brother Darwin Longstreet?"

Harry lowered his face. Fear crawled up his spine. "Darwin is mean. He was in your attic looking for his gold. He wants all of it so he can go to Mexico."

"Where's Darwin now, Harry?"

Harry looked around for a minute. "I don't know. He said he was comin' here when the sun set. He told me to be here, too. Maybe he won't come with all these people here. Maybe he'll stay away until the rain stops." He pointed up the hill behind the pond. "He comes that way and ties his horse up there, then watches until it's safe."

Lillian was busy at the stove when Woody entered the back door. She paused momentarily to look into his eyes. "Woody?"

He entered the kitchen and glanced to where Jimmy was playing with Mr. Whiskers. "I need you to go to town right now, Lillian. Fetch the sheriff, and take Jimmy with you. I've saddled a horse for you."

"What? Why?" She dropped the towel on the table and started to untie her apron. "Won't it be dangerous?" She paused lest she worry Jimmy. "I mean what with the thunderstorm."

"I can't explain now, but I ran across Harry while I was checking the grounds." He held up his hands when Jimmy jumped to his feet. "Don't worry, he's fine. And I think I've figured out the rest of the puzzle. But I need you to go to town now. As fast as you can."

He could tell by the look on Lillian's face that she was beginning to understand. She nodded very slowly, then smiled at Jimmy. "Go get your boots on."

Jimmy nodded and ran from the room. Lillian turned back to Woody. "Did Harry see something? Did he see Mr. Longstreet?"

"Darwin Longstreet is Harry's brother." She went pale. "Oh . . ."

He nodded. "Harry said he was supposed to meet him here at sunset. I'm going to get my men, and we'll hide out around the

444

property. I told Harry not to tell his brother that we're here. I don't want him spooked off. Harry said he always comes from the hill just beyond the pond. That should leave you and Jimmy safe to ride to town. Once you're there, stay there."

She squared her shoulders as Woody had seen her do on many a trying occasion. "I'm sure we'll be fine."

He pulled her into his arms and kissed her hard. "Ride fast and don't stop for any reason. The storm's nearly passed and hopefully the ground will soak up the water, since it's so dry."

Lillian looked into his eyes and kissed him again. "Please be careful."

The hours ticked by. The storm was long gone and the sun moved across the western sky. Soon it would be dark. Woody and his men had taken up positions all around the grounds to wait for either Longstreet or the sheriff. But neither had come. Woody tried not to worry, but he couldn't help it. He tried to pray, but all he could get out was, "Please God, help." He hoped it was enough.

After another two hours a real sense of fear set in. Twilight had fallen, and it wouldn't be long before the skies grew dark.

That would make it hard to see Longstreet
and Harry when they came. Woody told his
men all about Harry and admonished them
to do nothing that would cause the boy
harm. However, if it was dark outside, it
would be almost impossible to know who
was who. Not only that, but worse still was
the growing sensation that something wasn't
right. Woody felt it all the way to his bones.
The sheriff had plenty of time to get here.
Where was he? More important, where were
Lillian and Jimmy? Had they run across
trouble on the way? Had Longstreet somehow fooled them all and come from a direction other than the one Harry had suggested?

CHAPTER THIRTY-ONE

"Wake up, lady. It's time to go."

Lillian struggled to open her eyes. Then the pain hit her. Her head hurt as if someone had hit her with the trunk of a tree, and her body ached from lying on top of the rocky ground. She sat up and realized her hands were tied in front of her and a kerchief had been placed around her mouth as a gag.

"Now you're gonna cooperate with me," the fierce-looking man declared. He yanked her to her feet. "Understand?" He pointed to the crumpled body of Jimmy. The child had been bound and gagged just like she was, but also blindfolded. He wasn't moving, and Lillian feared the worst.

She tried to protest and edged toward Jimmy, but her words were nothing but garbled moans.

"The kid is fine, lady. But he won't be for long if you don't do exactly as I tell you.

Now the sooner you get that in your head, the sooner we can get to work." He smiled and leaned in, nearly sickening her with his whiskey-scented breath. "And the sooner we get what I'm after, the sooner we can get back here to the boy. Understand?"

Lillian had no idea if Jimmy truly was all right, but she nodded. She couldn't remember what happened, but she remembered riding hard and fast with Jimmy. They were going after the sheriff. The rain had made the road slippery. The horse faltered, and Lillian lost her balance. She looked at her captor, all of a sudden realizing who he was.

Darwin Longstreet grinned back at her. "I think you understand real good. Now come on." He pushed her toward the mouth of the cave.

Lillian looked around, trying her best to memorize where they were and how she might get back to Jimmy. Longstreet had made a fire and lit several torches, one of which was near the entrance to the cave — or was it a mine? Hadn't Harry said he lived in a mine?

Longstreet hoisted Lillian up atop the same horse she'd ridden earlier. She gripped the horn tight, fearful she might very well fall off. She glanced back in the direction they'd come and realized it was difficult to make out the light from inside the cave. It seemed Longstreet had created the perfect hideaway for himself. She worried about Jimmy and worried about what he would think when he woke up alone, blindfolded and bound.

Longstreet mounted his own horse, then grabbed her reins and pulled the horse to follow his. "I'm figurin' by now your men are out looking for you on the road. We're gonna make our way back to that fancy house, and you're gonna help me retrieve what's mine — and if you dare make any noise, you and that kid will both be dead."

Lillian tried to remember the path they were taking, but it was dark and almost impossible to make out any landmarks. *Please, God, keep Jimmy safe and help me to get back to him. He'll be so afraid if he wakes up alone.*

They wound round and round. It seemed the trail went in circles as far as Lillian could figure out. Most of the trip was downhill — at least she felt like it was from the way she was pulled forward.

Longstreet finally halted, and after wrapping her reins around his saddle horn, he jumped down and walked away. Lillian stiffened at the sound of an owl from a nearby tree. Longstreet was gone only a few minutes before he came back and dragged her from the horse.

Pulling on the rope in his hands, Darwin tugged her closer. "Come on. And not a peep outta ya, ya hear? If anybody is still down there, I don't want them to hear us comin'."

She nodded, still gagged and bound. Lillian didn't know if he could actually see her nod, but he moved out and took her with him. She smelled the pond as they passed close by. There wasn't even so much as a sliver of moonlight to help her see, but her eyes were adjusting to make out the dark shadowy trees overhead. They were heading for the house. That much she was sure of. Apparently there was still something there that Longstreet was after.

When they reached the well, however, he stopped and whispered into her ear, "Not a sound." She shivered and pulled away. "Just wait, missy. I'll really make you cringe later." He tightened the rope around her wrists.

"I have a fortune in gold down this well. There are two bags, and you're gonna go down there and get them for me. Now I'm gonna put a rope around your waist and lower you down. As soon as you have the bags, yank on the rope and I'll pull you up."

Lillian wanted so much to cry out, but

she knew if she did, she'd never see Jimmy or Woody again. She prayed without ceasing for help — for courage — for strength.

Longstreet fastened the other rope, then lifted her and set her on the edge of the well. She almost slipped into the abyss because of her bound hands, but Longstreet grabbed hold of her. To her surprise, he untied her hands.

"Now turn around and slide in there. I'll let you down slow, so don't worry. I ain't gonna let you fall. You wouldn't be able to get my gold if you did."

Lillian was small enough that she swung free of the wall only to crash back against it. Darwin was none too careful in his lowering. He might not intend to let her fall, but he was in a hurry all the same. She tried not to think of what all might live in the well. They'd seen snakes near the pond, but surely a snake wouldn't get itself down a well. Would it? She shivered.

Cold water swirled up around her. She feared momentarily that she might drown before she found the bags of gold. What if the well water was really deep? But just as she began to fret, her feet hit something solid. She tested the bottom and realized she'd come to the end of the well. By now the rope had slipped up just under her armpits. She pushed the annoying constraint down and tried to figure out what to do next. There wasn't a lot of room to maneuver, so she squatted down in the water and felt for the bags. It took some doing, but she finally managed to find one of them. Lifting it, however, was an entirely different matter.

She worked and worked to bring the bag to where she could have it in front of her. She got the idea of tucking the bag in between her and the waist rope. It was really heavy, but it just might work. Hugging the bag against her, she tugged the rope. Lillian's body hurt from the pull of the rope against her waist. She very nearly cried out against her gag as Darwin yanked her up out of the well. This was one time she would praise God for her corset. At least it had kept the rope from tearing apart her midsection.

He grabbed the bag. "That's one. Now go get the other." He all but pushed her into the well.

Lillian repeated the grueling process. The second bag wasn't any easier to lift. Exhausted and hurting, she didn't bother to do anything but tug on the rope and cradle the bag like a baby.

Darwin had her out of the well in nothing

flat. Lillian began to shake from the cold of the water and her fear. Longstreet didn't seem to notice or care. He heaved the bag over his shoulder, then turned and yanked her off the well's edge. He didn't untie the rope from her waist, but instead yanked it hard to point her in the right direction.

Lillian gave a quick glance around. Surely Woody had left someone there. But only silence and darkness could be found. She faltered in her steps, and Darwin gave the rope another hard pull. In no time at all he had her back up the hill to where the horses waited.

"Now, I'm gonna tie you to this tree, and you're gonna wait here all nice and quiet-like." He put the bag of gold down at her feet. He tied her to the tree and rebound her wrists before picking up the gold and tying it to the saddle of her horse.

"Now," he came much too close for comfort, "I'm gonna go get the other bag. You want that boy to be unharmed, you'll do nothing but stand here like a good girl."

She watched him disappear in the dark and immediately began squirming to free herself from the rope. He wasn't going to allow either her or Jimmy to live. That much was clear. Lillian felt the rope cut into her wrists as she moved against it. She thought the rope around her waist gave a little and turned in the direction that felt loose, but it was no use. Before she could do much of anything Longstreet was back with the other bag.

He secured the gold, then untied her from the tree and carried her back to the saddle. Her wet skirt clung to her, but Lillian knew there was nothing to be done about it. She held tight to the horn and prayed.

She had to come up with a plan. Once they made it back to the mine, she knew Darwin would kill her. And then he'd kill Jimmy. Lillian couldn't stand the thought of the little boy going through any more anguish. She *had* to do something. But what?

The ride back went fast. Darwin pushed their horses hard, and she had a difficult time staying astride with her hands bound and her skirt and legs wet. *Lord, help. Please send help.*

Maybe Jimmy had woken up and escaped. She could at least hope.

But when they dismounted and climbed up to the cave that was the opening to the mine, she saw him still asleep on the ground. Blindfolded and tied up. His little body curled into a ball.

Darwin kicked rocks and dirt at the boy.

"Wake up."

He threw Lillian to the ground and tied her feet again. Then he pulled out a gun. "Now, we are gonna wait for my idiot brother to get here, and you two are gonna do exactly as I say, got it?"

Jimmy squirmed on the ground next to her. He seemed agitated.

Lillian wished she could comfort him, but she couldn't reach out to him or even speak to him.

The boy wiggled some more and grunted through the gag.

Darwin laughed, leaned over Jimmy, and yanked off his blindfold. "That's right, kid. Ya know me, don't you? Recognized my voice, didn't you?"

Jimmy's eyes adjusted to the light and then narrowed in anger.

Lillian's stomach tied up in knots. Jimmy's reaction confirmed that this *was* the man who had killed Rebecca Colton. He'd witnessed it.

His face was no longer pale and drawn but red with anger. He grunted through the gag some more. Wiggling his jaw and mouth, Jimmy finally managed to move the gag and screamed. Loud and strong.

Darwin slapped the boy and tried to replace the gag, but Jimmy bit him and then screamed some more.

Lillian lunged forward on her knees, trying to get between Darwin and Jimmy. Longstreet slapped her down, but the action caused him to lose his grip on the pistol.

"Put your hands up, Longstreet!" the sheriff's voice boomed from the opening of the mine.

In one fluid motion Darwin's arm was around Lillian's throat, and he pulled her to her feet, using her as a shield. He'd lost his gun, but he now held a knife to her face, the cool of the blade pressed against her cheek. "Back off, sheriff, or I cut her to pieces."

"Don't do anything stupid, Longstreet. We've got you outnumbered."

"I don't rightly care. But I think you do care about this pretty lady here, and I'll kill her."

"Don't hurt her, Longstreet!" Woody's voice echoed off the walls.

A gun cocked behind them. "You killed my mama!" Jimmy's voice. Scratchy but strong. It brought tears to Lillian's eyes. She'd never heard him speak.

Darwin turned sideways and backed them up against a wall of the mine. She could see the sheriff, Woody and his men at the entrance, and Jimmy with a gun in between his bound hands on the other side. Pointed directly at them.

"You *killed* my mama!"

Darwin laughed. "And I'm gonna kill her, too, if you don't put that gun down."

Lillian felt the blade move to her throat.

"No. I won't let you. She's my new mama and you won't hurt her. I won't let you."

She felt her heart race. She'd never seen Jimmy like this, and it scared her more than anything else ever had. He was so small, but he was holding a gun, and while she knew Woody had taught him how to handle it, Lillian also knew the stress of the situation would only serve to make Jimmy careless. Without giving it another thought, Lillian sucked in a breath and slammed her head back into Darwin's. She heard the cartilage of his nose snap. The jolt knocked them both around, and Lillian lost her balance. With her hands and feet still tied, she couldn't do anything but fall.

The sheriff and Woody took that moment to lunge toward them. In a scuffle on the ground, Lillian felt a sharp sting to her arm. The knife. Where was it? She didn't care if she was cut, as long as Darwin didn't have it.

Darwin was spry and landed punches to

both the other men, but another gun cocked right next to Darwin's head this time.

Sam spoke. "Now, Longstreet, you've got three more pointed at your head. I suggest you give up." The crew boss looked over to Jimmy. "Son, you did real good, but you can put the gun down now."

Jimmy shook his head. "No, he killed my mama." Tears streamed down his face.

Lillian grabbed the knife from underneath her and cut the rope at her feet. She walked over to Jimmy. "It's over, sweetie. Let the sheriff take him to jail."

"He killed my mama." Sobs now shook his frame.

"Put the gun down, son." Woody came closer.

Jimmy stood frozen, the gun aimed at Darwin's chest as the sheriff cuffed the man. It was almost as if he couldn't hear either one of them. Lillian bit her lip. Surely he wouldn't fire.

"Jimmy. Jimmy. Jimmy." Harry's voice called out. "Jimmy, please don't shoot him. He's a bad, bad, bad man, and he's done really bad things. But he's my brother and I love him. Please." Harry knelt beside Jimmy and wrapped his big arms around him. "Please don't shoot him. Don't be mean like he is. Don't be bad, Jimmy."

Jimmy sobbed harder and then finally lowered the gun. Woody quickly took the pistol from him and carefully uncocked it. Jimmy fell into Harry's arms and cried. Woody and Lillian moved forward at the same time and wrapped them both up in a hug.

It was finally over.

CHAPTER THIRTY-TWO

A couple of weeks later the trial for Darwin Longstreet was swift and to the point. Woody sat with Harry and listened as the judge declared Darwin's fate. They had decided the situation might be too much for Jimmy, so Lillian had taken him to the general store.

The judge looked down at Darwin Longstreet and shook his head. "You have proven yourself as a menace to society. Therefore, I sentence you to be hanged by the neck until dead. Sentence will be carried out immediately." He pounded his gavel and exited the room. The few people who'd come had risen for the judge, then quickly shuffled out, leaving Woody and Harry with Darwin and the sheriff.

"Brother." Harry reached toward Darwin.

"Get away from me, stupid." He spat at Harry. "I hate the very sight of you. You should've died a long time ago." The sheriff jerked him away and headed out the side door with Darwin calling insults at Harry and anyone else he could.

Fat tears rolled down Harry's broad face. Woody put his arm around his shoulders. "Don't you give it a second thought, Harry. You aren't stupid. You're amazingly wise and pretty smart."

"But he's my brother and he hates me." Harry was still looking at the door where the sheriff had taken his brother. "He's gonna die."

Woody nodded. "Yes. And for that I am sorry. Not sorry that justice will be done, but sorry that you will be hurt."

Just then Jimmy and Lillian returned. Lillian had a newspaper tucked under one arm and Jimmy under the other. The boy would hardly let her from his sight. She had a smile on her face, and that always seemed to act like a balm for Woody and now apparently for Harry.

"You look happy, Miss Lillian. Did something good happen?" Harry sounded so hopeful, and Woody couldn't help but pray that Lillian would have something good to say. Perhaps Mrs. Goodman would be able to rejoin them at home.

Lillian gave Harry a hug as Jimmy went to wrap his arms around Woody's waist. "It sure did. Mrs. Goodman gets to return home with us today."

Harry jumped up and down and clapped. "Mrs. Goodman is so nice. She gave me a hug."

Lillian laughed. "Yes, she did. And once she's better, I'm sure she will give you lots more." She caught Woody's eye and gave him a special smile before turning back to Harry. "But there's more good news, too. Do you remember I told you that my grandfather was sick?"

Harry nodded. "But he didn't want to see you." He frowned. "Darwin said he hated the sight of me. He wished I'd died."

Lillian patted his hand. "Harry, Darwin's mind isn't right. He's had a lot of hate eating away at him most of his life. I don't think he meant a word he said to you."

This caused Harry to perk up. "Do you really think so, Miss Lillian?"

She nodded. "I do, so don't be too sad. I think that Darwin — maybe when you were both little boys — before the hate took over, well, I'm certain he must have loved you very much. And we know that there's still a chance for Darwin, because God loves him very much. We just need to pray for him to turn to God in his last hours."

Harry nodded. "Yes. Yes. Yes."

Woody met her gaze and shook his head. She was something else. "So what's your other good news, wife of mine?"

She held up a telegram. "Remember I told you that Stanton notified me that Grandfather was sick and told me I should come?" Woody nodded. "Well, I sent a message back because I knew I couldn't just up and leave you boys to take care of yourselves and Mrs. Goodman. I didn't know what to do. And after Darwin was arrested, I sent another telegram telling Stanton that enough was enough. Since Grandfather was sick and could do nothing about it, I wanted Stanton to sit and read to him every one of the letters I had written."

Woody laughed. "That sounds just like you."

"Well, it did the trick." Lillian crossed her arms against her beautiful lace shawl. "Stanton said the letters perked up Grandfather to the point that he began to take food and medicine again. He said Grandfather wants to see me — that he loves me."

Harry clapped his hands. "Good. Good. Good."

Lillian laughed and nodded. "Yes. Yes. Yes."

"So when do you want to go see him?" Woody asked.

She drew close to him, and Jimmy went to stand beside Harry. She smiled sweetly at Woody and took hold of his arm. "That's what I was hoping to talk to you about."

"Oh dear. When you start in like this, I know it's going to be quite interesting — perhaps even dangerous."

"Nonsense. I just want for us to go see Grandfather as a family. You, me, Jimmy and . . . Harry."

"Me?" Harry looked at them with such hope that Woody could have never denied him, even if he wanted to.

"Of course you," Woody said. "You're a part of our family now. If that's okay with you."

"A family." Harry spoke the word with great reverence. "I have a family."

Jimmy gave Harry a hug, and to his surprise Harry hoisted him into the air and up on his shoulder. "You're my brother now," Harry told him.

Jimmy giggled and squirmed. "And my papa and mama are your papa and mama."

Woody felt tears dampen his eyes at the joy that radiated from the faces of his boys. "I think we should go have some ice cream and plan out our trip to Indiana."

"I like ice cream," Jimmy declared.

Harry nodded with great enthusiasm. "I

like ice cream, too." He headed for the door. "I know where we go for ice cream."

Lillian put her arm around Woody's waist, and he put his around her shoulder and pulled her close. They followed the boys at a distance, not caring at all about the spectacle they created.

"I like ice cream," Woody whispered against her ear, "but I like you even better."

"Funny you should say that." Lillian gazed up at him with an expression of complete adoration. "Because I like you better than ice cream, too. And I *like* ice cream. A lot." They hadn't had much time as husband and wife, but the look she gave him made him look forward to all the years ahead.

He chuckled. "It's a good thing."

"Oh, I nearly forgot," Lillian declared. "Mrs. Goodman sent this newspaper." She let go of Woody and pulled it from under her arm. She opened it and handed it to Woody. "There's a certain article she thought you would find amusing, especially with all the orders you've had coming in."

Woody read the caption she pointed to:

Olive Growers' Convention in Sacramento, California — Olives for All

He scanned the article and began to chuckle.

"Listen to this. It's a statement from

Dr. P. I. Remondino at the Olive Growers' convention. 'The modern American . . . will never know . . . a full tide of health until he returns to the proper admixture of olive oil in his diet. Until he again recognizes the value and use of olive oil, he will continue to drag his consumptive-thinned, liver-shriveled, mummified-skinned and constipated and pessimistic anatomy about . . . in a vain search for health.' " Woody laughed again.

Lillian giggled along with him. "That could be our next advertisement. Wouldn't *that* get the gossip chain going?"

He stopped in the middle of the street and pulled her to him.

She blushed a pretty shade of pink but wrapped her arms around his neck.

Leaning down, he kissed her nose. "I don't know about you, my dear, but I would prefer to stay out of the gossip chain for the rest of my life."

"Me too." She winked. "But I fear, Mr. Colton, that if you continue to kiss me in the middle of the street —"

He interrupted her with a quick kiss to her lips.

"— where everyone can see —"

This time, he kissed her a little longer, and her arms wrapped a little tighter around his neck.

"— while our boys are no doubt —"

He leaned in for another distraction.

"— no doubt already ordering three scoops of ice cream apiece —"

Another kiss. And a waggle of his eyebrows.

"— As I was saying . . . oh, fiddlesticks, what was I saying?"

He laughed and kissed her nose again.

A whistle from across the street drew their attention.

From none other than their pastor. Their friend chuckled and waved.

Woody drew his wife . . . *his* wife . . . closer and winked.

She sighed. "I'm guessing we will *remain* the talk of the town."

He kissed her soundly on the lips this time and looked around and smiled. "But you made a good point. We'd better hurry. We wouldn't want them to run out of ice cream before we got there." Releasing her from his embrace, he took her elbow and led her down the street while she laughed.

"Life will always be an adventure with you, Woody." She straightened her hat. "And I'm looking forward to every moment."

DEAR READER

We are so thankful for each of you — our readers. Thank you for taking another journey with us. What a joy it's been to hear from so many of you about *All Things Hidden* and to hear your excitement for *Beyond the Silence.*

Once again, our story is bathed in the historical detail and setting of a real place and time, but we also took some artistic liberty — this is, of course, a work of fiction.

Angels Camp, California, is a real place with an amazing history that goes beyond gold (just look up Mark Twain and the Jumping Frog Jubilee), and we had a wonderful time working on the research. The people of the Angels Camp Museum were a huge help, as well as the Calaveras County Historical Society.

There are real people we used in our story that we'd especially like to point out. Mrs.

Rolleri really was famous for her handmade ravioli. In fact, people would line up at the back door on Sundays with their buckets ready to fill. George Stickle and his brother Edward came to the area in 1849 and built their store in 1852. Although in the story we called it the Stickle Bros. mercantile, all photos show the sign above the store being labeled "G. Stickle." George was a fascinating character who we kept coming across in our research. In fact, in *A History of Angels Camp* it states that George had one of the "finest reputations of any man in Angels Camp. His Enterprises were always of top repute. He helped organize the first Republican Party in town, served as a school Trustee, and was postmaster for several years." While George's personality in the book is a creation of our own, we imagined that the real George Stickle just might have been that same champion for Harry.

We'd also like to mention Freda Ehmann, a German woman who experimented in California and actually came up with the process that is still used today for canning table olives. She became famous for it just a few years after the setting of our story. While we spent months immersing ourselves into the research for the olive farm, only so much of it made it onto the page. But we hope you enjoyed it as much as we did. We know we will never look at olives or olive oil the same again, especially knowing that so many of them are still picked by hand.

Again, dear reader, thank you. You are a treasure to us.

We pray you have enjoyed the journey,
Kim and Tracie

ACKNOWLEDGMENTS

It takes a team of talented people to put a book like this in your hands. And the team at Bethany House is beyond compare — from editorial to marketing to cover design and everything in between. They are incredible. Thank you — our BHP family.

In loving memory of Sharon Asmus — our beloved editor on both *All Things Hidden* and *Beyond the Silence*. Thank you, dear lady, for your years of service, and your encouragement.

To our husbands and families — we love you dearly. We couldn't do what we do without your love and support (and sarcasm, corny jokes, research, and brainstorming help)!

To the countless people who took our phone calls (and personal visits) in stride at the Angels Camp Museum and Calaveras County Historical Society and did your best to answer all of our questions — thank you!

But most important, to our Lord and Savior. May You be glorified in all that we do. Thank You for the gift of story and the opportunity to share our love for You and Your Word.

Now unto him that is able to keep you from falling, and to present you faultless before the presence of his glory with exceeding joy, to the only wise God our Saviour, be glory and majesty, dominion and power, both now and ever. Amen.

Jude 1:24–25

ABOUT THE AUTHORS

Tracie Peterson is the award-winning author of over one hundred novels, both historical and contemporary. Her avid research resonates in her stories, as seen in her bestselling HEIRS OF MONTANA and ALASKAN QUEST series. Tracie and her family make their home in Montana. Visit Tracie's website at www.traciepeterson.com.

Kimberley Woodhouse is a multi-published author of fiction and nonfiction. A popular speaker and teacher, she's shared her theme of "Joy Through Trials" with hundreds of thousands of people across the country. She lives, writes, and homeschools with her husband of twenty-plus years and their two awesome teens in Colorado. Connect with Kim at www.kimberleywood house.com.

The employees of Thorndike Press hope you have enjoyed this Large Print book. All our Thorndike, Wheeler, and Kennebec Large Print titles are designed for easy reading, and all our books are made to last. Other Thorndike Press Large Print books are available at your library, through selected bookstores, or directly from us.

For information about titles, please call:
(800) 223-1244

or visit our Web site at:
http://gale.cengage.com/thorndike

To share your comments, please write:
Publisher
Thorndike Press
10 Water St., Suite 310
Waterville, ME 04901